JIM CHAMBERS emanates from Derby in the East Midlands and is the eldest of three born to Dick and Barbara. His working-class roots are a source of pride, his father an enduring point of reference, the person Jim has most admired in life. But the world of butchery was not for him. Instead he opted for business, subsequently enjoying a career in the education technology market where he became a CEO in technology and training businesses and then non-executive chairman in ed-tech companies. Now more time rich walking and writing are his passions – perfect bed fellows. The *Paradigm Shift* novel was self-published in 2013, and foretold the Brexit outcome years before any referendum had even been mooted. Then *The Hope Affair* was published in April 2021 and *Urban Scarecrows* follows in 2022. Jim is a long-term Derby County fan stretching back to the glory days of Brian Clough's and then Dave Mackay's championship winning sides of the 1970's.

Jim lives in the Peak District of Derbyshire and is a family man who has been married to Barbara for over forty years. They have four offspring: Nicola, Andrew, Christopher, and Elizabeth and, at last count, four grandchildren.

G000082920

URBAN
SCARECROWS

JIM CHAMBERS

SilverWood

Published in 2022 by SilverWood Books

SilverWood Books Ltd
14 Small Street, Bristol, BS1 1DE, United Kingdom
www.silverwoodbooks.co.uk

ISBN 978-1-80042-209-4 (paperback)

British Library Cataloguing in Publication Data
A CIP catalogue record for this book is
available from the British Library

Page design and typesetting by SilverWood Books

CHAPTER 1: JOURNEY'S END – DESTINATION DAY -5

JUNE 2027

He glanced around at his fellow travellers. An old man sat glassy-eyed in the corner, trance-like. Two young guns sniggered, seemingly unconcerned. A lady with straggly grey hair fidgeted, wide eyes flicking from one person to another, but he doubted she was taking much in. A younger woman hid her face but was silent. She reached out as best she could, given her restraints, to the old man – her father? They were, all of them, packed together, feet and hands manacled. Dominic's nose twitched; the smell of fear mingled with unwashed clothes and sweat. And it was yet another hot, humid day in London – the mercury touching thirty-two.

He had not expected a fair hearing, nor mercy. The sentence was to be expected and duly delivered in short order; just a few hours to seal his fate. The courts were busy, efficiency their hallmark. He was resigned but still surprised at his own calmness, an out-of-body experience of detached curiosity. Now better to speculate on the backgrounds and experiences of his fellow prisoners than dwell on his own nightmares.

As the van bumped over the pot-holed streets it took perhaps thirty minutes to reach their destination. Even the young men fell silent as it backed up, soon coming to a halt. After a moment, the rear doors were flung open. Dominic blinked in the bright sunshine, feeling a wave of heat reminiscent of emerging from a plane into the Bahaman sun, shades at the ready. But this was a one-way ticket to a rather less salubrious destination: Wormwood Scrubs Prison. And it had lost its tag of HM, he noted wryly. Their welcome party was armed with guns; dog handlers with Alsatians straining at the end of leashes baring their fangs, slavering, barking their warning. He stumbled out into a courtyard along with the others, pushed and shoved by bullyboy guards wearing their red flag badges and crimson epaulettes on grey tunic uniforms. A young gun protested and received a gratuitous blow from the butt of an AK-47 as they were marched into the building, a holding pen.

'Listen up,' shouted an officer. 'You are all traitors, enemies of the state. You have no rights, no appeal, no lawyers to fall back on. Your sentence will be carried out as stated by the court but if anyone wishes to test our patience…'

The officer paused, let the sentiment hang in the air. He walked amongst them, stopping in front of one of the youths who stared back at him with a smirk, an arrogant shrug of the shoulders.

'There's always one, isn't there? Take him.'

The youth was dragged away, his body language changing in an instant; angry shouts turning to pleas for clemency, soon mutating into panicked screams.

And then silence.

The remaining youth looked around him, eyes wide, reality belatedly dawning.

They were shunted into another room, instructed to remove their clothes. They began to do so in stunned silence – men and women; inadequate torn screens offered little privacy; no respect afforded to the elderly. Or the disabled.

'Remove watches, rings, necklaces – everything; you've no need of ostentation where you're heading,' a guard shouted. Dominic glanced down at his wedding ring, twirling it round before easing it over his truncated finger; he had lost the fingertip in a moment of lapsed concentration early in his chef's career. He dropped it into the container, followed by an involuntary salty tear. Soon the box contained a gallimaufry of objects: signet rings, gold bracelets, crosses, engagement and wedding rings, a St Christopher's necklace, friendship bracelets, facial studs. Someone had even dropped in a false tooth, he noticed with bemusement.

'Get on with it, you,' the guard said to the young woman, who had been pulled into the background, her father attempting to pull the screen around her, vainly striving to guard her modesty.

'What are you waiting for? Shy, are we?'

'Not usually,' she said with some bravado, but the voice wavered. Her attempts to control her emotions were losing out as she trembled, tears brimming and spilling. Dominic looked up sharply, recognising the tone of voice. His heart missed a beat. She looked different shorn of her authority, had unsurprisingly lost all sparkle. She seemed to have aged years in a matter of weeks. He supposed that must be true of himself too. But, yes, it was her. Definitely. The memories flooded back, reminiscences of their first dramatic meeting; the context had been so different then, so nearly fatal. And then all the adventure, intrigue, derring-do. But ultimately so much pain. He caught her eye and thought he saw a momentary shock of recognition. She gave the barest shake of the head. Don't, seemed to be the message. And he understood only too well. That segment of his life now joined the other fragmented splinters. He gasped inwardly, managing to suffocate the life out of it bar the escaping of a heavy breath, a stifled groan.

'Showers that way,' the guard said, twitching his head towards the corner doorway.

The young woman grabbed a towel to wrap around her waist, put her shoulders back and drew herself to her full height, stoic in the face of such obscene abuse. Dominic's heart went out to her once more as she joined an older lady and an elderly man who struggled in vain to cover themselves, each caring for the other. Their love was a heart-warming display of human emotion in the midst of such callousness. But they held their heads as if in shame at the stripping away of their last shreds of dignity, ageing flesh left hanging, bellies and shoulders drooping. A hush now prevailed as the entire group shuffled forwards, leaving piles of clothing behind. The group grew tighter together to find succour in numbers, just as shoals of fish form balls as protection from their predators.

Now freshly showered, Dominic quickly donned a coarse white prison uniform emblazoned with a large black T, grateful for the small mercy of covering up and restoring some semblance of decorum. The entire group was gathered into another room. Dominic looked around him: a windowless cell with a single electric bulb hanging by a frayed flex, a round-faced clock loudly ticking the minutes away, buckets acting as latrines in two corners. The walls and ceiling were grey, the floor of a rough, bare concrete construction – blood-, urine- and faeces-stained by the look of it. There were perhaps twenty enemies of the state crowded together, the females gravitating towards one end. The young woman joined the other females, sitting on the periphery of the group, allowing her father to squat beside her as a bulwark to the men. Dominic reached for the allocated blanket, carefully folding it; he used it as a cushion to sit on, plonking down next to the father. Dominic was drawn towards the old man's daughter like a moth to a flame. Proximity to her seemed important. And his head was suddenly filled with fragments of happiness, moments of tenderness, but also periods of bravery, steeliness, leadership. He was dragged back to reality as one of their group rushed over to the corner, giving in to the force of nature, his piss hitting the empty bucket; a sound that was likely to become all too familiar. His thoughts drifted back to all that was special in his life, of all the people he cared for, who cared for him. Pre-eminent amongst those were Rosa and Albert and Juan and… Then he cast back to the day that changed everything: for his family, his friends, and the entire nation. He shook his head as he recalled his naïve jubilation…

2019

Dominic woke early on what promised to be an ominous day, Friday 13th December 2019. He had known that a victory for the Labour Party was inevitable by the time he went to bed. But how large would the majority prove to be? His alarm went off on his smart phone. Reaching over he fumbled with the controls, sat up in bed and rubbed his eyes. He yawned and took a sip of water from the glass at his bedside. Gradually coming to, he reached for his mobile:

> **Labour Landslide:**
> *Latest forecasts indicate*
> *108 seat majority*

He nudged Rosa who groaned her annoyance, turning over to resume her slumbers.

Freshly dressed and refreshed, Dominic donned his apron and set about preparing a celebratory breakfast: fresh orange juice, coffee, pastries, tropical fruit salad and eggs Benedict. He set about pulling the dish together as a sleepy Rosa joined him, ambling in, scraping her fluffy slippers on the tiled floor, and pulling her dressing gown tight around her. Dominic rushed over, kissed her, and fussed, easing her into a seat. She scowled at him.

'You look radiant, darling,'

'What have you done?'

He smiled benevolently. His wife was not a morning person, but he was in a sunny mood and was not going to be subsumed by her grumpiness.

'I've prepared something special. And let's wash it down with a little fizz, shall we?' he said while opening a bottle of Prosecco and filling her glass.

'*Mierda*. Give it a rest.'

'That's not the spirit. What else can I get you?' Dominic asked as he set her plate of eggs in front of her. 'Fresh hollandaise of course.'

'How about a coffee and some peace and quiet? You're annoyingly sprightly this morning and what the hell time is it?'

'It's happened, my love, it's happened. We *won*! Labour back with a huge majority. Now we can get away from the incompetence, austerity—'

'Don't hold your breath.'

'Now then. We've destroyed the bloody Tories – a rout. My dad would be tickled pink. Sweet.'

'Bloody disaster if you ask me...' intoned a deep voice.

'Oh, hello, darling,' said Rosa, addressing their eldest son, who had just surfaced. 'You have the eggs, and you're welcome to the Prosecco too. I'm going back to bed.' But the effort seemed too much, as she sipped her coffee.

'Did you actually read the bloody manifesto before berating people on their doorsteps? What you're celebrating is the start of a revolution.'

'What nonsense, Albert.'

'Tobin and Connell are not so much Blair and Brown as Marx and Lenin. Let's hope they don't turn into Stalin.'

'No, no, no. I'm much more—'

'You always are, Dad,' said Albert, pushing his eggs to one side, quaffing his sparkling wine.

'Just you mark my words...'

But Albert just grabbed a Danish pastry, threw his dad a look, and stole out of the room.

DESTINATION DAY -5, 19.35
2027

Dominic was brought back to the present by a gentle nudge from the old man, who leant closer to whisper in his ear, 'Don't I know you?'

'Do you?'

'That celebrity chef, Dominic Diamond?'

'Dominic Green actually, but my business partner thought Diamond sounded better. DD seemed a decent brand at the time.'

'No accounting for taste.'

'Indeed. I listened to him too often. Not sure why but that's a long time ago now. All seems unimportant...good memory though.'

'My wife used to love you.'

The old man paused and sighed, his eyes clouding over. All of them would have their own stories, their own tragedies; too painful to recall, too excruciating to relate.

'Harry, by the way, and this is my niece, Celia.'

Celia? Really? Dominic glanced across and she shrugged. He did not ask. The two men shook hands briefly and Dominic intuitively knew the formality was ridiculous given the circumstances. His niece flashed him a half-smile, but her eyes conveyed her reluctance to engage.

'I'm trying to recall the name of that programme – no don't tell me, it's coming. *Diamond Delight!*' said Harry.

'Nearly—'

'*Diamond Delicacies.*'

'Well done. Is Celia alright? A terribly embarrassing ordeal for her, back there.'

'Bastards,' said Harry. 'But she exposed a few of their sorts before being caught. I caught a few of your podcasts. Inspirational.'

'Celia must have been courageous to land here…'

'You've no idea but…' And suddenly he was relating her exploits. Dominic listened with interest. Celia tugged on her uncle's sleeve, shaking her head. He was not to be silenced but she glanced across at Dominic and put her finger to her lips. *Please,* flashed her eyes.

CHAPTER 2: CAMPAIGNING

18TH DECEMBER 2019

Dominic had slept restlessly ahead of what promised to be a hectic day: the last day of electioneering. He had been lined up to broadcast on radio and television, bite-sized slots to lend some celebrity sparkle to the Labour Party's final attempts to woo the voters; to end Tory austerity and supplant it with radical reform. As he munched on a piece of toast and marmalade and sipped a strong mug of coffee, his mind cast back to his childhood. The penury of a mining community brought to its knees by a politicised assault on the mining industry was still vivid; it still provoked strong anti-Tory sentiments in old mining communities today. He recalled the strikes, the violence perpetrated by the police in their attacks on organised protests. Most of all he mourned the death of his father from pneumoconiosis. He had seen his father wither and diminish before his young eyes. He had vowed then to extract revenge, and the time had come. Deep down he knew he was conflating two separate disasters. But the sentiment remained, the emotions powering his latent political activism. He struggled to understand how Albert could ignore the cruelty that had inflicted such hardships. How could he deny his own family history? But he remained hopeful his eldest son would see the light. And Dominic liked to think his father would be proud of his success despite their impoverished roots. Discovering a passion for all matters culinary, to rise to the top of that profession would have been celebrated. And now to put the icing on the cake.

Dragging his mind back to the present he re-read his diary for the umpteenth time: interviews, campaigning, a dinner for the activists...

He studied his crib sheet carefully, rehearsing the soundbites to repeat as often as possible. Apparently, repetition and impassioned grandstanding was prized above intelligent discourse. But snippets of his backstory were encouraged.

Dominic did a final bathroom run and packed a washbag of essentials for the day: favourite aftershave, moisturiser, comb, toothbrush. He studied himself in the mirror, adjusting his red tie and admiring the matching red socks and braces – taking a leaf out of Brandon's book. Applying gel to his hair, a final comb, he stood back and nodded his satisfaction. Then a swift goodbye to an unreceptive Rosa.

The morning passed in a whirlwind of frenetic interviewing, slogans, ardent pleas to the British public: the introduction of voter ID into polling booths was labelled a sinister Tory plot to disenfranchise working-class, disabled, and ethnic minority voters; time to end Tory austerity, invest in public services, save our NHS, supply broadband for all; time to nationalise the railways, scrap tuition fees; time to eradicate billionaires. He steered clear of the elephant traps of economics and affordability; preferred to declaim social injustices, inequality of opportunities, racial and gender discrimination. Dominic knew that his appearance was an asset, knew that the camera was kind to him; his square jaw and swarthy good looks were appealing, as were his working-class roots. And he had legions of followers from his culinary programmes.

He trudged up the garden path to their Georgian town house carrying spare leaflets. It had been a long day, a good day. The prospects seemed good if his afternoon of canvassing was anything to go by. Time for a quick shower before then heading to his final meeting. As he fumbled with his keys the door opened and Rosa ushered him in.

'Thanks, love. Wow, you look great. Did I forget something?' said Dominic, racking his brains to recall any family commitment that may have slipped his mind.

'Dinner with my partners. Remember? You were much too busy on matters of state to spare your time,' she said.

And it all came back to him. Her partners at Flight Legal and their spouses were dining at The Goring, the culmination of a long planning exercise. Dominic searched his memory in an attempt to recall the details. He really ought to pay more attention, but he had been preoccupied in doing his bit for the country. And tomorrow was the day it would all happen. Hopefully. But he still felt guilty at not supporting her; it would certainly have been a more enjoyable occasion than meeting with fellow activists at the local constituency office of the Labour Party's candidate, Joseph Stubbings. But he had given his commitment and there would be other occasions to enjoy the delights of The Goring, he had suggested.

'What time are you heading off?' he asked.

'In about thirty. You will soon be free to play with Joseph's little helpers... or...whomever.'

'I thought we'd moved on from all that?' Dominic said, sighing.

'*You* might have...'

'Please, Rosa, how many times do I have to... Oh, come on. Let's have a swift G&T to kickstart your evening, a loosener. What do you say?'

Rosa glared at him, tossed her hair back and headed to the front lounge to join their elder son, Albert. Dominic took that as assent and busied himself with the drinks, not forgetting the lime and, for good measure, rosemary, and mint.

'Hi, Dad. How was it on the doorsteps?' asked Albert, who was sprawled on their sofa, a bottle of beer within reach.

'Really positive actually. Lots of supporters, lots of people asking for autographs too. Not sure that went down too well with Joseph after a while. But we can be pretty confident of the right outcome.'

'The right one for you maybe. But for the country? I wonder,' said Rosa.

Dominic and Albert both looked at her in surprise. It was not like her to offer a political view.

'It'll be a disaster,' said Albert.

'Here we go again...'

But Dominic was cut short by Rosa. 'I couldn't care less about party politics, but I do care about the impact your lot has had. Look at poor Neta Kahn round the corner – relies on a food bank to feed her kids; Dennis Pomfrey was turfed out of his part-time job and can't make ends meet. And have you noticed the number of homeless on the streets?' she said directly to Albert.

'Couldn't agree more...' began Dominic.

'And as for *your* lot, Dom. The business world is preparing for mayhem. We've been working with economists in assessing the likely impact. It's not pretty, which is why in the last few months we've ramped up corporate law practices in France and Spain. Family law and litigation should be okay, may even do well if the worst of our scenarios comes to fruition,' said Rosa.

'Sounds interesting, Mum. Tell us more...'

'The best we can hope for is higher taxes, a new wealth tax, renationalisation of utilities and rail, sky-high corporation taxes. But the impact will stifle growth and investment. We've already seen M&A activity plunge by twenty percent in anticipation. We fully expect it to seize up almost completely with the inevitable introduction of capital controls.'

'No, I don't believe it. You wait and see. It'll be fine,' said Dominic.

'Get real, Dad.'

'And I'm talking about the most benign scenario…you should see the other plans. *My Godddd*. We *have* to be ready,' said Rosa.

'Welcome to the Tories,' said Albert to his mum, before smiling in victory at Dominic.

'Not on your life. I really don't care which tribe rule the roost. But I *do* care about what it does to vulnerable people. And I care what an attack on business by an ideologically motivated Labour Party does to the economy and I most certainly care about what happens to our legal practice…'

'So who gets your vote, Mum?'

'That, my son, is between me and the ballot box – and that sounds like my taxi,' she said to the sound of a honking horn. 'Oh, and by the way…'

'Yes?' said Dom, helping her into her coat.

'I've been asked to become the next senior partner.'

'That's amazing, darling. Simply wonderful. So sorry I can't be with you this evening.'

CHAPTER 3: DISCORD

MONTHS LATER

He settled into a seat in the centre of the carriage, squashed between a large man in a soggy raincoat and a young lady with facial studs and tattoos, thudding music leaking from her earbuds. But it was a bonus to get a seat on the packed Tube. Dominic scanned the headline story on the front page of the *Evening Standard*: prison reforms, reducing recidivism. For once, the downturn in the economy had been elbowed out of the spotlight. Unusually, the paper seemed to see merit in a government policy while casting doubt on its ability to make any tangible difference in even the medium term. But reading was a challenge as the Tube jolted and trundled on its way with the oppressive crowding of wet, tired humanity pressed together like sardines. Dominic's mind turned to the growing challenges in his business life. Thank goodness Brandon was there to navigate the economic perils, the woes of the onset of the crisis; just one month away from it becoming an official recession. Dominic stayed away from the profit and loss account and balance sheets and cash flow statements, which confused and bored him. But there was no denying the drop off in business. Fewer customers were venturing out to their high-class restaurants and the jewel in the crown, their Michelin-starred restaurant, Diamond's, in Mayfair. He sighed, recalling his own words that foresaw a short period of adjustment as the new government pressed on with their reform agenda. And the nature of the constant narrative against capitalist excesses, for higher business taxes, and for an assault on corporate greed was unhelpful and seemed to tar all with the same brush. He also reflected on his own finances as the hiking of taxes was impacting his business, although as a high earner himself he accepted the social fairness of paying more. Rosa had also asserted that the business community was hunkering down: reducing investment levels, shedding staff. His thoughts were suddenly interrupted as the train juddered to a halt, causing an old man to lose his handhold on the overhead strap. He mumbled a curse, quickly followed by an apology to Dominic, in whose lap he had fallen. It was Dominic's stop anyway, so he eased his way past the pensioner and through the throng to step out onto the platform, making his way to the exit on autopilot.

Having shed his coat, towelled his hair dry, combed and gelled it, he examined his image in the mirror, adjusted his collar so that it showed just above the crew-necked sweater – just as he liked it – and went in search of his family. The kitchen was quiet and orderly; everything in its place, granite work tops uncluttered, stainless steel sparkling. He flicked the switch on the kettle, resisting the temptation of an early evening beer. Glancing over at the blackboard on the far wall was a message from Rosa reminding him she would be home late that evening; a microwave meal could be found in the freezer or there was fresh salmon in the fridge. But he decided to order a curry takeaway. Grabbing his mug of coffee he meandered into the lounge where he encountered clear signs of young male adults: discarded pullovers, car magazines, TV and video controls lying abandoned on the coffee table. He found Juan at the formal dining end of the elegant Georgian room, where two rooms had at some point been knocked into one: Juan hard at work, bent double over a large banner.

'What's the cause this time, Juan? Hong Kong? Or saving the planet or liberating Muslims in China perhaps?'

'Poor banter, Dad. Good day?'

'Okay, but quiet, so I left Bill to do the evening service. Business could be better.'

'Told you,' said Albert, who came in clutching a beer; slumping onto one of the sofas, he kicked off his slippers, stretched out and clicked on the television. He muttered, 'Bloody Marxists.'

Dominic ignored the sentiments; he could do without an argument with Albert, so he encouraged Juan to tell him what he was doing.

'XR demo tomorrow,' said Juan.

'XR?'

'Extinction Rebellion. Remember what that's all about, Dad? Just the small matter of global ecological disaster. Have you seen what they're doing in the Pennines and the Welsh Mountains? Amounts to wilful destruction of the environment. To hell with the wildlife, fragile moorland habitats. Do you know...'

'Okay, I get the gist. Good that you care but I'm not sure the protesting and demonstrations and disruption of the livelihoods of working Londoners actually helps. Without even going into the anarchists that inevitably latch onto these things as an opportunity to turn a demo into a riot. Anyway, what's happening there? Must have passed me by.'

'Prison building programme,' said Albert.

'Ahh, of course. Actually there's a documentary on this shortly. Let's tune in. I think I'll join you in a beer as well. And I've ordered curry for the three of us, by the way.'

'Great idea,' said Juan.

'A big match on later, Chelsea versus Spurs. Don't want to miss that,' said Albert.

'At least you two will be on the same side for once,' said Juan.

'Joining us?' asked his brother.

'Nope. Off out...to save the planet,' he added with a smirk.

'But time for a beer and a curry first?' suggested Dominic.

'Always! And I'd like to watch that documentary too.'

'You? Don't tell me you're getting political now?' said Albert.

'Nope but I'm hoping there'll be an environmental angle. Also pissed off with what's happening at the moment. People are really suffering. Have you noticed Harry round the corner?'

'Who?' asked Dominic.

'Just a homeless guy, Dad. You obviously haven't even noticed him let alone helped. Thought you were the socialist?'

'*Champagne* socialist,' added Albert.

'Give me a break, lads. Curry's here.'

In Rosa's absence they took the takeaway into the lounge. Ploughing through chicken jalfrezi, beef madras, salmon tikka, lamb dansak, tiger prawn korma, rice and naan breads they listened to the introduction to the programme: an overview on the reforming zeal of this radical government, the downturn in the economy, its impact on business and unemployment levels and on the prison reforms. Juan leaned forwards as aerial photographs showed swathes of moorland turned into building sites: the scars on the landscape of the construction of access roads, the demolition of farmhouses and village abodes. An interview with an expert in prison reform was met with exasperated sighs from Juan, exclamations from Albert as he spoke of the decades of neglect of the prison service: of overcrowding, of poor education, the prevalence of drugs, understaffing.

'What's up with you two? This has to be good, hasn't it? You're both liberal young men with a social conscience. Why aren't you applauding? More capacity, investment, educational programmes all designed to take the pressure off the system and open up opportunities. What's not to like?' said Dominic, breaking his promise to himself to simply listen for the sake of family harmony.

'Albert? A liberal? Ha – not a liberal bone in that reactionary Tory,' said Juan.

'Go to hell,' replied his brother, taking a swig of beer and offering his brother the rods.

'The environmental impact will be enormous. And what about the local villages? They'll be destroyed. Think of the destruction of the habitat of lapwings, skylarks, curlew, red grouse, adders. And the heather and crowberry and...'

'Alright, David Attenborough...' interjected Albert.

'Let's listen,' said Dominic as the experienced broadcaster, Fred Star, began interviewing a Home Minister, Ralph Strong.

FS: Your prison reforms are coming under heavy criticism with particular focus on the government riding roughshod over local democracy; subverting public consultation and planning. What do you have to say, Minister?

RS: The policy is to reduce recidivism, to create a more constructive environment for reflection, for education and re-skilling, for rehabilitation and opportunities. For too long prisoners have emerged with addictions more acute than those they took into prison. For too long we have turned perpetrators of minor crimes into hardened criminals. For too long we have simply chosen to punish offenders.

FS: We've heard this all before, haven't we? Why will it be any different this time?

RS: Because of our massive investment in new prison building with the very latest designs and our commitment to education and skills. We are the party who help the disadvantaged who sometimes find themselves on the wrong side of the law. The emphasis will no longer be on punishment but on the development of the individual. We are building into the designs the health and well-being of our offenders: their physical and mental health, their fitness, their spiritual well-being, their education, and re-skilling. We're determined to reduce recidivism.

Rehabilitation centres rather than prisons. And *this* government means it.

FS: The ideology, the commitment…the ramrodding through of radical changes despite legitimate concerns of the wider public is regarded with trepidation and the protests of the public are growing. Surely you must take public opinion with you or ultimately fail?

RS: The media's attempt to present every change in a negative light despite the clear mandate given by the British public is wearing thin, if I may be so bold…

FS: Our job is to…

RS: *No.* Hear me out for once. I won't be interrupted. What you mean is the media seeks to hold us accountable on behalf of the establishment, with your own take on what the public really wants. Let me be clear. For those who choose to resist changes to the status quo I say your protests will fall on deaf ears. We will *not* be deflected from implementing that which we were voted into office to do. If you're an ordinary citizen or disadvantaged in any way then you will have much to celebrate. We *will* invest in our infrastructure; we *will* remove poverty and work tirelessly to assist the disadvantaged sections of society; we *will* redistribute wealth.

FS: That's a fine speech, and people will make up their own minds, but before our time runs out can I bring you back to the building of new prisons. How can you defend the uprooting of local communities, the destruction of swathes of moorland in areas of outstanding natural beauty?

RS: We are going to extraordinary lengths to minimise the impact, working with the various bodies to help repair any damage.

'In other words sod the environment,' said Juan.

'Yeah. And democracy…' said Albert.

'I despair, guys. This is surely a policy we should all celebrate? I like the vision.'

''Course you do, Dad,' said Albert.

'Footie time,' said Dominic, sighing.

'And time for me to go,' said Juan.

CHAPTER 4: FRIENDSHIP

Dominic glanced around the kitchen, satisfying himself that everything was on track for the lunchtime service.

'Bill, I need to pop up to the office – hold the fort, would you? The demi-glace needs refining and the consommé finishing.'

'No problem, Chef.'

'Jen, all under control on your section? The panna cotta? And the...'

'Got it, Chef. Don't suppose we'll have many covers today though.'

Dominic joined Brandon in the office. They needed to talk, take stock. While they were equal partners, the office was an alien environment; it felt as if he had been summoned to the headmaster's study. Dominic, having removed his apron and chef's hat, found Brandon at his large desk, poring over papers. His partner was wearing his trademark red braces and looking dapper in his business suit. Brandon took a sip of coffee, poured Dominic a cup and came to join him at the small glass table. They eased themselves into leather chairs.

'Flying the red flag?' said Dominic, taking in the red socks.

'Hardly...ever the politician?'

He was not going to be baited by his partner today and changed the subject, but quickly found himself mired in what Brandon called harsh commercial realities: profit and loss statements, balance sheets, cash flow projections. He referenced recent reports of the Bank of England and the Office of Budget Review. It was all gloom and doom, the outlook presenting a dark future.

'You do like your business jargon, don't you? Surely the assumptions are too gloomy, the projections unnecessarily grim? Anyway, what are you actually proposing?'

'Unless trade improves very soon, we'll have to start letting people go—'

'Sacking them you mean?'

'Three of the restaurants are in jeopardy. We may have to close them down, consolidate our operation. And if the bank isn't more helpful it could get worse than that.'

'We must do all we can to keep staff on. This is just a temporary blip. Things will look up.'

'Which is why I run the business and you run the kitchen. Things are getting worse by the day; it's impossible to see how we can survive without changes. I need you to realise how bad things are.'

'There was always going to be…'

'Wake up, Dominic.'

Heading out to meet Bill at one of his favourite haunts, Dominic fished his mobile out of his pocket to see what the alerts were all about.

> **Rehab Centres:** *Opposition leader, Norris Jinks,*
> challenges the government over prison reforms.

> **Recession:** *Two consecutive quarters of negative growth*
> means the UK economy has now formally entered a recession.
> GDP expected to fall by four percent this year.

> **Unemployment:** *Soars to three million.*

He found Bill in his usual corner eyeing a pint of bitter lined up for Dominic. They shook hands and Dominic took Bill's empty glass, soon returning with a frothy new pint.

'Cheers, mate,' said Bill, raising his glass.

'Good health.'

'How was Brandon? Tell you the country's going to the dogs, business in decline?'

'Something like that. Much too pessimistic for me. But looking at the news on the economy I'm beginning to wonder. Let's change the subject. How are Jake and Vicky?'

'Bloody expensive, argumentative.'

'Perfectly normal then?'

'Exactly. Yours?'

'They don't get much better as they get older, Bill.'

'Thanks for that. I thought you were Mr Optimistic?'

'Albert's bloody fixated on our supposed Marxist government...'

'He's got a point.'

'And Juan's his usual argumentative self. Trying to save the world from global warming this week.'

'Rosa?'

'Oh, you know. Lovely, volatile, impossible... But at least she has her career. Doing really well. I'm dead proud of her...'

'Told her recently?'

'I'm sure I have, but I'm not flavour of the month. Doesn't matter what I say. Getting bloody fed up with it if you must know.'

'Once you transgress, mate... Rosa still giving you a hard time?'

'It's all so long ago. I struggle to understand why she keeps harping on about it. I've done the mea culpa bit, apologised until I'm blue in the face. I thought we'd moved on, but it keeps resurfacing.'

'It's a big hurdle to overcome.'

'Hey, it was a brief fling...over in the space of three months. There comes a time when you just have to draw a line. Anyway, how come you're suddenly Mr Enlightenment when it comes to the fair sex?'

'I just think you've reason to tread carefully.'

'Christ, mate, I get this at home. It was nothing; it's been over for years. She's got to get over it.'

'Easy for you to say though, isn't it? Whatever you call it is hardly the point. It's how Rosa sees it. She's still hurting, mate. You can't blame her either...'

'Blimey, wisdom as well. Careful you don't lose your Neanderthal image.'

'And your reputation with the ladies isn't exactly helping. I mean what about...' said Bill, draining his glass.

'Don't go there! Absolutely nothing in it...and don't look at me like that. Crikey, thirsty as well as cranky tonight? Another?'

'My shout,' said Bill, and he went off to join the throng at the bar, leaving Dominic with his thoughts.

The sun was still beating down as Dominic strode along the almost-deserted beach. He paused on his walk to admire a young woman disrobing, revealing a shapely figure in a yellow bikini. The wind whipped at her hair as she piled her clothes up, draping a towel over them. She turned and ran towards the sea, soon diving into the surf. Dominic smiled and walked on but glancing back he spotted the raised hand. He sensed her panic and realised she had been caught in a riptide. He recognised the signs: the dark patch of water, the break in the surf, the rippled surface. And this one appeared to be heading straight out to sea. He watched and hoped she would know what to do but it was soon evident that she did not. He felt the push-pull of uncertainty, of his *own* panic. You're trained for this, he told himself. And it seemed suddenly like an opportunity to become the hero; to help balance the scales given his earlier cowardice. His friend Tim often came to mind, especially in moments of self-reflection. He had let him down so badly. So many years ago, now, but the memory still haunted him.

'Penny for them?'

'Mm.'

'Going back over it? So was she worth all the pain? Sorry if I came on a bit strong. Not a great day all in all…but she obviously made quite an impression. More than just a fling wasn't it, mate? Or was it simply about sex?'

'It was all about that at first. But we connected. It became much more – at least it did for me. But I had to put Rosa and the lads first. You do realise I've never told another living soul about all this… Oh, shit, you didn't share it with Sue did you? I don't need that, and it would put her in a difficult position being so close to Rosa…and if Rosa thought I was talking to anyone about this – well, doesn't bear thinking about.'

'You know what – you take the bloody biscuit, Dom. What sort of a position did you put *me* in? I can't think of anything else I've ever deliberately kept from her…'

'Sorry. Let's talk football.'

'Nah. I'm done. Must get back. See you tomorrow.'

CHAPTER 5: CONFLICT

Having shaved and showered, he applied the cologne, moisturiser, and blow-dried his hair. Donning the faded jeans, button-down shirt, and waistcoat he combed a few errant strands back in place. Grabbing a favourite dark blue jacket he was ready. He had a spring in his step, looking forward to this evening after another fairly slow day at work. And it sounded as if Rosa had just got home. She was working long hours at the moment, and he wanted to catch up with her first. Perhaps Bill had a point. Bounding out of the bedroom he passed Albert on the landing.

'Good look, Dad. Not overdone the aftershave have you?' he added, wrinkling his nose. Dominic smiled and patted his son's shoulder as he made his way downstairs. He found Rosa in the lounge opening the post. Dominic bent and kissed her head, plonking down next to her. She half-smiled and handed him the latest letter from HMRC. 'Yet more tax to pay with wealth taxes on the horizon too. My *Godddd* – all the top earners will head to the continent or USA...happening already. What's the matter with these people? Why the hell can't they understand basic economics?'

'A difficult day, love?' asked Dominic, scanning the letter.

'A good one actually, just incredibly busy. I'm bushed. But at least we're narrowing in on a plan. Off to France and Spain in a nutshell.'

'Ramping up corporate law over there?'

'Moving our head office to Paris in all probability. We'll reduce our UK corporate law team to a skeleton, whilst expanding in France, Germany, and Spain. Mergers and acquisitions have ground to a virtual standstill. Our top lawyers are making noises about moving anyway because of the penal taxes here. Oh, I've had enough for one day. Think I'll grab something to eat, then have a bath.'

'You take it easy; I'll fix you something. Risotto okay?'

'Sounds wonderful. Thanks, Dom.'

He moved towards the kitchen, stopped in his tracks and turned round to say, 'I really am proud of you. You do realise that don't you? And soon to be senior partner too.'

'Yeah, amazing Mum,' said Albert, as he joined them.

Dominic busied himself with her supper, soon presenting her a tray with a wild mushroom risotto, a side salad, and a large glass of Chablis. He poured himself a small glass too and sipped as she relayed her day, the work with senior colleagues and the economist they had employed to advise on the likely impact of government reforms. Dominic listened.

'Not leaping to the defence of your tribe? Still happy with the direction of travel?'

'Not totally. It's been a difficult week, so just looking forward to seeing the lads tonight.'

'Darts?' said Rosa, looking at him intently, her dark eyebrows fusing.

'*Darts.*'

'You look good,' she said, looking at him quizzically.

'Enjoy your bath. I won't be late.'

As Dominic busied himself in preparation for his working day he caught up with news of the growing unrest on the streets of London. He switched on the *Today* programme as he sat nursing a cup of coffee and a banging headache. He really needed the aspirins and caffeine to kick in and paid scant regard to the commentary on the economy and news of mayhem on the streets of London. Rosa was an unusually early riser this morning and sat quietly brooding. Over what, Dominic hardly dared ask. The woes of the economy would soon pass, he muttered; business would pick up. Rosa scoffed in disdain. Hearing footsteps, he looked up and smiled at Albert.

'Morning, Dad,'

'Good morning, son. Ouch, that shiner looks painful. What were you up to last night?'

'A beer or two too many. Fell over and, yeah, it's sore. Bloody awful day at work; was drowning my sorrows. Been made redundant and there's few vacancies for chartered accountants at the moment. The country's going to pot. And Sally's struggling too.'

Rosa did not seem to take in what he was saying, seemed lost in her own world for the moment, but on noticing the black eye was soon fussing.

'Have two of these,' Dominic said, throwing him the aspirins.

'In need yourself, were you? Darts again?' asked Albert with a smile. Was his son mocking him?

'Mm. Washed down with a particularly good bottle of claret.'

'Thought gallons of beer was darts natural bed-fellow?' A smirk this time. And was the choice of words, the inferences deliberate? Rosa looked about to enter the fray but changed her mind. 'Par for the course these days isn't it, Dad?'

'Hey, let's just remember who sports the black eye here shall we...'

The two of them sat on opposite ends of their granite-topped breakfast bar. Dominic worried about their relationship, struggling to reach his headstrong son. But Albert had been uncannily prescient in forecasting the deprivations the new government would usher in. And the news delivered by the B&O speakers in the corner of the spacious kitchen was gloomy: demonstrations had turned to rioting in Trafalgar Square and opposition leaders were vociferous in their condemnation. The government had succeeded in uniting opposition political parties into a single opposing voice; all bar the Scottish Nationalist Party, who supported the Marxist policies and the revocation of Article 50 to ensure continued membership of the European Union. Other parties broadly aligned with the Conservative's leader, Norris Jinks – impossible to imagine just a short while ago.

'I have to admit that—'

'Yeah. All going tits-up, isn't it?'

'I'm still confident things will look up. We need to listen to the protests though… Hey, were you at that demo yesterday? I hope you didn't get dragged into the fracas.' Dominic looked sharply at Albert, assessing his black eye, noticing cuts and abrasions to his face and neck and on swollen hands as he reached for his coffee. 'Sure you just fell, Albert?'

'Tip of the iceberg. Got to do something. Even *you* must see that. A real threat to our liberty. Tobin and Connell are on a mission, the realisation of a lifetime's dream. And they have Mobilisation behind them – that manipulative, all-controlling arm of malevolence.'

He referred to the organisation created to advance the cause of British socialism, to mobilise activists, manipulate and manage social media channels. And it had become an effective, well-oiled machine – one given to expounding extreme policies while walking the tightrope of credibility to ensure the election of the Labour Party.

'Now you *are* exaggerating. Come on, let's listen to this broadcast. They're interviewing Jane Connell. I quite like her.'

Albert looked askance at his father and cast his eyes heavenwards, Rosa watching. Dominic turned the volume up as Fred Star began the interview.

FS: Welcome, Minister.

JC: Hi, Fred.

FS: Perhaps we should take the opportunity to ask about your new position as minister of communications. Some see it as a demotion.

JC: Ha, ha, ha! Very droll. The serious point here is that we in the government really must become rather more adept at communicating our messages without allowing the opposition to spread their mischief; fake news aided and abetted by the mainstream media is becoming an acute problem. Your bosses at...

FS: Is the revoking of Article 50, and the threat to the Union – both contrary to your promises – fake news? Can you comment on the imminent abandonment of Northern Ireland? Payback to your friends in the IRA and...

JC: Yes, most of that is indeed fake news, inflammatory too. We have a statement soon to be made on the Union and retaining membership of the EU is in the best interests of the economy; we are standing up *for* the British people.

FS: So why is the economy in a downward spiral? We were enjoying growth prior to the election but are now mired in recession with rising inflation. And unemployment, despite all your assertions to the contrary, is up to...

JC: Calm down, Fred. You mustn't get so het up, it really isn't good for your blood pressure. I do so worry for you.

FS: Can you comment on last night's protests in London, the riots in Birmingham?

JC: On the economy there was always going to be a period of adjustment as we set about transforming our nation: restoring socialist values, unwinding the gains of self-serving rich capitalists. And this has been made all the more painful by the desertion of the wealthiest in our nation, people who value their own prosperity above their love of country or fellow citizens. We will be better off without them in the longer term.

FS: But ordinary families are struggling as we approach the next general election. Every opinion poll is forecasting a victory for the Tories. The riots and protests would suggest your time's nearly up. Is your experiment not an abject failure? Your tenure nearly over?

JC: *Sigh.* We will shortly be announcing measures to consign unemployment to the history books. You should expect to see a significant strengthening of our national police force, the formation of new sections of our internal security, a strengthening of our borders, a streamlining of communications and news agencies. And as for the protests, I refer you to my earlier comment about fake news. We will not allow the opposition to continue to incite...or the BBC to sustain the propaganda. I won't comment further now...no, Fred, bluster away if you will but you will have to wait for an imminent announcement as to new arrangements.

FS: Okay. Changing tack, can I ask your thoughts about the importance of planning and local democracy? I refer, of course, to your prison reforms.

JC: Ralph Strong set out the position very clearly. All I would add is that our commitment to radical reforms of the prisons is a passionate desire to improve society, to improve education and opportunity for those who have fallen the wrong side of the law. Hence the building of *rehabilitation* centres. Why is this not receiving the admiration of the BBC? One has to wonder about political bias. And on local democracy and planning your claims are false. We conducted a consultation exercise which was used by all the usual pressure groups and by those directly affected by the changes. Their views have been heard. All of this is consistent with our manifesto.

FS: So your answer to the environmental lobby is hard luck?

JC: Not a bit of it. *Sigh.* Our green credentials are strong.

'Why is no one asking the right question here? Sounds like political prisoners are destined for these so-called rehab centres to me,' said Rosa, suddenly. Both Dominic and Albert turned sharply towards her. But she threw up her hands in apparent despair and padded off to the lounge.

FS: Before you go, I have another guest to draw into the conversation. Good morning, Thomas Higginbotham, Shadow Chancellor of the Treasury.

TH: Good to be here, Fred, and hello, Jane.

FS: Do you welcome the Minister of Communication's elimination of unemployment?

TH: Quite the reverse has happened, and promised measures are vague. She's had nothing to say about the recession or the dearth of business investment, the falls in productivity, our increasing isolation from the civilised

Western world. Foreign inward investment is a thing of the past and company after company is announcing their move to the continent. I fear that progress towards a Marxist state is happening at pace.

JC: You'd better believe the old ways are over, Thomas. A new order is being established; a socialist society will breathe life into the UK. We will work tirelessly to eradicate inequality. We will dismantle all barriers placed in our way.

TH: All the usual huff and puff. All the usual dogma with no evidence whatsoever to support the assertions. And, Fred, the fake news comments and threatened streamlining of news agencies sound sinister to me. I'd remind you they come on top of the nationalisation of the major UK telcos which was not featured in their manifesto. And can Jane shed light on the new structures going up in remote areas of the Northern Pennines and in the Welsh Mountains? Are they a UK variant of the concentration camps for Uighur Muslims in China? On all these questions, I challenge you to meet me face to face, Jane.

Dominic and Albert again exchanged glances.

JC: Ha, ha, ha. It's good to have a laugh first thing in the morning and I hope you feel better for getting all that bile off your chest, Thomas. I tell you what, why don't you come around to my office for a chat? I'll give you advance sight of our plans. Now, I can hardly say fairer than that, can I?

TH: Name the time.

JC: Okay, two this afternoon?

TH: Well…let me see… I have a meeting with…

JC: There you go, listeners, a genuine invitation and he's too busy. Ha, ha, ha.

TH: I'll be there.

Just then a thumping at the front door demanded their attention. Albert stayed rooted in his chair, as Dominic went to investigate. He stepped back in surprise at the sight of his early callers.

'Sorry to disturb you, sir. Does an Albert Green live here?' the constable asked, checking the name in his notebook. His older colleague looked on, shuffling from foot to foot and sighing.

'Yes, hang on.'

He shouted and Albert soon hove into view, his face like thunder.

'What is it?' asked Albert, as Dominic withdrew a few paces.

31

'May we come in? We need to ask you a few questions?' asked the young constable.

'*No*, you may not. What about, anyway?' said Albert.

'Last night. Where were you?' said the senior policeman, pulling his colleague aside.

'Nothing to do with you…' said Albert.

'*Albert*! Be civil,' said Dominic from the shadows.

The constable reacted by pushing his way into the hallway. But Albert told him he had no right to enter without a warrant, placing a hand on the policeman's chest.

'We aren't a police state just yet. Bugger off…'

The policeman shoved Albert roughly.

'Please calm down, everyone,' said Dominic, but his words were ignored as Albert responded angrily, striking back. The policeman lost his footing, was sent sprawling. Dominic recoiled, edging deeper into the hall. As the policeman struggled to his feet, a thin line of blood trickled down his cheek and he sported a cut lip. Albert made to slam the door, but his adversary lunged, made a grab for Albert, manhandled him outside. He was quickly arrested and cuffed, read his rights on the move.

Dominic looked on in horror, shaking at the onset of conflict, as his son was dragged out and unceremoniously bundled into the police car. Just as the door was slammed shut, he pulled himself together enough to shout to his son, 'I'll phone someone, Albert.'

Rosa appeared at his side, still in fluffy slippers and dressing gown.

'What on earth?'

Dominic's heart hammered in his chest; a wave of nausea swept over him. What had Albert done? Why could he not just answer the bloody questions? They stared in astonishment as the car sped away.

Dominic and Rosa speculated as to what their passionate, impetuous son had been doing last night. Dominic could guess. He needed to find a way of reaching out to him; persuade him that things were not so bad, that it would all come good in the end. Rosa was sceptical. But Dominic ploughed on. He resolved to try to talk sense into Albert.

'It'll be a first, if that works,' said Rosa.

'He'll come to his senses, apologise, and then hopefully they'll let him go with a warning. I'm sure he will, Rosa. It'll be okay, just you see.'

Rosa looked at him through narrowing eyes, muttered a profanity in her native language and reached for her mobile.

Ping.

> **Jinks Warnings:** *Major speech scheduled for noon.*
> The leader of the opposition will highlight the growing
> unrest as reforms hit the economy hard. He will point
> to the unrest in major cities and the need for the
> government to listen to the growing wail of protest.
> Jinks will pledge the support of the Conservative Party
> to fight Marxist ideology, the abandonment
> of the Union and the cancellation of Brexit contrary
> to the democratic referendum vote of 2016.

Dominic sighed as he replayed the earlier scene in his head. Rosa emerged half an hour later, having showered and dressed. She shunned the offered coffee.

'I've spoken to the solicitor,' Rosa said.

'What did he think? A reprimand before being sent on his way?'

'No chance,' said Rosa. 'If he's struck a policeman, they'll charge him for sure.'

'They're exaggerating; it was a bit of harmless pushing and shoving and he fell.'

'*Sure!* You're driving me mad. What planet are you on?' she said.

'Come on, Rosa. These are tough times. We've got to be strong.'

'The damned country is in turmoil, Dominic, and now Albert…'

'I know, but we'll pull through, we just need to rediscover our old magic, Rosa; you and me…'

'*Mierda.* Sort yourself out and then maybe we can do something about *us*…maybe. I don't know,' said Rosa.

'There's nothing to sort out other than Albert's plight.'

'I don't have time to talk about this. I'm bored with the subject anyway. But I've just about had enough. Your business is in the doldrums, mine is in retreat, we're poorer by the day, we continue to drift apart and…'

'Please, Rosa, please stop this. I love you; I've always loved you, I always will. I made one mistake years ago. I just don't know what else I can say. And please don't join the doom-mongers and doubters. *Please.*'

'*Ha!* Tell me what the hell there is to be optimistic about? It's not stopped raining for weeks, it's cold, business is going up in smoke, Albert's in jail...'

'Rosa, I love you dearly but—'

'For *Godddd's* sake won't you take your rose-tinted specs off. Let's take the kids. Let's move. Away from this mess, away from your...your...'

'To Spain I suppose?' said Dominic, trying to cut off that avenue.

'Of course. Or France. We've spoken about this many times; now's the time to do it. You said yourself the business needs a new direction. Set up in Girona. Albert's out of work, so maybe he and Sally can join us; it might be the break he needs. He might even take an interest in catering, work with you. Before he lands himself in serious trouble. And Juan finishes university this year, so the timing's good for him too. And I could transfer to the office in Barcelona.'

'Maybe you're right...'

'My Godddd! My *Godddd*! At last. Let's do it, let's escape this hell. I'll ring the estate agents and...what's wrong? Why the grimace?'

'Hold on just a second. I said *maybe*. I need to speak with Brandon, and we'll have to plan carefully for something like this. We can't just up sticks and move. And anyway, the market's on the floor, so let's bide our time...'

Rosa brought her balled fists down hard on his chest in frustration and was soon in full flow. She ridiculed his optimism, his weakness, his philandering. She would not listen to his denials, his appeals for her to be reasonable.

'Do what you like but if I take up the senior partner position I'm heading for the continent. Perhaps we're done anyway...*Darts*. Ha! Hope she appreciated the expensive cologne.'

Juan and Ellie were welcome interventions as they crept sleepily into the room in dressing gowns and pyjamas, clutching mugs of coffee. Juan and Ellie were at university: their son at Exeter, Ellie at UCL, home for a few days. They listened in silence to the news of Albert's arrest, Ellie offering sympathy to Rosa. Juan sat and brooded. He wore a frown and shook his head gently. At least their appearance was a welcome distraction.

Just then the telephone rang, and Dominic left them to take the call. After a short conversation he re-joined Rosa in the lounge, the youngsters having gone back to bed. Rosa sat smouldering with knitted eyebrows, a scowl darkening her features. Her eyes flashed her displeasure. Dominic sat down and took hold of her hand.

'And?'

'Your guy tried to reach you, but your phone must be on silent. Albert's been charged for assaulting a police officer.'

'My *Godddd*! I told you, I told you. I'll *keeell* him…'

'He should be home later.'

'What's the penalty? Does he go to court? The bloody young fool.'

'His solicitor says he could face up to six months in prison—'

'My *Godddd*!'

'But that's unlikely. He'll probably get a severe reprimand and a fine.'

CHAPTER 6: INTERVIEW

He made a call to Brandon on his way into work. *No it cannot wait. Yes they needed to talk.* Less than an hour later he was assailing Brandon with a proposition. A restless night's sleep had followed Rosa's words and he was resolved to doing what he could to steer their relationship out of choppy waters. Come to think of it, the seas were stormy more often than not, threatening to overwhelm. He found Brandon checking through bills to pay, demands from accounts overdue, and he told Dominic that some of their suppliers were calling it a day. Dominic had hoped for a more positive start to their conversation but decided to press on anyway.

'Rosa and I have been thinking. Why don't we transfer some of the operation to Spain, say to Girona? We have good people, talented chefs who can keep London ticking along until we get through to the other side. Now must be a great time to do something radical, don't you think?'

'Crazy idea, that's what I think. Where would the investment come from?'

'Can't we talk to the banks, put up a business case?'

'And what would that be? Have you a plan?'

'More your forte than mine...but we could open a restaurant in Girona. There's a really vibrant gastronomic culture there. And we could do more broadcasting in the region. You know, something like...*Diamond in Iberia...*'

Brandon looked at Dominic aghast, threw his arms up in despair and exhaled. Not for the first time Dominic wondered what he did to Brandon, to Rosa, to Albert, all of whom were driven to exasperation from well-intentioned suggestions. His partner paced around the room, before coming to a halt at the window, gazing outwards. Dominic watched his partner's reflected image intently.

Brandon was silent for a few moments and then, apparently addressing the outside world, he said, 'Such an innocent. When will you grasp what's happening – if not to the nation, to our way of life, to the economy, then for goodness' sake at least come to terms with our own predicament. Do I really need to spell it out? So be it. Much more of this and it will be the end of the road. Bust. Bankrupt. If I could find a buyer now, then we would have to sell. But who's going to buy any business, let alone a failing upmarket restaurant chain serving the well-heeled? As for starting afresh in another country… however appealing it might be to escape… Can't you see? Banks aren't lending, we've no liquidity, private equity is in hibernation. The country's going to hell in a handcart.'

'Surely, we can…' Dominic stopped mid-flow as Brandon spun round, his face almost as red as his braces. Dominic quickly raised his hands. 'Okay, okay I get it. So, what do we do, Brandon? I could see about another television programme, maybe.'

'I've tried these last few weeks, but even the BBC have no money. Would you believe they've even begun to tax them, to rake off the licence fees? Unbelievable. They're taxing a tax! Who came up with that wheeze? And programmes extolling the attractions of high-class cuisine or travel or property-owning have all been declared decadent, an insult to the working man, to their new order.' *Ping*.

'There you go, right on cue. Read that,' Brandon said, handing Dominic his phone.

Breaking News
The government confirms wealth taxes on property
above £1M in addition to the hike in tax rates.

'Crikey. We can't be surprised though. It was in the manifesto. Not ideal, mind.'

'The master of understatement as ever. Bad for business, unbelievably bad. But I have an idea. Quite creative, although I fear you may regard it as a bit unsavoury. It should buy us some time. Needs must and all that.'

As he headed towards the television studios, he ruminated on the conversation with Brandon. It was always a long shot. At least he could tell Rosa he had tried. But he needed to pull himself round, get back on the front foot in time for the interview he had been persuaded to hold with the local news magazine programme. It was not a big deal. He was used to the media and knew that a positive mindset was essential. But this time he had no prior knowledge as to the precise nature of the questioning, no inkling as to what the primary focus was going to be. He would have to wing it.

He was shown into a familiar studio but had left little time for any preparation other than the cosmetics: powdering his face, checking his hair, straightening his tie. He secretly enjoyed the pampering and needed to look his best for his followers. The briefing was cursory: just a general view from a Labour Party activist, local businessman and celebrity chef. It was one of a number they were conducting over the course of a week, for their daily *London Today* evening slot.

He was shown into the studio; he picked his way between the cameras and the usual broadcasting paraphernalia to take a seat in a bucket chair opposite his interviewer. He sipped from a glass of water and was soon given the cue. Rosemary Staples summarised the downturn of the economy and set out how *London Today* would examine the impact on local businesses. Dominic watched her closely as this diminutive, grey-haired, middle-aged lady delivered her lines in a conversational, mild-mannered tone. She could be anybody's favourite, slightly dotty aunty. Rosemary then went on to welcome Dominic Green, aka the celebrity chef Dominic Diamond, placing the emphasis upon his celebrity status.

RS: Are you pleased to have the government you argued so passionately for, Dominic?

DG: I'm delighted to see socialist ideals at the forefront of a radical programme of change which is long overdue. I'm no politician...

RS: Oh, come now. That's exactly what you are. You're an activist with a passionate zeal to rid the country of the Tories, are you not?

DG: Well, I'm certainly pleased to see the back of the Tories, the end to austerity.

RS: And how's it going so far, would you say? Marks out of ten?

DG: It was always going to be challenging at first; a pause in economic growth was likely. We all knew that.

RS: The recession, unemployment approaching three million, inflation... all part of the medicine you mean? What's the impact on your business? On you personally?

DG: Challenging, but we'll be okay.

RS: Your business partner is on record as having said you're on the verge of bankruptcy? Is that what you mean by challenging?

DG: An overstatement. We always expected a downturn.

RS: That's not what you said prior to the election. I have a quotation here...

Dominic ran his finger between collar and neck; he felt hot and took a sip of water as she read aloud his own words. He twiddled with his wedding ring, and unconsciously rubbed his truncated finger.

RS: I ask you again for your marks out of ten?

DG: I'm confident we'll get through this, and the country will emerge all the stronger.

RS: Okay, you clearly aren't going to answer the question. Can I ask for your comments on the prison reform programme?

DG: This is an area in which I can claim no expertise or particular knowledge, but the policy is admirable. As I understand it, this is all about reducing recidivism, about...

RS: And what about *how* this is being done. Are you not concerned at the government pushing it at break-neck speed through parliament? Is this not to deny democratic scrutiny? And how concerned are you about the environmental impact? And what about the reports about these so-called rehabilitation centres becoming little more than correction centres to brainwash political dissidents?

DG: I repeat – I strongly welcome the thrust of the policy. But I must admit...

RS: Yes? Some unease about the *where*, the *how*, the *impact*?

DG: Well... I do have reservations in these areas. There have been errors in the rush to implementation, which makes others question government's motives. I think this is unwise. But of course there's so much to do, much that needs to be changed.

RS: And of the environment? Any concerns? Your youngest son is an ardent supporter of Extinction Rebellion, is he not?

DG: I won't talk about my family, and I'd be grateful if you'd respect their privacy. But of course I have concerns about environmental impact. In fact, I would go so far as to appeal to the government to adjust their course. Brown field sites would be wiser.

RS: Thank you, Dominic.

Rosemary smiled at him, and he withdrew from the studio as the cameras focused in on the presenter. As he made his way towards the exit, he turned sharply on hearing Rosemary Staples' summary.

RS: Well, we've heard first-hand from one of the leading celebrity activists for this socialist revolution. He condemns the government's approach – the devastating ecological impact, the abuse of democracy and local planning. Tomorrow we bring you…

'That's not right. You're putting words in my mouth, taking my comments out of context.'

But it was too late. And while Dominic fumed in the adjoining room, he watched on the screen the return of the avuncular aunty persona. An assistant editor thanked him for his contribution, assured him he had been excellent. He looked great too. *Can see why you have so many admirers.* He allowed himself to be mollified by her praise. Then she voiced admiration for his bravery in speaking out so clearly. That worried him. It worried him a great deal.

Later that evening Dominic looked at the tweets in horror. He had inadvertently provoked a fire storm as environmentalists proclaimed his wisdom, while vile, abusive messages lambasted him on his censure of the Labour government: turncoat, traitor, capitalist pig. He was horrified, and felt compelled to offer a tweet himself in an attempt to calm the outcry:

#Equalityofopportunity
Diamond
Full marks to the prison reform policy: reduce
recidivism by embracing education – create
opportunity for disadvantaged in our society.

But the outpouring was in full flow, and his own protestations seemed to serve only as an incentive to those who regarded his comments as a heinous crime designed to undermine the left-wing revolution underway. The more he tried to assert his support, the more the abuse flowed.

CHAPTER 7: DESTINATION DAY -5, 21.14

2027

The night noises of fellow inmates rendered sleep impossible: screams from vivid nightmares; farting and grunting and swearing; and pissing and shitting in the buckets in the far corner. His own nightmares had brought on cold sweats, spasms that jerked him into full consciousness in a blind panic. Recurring images of *urban scarecrowing*. He distracted and comforted himself with memories of the early days with Rosa. As he'd ambled into the outdoor kitchen set on the beach at Empúries, in the Costa Brava, where the programme was to be filmed, he had been struck by the beauty of an assistant to the producer, an expressive young lady with lustrous black hair and dark eyes given to flaring their warning to those who incurred her wrath. She'd been wearing a tight red dress and sandals; she looked stunning. Her first words had been to castigate him for being late *and stop slouching, will you?* He could not recall exactly what he had said in response but knew it had been some casual quip which earnt him a flaring of the nostrils, hand gesticulations and a swift *mierda* for good measure. But they quickly hit it off, the laid-back Englishman and the fiery, intelligent Spaniard. Their mutual love of food and wine, together with strong family values, had always been the threads that bound their relationship. Oh, Rosa...

But Dominic's reverie, his escape from his hell, was abruptly terminated by the banging and clanking and creaking of the door to their cell, through which marched two guards, Pock and Shorty; so labelled by the veterans. Acne-scarred Pock was a squat, thick-set, brutish man who seemed to relish the wielding of his thick leather boots: gratuitous, bruising kicks. He was accompanied by a tall, lanky guard.

'Jimmy Bell, it's your lucky night,' said a smirking Shorty, as a meal of something approximating roast beef was placed in front of him by a third guard, a gloopy gravy already skinning at the edges. The soggy, doughy mess in the middle was presumably a nod to a Yorkshire pudding. Jimmy looked up from his prone position with wide eyes; he opened his mouth to say something, but only a wail of despair escaped.

'And Sharon Briggs and Tom Handley,' added Pock, grinning as he watched their reactions. Tom muttered angry sentiments impossible to decipher; Sharon broke into a defiant scream before collapsing in tears, unable to handle the enormity of her predicament.

Dominic watched the drama play out with increasing dismay and horror, emotions close to boiling point at the display of human trauma stirred by taunting, sadistic cruelty.

'There's no rhyme or reason,' whispered a middle-aged man to Dominic's right. 'Jimmy's been here over a week, Sharon just two days. A half-decent meal signifies only one thing.'

'And you? How long have—'

'Ten days. Overdue. Name's Simon. No time for us to become friends. Quite expected to be a recipient of...' He nodded at Jimmy's tray of food. 'The ability of mankind to inflict such unspeakable horrors on so many of their fellow citizens never ceases to appal me. I guess we are all expendable in the quest for equality. *Ha*! Why does egalitarianism have to dress in brutish terror? Is this what Marx really had in mind? And Pock and Shorty there – they're just kids. Probably half-decent young men deep down. They've all lost their way... we should find it in our hearts to...' Simon shook his head sadly and paused, but his whisper had been overheard by a young man close to them.

'Bollocks to that. Evil bastards.'

'Your finding good even in this situation does you credit, Simon. I'm afraid I struggle to reach such heights. I used to be the eternal optimist once. It drove my family mad. Mr Micawber, they used to call me. Apparently, I was naïve and unrealistic. Events have sadly proved them right... Tell me, were you a cleric before all this, perhaps? A religious man?'

'Barrister and lay preacher.'

'So why on earth...'

'A long story. The long and short of it is that the judiciary, along with every other institution, has bowed to the will of the government. So, judges and all associated with the legal system escape scrutiny to live near-normal lives. For now. I did what little I could to argue for justice, which didn't go unnoticed.

And my sermons didn't find favour. Apparently, I was preaching propaganda! The irony's delicious, don't you think?'

Just then, the third guard returned with plastic beakers of water, which he plopped down carelessly, disregarding the spillage; a basket of bread and cheese was also dropped into the middle of the room. The guards watched as some of the inmates threw themselves on the provisions.

'Animals,' sneered Pock.

Shorty took the opportunity to kick the backside of one of the prisoners, accompanied by a rash of expletives, which amused his colleague; their laughter gradually faded as they left their charges to their rations.

Dominic looked on in consternation as Jimmy cast aside his tray, placing his head in his hands, weeping quietly. Tom shouted an obscenity after the guards. But it was false, inconsequential bravado offered up to a thick steel door. Sharon sobbed noisily, and an older lady tried her best to offer comfort while two of the others tucked into the discarded meals.

CHAPTER 8: HANGOVER

EARLY 2020S

Dominic had spent much of the night tossing and turning, his mind tussling with Brandon's business diagnosis, with Rosa's strictures, his head fuzzy from too much wine. As he reached for the paracetamols he groaned. He stumbled to the bathroom and took a long, cool shower. Standing in front of his mirror, he took in the rheumy eyes staring back at him. It was beginning to dawn upon him that things were unlikely to improve. Rosa was still struggling to forgive his transgressions and was even given to threatening the end of their marriage. He could not believe she really meant that, but knew he had work to do to repair trust and rediscover the mojo of their relationship. He had to work harder on this front. Meanwhile, his business was disintegrating, his son was in trouble and his volatile wife wanted to escape to sunny Spain. Who could blame her on that score, at least? And in the country, the volume of protest, abuse, rioting could no longer be dismissed as a temporary phenomenon. All that he had built over decades now seemed in peril. Yes, he lived in an expensive and desirable property: a four-storey Georgian town house in Notting Hill. But he had a large mortgage that needed to be paid. Both he and Brandon had taken hefty salary reductions, so he was eating into his savings every month just to meet outgoings. And the collapse of the property market meant that any sale would simply crystalise huge losses he could not afford. What to do?

Slurping his orange juice, he scanned the latest news on his phone.

> ***Riots Erupt:*** *Warring factions on the rampage as large swathes of Sheffield, Leeds and Manchester cordoned off following last night's riots. Sixty people injured, four seriously and one in a condition described as life threatening.*

Location of Shadow Chancellor a Mystery: Where is Thomas Higginbotham? Following his appointment with Jane Connell in Downing Street no one has seen or heard from him, according to the Conservative Party.

Freak Storm: Glasgow deluged as high winds, torrential rain and hailstones submerge the Newton Mearns area of the city.

House Prices: Demand for homes in London and the South East collapses as foreign investors look elsewhere. Price reductions of up to twenty-five percent recorded in London.

Fake News: The BBC and the paper media are accused of fake news by the new minister of communications, Jane Connell.

Just then, the 08.10 broadcast was starting, and he tuned in to Fred Star's dulcet tones welcoming the Minister of Communications, Jane Connell, to the programme. But today his voice seemed scratchy, sandpaper dry, devoid of the usual velvety richness associated with the veteran broadcaster.

FS: Before we ask you about your recent statements, Minister, can you comment upon your meeting with Thomas Higginbotham, Shadow Chancellor. Our listeners will recall you inviting him to meet with you. No one seems to have seen hide nor hair of him since.

JC: Good morning. Sadly, there's nothing to report. The dear man obviously decided he had better things to do than meet with me. He failed to show.

FS: But we have footage of him striding down Downing Street, disappearing inside Number Ten. Who did he see, if not you, and why have we not been able to track him down since?

JC: You're mistaken. In fact, I have a video clip here which I'll post online for you to study if you wish. It's date-stamped and shows Thomas slipping into Diamond's, a decadent restaurant in Mayfair run by that rich celebrity chef, Dominic Diamond; a self-publicist made rich off the fat of his downtrodden workers. And you will note that this was the precise time at which Thomas

Higginbotham was due to meet me. And look – I even have a copy of his bill. This is what we are seeking to escape from, Fred. He and a colleague had an expensive lunch which cost over five-hundred pounds: lobster, prawns, beef fillet, salmon en croute, Grand Marnier souffle, cheeses…and let's not forget the two bottles of Chateau Rothschild. Here we are, Fred. Even footage of them stumbling out of the restaurant later that afternoon. This is what the privileged capitalists get up to whilst the normal working man suffers impoverished wages to keep them fuelled on their red claret.

Dominic gasped at the mention of his own name. He smelt a Brandon Scam. What's he done? He was aghast that he should be explicitly mentioned. Albert was staring open-mouthed at his father. *Was it true?* Albert wanted to know. But as far as his son was concerned, choosing lunch over the company of Jane Connell showed eminently good judgement.

'Heard about your interview, Dad. Interesting. A rapid U-turn. About time too.'

'Don't you start. It was no such thing. I voiced my support…did you not see it? That bloody interviewer just took my words out of context.'

Dominic racked his brain to think back to the lavish lunch suggested, but he could not know who was in the restaurant. Brandon had mentioned something about a senior politician, but it was not unusual for them to cater for public figures: politicians, actors, business moguls.

FS: There must be some mistake. He can't have been in two places at the same time.

JC: As you say. Fake news, Fred, fake news. It must *stop*!

FS: Let's move on, Minister.

JC: I think that might be wise. We would remind you that this government was elected in a landslide by *The People* to radically overhaul the outdated, capitalist order of the UK. This we are doing *exactly* as promised. But the ingrained prejudices of the establishment elite are dragging its feet and obstructing us every step of the way. The use of fake news is a daily occurrence, and we will take whatever steps are necessary to eradicate it. Action will be taken to rid our society of privilege, of inequality, of social tension, of poverty, of homelessness. The profit motive must give way to social justice and equality. These points will be elaborated upon in an essay that is to be published in every newspaper in the country and distributed widely in public places. And the

BBC and mainstream media must mend its ways.

FS: Your warning sounds sinister. It's not fake news. Our job is to hold the government to account for—

JC: Enough! If the rich American and Australian owners of the paper media fail to take heed, we will ban them.

FS: That sounds like censorship—

JC: Similarly, the BBC, ITN and all the others. You should not underestimate the will of this government.

FS: I doubt anyone does, but normal, reasonable people are up in arms, Minister: Middle Englanders, if you like.

JC: Again, I plead a sense of perspective, Fred. Let's take a step back for one moment. I realise many are struggling with the changes underway, but this is about rebalancing the scales... There's bound to be some difficulties and the government will do all we can to assist those in genuine hardship. But don't talk to me about the bosses, the establishment, the rich...talk to me about the workers, the impoverished who deserve better. And I promise you they *will* get social justice; we *will* redistribute wealth in this country. It's what we *promised*. It's what the electorate voted for. This is democracy in action.

FS: Listeners will note your lack of empathy for those losing out. I must press you. When will you at least compensate them?

JC: Our empathy is reserved for the downtrodden workers, the poor, the destitute. Move on...

FS: Then can we ask you about your oft-stated plans to eradicate unemployment and strengthen our security and police services?

JC: As we set out only yesterday, our police force will recruit a further sixty thousand staff; a new internal security force, Socialist National Police Service, has already been created and will expand to ensure a presence in every town and city throughout Great Britain. Conscription will commence from next month. Every single young person under the age of thirty will be required to serve in either the SNPS, or in the STS, the State Technology Service, or in the armed forces. They will serve a minimum of twelve months after which they will be allocated a work position as determined by national need.

FS: Allocated?

JC: According to national needs. Why the surprise?

FS: So, you will allocate roles contrary to an individual's wishes? Government will dictate the career paths of our youngsters? That defies any normal definition of justice, fairness, liberty...

JC: Not at all, not at all. You do so like to dramatise. Of course, we will take account of every person's preferences and skills. But in the final analysis the needs of the *State* are paramount.

FS: Surely this fuels the fires of those accusing the government of an inexorable move towards a totalitarian, one-party Marxist state. For how much longer can you ignore the protests across the country? When will the government listen and engage in reasonable, rational dialogue? Your statements have sinister undertones, Minister.

JC: Again, I note that the BBC chooses to refer to the prejudices of the privileged. Why don't you highlight the demonstrations and parades of the revolutionary workers. They are also in daily evidence in most cities. Why don't you air the grievances of the workers in whose name we are revolutionising society? Millions have been marginalised, subjected to poverty wages, denied opportunity. What you are referring to is the squealing of the rich as resources and priorities switch.

FS: We do report on the protests of both sides of this argument. Please answer the charge that your announcement this morning may be received as being sinister and malevolent in intent.

JC: Ha, ha, ha. Not a bit of it. The idea of eradicating unemployment will surely be welcomed by everyone, the notion of more effective policing to reduce crime also, and the need to harness the excellence of British technology capability for the benefits of the state is surely unarguable?

Dominic and Albert listened in silence, occasionally flicking through the newspaper articles and lurid pictures of rioting. Bloodied figures holding banners calling for the overthrow of the government; young men and women brandishing batons, rocks and petrol bombs as raging battles ensued around burnt-out cars on the streets of British cities. Both sides seemed equally enraged, divided, engaged in a spiral of violence. He was shocked at the eruption of violence, although the anti-government sentiments seemed to Dominic understandable, but they only served to inflame opinion and the truculence of ministers. The announcement of the increase in policing numbers was likely to be perceived as a further strengthening of the resolve of government to hold their line – to fight any and all opposition. As for the role of an internal security force, the SNPS, the remit of this new force was opaque. But it seemed ominous.

'And what do you make of the STS, Albert? You understand more about technology than me. What's that all about?' Dominic rubbed his forehead in a vain attempt to ameliorate his stabbing headache. He looked at his son, whose face seemed set in a permanent scowl these days.

'Another darts evening last night, Dad?'

'Something like that. And business is difficult. Teetering on the brink if I'm to believe Brandon.'

'What will you do?'

'What can I do? What can any of us do. Grit our teeth and see it through...'

'That's a cop-out, isn't it? We've got to act, make this bloody government change course,' said Albert. He banged his fist on the table to underline his point.

Dominic sighed, wearily. He had heard it all from Rosa. And Brandon. They all seemed to advocate either escape or confrontation. But neither option seemed to offer any lasting solution. They had not thought it through. 'Getting back to the announcement. The STS – your thoughts?'

'There are rumours of plans to cut us off from the internet—'

'Can they do that?'

'It happened in Iran and in Pakistan. The Chinese control technology channels too. And social media platforms may also be cast adrift in favour of creating our own platform. I've no idea if that's likely or how long it would take, but Whitehall has been working secretly with technology clusters in various universities over the last twelve months. Sally has a friend who works in a technology hub in Cambridge, attached to the uni there. Apparently, they're all sworn to secrecy, but these things get out. Dangerous though – clink beckons for any worker caught divulging details.'

'Our universities are amongst the most respected in the world. They'd never engage in anything that...'

'Most are short of funds. And anyways it's all dressed up in special research projects, and do I need to remind you of the prevailing left-wing bias of the university elite? Dad, we have to *do* something... By the way, I have my court hearing later today.'

'Oh, my *Godddd*!' cried Rosa, who had drifted in. 'Why you not tell us? What time, where is it? I must get dressed and...'

'Whoa there, Mum. I'll be with my solicitor and I'd rather you weren't there.'

'Too bad. You go without me, I *keeell* you. I love you, Albert. And what are you doing looking so sorry for yourself?' she said, turning on Dominic. 'Do you not care that your son is to be imprisoned – tortured for all we know?' She threw up her arms in dramatic exasperation, muttered obscenities in Spanish; cojones were mentioned once or twice before she grabbed a pile of clothes and left the room, spitting venom in all directions.

Dominic and Albert exchanged glances and burst out laughing. Rosa in full flow was a sight to behold, but her remonstrations and over-the-top narrative seemed to prick the moment.

'It's this afternoon by the way, two thirty. It should be okay. I just have to dress smartly, eat lashings of humble pie and hopefully escape with a suspended sentence, possibly a fine.'

'Makes you wonder if a flat cap and boiler suit might not create the better impression,' said Dominic.

'Very good, Dad. I'll go and find Mum, have a chat.'

'But seriously, are you okay? Your mum and I will be there. Try stopping us. You might not be so worried but…'

'I'll be fine.'

Despite the momentary light relief provided unknowingly by Rosa, Dominic's mood was sombre as he reflected on his son's courtroom appearance. Hopefully, Albert was right – a rap on the knuckles and community service. But he would be there for him. Of course he would. And as he heard Albert trying to reassure Rosa, Dominic's mind drifted back to what his son had said. Albert's passionate assertions of the need to "do something" were understandable. But do *what?* The interview with Jane Connell was shocking – it seemed to portend more dangerous news. It almost seemed as if she was taunting the media to dare the government to be even more extreme. And the growing clamour from their left-wing activists was becoming ever shriller, their actions more and more violent. Only last week a Conservative member had been attacked in his constituency office and hospitalised. It was news that had little airing, which seemed to say something about how inured the country was becoming to what would once have made the headlines. Oh, come on, Dominic, stop being so gloomy. Perhaps it was just the result of the hangover and a bad night's sleep. That and worrying about his son's plight.

CHAPTER 9: REPERCUSSIONS

Dominic emerged from Bond Street Tube station, and ambled along the well-trodden route, hardly aware of the constant drizzle and cold wind. He was trying to pull himself out of his torpor. On impulse, he dived into a coffee shop. But not even the caffeine fix sparked him into life, and he found himself increasingly despondent listening to a heated argument between two youths: one extolling the virtues of long-awaited social changes, the other delivering views he constantly heard from Albert and Brandon.

Ping. WhatsApp messages.

> **Albert**
> *I'll be fine today, Dad. Look after Mum. Watch out for Juan. Getting dragged into FF. You know how he's always spoiling for a fight!*
> **Albert**
> *Rich coming from me I know!*

Dominic smiled. His son had some of his mother's temperament, but he liked to think they were a close family for all their disagreements. And what's this about FF and Juan? Something else to worry about no doubt. *Ping.*

> **Albert**
> *Juan told me about this guy, Dad. Seb via Seb999@hotmail.com.*

Albert

Speak to him. He can help.

And now what's he up to? All very cryptic. Sighing, he finished the last of his flat white, pulled his collar up and trudged out. As he rounded the corner, approaching Diamond's, he stopped short on seeing a noisy, angry crowd carrying banners proclaiming the merits of socialism. What had sparked a demonstration here? It was perfectly normal to find such protests in Trafalgar Square, at the Palace of Westminster, at the US embassy and even outside Buckingham Palace these days. But not in Mayfair. His eyes alighted on messages denouncing hedonism, privilege, the decadence of the elite – of placards proclaiming: '*Snouts in Trough*', '*Gluttonous Rich Bastards*'... But why outside his restaurant? Then it struck him, as a placard with his name emblazoned across it hove into view. He had been named. And, as far as the protesters were concerned, also shamed. He knew instantly who was behind yet another scam. *Brandon*!

A solitary policeman keeping an eye on proceedings stood on the periphery. And then two youths recognised Dominic and he found himself surrounded by angry, red-faced guys brandishing fists in his face, pushing and shoving. He was shocked at their cold hatred; one youth so animated his spittle projected from screamed abuse. He felt the same stabs of fear, the same flight instinct, the same clammy hands as he had all those years ago. There was no escape for Dominic now, just as there had been no escape for poor Tim. Dominic noticed staff at the restaurant door, so breathed in deeply, put his head down, hands in pockets, and edged towards the entrance. He was jostled and jeered. A violent shove from behind caused him to lose his footing – next minute he was sprawled yards from the threshold. A jubilant cry went up; the chanting and jeering grew louder. Prostrate, he was now easy prey; he was assailed by violent kicks, placards raining down on him. Pulling into a tight foetal ball, he covered his head with his hands. Now he was receiving the same treatment as his blood brother, beaten mercilessly all those years ago. His failure to find courage in the face of violence then had consigned Tim to the same fate that was his today. Perhaps this was his comeuppance. At that moment, the burly policeman deigned to enter the fray, managing to part the group to reach him.

His assailants pulled back but continued to scream their howls of protest as the policeman pulled him to his feet just as the front door swung open, helping hands enabling him to crawl inside.

The restaurant manager, Gina, and his sous chef, Bill, rushed to him, administered first aid to facial cuts and bruises, persuaded him to drink sweetened tea, tried to calm him. His nerves were shot through, and a proffered brandy was eagerly despatched. When Brandon appeared on the scene, he got short shrift. Not now, Brandon. You have a lot to answer for.

Albert was later found guilty of assaulting a police officer and sentenced to four months in a rehabilitation centre. Dominic and Rosa looked on disbelievingly as their son was led away in handcuffs. The solicitor pulled them into an anteroom to explain that this was a relatively new initiative with several centres being daisy-chained across the bleak Pennine uplands and the Welsh mountains. The emphasis was upon re-education, skills, health, and well-being, all designed to improve opportunities for employment. But there were no visiting rights and the content of the educational programmes and nature of the regime, of life inside these institutions, was opaque.

'Sentences are for a minimum period with no upper limit, no remission for good behaviour – quite the reverse – the period served depends upon the willingness of inmates to learn the error of their ways,' said Rosa.

'How do you know that?' asked Dominic.

'I examined the legislation with one of my partners, of course. You might deal in blind faith; I deal with legal realities.'

'But three months to learn the folly of striking a policeman?' asked Dominic.

'*Bastards*! He'll be force-fed propaganda, dawn to dusk,' said Rosa.

'Surely not but...*you* must know,' stammered Dominic, appealing to his solicitor.

'I don't, but there are rumours. Completely unsubstantiated—'

'And?' said Rosa.

'Not here,' the solicitor said, glancing nervously around.

Stepping outside, he saw a large, noisy crowd had materialised, and Dominic feared a re-run of this morning. Rosa looked around her, opening and shutting her mouth without speaking. They paused for a moment, and fortunately this time there were police on hand to create a path through to waiting taxis. Dominic noticed there were two distinct factions: the socialists sporting badges with a large red M and their black-shirted opponents. On the periphery were a few supporters who were chanting his name, his image smiling from posters held aloft. As objects rained down on them they were bundled into a taxi; it gently pulled away, at first buffeted by protesters until police managed to drag them back. As he glanced through the rear window, he saw that the different groups had turned on each other, the police struggling to restore peace and order.

'What's the world coming to? Are you alright...?' It was then that Dominic noticed blood oozing from Rosa's head, tears trickling down her cheeks. He insisted they head to the nearest A&E department, but she was having none of it and they continued their journey homebound. Just a scratch, a plaster will do the trick. Her tears were angry tears. Their solicitor was also visibly shaken, checking himself out for cuts and bruises.

'Did you see those badges?' asked Dominic.

'Mobilisation. Tobin and Connell's pet rottweilers: the vanguard of the socialist movement, the drive behind the membership explosion and lurch to Marxism.'

'They *bastards*. Missionary in zeal and with a once-in-a-lifetime opportunity to revolutionise our society, our economy and redefine democracy,' said Rosa.

'Well, that's certainly one interpretation,' said Dominic, surprised at her insights. He added, 'But I've not seen the badges before. Are you sure you're okay, Rosa?' He fussed, alternately dabbing at her cut, and stroking her hand until she haughtily pushed him aside.

'It's not only the activists that wear their colours now. It's the sign of loyalty, a badge of honour if you like,' said the solicitor, taking no notice of Rosa's gash, of Dominic's dismay.

'Ha, honour? They don't know meaning of words. My *Goddd*!'

'Wrong word. I fear it will become a must-have accessory for a peaceful life. Every SNPS member will sport them along with their red flags.'

'You seem well-versed,' said Dominic.

'I have clients of a political persuasion and, well, politics is something of a passion of mine,' he said, smoothing his trousers before removing his glasses to burnish them, then pulling a comb through his hair. It occurred to Dominic that his legal adviser had a narcissistic vanity he found discomfiting: his first reaction had been one of self-interest, restoring his well-groomed appearance.

'Oh, you've been hurt, my dear. Are you alright?' asked the solicitor of Rosa.

'Yes...and don't *my dear* me.'

'Who are these clients?' asked Dominic, quickly.

'You will understand the need for client confidentiality. After all, you wouldn't want me quoting our exchange to anyone else. Important people, influential people – I wouldn't want to incur their ire. But you mark my words. Young professionals will be wearing these badges as in mediaeval days women wore garlic to ward off vampires. I fear that every government building, council office, social housing estate will also have Mobilisation eyes – essentially party members to spy on staff, residents, neighbours to report disloyal behaviour.'

'You exaggerate, surely? This is not the 1930s. And it was only this morning that the SNPS was announced—'

'True enough but I've seen the planning of this, documents that set out the details, mock-ups of uniforms: grey tunics with small red flags on each lapel and a bright red M sown into the left breast. Of course, it would be the *left* side wouldn't it! Now I've said more than enough. Making a judgement call about your likely political orientation. I'd be grateful if you'd say nothing of this exchange. I really must learn to curb my tongue, put a lid on my passion. A word to the wise, dear clients, share your views with no one; beware of Mobilisation's eyes and ears.'

'Can we get back to our poor son's plight? The rehab centres,' said Rosa, a rush of blood flushing her cheeks.

The solicitor gave them a few details and promised to make enquiries as to Albert's likely location as the taxi drew to a halt outside their house. Dominic, spotting a small group at the end of the street, quickly bade him goodbye, rushing Rosa inside.

While Rosa busied herself in the kitchen, he pulled his mobile out and re-read the messages that Albert had last sent him. Who was Seb? He was intrigued. A tentative enquiry could do no harm, surely. He was tired. Rather than weigh the pros and cons he sent a brief note on impulse. Ten minutes later – *ping*. WhatsApp. An invitation to join a group labelled, simply, *Seb*.

Seb
Albert said you might contact me. Good move. Meet me at The Bell, Monday week 20.00. I know what you look like.

Dominic
What do you want to talk about?

Seb

Let's meet. Ok?

Dominic

Ok

Seb

See you then

CHAPTER 10: HARTLEY

Albert and six others stumbled out of the police vehicle after a long, bone-jarring journey devoid of interaction, refreshment, or facilities. As their eyes adjusted to the light they found themselves in a razor-wire-enclosed compound with another fifteen or twenty young men. The air was damp and chilly as low, soporific cloud engulfed the prison. Beyond the wire and the snarling Alsatian dogs and the security towers was wild, boggy moorland. But the young men saw only the structures that towered in front of them: two massive, golf-ball-shaped, two-hundred-feet-high domes.

Handcuffs were removed, and the prisoners rubbed at their sores and abrasions as they gazed upwards, necks craning to take in what was before them. They were directed to a smaller, opaque dome in the outer courtyard, formed into a line and directed into a clinical, white changing room. Polite notices requested their silence. 'Welcome to Hartley' announcements played from hidden speakers. They removed their clothing as requested, shoving trousers and shirts and pants through a hatch. Donning their allocated institutional pants and a grey tunic uniform adorned with small red flags on the lapels, a red M on the left breast pocket, they were stripped of any remaining jewellery and watches. They shuffled forwards in single file to the clinical area where a masked, white-coated operator quietly instructed Albert to extend his left arm; a loaded syringe was inserted into his forearm, and he was directed to enter the next cubicle. Another white coat reached for a scalpel and asked Albert to raise his left arm, but he pulled back, gasping shock. Reassuring tones asked him to extend his arm again. There was no escape, no explanation, no choice; nor were there raised voices or threats. Reluctantly, he did as instructed. A swift incision was made, a chip inserted. The white coat in the following cubicle applied sutures. In the final bay he was asked to hold out his right arm, and a stamp was quickly applied. His eyes opened wide as he read the indelible inscription, Matthew 2225.

He joined the conveyer belt of new prisoners and the heavy metal gates creaked open and then clanged shut behind them as they left the wire compound. They were led towards the larger of the two domes, through opaque glass doors that slid open and closed silently as they entered a vestibule within this main edifice. The extraordinary interior was now revealed: disorienting domes within domes, pathways that led in different directions to other domes of varying sizes, like a series of large and super-sized mole hills: a futuristic world. As they were led over a vast tarmac square they could see diminutive prisoners or soldiers marching in step on the far side, halting on a single barked instruction. Pressing on, they gazed at two glass domes just beyond and to the far right of the square where they could just about discern three tiers within, dotted with people in white coats, some in scarlet and others in grey. As they were escorted beyond the square they came across a greened area, a parkland scene at the periphery of which were scattered further domes of differing dimensions. They were now able to see other prisoners going about their business, accompanied by men in white coats, some of whom carried small black bags.

Everything was orderly. There was the sound of birdsong, but no birds. The sky was blue and the light golden, the mist and grey and damp of the moors having been cast aside. And the temperature had climbed from the six degrees outside to nineteen or twenty in this new outside. And fragrances assaulted their nostrils, although there were no roses or azaleas or aromatic plants of any description to be seen. Glancing to their right they could see green hills, which on closer inspection were projected images of the hills of the Cotswolds or the Chilterns or perhaps the Peak District on a sunny day.

They trooped forwards and a new set of doors slid open. Stepping into a large lecture theatre, they saw their designated seats were located in the middle of the tiered auditorium. There were perhaps another hundred prisoners all sitting in complete silence, some shuffling nervously, looking around. The lights soon dimmed, and they were pitched into darkness momentarily until spotlights illuminated the stage before them as a man dressed in black – black suit, black polo-necked shirt, black shoes – walked slowly onto the dais and stood behind the lectern. Spotlights picked out three others, similarly attired, sitting at a large swooping table to his left.

One of Albert's group broke the silence that cloaked them, and a few colleagues laughed. Albert turned sharply as a bright white light singled out the culprit, who stopped talking immediately, fidgeting his discomfiture. Nobody spoke. The body of the room returned to complete silence and still the light shone. And then it snuffed out, plunging them once more into the obscurity of darkness.

'I'm Professor Hughes, Principal of Hartley Campus. Welcome, gentlemen. I am proud to head up the educational and skills delivery of Hartley, an educational concept that draws on best practice from around the world from university, college, and apprenticeship settings. More of this shortly, but first let me introduce you to our leader.'

A general murmuring broke out, which prompted Professor Hughes to raise his hands. 'Please, gentlemen, you will hear of our philosophy and of the rehabilitation methods and inspired teachings in a moment, but this institution does have two fundamental guiding principles – contemplative silence and respect.'

Albert muttered something to his neighbour and almost immediately he was illuminated from above – a strong, piercing, narrow beam of light.

'Please stand and declare your name,' said one of the professors at the table, who seemed to be studying and manipulating his tabletop.

'Green. Albert Green,' Albert said, in a wavering voice.

'Your Hartley ID please?'

Silence.

Albert turned to the prisoner to his left and the light turned red, two orderlies in starched white coats carrying small black medical bags materialising at his elbow. Neighbouring students shrank back, and heads turned away from the white coats. The air bristled with tension.

All eyes focused back on Professor Hughes, whose own features had tightened, his eyes narrowing. Without turning his head, his eyes bored into Albert as he said softly, 'Play it.'

The touch screen was tapped and instantaneously Albert's voice rang around the hall.

'What a load of bollocks...'

Albert appeared shocked at hearing his own voice.

'Another breach and you will experience for yourself the therapies of our ICU. Matthew 2225 is your new identity, and you will kindly adopt this here. Now, if you will permit us, we shall proceed. Please remain silent; rediscover self-control and respect for those who are here to *rescue* you. Should you need help conforming to our standards, then be reassured that the full range of Hartley's sophisticated therapies will be made available to you,' said Professor Hughes. His tone was cold, his eyes lasering in on Albert. At last the light clicked off and Albert exhaled in the darkness and lowered himself into his seat.

A brief pause followed and then Thomas Tobin, their prime minister, appeared in their midst: a hologram. He proceeded to speak in a low voice while referring to his black book, which had been commonly dubbed Tobin's Tome. He spoke of the will of *The People*, of the embracing of values of common decency, fairness, and equality irrespective of gender, background, class, religion, race or colour. Turning to the rehabilitation centres and the programmes that the assembled students were beginning to experience, he spoke passionately about reducing recidivism, of embracing learning and skills, of saving those who had strayed – and he pointedly indicated that all of those assembled had offended the state and needed educating.

'These institutions are a classic example of what is possible when the state operates the levers of power to exert the will of *The People*. We embrace rehabilitation and shun punishment. We respect all backgrounds and embrace whatever faith or religion you may belong to with the one proviso that it's not used as a vehicle to oppose or resist the will of *The People* or undermine the state. This institution is focused on your education, social development, physical and mental health and well-being and spiritual needs...'

They were then conducted on a virtual tour of the facility, gaping silently, perhaps unbelievingly, at the scale of the campus, the modernity and clinical nature of the structures – the domes given over to education: the tutorial rooms, lecture theatres, workshops and libraries; to the health facilities: the consultation and diagnostic rooms, sick bays and ICU; to the spiritual areas: Muslims in a mosque, Christians in a small church and pods set aside for prayer and contemplation; to the recreation domes where physical exercise took place in the gyms and pools, the running tracks and athletics facilities, on the football pitches and cricket pitches; the restaurant domes and the capacious sleeping domes each of which contained pods with bunks to sleep twelve. This was their new, surreal, world.

Professor Hughes once more took centre stage and made his final announcement in hushed tones. 'Gentlemen, I hope you are impressed. No expense has been spared. You will shortly be escorted to your new abodes. But before then let me formally welcome you to the Socialist National Police

Security, the SNPS, into which you are honoured to have been *conscripted...*'
He paused as muttered protests broke out and the room became filled with
dazzling, white light as orderlies walked amongst them and officers in uniform
lined the auditorium. Silence quickly followed. The officer resumed in a thin
voice, 'Cadets...please let me remind you for the *last time* of the fundamental
principles of silence and respect. You have been found guilty of crimes and
earmarked as potential *enemies* of the state. Your term of sentence is a mere
guide. You should not rely upon there being a release unless you satisfy our
criteria. In the name of *The People*, any enemy of the state is isolated from
society until we can rehabilitate and then re-integrate. Hence the marvellous
facilities you observe here. Let me impart some free advice. There are only two
pathways available to you; firstly to work hard and integrate into the SNPS –
for which you'll be rewarded with promotion and the honour of serving the
state in the eradication of its enemies, the SNPS's sole raison d'être; secondly,
to embrace your education and secure an apprenticeship that will befit you
in re-integrating into society. I and my team will strive every sinew to assist
you on this journey. I urge you to positively embrace the programmes and
you will find fulfilment, new skills, and a bright future. But those of you who
are slow in adapting to your re-education or who choose to kick against the
system will endure a prolonged sojourn, a needlessly unhappy experience.
The choice is yours.'

CHAPTER 11: DIVERSIFICATION

Dominic and Rosa had tried in vain to find out how Albert was faring and where he was being "re-educated". His due time for release had come and gone. Not even their solicitor had been able to shed any light on matters and, worryingly, there were stories, rumours of people not emerging from such centres. Their MP was unable to help, despite asking questions in the House of Commons, as did many other opposition MPs. Government had shrugged off the challenges, dismissing them as another example of scaremongering, fake news.

Dominic settled down to watch the extended early evening news on the brewing constitutional crisis and outrage across the political spectrum. Prime Minister Thomas Tobin had made a stark announcement to the Commons that the House of Lords was to be abolished and replaced by an appointed upper tier. The PM remained calm, adopting an almost bemused air as angry scenes of incandescent opposition MPs erupted. After the third suspension by the speaker, an unruffled Thomas Tobin elaborated that the Upper House was to be a twenty-four-person executive with legislative powers, headed by The Leader, who would appoint the executive team. Advice would be taken from the House of Commons. The elected chamber was to prepare legislative instruments as directed by the Upper House using the well-established committee system. Dominic listened in dismay as the PM was challenged by Norris Jinks.

'The outrage of all opposition parties is palpable, Prime Minister. There's no precedent for what you propose, you outline no consultation, no safeguards, no process. There will be rebellion in this country if you aren't...'

'I note that the Right Honourable member seeks to incite, and I respectfully ask him to withdraw,' said Jane Connell.

'What process do you propose? Constitutional change demands a commission to carefully consider options, implications and conventions before being presented to the House in a Queen's Speech for subsequent debate.'

'It *will* be presented in a Queen's Speech. As to timing, I will return to the House to advise in due course,' said the PM. 'But we will not be trapped into a long procedural process designed to divert us from our will. It is *The People's* will that is our guiding light, our mandate. This government will not be blown off course. The radical reform we promised will take place and we intend to increase the speed of change, which, comrades' – the PM turned to encourage his own MPs amassed on the benches behind him, provoked cheers, the waving of order papers, and brought most to their feet in thunderous applause – 'is long overdue; the *socialist revolution* will prevail despite the best efforts of my Right Honourable friend opposite who seems determined to stoke opposition, inflame opinion, thwart the democratic decision our great country made in 2019. Social justice and equality are our compass bearings. We won't rest until these irrefutably moral standards of common human decency prevail.'

'And *we* will strain every sinew in every muscle to thwart your lurch to Marxism, the abusing of democracy, the insulting of this House and her traditions. We will speak up for human rights, democracy and the freedoms you seem intent upon eroding. The country won't stand for much more of this. Opposition will grow and I fear that violence will erupt on the streets. The blood of decent, British folks will flow in the gutters,' said Norris Jinks, tossing his ginger locks, his words evoking Enoch Powell's rivers of blood speech of 1968. Jinks' passion was infectious: a rallying cry in the chamber.

'You heard him, comrades – he sets *his* will against that of *The People*. I warn you, my Right Honourable friend, there will be repercussions if you and your party continue this call to arms against the elected government. Don't say you haven't been warned.'

The tumult was such that the Speaker eventually made himself heard to suspend parliament for the day, members crowding out of the chamber in high dudgeon. Some of the more passionate MPs lost all sense of decorum, soon scuffling, throwing largely ineffectual punches. The chaotic scenes were broadcast across the nation and the streets of Westminster were soon awash with warring groups: Marxists, trades unionists and socialists on the one side, opposition supporters, right-wing nationalists, anarchists on the other.

Over the coming days unrest spread like wildfire and most cities and towns experienced demonstrations, riotous assemblies, and violence, resulting in extensive knife crime, mutilations, gun crime and deaths on the streets of London, Bristol, Birmingham, Manchester, Liverpool, Glasgow. Hospitals were overrun, shops looted, cars and buses set alight in barricades as urban warfare erupted. The police struggled and failed to curb the explosion of violence, carnage, criminality. The self-proclaimed Workers Revolution group proudly wore their red Ms, waved their red flags and banners and increasingly brandished machetes, knives, and guns. Set against them were a ragtag of right-wing activists dressed in black, waving Union Jacks proclaiming their support of Norris Jinks who was becoming a totem figure. The police strove to regain public order but appeared to come down more heavily on the right-wing extremists, most newspapers claimed.

Dominic scanned his news app:

> **Northern Cities in Flames:** *scenes of mayhem flared across the streets of major cities. Hospitals and police resources stretched as casualties mount from running battles between far-right protesters in black shirts and Mobilisation activists. Casualties mount.*

> **Jinks Leads Rebellion:** *Norris Jinks appears in rallies as the rebellion against government reforms gains traction.*

The declaration of a state of emergency seemed likely to most political commentators but was not forthcoming. Nor were the army called in, despite the appeal of senior political figures, business groups, the media. Church leaders of all denominations appealed for calm, peace, and restraint. Tobin and Connell were not to be seen. Norris Jinks dominated the political stage, featuring on the BBC and other terrestrial and satellite news channels and in the paper media. He was also high profile at public gatherings calling for the government to change course, to restore order, to return the country to normality, to put their extreme plans to one side and show leadership. Still no response. The clamour for radical change was strident, the opposition to it growing ever shriller.

> ### Archbishop of Canterbury Appeals for Calm

> **Army on Standby:** *Government leaks suggest that troops will soon be called in to restore order*

And gradually peaceful demonstrations of the professional classes appeared, striking a different, lower key. Eschewing violence, a libertarian movement began to flourish calling itself Peace and Democracy – PAD. Lawyers, accountants, doctors, shopkeepers, priests, managers, media figures took to the streets in non-violent protest. They merged at a rally in Sheffield and set out on a journey to Westminster: fleets of buses, cars and lorries transported them from the outskirts of one city to another. They marched into the city centres. Norris Jinks and other opposition leaders addressed them at assemblies in Sheffield, Leicester, Northampton, Luton, Watford. Their numbers swelled, the media providing the oxygen of publicity.

Dominic and Rosa watched the footage on television, spellbound as the marchers entered Trafalgar Square, chaos prevailing as thousands joined their ranks.

'My *Gooddd*!' Rosa exclaimed.

Dominic simply shook his head as he sipped a mug of tea and nibbled on a freshly made scone.

But PAD's avowed intent was peaceful, he was relieved to see. They were not to account for infiltrators who stole their identity, waved their banners, voiced their chants – until suddenly stones and bricks and bottles were thrown at the police; rival gangs targeted each other, knives were drawn, and blood flowed in the streets of London. Just as Norris Jinks had predicted in parliament. As he was finishing a clarion call with a classical Jinks oratorical flourish, from a stage at the foot of Nelson's Column, a police charge on horseback parted the crowd. The target was evidently the Conservative Party leader, various shadow ministers, PAD leaders and celebrity campaigners. As they charged in to make their arrest, youths with bloodied knives received desultory blows from police batons and riot shields but were allowed to melt into the folds of the crowd to commit further indiscriminate havoc. The association of violence, blood, murder, and pandemonium with the opposition leader had provoked the government into action. Jinks was unceremoniously dragged away to a cacophony of protests and cheers: equal and opposite in volume as a pitched battle of the different protagonists ensued.

Dominic and Rosa took in the extended coverage until they could take no more. The scenes were depressing, the developing situation on the streets of their adopted city threatening. All this taking place in one of the most sophisticated capitals in the world. The pleasure of the arts: red carpet premieres, museums, opera, art galleries disrupted; attending West

End theatres meant running the gauntlet of intimidation, protest, violence. Tourists were no longer flocking to enjoy the history and traditions of London and were spending their dollars and euros elsewhere. The economy was in such turmoil that shops were beginning to display half-empty shelves as supply chains faltered, and inflation spiralled inexorably. Criminality and thuggery invaded their lives; much of this seemed the direct or indirect consequence of a government hell-bent on revolutionary change, whatever the consequences. All in the name of *The People*.

'I fear where all this is going, Dominic. We're no longer safe in our own home. Our Albert doesn't seem to be coming back anytime soon and what's Juan up to?'

'It'll be fine. Hopefully... Oh, I don't know, who does? I can't imagine why Albert's not home yet. Surely, he hasn't been misbehaving? He can be stubborn and principled but even he must see that you have to play the game to survive? And it would be nice to hear from Juan too. I wish he'd stay in touch. And at Diamond's, customers are becoming thin on the ground, Brandon's becoming ever more desperate, resorting to all manner of schemes to keep the business afloat,' said Dominic. 'We just have to believe, hang in there.' He sighed, reaching for his wife, but she shunned him.

'Or we *could* be realistic and deal with it,' said Rosa. She stood up, turned the television off and stood over him, hands on hips. 'So what are you going to do about Albert?'

'What *can* we do? Be reasonable, Rosa. I know you're...'

'Too right I'm worried, emotional, upset. But I'm also applying my mind to the issues. I'm meeting with that wretched solicitor of ours tomorrow and talking to one of my partners. There has to be some mechanism to work out access. Denying visitation rights must be in contravention of his human rights. And where's Juan? What's he up to? I'm going to put feelers out through Ellie and their mates. As for your business, you have to deal with the challenge yourself, work out some sort of contingency plan. I can't do that for you as well. Are you content to put your head in the sand and hide behind Brandon? I just don't understand you anymore...'

'We'll be okay. Everything will come right somehow. Something will turn up,' said Dominic, trying to be reassuring, bringing to the fore as many of his Mr Micawber traits as he could muster. Rosa scowled, uttered a profanity, grabbed her book, and opted for a long soak in a hot bath.

*

Dominic opened his front door a crack, still on the chain. He surveyed the street. It seemed calm this morning and, pulling his coat up high and donning a trilby, he slipped out. All seemed quiet. He looked up to see Rosa watching from their bedroom, directly above the boarded-up lounge window: a brick wrapped in a threatening note had shattered it. The police had not wanted to know. *You shouldn't court publicity.* The glazers could only promise to try to repair it within the week; it had now been two weeks, so at least one trade was doing well. He waved to her, but she just stared. A good night's sleep had replenished his reserves of positivity; it was too easy to be overcome by the relentless flow of bad news. This was Great Britain, one of the most advanced and respected nations on earth. He wrenched his thoughts away from crisis, determined not to be dragged down into the abyss of doom and gloom. And Albert would surely soon be released. They had to believe that.

He briefly pondered his mode of transport this morning. He had tried every conceivable way: a taxi was extravagant currently, he felt exposed on a bicycle – his fitness levels also a deterrent – and the bus route was not straightforward. So, it was to be the Tube today. He settled for pulling his collar up high, his hat perched precariously; he wore a pair of largely redundant thick, black-framed spectacles and hid behind a newspaper while trapped in the subterranean confines. Emerging at Bond Street unchallenged he breathed out a huge sigh of relief. As he walked briskly through Mayfair he took a call from Bill just as he was approaching Diamond's. Did he fancy a coffee away from the ranch? He did. Dominic suggested one just behind Oxford Street, but Bill told him it had closed.

'When did you last walk down Oxford Street?' asked Bill.

'Not for a few weeks, I guess.'

'Be prepared for a shock. See you at Rafa's Coffee Emporium.'

Just then he was assailed by a small group holding placards and his heart sank. It had been going so well. But then they cheered and shouted his name. They were supporters. What a relief. Emerging from within the ranks of the group a young lady approached him.

'Dominic – Louise Chapman from the BBC. Can we have your thoughts please?' said the diminutive reporter with a shock of red hair.

'No comment.'

'Not even for your supporters?'

'It's pleasing that at least some people seem to think positively of me,' he mumbled, looking around at the group of about a dozen mainly middle-aged women. He smiled at them and shook a couple of hands. 'Thank you so much for your support.'

'Who were your attackers the other day? What can you tell us?' the reporter asked.

'I've no idea why my name was dropped into a political programme and… I just don't want to say anything. No comment. *Please*,' Dominic said, smiling an apology and beginning to walk away. But he stopped in his tracks and, turning back to the vivacious reporter, said, 'Please just know that I'm a Labour voter. I rejoiced at the election victory, but I'm shocked by what's happening now: the turmoil, threats, and violence. The cranking up of rhetoric by all parties is just leading to a spiralling of the troubles. Can't we return to normality? Let's use some common sense… *And* the return of my son,' he added.

'He was sentenced for assaulting a policeman, wasn't he?'

'A trumped-up charge and now he's in some rehab centre.'

'Where? And for how long?'

'You tell me. Contact's forbidden, his location's a mystery. And as to his treatment we can only speculate and pray. But exactly what is a rehab centre?' he said. 'And are my son's basic human rights not contravened by denying him visits from his family?' added Dominic, recalling Rosa's tirade of a few nights ago. She had more than a point.

'Good questions, Dominic.'

'Please excuse me, I must get on.'

Turning his back on her, he smiled as he took in her report.

'Reporting live for BBC London outside Diamond's, you've been listening to the celebrity chef, Dominic Diamond aka Green. Name-shamed by Jane Connell, Minister of Communications, for merely doing his job. Zealots took this as their cue to stage a protest, culminating in a violent assault. Will the police investigate and bring the perpetrators to justice? His son has been sentenced to spend time in a so-called rehabilitation centre. What are these centres really about? Why is the location of prisoners not declared? Viewers will want to know what their purpose is, how many are currently incarcerated. And Dominic asks why the government can't tone down the rhetoric to counter the escalation of violence? *Good questions!* We look forward to a response by the government. This is Louise Chapman, political correspondent…'

Dominic picked his way along a quiet Oxford Street. Demonstrations had not reached this part of London so far today. But the sight of boarded-up shops, large department stores and coffee houses was surprising. A homeless village that had sprung up just behind the shopping areas was depressing. Mid-morning and it was still populated by men and women and pet dogs lying on blankets with cardboard and cloth awnings. Some were almost comatose, zombie-like figures. Others drank from bottles of cider, cans of beer. Bustling past the prone figures, stepping over the discarded bottles and decaying rubbish, dropping a few coins into proffered tins, he stepped inside Rafa's with relief. Bill waved from the corner, and he noticed that Gina and Brandon were also there. Unbuttoning his coat, he wandered over, frowning his consternation, the day only a few hours old, but already full of surprises.

'I thought we'd solved the homeless and unemployment issues,' said Dominic, shaking his head. 'And what's this – a staff meeting? Hi Gina, Bill. What the hell are you up to now, Brandon?'

'We've been watching you on the box actually,' said Gina, pointing to the large screen in the corner. Dominic was supposed to be lying low as his media profile was working against him currently but had been drawn to a pretty face and the camera and his quest for answers had overcome his intentions. Gina and Bill both expressed disgust at how Dominic had been treated and spoke warmly about his interview.

'Did you listen to that toerag, Jane Connell, the other day? A dangerous one that. Well done, Dominic, about time someone stood up to these bully boys,' said Bill.

'Keep it down,' said Brandon, his eyes signalling the interest of a neighbouring couple.

'All I want to do is get on with life, look out for my family. Why's that impossible these days?' he said. 'What's happening with the world? Oxford Street's depressing and the shanty town back there...'

'You've not seen the half of it. You should head down to King's Cross. Almost lawless after dark with tramps and pimps and prostitutes and pushers and druggies,' said Bill. 'Petticoat Lane's become a black market too.'

'Always was, wasn't it?' said Brandon.

Looking around them, Dominic noted that Rafa's was now a tatty, dreary venue – not helped by the public squalor adorning its doorstep. And Dominic's eyes cast heavenwards as he took in his business partner's attire, discordant with the surroundings. Today the tie was gold-coloured and the flowing top pocket handkerchief blue with yellow spots all setting off his navy-blue, pin-striped suit. The ubiquitous red braces were flexed as he chatted, as a boxer flexes his biceps.

69

'Is there a point to this gathering?' asked Gina.

'You took the question off the tip of my tongue. What are you up to now?' asked Dominic, whose sunny mood had dissolved. *Ping.*

> **Breaking News:** *Celebrity chef Dominic Diamond accuses police of trumped-up charges against his son. Albert was sentenced to 3 months in rehabilitation centre, location a mystery. What is the purpose of these centres asked Dominic Diamond? No government minister was available for comment.*

Brandon declared that the business was haemorrhaging cash, and this month's salaries were in jeopardy. But there was an opportunity to augment their earnings.

'I bring you some good news,' said Brandon. 'Sullivan's have gone bust.'

'And in God's name how's that good news? I know most of the guys and gals who work there,' said Bill.

'We owed them a couple of grand.'

'So, we pushed them out of business?' said Gina.

'Not a bit of it. The debt's not been due for long. Their demise is nothing to do with us, but there's no denying it helps with the old cash flow,' Brandon said, smiling broadly, while straightening his tie.

'I refuse to rejoice at the distress and misfortunes of others. Goodness knows there's more than enough misery to go around these days. So what's this scam of yours? And why aren't we having this conversation in the office?' said Dominic.

'A tad pompous, my friend… The thing is, I suspect we're being bugged.'

The statement was met with momentary silence. Then the damn broke and incredulity was expressed in their different ways, all speaking simultaneously. Brandon's answers were opaque, evasive. Dominic was used to such diversions from his business partner and promised to return to the issue of bugs later. Brandon eventually explained that Dominic's professional services, assisted by Bill and Gina, were required at government gala dinners, but offered no details.

'Absolutely not,' Gina shouted, standing up unexpectedly, sending her chair crashing. She threw her arms in the air and headed for the ladies', muttering indignantly. Bill and Dominic were equally vehement in their refusal to contemplate the proposal.

'You've sold us out!' accused Dominic.

'Not a bit of it. We need to balance the books, that's all.'

'They'll pay pennies if anything at all,' said Bill through gritted teeth.

'When I say balance the books…look, guys, we need to curry some favour with our ruling masters. I'm afraid you aren't the flavour of the month, old bean, no matter how talented you are. But the leader is apparently a secret fan of yours, if somewhat disappointed that you're fuelling the excesses of the decadent and privileged classes… I know, I know, all rubbish and terribly distorted but I'm afraid different rules, different paradigms prevail today. The worldview has changed, old orders dispensed, the elite of today are those extolling the virtue of the great unwashed. Social justice and all that. It's de rigueur to denigrate Eton, the old boys' network, private anything whatsoever, Tories, caviar, etcetera, etcetera. But they still have to entertain foreign dignitaries, royalty, their party stalwarts – after all, I imagine the espousing of so much egalitarian claptrap is quite exhausting for the old darlings…'

'Hypocritical bastards,' said Bill.

'I know. Ours not to reason why. But we must survive. Could do with a few brownie points, get them to call off the dogs of war, their revolutionary fanatics.' Brandon sat back and beamed benevolently at them. 'What do you say?'

'No way,' said Gina.

'Fuck off,' said Bill.

'We need to talk,' said Dominic.

'Quite understandable. Natural reactions. But – well, your first gig's tonight and you get access to the kitchen in an hour's time. Let's just pull together, team. Do this and then talk. Let's just try it on for size, shall we?'

'*No!*' Bill and Gina shouted in unison. Dominic sighed and sat back, resigned to his destiny. Fatalistic.

'Good, that's settled then… And here's your taxi – fee paid by Her Majesty's Government.'

CHAPTER 12: CHEQUERS

Dominic and Bill piled into the limousine, a plush long-wheel base Jaguar. Gina had refused to have anything to do with the project and stormed off, much to the chagrin of Brandon. Dominic admired her spirit, was tempted to do likewise, but given the problems the business faced he persuaded Bill to join him. Conflict with his business partner would hardly help anyone, and he could do without yet another front opening up. As their peak-capped chauffeur opened the door to the black Jaguar XJ, Dominic turned to Brandon with raised eyebrows, *what the hell?*

Dominic and Bill turned their backs on the surrounding squalor and climbed into a luxuriously cocooned interior: soft leather, suede panels, background classical music. They had no idea where they were headed; all enquiries were waved aside, and their driver pressed a switch that raised the glass partition between the front and rear seats. The limo was soon picking its way through the streets of London onto the A40 and onward to High Wycombe from where they seemed to glide into the Chiltern Hills. As the car nudged through and beyond the pretty village of Ellesborough, the glass partition slid down, the chauffeur turning the mirror to watch their reactions. They took in the beautiful parkland setting as the car slowly crunched up the gravelled driveway in stately fashion towards a grand sixteenth-century manor house. After navigating its way around the side of the mansion, it came to a halt at the rear of the property, where they were met.

'Welcome to Chequers, gentlemen – the country residence of the Prime Minister of Great Britain. I have the pleasure of being the house manager and will give you a brief tour.'

Dominic noticed the suit, the aristocratic accent, the lofty disposition.

'Why are we here?' asked Bill.

'All will become clear in due course, but you are greatly privileged, gentlemen,' he said, casting them an imperious look accompanied with a sniff. As he showed them inside, they took in the grandeur of their surroundings.

'It is thought that the name of the house derives from an early-twelfth-century owner of the manor of Ellesborough, and the current mansion you are stood in was remodelled around 1565 by William Hawtrey. Lady Mary Grey, the younger sister of Lady Jane Grey, married without consent and was banished from court by Elizabeth I. She was confined at Chequers for two years and the room where she slept from 1565 to 1567 remains in its original condition. In the eighteenth century the owners were relations to Oliver Cromwell, would you believe. A house steeped in tradition, dripping history.'

'Blimey, a history lesson,' said Bill, drawing an oily smile from the house manager.

'So, when did it become the Prime Minister's home?' asked Dominic, nudging Bill.

'During the First World War it became a hospital, then a convalescent home for officers after which it became the PM's abode in 1917, Mr Diamond.'

'Green. Dominic Green.'

'Of course, how forgetful of me... The gift to the nation was made after discussions with David Lloyd George and became official under the Chequers Estate Act 1917.' Glancing at his watch, he bestowed a benevolent smile, announcing that time was slipping away.

'And in answer to your original question, Bill, you will be cooking for the Prime Minister and his recently announced executive team. It really is a great honour and is at the special request of the Prime Minister himself; he's apparently a great fan of yours, Dominic. May I call you Dominic?'

'Of course.'

'And I'm Bill.'

'Yes, you would be,' he said, casting a glance in Bill's direction. 'There's to be a special dinner tomorrow evening to mark the occasion. I understand the monarch has been invited.'

'Blimey!' said Bill.

'As you say, a great honour, Mr... Mr?' said Dominic, heading off Bill.

'Hutchings.'

'Do you have a Christian name?' asked Bill.

'Let me show you a few menu suggestions and your kitchen,' said

Hutchings. As they followed him down the corridor, Bill smirked and offered a gratuitous verdict, 'Pillock!' Dominic gave him a reproving glare. As they made their way towards the kitchen a wave of youthful female laughter struck a wholly different note to the reverential atmosphere of the grand house and the stilted conversation of their stuffy guide. Turning the corner, a small group of young women chattered and giggled, brushing past them. Dominic quickly turned on his heels. He recognised one of their voices, thought he knew one of the girls. And then it came to him. 'Ellie? Is that you? *Ellie.*'

She stopped and recognition skidded across her face. She skipped back to plant a light kiss on his cheek. 'Hi, Mr Green. You here for the big do as well?'

'What a surprise. What brings you here? Have you seen Juan?'

'*Ellie,*' shouted an older lady in charge of the group.

'Gotta go. Duty calls,' she said lightly, as she ran back to join the others, shouting back to him, 'Not seen or heard from him. *Laters.*'

Dominic was taken aback but recalled her saying something about waitressing for pin money.

'Juan's girlfriend,' he clarified for Bill.

Dragging himself back to his situation he realised that he had not called Rosa. He was anxious about her, had promised to call. He pulled his mobile out of his pocket but there was no signal. Apparently all mobile and telecommunications signals were blocked for security reasons.

'I really need to call my wife. She hasn't been well. Our son, you see. Away,' Dominic said. Hutchings inclined his head and led him to a small office where he was left alone to use a retro telephone: a large black Bakelite device with a dial. Rosa answered quickly and he was treated to a torrent of angst-laden emotion, which was hard to decipher. He sat down heavily in the leather chair and eventually succeeded in calming her sufficiently to understand what was going on. Albert. She had received an unexpected call. He had been allowed a single phone call to explain that his release had been delayed indefinitely. *Nothing's certain. You never know.*

'I don't understand. Why? How can they do that? Where is—'

'Oh, Dominic,' she said. 'He sounded so flat, so ill, broken. Not our Albert at all. What have they done to him? Those *bastards!*'

The tears abated long enough to allow her anger to surface, and she let rip with gusto. Eventually he managed to elicit from her that Albert was allowed one brief call a month. Dominic said he would get back home as soon as he could.

'I'm so worried about him. Try as I might I haven't been able to find any loophole in the law that would allow us to appeal or to demand visitation rights. The penal reform people just say they can't help. Nor can the various charities. Or the church. Our MP says he's powerless...and meanwhile...where are you? What are you doing?'

'I'm not allowed to say. Some project Brandon has me working on.'

'And that's more important than your son? Your wife?'

'That's not fair, Rosa. Look, I know you're worried. You have every right to be. So am I. But I can't drop everything. I just can't. Please understand.'

'All I understand is that you do nothing but wring your hands and dance to Brandon's tune. You're supposed to be the man of the house. *Ha*!'

'Rosa...'

But it was too late. She had slammed down the phone.

He sat thoughtfully for a moment, still holding the phone when he heard a faint click on the line just before replacing the receiver. Dominic, shaken by the whole conversation, frowned, and sighed deeply. At least limited communication was now possible. That was something. He tried to repair his mood, once more don his cloak of positivity, but it was like struggling into a rediscovered, long-lost favourite suit; it had lain dormant at the back of the cupboard for too long and he had outgrown it. But apart from meagre contact with Albert they did not seem any further forwards. And why could he no longer connect with Rosa? She seemed so distant, so alienated. Why could she not see that if their MP, the church, the various charities could not assist, and the law was impregnable, he was unlikely to succeed where they had failed?

Returning to the kitchen he bumped into Hutchings who cocked his head to one side, leant a sympathetic ear to Dominic's demands but insisted that transport back to London was not scheduled; impossible to arrange.

'That's ridiculous. Look, the car's still at the back,' he said, spotting it through the window. 'Our driver was sipping a mug of coffee a short while ago. He can't be far away.'

'I have my instructions, sir. Now may I suggest you focus on the menu and your, what do you chefs call it, mise en place?'

'I really do need to get home, so if you—'

'Quite impossible, I'm afraid.'

Dominic glared at him angrily. 'Then I shall walk back to the village and arrange my own transport. We came here out of the goodness of our hearts, contrary to our better judgement. My son is being held by the authorities, illegally as far as I can see. We've no idea where he is or how he is – still don't.

And my wife is beside herself – as you will know from having eavesdropped our conversation. Now do I have to walk back or are you actually going to help? And as for your bloody dinner – call out for a microwave meal!'

'Atta boy!' said Bill, who had joined them.

'Mr Green, I have my instructions and as for you going anywhere…well, that really is *completely* impossible I'm afraid. We had imagined you would wish to spend much of this evening at work, so accommodation is arranged in the house. You'll find the bedroom suite most comfortable, I'm sure. Your business partner kindly provided your own knives, tools of the trade as it were, freshly laundered chef's whites, hats. Everything. And we have night-time attire, toiletries, and all that you could possibly need. Even your favourite beers so you can enjoy a glass before you retire. Your partner has been most helpful, don't you think?'

'I'll *swing* for Brandon,' said Bill.

'The prime minister of Great Britain has requested your service. It's like a royal command, my dear chap. Now…the menu?'

Dominic's face flushed, but he said nothing. Bill pushed him out of the way and grabbed a shocked Hutchings by his lapels before a hovering armed security policeman intervened.

'I'll consult with my superiors,' said Hutchings, the detached air of superiority slipping as he looked at them with wide eyes before slinking away.

On his return Hutchings was flanked by two burly policemen and he confirmed that it was impossible to leave prior to the dinner function tomorrow night. He and Bill were effectively under house arrest and had little choice other than to comply with the arrangements. Bill ranted and swore. Dominic in turn pleaded, threatened to withdraw his labour. But Hutchings was unmoved, and it became clear to Dominic that he was doing no more than what his masters demanded. But he could make another call, which was something. Not that he looked forward to *that* conversation.

CHAPTER 13: HOME

Dominic, bleary-eyed, stumbled into the kitchen intent upon making Rosa
a cup of tea. His mind was alternately preoccupied with the events of two
evening's ago at Chequers and the state he had found her in when he got home.
That Rosa could be emotional, volatile, given to mood swings was one thing –
but this was on a whole new level. He tried everything he knew but consoling
her was impossible until, exhausted, emotionally drained, she fell asleep on the
sofa. He had sat with her, stroking her hand until he was sure she was asleep.
After covering her with blankets, kissing her forehead, he had eventually gone
to a lonely, cold bed. He shared her despair over Albert's position but was
powerless to do anything despite her strictures. They simply had to hope that he
would serve his time, behave sensibly, and this period would pass. Meanwhile
he was deeply troubled at the events he had witnessed while on Brandon's ill-
fated project. And he felt utterly helpless. He had to do something. Perhaps he
should ring the police despite the unambiguous warnings. But he could not
imperil his son's safety.

The Chequers scenes flooded back. The monarch had not attended
after all. It was just as well, thought Dominic, as he surveyed the antics of the
mainly male group of politicians and loyal activists. Jane Connell was a notable
exception; she seemed to float around imperiously, exchanging ribald jokes
with fellow politicians, encouraging behaviour her public persona vehemently
opposed. Yet another example of hypocrisy, her virtue-signalling exposed. As
the night wore on, the copious volumes of alcohol consumed provoked careless
power talk, the boasting boorish, the proclaimed plans stretching credulity.
The feast rapidly took on the flavour of a sixteenth-century royal court. The
high-necked grey tunics, which had become common place in government,

had been forsaken for the evening by everyone other than Thomas Tobin. More flamboyant, informal dress prevailed. And the buffet table groaned with whole salmon in aspic, beef Wellington, ribs of rare roast beef, crowns of lamb, lobsters, langoustine, pheasants... Hardly the fare of the proletariat or the stuff of egalitarianism. Comedians entertained the group: crude, foul-mouthed humour. The young waitresses were modestly attired but nonetheless attracted attention, wandering hands a constant challenge; most did what they could to repel unseemly advances, although some were less bothered. He was shocked at how Ellie was targeted by a small group of middle-aged politicians and officials: no doubt husbands and fathers who should know better. Certainly, she was a pretty girl who attracted male attention. But she should not be subjected to such naked abuse of power and nor should the other young girls. His gaze was caught by Ellie as she pushed away an uninvited hand, smoothed down her skirt and looked embarrassed at having her boyfriend's father witness such events. What on earth would Juan say if he knew? What should Dominic say? Nothing probably. What could he possibly say or do?

Dominic and Bill carved the beef as the party gathered pace. Was that really the chancellor of the exchequer cornering one of the girls? Another more compliant waitress sat on the knee of a treasury minister feeding him grapes and morsels of pheasant as his hands explored her shapely form. And the head of Mobilisation dad-dancing, hands gripping inappropriately whenever his partner ventured close.

As the champagne, wine, beer, cocktails flowed, the music became louder, the dancing and cavorting more extreme until at last Dominic and Bill were able to escape their duties. Having withdrawn to their bedroom they hoped for peace and quiet, time for reflection, a beer and sleep. But one of the young ladies had evidently been escorted to a neighbouring room. The noise levels increased, the sound of furniture being pushed against the wall, drunken laughter. It soon became evident from the whooping and jeering that more than one of the men were subjecting her to more than she could possibly have signed up for. Dominic and Bill exchanged anxious looks. What should they do? And then her squeals morphed into cries of anguish, pleas to stop, protests brushed aside until her screams became impossible to ignore. With a jolt, Dominic suddenly recognised the voice and stood up urgently. Surely not? Dear God, what's happening? But now the laughter and merriment were pierced with female cries of protestation, anguish, pain. Male voices egged each other on; coarse, foul-mouthed encouragements proffered. There seemed to be a frenzy of activity, pandemonium. Dominic and Bill, still wearing their chef's whites, swung open their bedroom door. Venturing into the corridor they edged along but were pushed back by an aggressive security policeman, stopped in their tracks. Dominic was ashen-faced and shaking. His wavering voice demanded the policeman intervene. *Back off.* Bill forced his way by and pushed the door open. The security officer grabbed Bill's shoulder, wrenched him round and struck him. Hard. Dominic stared open-mouthed at the revealed scene; naked male buttocks thrusting, the naked waitress lying prostrate on the bed, bloodied, and wailing as three others pulled up their trousers.

'*Ellie*,' he shouted. Dominic rushed towards her, intent on lending some assistance but was caught by the collar and yanked back by a second security officer.

'Bastards, you *bastards*,' yelled Dominic, pointing at the offending men. He was shoved back into his room where he found a bloodied Bill on the floor, cursing. The door slammed behind them; a bolt slid across from the outside.

They looked at each other, hardly believing.

Prisoners at Chequers.

The first since Lady Mary Grey in the 1560s?

He and Rosa sipped their tea in stony silence, until eventually Dominic blurted out his Chequers experience. He swore Rosa to secrecy, having been shocked at the ill-concealed threats, the references to both their sons. She sat transfixed, unusually offering no comment until he had finished.

'What did you do then?'

'Insisted on reporting it to the police.'

'*And?*'

Dominic recalled the scene with Hutchings and the security officers.

Their protests had been in vain; they had no means of contacting anyone. At long last the noise abated; the whimpering sobs faded. The poor girl must have fallen asleep or maybe she had been taken somewhere for her medical needs to be attended to. How on earth would they repair her mind? Eventually they succumbed to a short period of sleep.

All too soon dawn broke. Time to face another day. Having dragged themselves out of their beds they sat wearily, looking at each other, despondently shaking their heads. Bill sported a rapidly blackening eye with swollen eye lids, cuts on cheek and lip. Dominic's ribs ached; a couple almost certainly broken. He strapped himself up as best he could, glanced in the mirror and thought he had aged ten years overnight; deep shadows, bags below blotchy eyes. The sound of a bolt being slid back was followed by a gentle knock at the door before a head appeared to inform them they would be expected in forty minutes; time to shower and change. After a while they were summoned to meet with Hutchings, who exuded superficial gentility and professed his admiration of the chefs. It dripped with insincerity. Dominic loathed the man.

'I need to speak to the police,' said Dominic.

'That would be most unwise, quite impossible. Now the schedule for the day is a light lunch for—'

'*No*! We saw the assault of a young woman; raped by four men. Ellie. And we recognised the men. I demand to talk to the police and refuse to work here another moment.'

'I'm sure you must be mistaken but let me ask the senior security officer here to take your details. Are you sure you wish to pursue this avenue? Are you not mistaken? Perhaps you had a drink or two too many yourselves. And why not? You worked hard...'

Bill had been unusually quiet, but leapt to his feet, lurching at Hutchings, who recoiled. The attendant security officer stepped in. Hutchings exhaled loudly and left, soon returning with DI Franks. He insisted they sit and calm down. Sitting opposite the chefs, wearing a blank expression, DI Franks slapped a document on the table. A signed letter: their engagement letter, countersigned by both Dominic and Bill. He made no comment, simply allowing the document to sit quietly, a brooding presence. And as their story tumbled out...Ellie...attacked...screaming...bloodied...*rape*...he stared at them, unmoved by their demeanour or words.

'Aren't you going to record this? Write it down?' asked Bill, glancing at the redundant pen resting on the table.

'The lady you claim was assaulted – her name?'

'I told you, Ellie. Ellie Sergeant,' said Dominic.

DI Franks scanned a list of names he produced from a file.

'No. We had no such person in the house.'

'I spoke with her in front of Hutchings yesterday...didn't I?' Dominic looked for confirmation.

'I can't say I recall...'

'You're...you're unbelievable. Last night the banquet descended into some sort of...of...*orgy*,' Dominic stuttered, his shaking hands gesticulating. 'And the crime took place next to our rooms. A security officer was present. He saw what happened, heard her screams, did nothing. He assaulted Bill and me.'

'There were no security officers in that part of the house. It was far from the banquet and guests and politicians. Are you sure you weren't having a nightmare?'

'Both of us? Don't be absurd.'

Their exchange did not seem to be going anywhere, the chefs becoming frustrated, the policeman's demeanour mutating from blank neutrality to irritation. DI Franks eventually stood, held up his hands and called for silence. 'I think we've heard quite enough. We had no such woman of that name working for us here, never have. None of our security officers can corroborate any part of your story. You have work to do, as do I.'

He stood and nodded to his colleague who opened the door for him. Bill stood in his way, his face reddening, eyes bulging. He placed his hands on DI Franks' chest.

'Yes? *Really?*'

DI Franks allowed the shadow of a smile to crinkle the corners of his mouth; it never reached his eyes, which narrowed and flashed warning signals. Dominic pulled his sous chef back and the DI walked casually towards the door, turning around a few steps short of the threshold. 'A word of caution, gentlemen. I've heard you out patiently, tolerating your belligerence. Do I have to remind you of the contract you signed? Do I have to remind you that you're bound by the Official Secrets Act? You have a duty to the State, to *The People*, to our elected government. Any word about any of your absurd claims or anything you believe you may have seen or overheard will render your positions fragile. Your wife works as a secretary in the Home Office, I believe, Bill? And you, Dominic, would be wise to remember that your eldest son is in the care of the authorities. You will no doubt be keen to see him home sometime soon. Oh, and how's Juan?'

'*Bastards!* What you do now?'

'What can we do? The threats to our sons were...'

'So, you do nothing? *Nothing?*'

Dominic poured whisky into a tumbler and took a glug. He never usually drank in the morning. He looked despairingly at her. No longer was she slumped in the chair. She was all action, adrenalin charged.

'Bastards. That poor girl. You should be ashamed of yourself. *Gutless.*

Grow a pair, Dominic.' He coloured and blenched at her tirade. Rosa stormed out, returning a moment later while shrugging on her coat. She glared at him, her eyes blazing.

'Where are you going? Please calm down. Let's think carefully about the next steps.'

'Whilst you think yourself in circles and wring your hands I'm off to find Ellie. That poor girl.'

'But we don't know where she lives. What good will it do? Think about the threat to our boys. And what did he mean about Juan?' said Dominic, looking at Rosa in amazement as she strode over, picked up his whisky and threw it down her throat.

She slammed the glass down, glared at him, threw her hands in the air and spat her words at him. 'That poor, sweet girl. You think some bully's going to frighten me off? I know where she lives, who her flatmates are and where her home is too. Unlike you, I talk to her, listen to her. You should try it once in a while. So, whilst you sit and mope, feeling sorry for yourself... I'm off to find her and then off to Exeter to find our Juan. As for you, *shame on you, Dominic Green.*' With that, she slammed the door behind her, only to storm back through moments later with another volley. '*Mierda!* Take a hard look at yourself. Where's my Dominic? Man up.'

CHAPTER 14: HARTLEY

Albert squinted; he pulled the bed covers over as the pitch blackness of his sleeping pod was suddenly bathed in a painfully bright light, signalling the start of yet another day. They had thirty minutes to shower and dress, a countdown emitting from ceiling and wall-embedded speakers. Pod inmates shuffled around each other, eyes locking in silent communication or darting away in fear of offending the so-called fundamental principles, faces etched with worry or smiling their contentment, the occasional shrug of a shoulder, body language their only means of communication without automatic sanction. The ubiquitous grey tunics were pulled on, the coarse material chafing, and they were escorted out of their pod, a low beep sounding as they were scanned out, past sleeping pods still in darkness.

Beep. Stepping out of the sleep dome they ventured outside; the inside outside. Golden light bathed the parkland and birdsong tweeted until drowned by the distant yapping of dogs. Albert looked askance at his colleague, Red Hair – named by Hartley as Peter 1671 – who shrugged as if to say, *what can you do? It's all false, all a façade.* The exchange was not missed by their escort, who spoke quietly, no more than a murmur and to no one in particular. He did not speak directly to Albert, nor to Red Hair. But the illicit exchange had been logged. The twelve cadets were soon met by Junior Sergeant of State Security Thompson, and they were marched into the tarmac parade ground for their daily drill, where they joined rows of other cadets assembled. Matthew 2225 and Peter 1671 and James 4646 and Talah 3787 and John 1516 and Thomas 2525 and Umar 1314, and the other members of Albert's sleeping pod, marched to their allotted positions under the watchful eyes of Captain Jenkinson and his officers. The daily drill was enjoyed by some, endured by most at the start of each day before breakfast rations and the work or fitness or education routines, which were to be interrupted only for a brief lunch before more of the same in the afternoon. A sullen acceptance of their new regime imbued most; a few foolhardy souls objected and were referred to the care of the medical director and his staff; others thrived on the disciplined routine. Albert kept his head down. To comply was easier than to resist and he could look forward to a brief period of leisure at the end of the day where some element of choice could be exercised: the libraries or the sports arena or the spiritual areas for prayer and contemplation.

Having conducted their drill routines, the white coats led them onwards. Walking was brisk, but fell short of a soldier's march. They weaved their way on the designated paths passing across the face of the library – a large glass dome inside which could be seen three tiers with inmates browsing permitted literature and librarians in scarlet uniforms going about their duties. Some cadets seemed to be staring into the distance with blank faces, staring at nothing in particular. Librarians skirted around them, while orderlies maintained a close watching brief. Leaving the library dome behind, they were marched between two of the education domes containing lecture rooms. In contrast with the library these were opaque: white golf balls. As they crossed The Green – a large open, public-park-like space, in reality Astroturf edged with virtual flower beds – they glimpsed the spiritual areas to their left, just making out the shape of the mosque, and to their right the Olympic-style geodesic sports dome, which towered over the smaller lecture room structures at the edges of The Green.

The doors of restaurant one swished open. *Beep.* They were directed to the purple zone to join the queue for breakfast: fruit juice, milky tea, fresh fruit and two rounds of toast with preserves – before joining dozens of others in the main body of the zone. To their right they could see the outer fringes of the red zone where inmates appeared to be eating lunch: sandwiches and chips with a cold drink. Hartley time was specific to differing groups of inmates and determined by the diktat of the administration, by considerations of efficiency and control. Time discernible only by routine.

'The tea's drugged,' muttered Red Hair.

He stopped short as two orderlies homed in. A wide-eyed Red Hair was escorted away. To where? They could guess – many others having had similar experiences.

*

84

By the end of the first week they sung out, unthinkingly, the red flag anthem that signalled the start and end of the day's lessons:

> *The people's flag is deepest red*
> *It shrouded oft our martyred dead*
> *And ere their limbs grew stiff and cold*
> *Their hearts' blood dyed in every fold…*

> *We'll keep the red flag flying here*

One of the cadets seemed to spend more of his time away from the group. He was a mouthy, spirited lad. His downfall was an indomitable soul. Albert had come close to treading a similar path. He had learnt from an earlier session though…

'What must private ownership be replaced by?' had enquired an educator.

'Co-operative ownership,' had been the rejoinder of the group.

'I didn't hear you, Matthew 2225.'

'No, sir.'

'So what have you to say? Speak up. What's on your mind?'

'I don't want the needle, sir,' said Albert quietly, watching the professor's hand hover over the red button.

'Please feel free to speak. I'm keen to hear what insights you can provide.'

'And you won't—'

'No. Speak,' said the professor, leaning forwards with eyes that had come alive.

'Well, the thing is, well, Marxism, extremes of left or right for that matter just don't work,' Albert said, pointing to failed regimes throughout history: Lenin, Stalin, Mao, Castro… Hitler, Mussolini, Franco, Pinochet… 'Churchill said something about capitalism in a democracy being imperfect but the only system that works.' His voice had raised, his body language had become more aggressive. Cadets' eyes burned into Albert as he stood defiantly, recalling long-past history lessons.

'Dear God forgive us the kindergarten history, student politics, the rantings of a long dead, grossly overrated racist.'

'The saviour of our country, sir. From both Nazism and communism,' Albert shouted.

'And you would liken the work of Tobin and Connell to the likes of Hitler and Stalin? Tell me, did Stalin or Lenin or any of the other examples you may like to cite embrace all religions? I think not. Did they have the mandate of *The People* from democratically held elections? Did they operate in a parliamentary democracy? Meanwhile, Tobin embraces the teachings of Jesus, of Muhammad, is tolerant towards all religions. The modern socialist model adopted by our government is wholly different to any that has gone before. The treatment of the disadvantaged, the poor, disabled, mentally ill; the eradication of racism and homelessness and unemployment is in the mould of Jesus himself.'

'Ha! It doesn't work, won't work, can't work,' responded Albert angrily, shaking.

'You will clearly only learn the hard way, Matthew 2225. From the off your recalcitrance has been noted. But we have the means of helping you overcome your ignorance, of helping you to come to terms with a greater wisdom. We view it as our mission in life to help you misguided, offending young people become model citizens, re-educated into the new order.'

Albert glared at him, snorted his derision.

Mouths opened; eyes widened as the confrontation developed.

'China's Xi Jinping, North Korea's Kim Jong-Un, Venezuela's Nicolas Maduro...' continued Albert in a raised voice. The permitted argument and debate had been surprising but had given way to emotion as a surge of pent-up pressure released itself in his words, his mannerisms; his face contorted, eyes blazing.

The professor pressed the button on his desk as the tension rose.

A pair of burly white coats materialised.

One of the cadets rose to his feet, a flush of anger blazing his cheeks. It appeared that he was about to leap to Albert's defence. Just then the door opened, and two junior sergeants of state security entered. One approached Albert, the other headed towards the other cadet, known by his Hartley ID as Peter 2979. His support began to leach at the obvious threat, his expression changing in an instant from aggression to uncertainty. The medical bags were opened, syringes extricated and tested.

Peter 2979 sat down sheepishly.

Albert's anger was instantly replaced by fear, and he raised his hands in supplication. 'Please. You promised...'

'Very well...a narrow escape for you, Matthew 2225. You have been warned.'

*

'*Matthew 2225* pay attention. Private ownership must be replaced by what?'

Albert snapped back into the present and answered smartly in an even tone devoid of emotion.

'Co-operative ownership.' The tone was subservient, his answer was repeated by the group.

'Who owns the means of production?'

'Workers,' the permitted answer.

Albert kept his head down, learnt his red flag anthem, chanted his Marxist mantras. They learnt of the merits of a classless society where everyone was equal, all resources and forms of production controlled by government, of the quest to free the exploited proletariat. Discussion was not part of the education process, no alternative views sought – or offered. The absorption of the ideological dogma was assumed by the ability to recite it. Being word perfect in the interest of self-preservation advisable, rather than revelatory. Some would no doubt wholly concur with the teachings, some would not. It was impossible to discern sincerity; impossible to discern insincerity. Control of emotion and speech was a survival technique learnt quickly. Those who failed to grasp this were referred for therapy, many disappearing for days on end, returning as shells of their former selves.

Drilled into them was the Marxist slogan that they would repeat every day:

From each according to his ability, to each according to his needs.

The people's flag is deepest red
It shrouded oft our martyred dead
And ere their limbs grew stiff and cold
Their hearts' blood dyed in every fold…

We'll keep the red flag flying here

Albert was shown into a small tutorial room where he was met by a professor seated at the head of the table.

'Sit down, Matthew 2225,' said the professor.

He sat without comment and stared blankly at his interlocutor.

'You may converse in this session – the start of your essential community re-education. I take it you recognise this street?' said the professor, as he hit a key on the tablet embedded in the table.

The wall in front of Albert lit up and he was propelled back into Notting Hill, and there was his father stepping out of his front door. Next minute they were in Mayfair as Dominic paused at a car showroom of Bentleys and Aston Martins, and then the recording fast-forwarded to Diamond's. Albert opened his mouth and seemed to be on the point of saying something but shrank back. He looked quizzically at the professor, who was watching him intently. Next moment the film showed lobsters and fillets of beef being served to affluent customers who were immaculately attired and bejewelled. But wait, now they were in a rubbish strewn, filthy side entrance close to the street where Albert lived. A middle-aged man was sipping from a bottle, a tin in front of him was set on a blanket, which caught the stray coins and buttons and spent travel tickets thrown in the vagrant's general direction. Most passers-by ignored him as if he were not there. Some offered abusive invective, which made Albert cringe. A young female charity worker shooed away an unwelcome, unkind youth who chose to throw an empty can and takeaway garbage directly at the man. She approached him with a coffee and a sandwich and kindness.

'Meet Colin, a war veteran,' said his professor.

And then his father hove into view and he watched him walk past without even glancing. His mother, Rosa, was also caught on film: she stopped and had a brief exchange, reaching into her purse to extract a coin, which she placed carefully into the tin before scurrying on. The camera followed her progress as she turned a corner and headed to her own house: the large Georgian town house with the red door.

'What do you glean from this, Matthew 2225?'

'What do you want me to say?'

'Just tell me what you see.'

'A homeless person down on his luck? My mum and dad...'

'Does the contrast in their circumstances not strike you?'

'I see what you're doing. But my dad was a working-class man who made his own way in the world. A miner's son with a talent for...'

'And he earns hundreds of thousands of pounds. Or should I say, he's paid these vast sums whilst Colin lost his leg and his mind in Afghanistan in the name of his country and is rejected by society. His world fell apart; retired from the army he couldn't find employment and his wife soon left the crippled veteran to, and I quote her, "sort himself out." The state paid him a measly amount until he lost his house. He became homeless, fell between the gaps in the state benefit system. These are the edited highlights. What do you think of a society that pays vast sums to a chef, and yet treats a war veteran in this way?'

'I feel sorry for—'

'He wouldn't thank you for your sympathy. He might appreciate a share of the spoils, a decent meal, a roof over his head...'

Suddenly, the wall flashed images of other locals, ethnically diverse, all with stories of having dropped out of society or being on the point of doing so: men and women with drink or gambling or drug addictions; disabled and mentally ill patients rejected by the world of work; homeless war veterans like Colin; working single mothers struggling to make ends meet while holding down multiple jobs...

Albert was asked to study their life stories, to ask himself fundamental questions as to how a capitalist society could allow such squalor and deprivation and despondency to exist unchecked alongside wealth and privilege. 'All this has been allowed to develop with sticking plaster solutions to salve consciences for decades. Until now. Thomas Tobin's Socialist Labour Party is committed to changing this. It has the mandate, and in future the state will allocate a fair and equal value to all members of society. No longer will CEOs in big companies be allowed to pay themselves twenty, thirty times the salary their workers are paid. Nurses will be valued equally with NHS managers and doctors and consultants and cooks and cleaners and...'

'Okay, I get the point. But if you remove aspiration you destroy the economy. Why should a well-educated, talented manager of a large company take all the responsibility and stress that goes with that, if they are to be paid what their cleaner's paid? Where's the incentive? It doesn't make sense,' said Albert.

'You have much to learn, Matthew 2225. I can see that your stay at Hartley is likely to be prolonged. I'll leave you to get to know these good and worthy people,' said the professor. He rose to his feet and offered his final thoughts. 'You will be asked to relate all of these life experiences and to explain what you have learnt from all this by one of my colleagues.'

He reached the door and turned back to Albert. 'And if you think the running of a company is more stressful than the desperate lives of Colin, Sharon, Darpan, Aisha and all the others, I look forward to you explaining that. Shame on you, Matthew 2225.'

CHAPTER 15: CONTACTS

Lunch service was in progress on yet another quiet day. Diamond's was managing to limp on; two staff had not been replaced and Brandon had cut costs wherever he could. Supplies were becoming difficult to source and their menu became mediocre and less high-end as they adjusted to lower demand. Those who could still afford plush restaurants, high-class cuisine and top prices could not be seen to afford them. So the menu was adapted to feature traditional British fare: steak, kidney and oyster pie, Lancashire hot pot, beer-battered fish and chips…

'Your girlfriend's here,' shouted Bill across the kitchen, grinning from ear to ear.

'Asking for you,' said Gina.

Dominic wagged a threatening finger at Bill, suppressing the smile forming at the corner of his mouth. He removed his apron as he headed for the restaurant. It was nearing the end of service and he relished the thought of seeing her again. He spoke to a couple who were just paying their bill, asking if they had enjoyed their meal, and walked towards her. As he approached she smiled, and raised an eyebrow, wine bottle hovering over a spare glass. *Yes please.* She was accompanied today, a woman with her back to him. And then her lunch companion swivelled in her chair, her bright blue eyes lasering onto his and she gave a wide, beaming smile that stopped him in his tracks. His palms were suddenly moist, and his cheeks flushed.

'I don't believe it… *Rebecca.* What on earth…?'

'Hello, Dom. It's been a while hasn't it?'

Dominic absent-mindedly accepted the glass of wine and plopped down in his seat, took a gulp, not really tasting the wine, needing to gather his wits.

He looked from one to the other in disbelief.

'Dear Dom. How good to see you. You've already had the pleasure of Rebecca,' said Stephanie, wearing a teasing half-smile, eyes glinting.

'You must forgive me, Dom. I wanted to surprise you,' said Rebecca.

'Well, you certainly did that. I just can't believe...'

'So you said, darling,' said Stephanie, clearly enjoying his discomfiture. She placed a hand over his, leaned into him and kissed him lightly on the cheek. 'I shall forgive you neglecting me on this occasion. So tell me, you two, was it *very* illicit, this love affair?'

'*Steph*. You promised,' interjected Rebecca.

'Becks has told me all about it, Dom.'

'Ignore her. She's just stirring,' said Rebecca, turning towards Dominic.

Those eyes. He couldn't help remembering – the isolated, rented cottage overlooking the South Devon coastline, a week of blissful escape. Flip flops and sunhats and towels thrown in a heap as they kissed on the golden sandy beach. Unbroken sunshine, swimming, walking, laughing, chilled wine lunches followed by afternoon lovemaking. It had started out by accident – the two of them thrown together by force of circumstance. But it became something more intense. There had been something elemental about it – a sense that it was meant to be. It had seemed pointless to fight the forces of nature throwing them together: a seismic shift of tectonic plates. It just felt right. Despite being wrong.

Dominic sipped his wine, struggling to find something to say.

'It all sounds very dreamy to me,' said Stephanie. 'A dashingly handsome man saves bathing beauty, kiss of life, deep gratitude. Cue passionate affair between two gorgeous creatures. There's no need to be coy. We're all friends here. Quite the little love triangle, come to think of it,' said Stephanie, sitting back contentedly, looking pleased with herself.

'We were friends, Steph. Special friends,' said Dominic. He paused and added, 'What do you mean triangle?' Stephanie always spoke playfully, an impish ability making him feel uncomfortable one moment, special the next. What was she suggesting? There was no *us* as far as he and Stephanie were concerned. 'You two?' He frowned and looked from one to the other as they smiled knowingly at each other.

'We're partners,' said Stephanie, head cocked to one side, watching Dominic intently.

'Oh... *Oh*, I see.'

'We've shocked poor Dominic, Becks.'

'You're impossible, Steph,' Rebecca said. She reached for Dominic and her fingertips stroked the back of his hand. He felt a frisson of electricity charge through him.

'Don't know what to say,' he muttered.

'I'm sorry, Dom. I should have been in touch before now. Telling you like this was cruel. I shouldn't have allowed myself to be persuaded...' Rebecca said. She threw a dark look at Stephanie, who watched the exchange with her large hazel eyes, adopting an amused expression.

'I'll leave you two to chat. Must powder my nose or something,' Stephanie said, getting out of her chair and lightly resting a proprietorial hand on Dominic's shoulder as she headed for the lobby.

'How's Rosa?' asked Rebecca.

'Oh, alright. And your new high-powered job?'

'It was never that. Just an administrative job in the civil service. Rosa was the reason I called it off, you know. The real reason.'

'Not Stephanie?'

'*No*. That's happened only recently. You're not the only one taken by surprise, I might tell you. It wasn't in the plan. But then neither were you... I know this is awkward, but I hope we can be friends.'

'Of course. I wish...'

'I know... It's been great to see you, Dominic. You know how grateful I am for what you did. I'll never forget it.'

As he finished his wine Stephanie insisted they arrange another of their evenings, telling Rebecca that he was responsible for her culinary education. Dominic was struck by how open she was in arranging an evening with him, not that their relationship was anything other than platonic. He watched her then hook her arm through Rebecca's as they headed for the exit, chattering away.

Rosa was waiting for him as he opened their front door at the end of the afternoon, her agitation and impatience plain to see. Juan? Ellie? She sat him down, thrust a whisky at him, pouring herself a generous glass of Rioja. Rosa had spoken to Ellie's flatmates. Nothing. She's not been seen for days. But her stuff was still in her room. Next stop was her parents' house. Her father had been brusque to the point of rudeness, her mum embarrassed by his manner but no more forthcoming. Where was Ellie? she had asked. *What business was that of hers?* Rosa expressed concern about Ellie's health but was assured she was well, staying with her flatmates. *Really?*

'You tried, Rosa.'

'You know me better than that. You don't think I'm about to give up, do you? Her dad was lying – frightened, I think. I had another go at her flatmates, but just the same. So, I waited until Jenny...'

'Jenny?'

'One of her flatmates, obviously. Keep up.'

Rosa had followed her into a café and eventually engaged Jenny in conversation, overcoming her reluctance. As they left, Jenny urgently pulled her to one side. Ellie had fled to France. She did not know for certain but thought Juan might be with her. She hoped he was. She had been scared, was battered, and bruised – not facially but on her body and internally. Jenny was also worried about Ellie's emotional state and thought she was psychologically fragile. Rosa promised she would not tell anyone. Clearly all of them had been threatened or bribed. Perhaps both.

'Juan's in France, is he? Why's he not been in touch?'

'He *has!*' she said triumphantly. 'But he's scared too. I couldn't get much out of him. He's with Ellie, they're safe and renting a cottage in Brittany. He mumbled something about you and Albert getting into so much trouble had reflected badly on him, created problems: a mild beating, threats from the university and warnings to lie low. It sounds as if the university campus is tinder bag.'

'Box. Tinder box.'

'*Whatever!*'

'Did he say anything about the FF?'

'Who?'

'You know... Freedom Fighters – the government calls them a terrorist organisation, they say they are fighting for democracy, for freedom... Albert said something about Juan getting involved,' said Dominic.

'No, he said nothing about that. My *Godddd*, we don't want that.'

'No. How's Ellie?'

'How'd you think? She was raped, *gang raped*. Remember?'

'Come on, Rosa, give me a break.'

'You don't deserve it. And did you find those cojones? *Ha!*'

'Oh, for *Christ's* sake,' he said, getting to his feet and glowering over her. Rosa sat back and looked at him quizzically. 'I've just about had enough of your

Latin temperament, your tantrums. My business is going down the pan, my partner's off his head, I've been beaten up by a mob, insulted and accused by government ministers, threatened and...why are you smiling?'

'It's good to see a bit of spirit. About time.'

'And I've given an interview to the *Times*. I'm seeing Seb this evening and then darts,' he said sharply. 'Not sure what time I'll be home.'

'No problem. My flight goes in two hours' time. Must get moving.' She stood, pecked him on the cheek and said, 'We've got a lot to sort out, Dominic. You and me. But I'm prepared to put that to one side for now, for the sake of the boys. *Our* boys. We have to fight for them. Good to see you taking steps in that direction – even if they are only baby steps.'

He found Stephanie sitting demurely, sipping wine, in the corner. She seemed lost in thought until she spotted him; she offered her enigmatic half-smile as a greeting. A contemporary Mona Lisa, but with sparkling eyes to lift his spirits. His heart skipped a beat. She was a beautiful woman: slim, brunette with hazel eyes and tonight she wore a tight-fitting emerald, green dress, which suited her colour just as Rosa's choice of red and black suited her. He kissed her on both cheeks and as he sat down, she covered his hand with hers, gently squeezing. He made no move to withdraw, the intimacy and warmth a balm to recent events. A welcome distraction from a disruptive world, however fleeting.

'I've been looking forward to seeing you, Dom. No sharing you with Rebecca this evening. I have you all to myself. And what a quirky, atmospheric restaurant you've chosen. Quite the romantic, aren't you? It would seem I need to be on my guard this evening. Although there again...' Her words dried up and her head tilted, eyeing him from an angle.

'Err... Why do you do that? Always unbalancing me.'

'Surely not. You seem stressed. A glass of wine is my prescription. And how was the irascible, latter-day hippy, Seb?'

'There you go again. How do you know...'

'You shouldn't underestimate this mere slip of a girl, you know.'

'Mm. It was a strange encounter. Cryptic. Vague. Confusing. Piecing it together was like plaiting fog. Not sure it's for me though. He hints at contacts in high places and rebellious zeal but is short on details.'

'He's gauging your reactions, testing your mettle, seeing if you can work it out. And how much more in the way of a crisis do you need?'

'And he keeps referring to cells – as if it's some sort of resistance movement.'

'Funny that. What do you think he may be resisting? That's not so hard to work out, is it? Not beyond our celebrity chef to fathom?'

'Now you're poking fun at me.'

'No… Well, just a little maybe. But you only get to speak to Seb by recommendation. It's not his real name of course.'

'But it was Albert, my son who—'

'Yes,' she said, and this time her smile disappeared altogether. She grabbed his hand again and squeezed tightly. 'He's being stoic, sensible, you should be proud.'

'We always have been…hang on – what are you saying? How do you know he's… What do you know?'

'*Contacts*, Dom. Now, let's eat.'

'You can't leave it at that. I'm not hungry anyway. It's one disaster after another, and now you're being every bit as baffling as your Bohemian friend. If you or he think I'm made of the sort of stuff that blows up bridges and shoots people – well, speak to Rosa. She'll put you straight on that point. Come on, Steph, you can't lay claim to knowing what's happening to Albert and then leave me hanging.'

'I'm not aware of anyone shooting or playing with explosives. No, it's more of a cerebral, modern world war, you might say. There's definitely a place for celebs of all sorts who have a message to resonate, a fan base. And you will hear very soon that Norris will be given his liberty.'

'Jinks? Can we talk about one thing at a time? And your name-dropping isn't going to distract me from my son. What *do* you know?'

'Later. We need a bit more privacy than is afforded here,' she said in a lower voice, leaning towards him conspiratorially. 'Let's have one course, another glass and then head to mine.'

'Okay, I suppose so. Will Rebecca be there?'

'Still smitten? That's not allowed. I want you all to myself.'

'*Steph!*'

'She's with her mum for a few days. Had a stroke, poor thing. So, all will be quiet. We won't be interrupted if that's what you're worrying about. And with Rosa off to France…'

'Good.'

'Not quite the response a vulnerable girl might have wished for. But I'm sure you'll be gentle…'

'I didn't mean that at all. You know I didn't. Oh, God. Look, all I meant was that I want to hear about *Albert*. Your honour won't be impugned; you'll be quite safe.'

'Another glass for Dutch courage.'

'Not needed.'

'I meant me!'

She soon called a truce, having finished their paella. Dominic picked at his food disconsolately, impatient for news of his son. Stephanie made up for it with light chatter: her flat in Mayfair, a play she had recently seen, Becca's mum…

As Dominic sank into a soft leather sofa, Stephanie splashed brandy into a glass and chatted about how life had turned sour, the horrors of the new regime; the deprivation inflicted on the hard-working people living a simple life. Words tripped off her tongue and he smiled as he admired her luxurious, sumptuous home, which sat in the middle of one of the most expensive residential areas in the world. Stephanie neither worked, hard or otherwise, nor led what most would regard as being a simple life. But she did seem well-connected, not something he had understood previously. Glancing around the room he noticed how tastefully furnished it was, with statuettes on the sideboard, and artwork adorning the walls. Dominic had recognised some of the watercolour paintings in the hall as featuring bays he knew well: Hope Cove and Thurlestone in the South Hams of Devon. He had half-wondered if they were Rebecca's, recalling hours spent on a headland with her easel and brushes and paint. Having found a few nibbles, Stephanie plonked herself next to him, kicking her shoes off and crossing one slim, toned limb over the other.

'Cheers,' she said.

They chinked glasses and he tasted the warm brandy, allowing it to linger in his mouth. He turned towards Stephanie, took her hand, and looked deeply into her hazel eyes. '*Please* tell me what you know about Albert.'

The mischievous smile was instantly replaced with sad eyes; a seriousness enveloping her.

'His sentence is being served in a sophisticated boot camp high in the Pennines. Conscription, if you like. It will only end when he either joins the SNPS or someone deems his re-education successful. Knowledge about them is scant, but I'm told the liberal, well-intentioned regime is but a veneer. Who knows what goes on in there. The only way out is via the national police really—'

Dominic blanched and gripped her arm. 'Please, God, tell me that Albert's okay?'

'We must hope he learns the art of survival.'

'How do we get him out?'

'We don't.'

'What will happen to him? I can't just...'

'Let's hope he puts his head down, goes along with the regime—'

'*Never*! Albert has his mother's Latin blood running in his veins. He's stubborn and principled, no way he will simply cower.'

'Then pray for divine intervention?'

Dominic sat and brooded for a moment, then turned back to her.

'Who?'

'I beg your pardon?'

'You said someone told you...'

'Ahh...can't breach confidences... Brandy?'

Stephanie poured liberal measures, tried to reassure him, but Dominic was downhearted. His eldest son in a so-called rehabilitation centre; a boot camp for bully boys in reality. And his youngest son had been beaten and was now holed up in France.

'I can't believe they're doing this. All our socialist dreams in tatters, destroyed by a government that's lost its way. I had hoped the extremism would be short-lived, that social democracy would soon be reasserted. But the extremes of control get worse by the day, the impact on society is penal. They've lost the trust of most fair-minded people, seem to be resorting to authoritarian measures. It's impossible to defend. Albert warned me, but of course I knew better...'

'It's all going to get much worse. Conscription into the SNPS has started; numbers are already measured in the tens of thousands. The rewards for those converting to the socialist cause within the SNPS are survival, safety, camaraderie; the repercussions for those who resist are severe. It's attracting thugs, hooligans, the dregs of society...'

'You make it sound like Nazi Germany. That can't happen in the UK, can it?'

'No? And we will soon become a one-party state.'

'*No*! How come you know so much?'

'I'm just guessing, reading between the lines...' She smiled at him. 'It's all very tiresome, isn't it? A night cap is what we need.' She deflected all entreaties for more information. They sipped another brandy and listened to Mozart, despite Dominic's agitation.

Then Stephanie stood, straightened her dress, and held out her hand, which he took meekly. 'Bed, I think.'

'I need to go home.'

'No, you don't. Come on, I can offer you a choice of bedrooms,' she said.

Stephanie was an unfathomable mix: one moment knowledgeable, serious, even insightful; the next light, teasing, flirtatious. A social butterfly with powerful contacts and an intellect that crept up and surprised, camouflaged in frivolousness. But her lightness and beauty were welcome escape routes from the darkness. His resistance evaporated and he trudged along the corridor holding her hand, the warmth and closeness reassuring – a life belt in stormy seas.

She turned to face him and kissed him lightly. 'Now you have a choice. To the left is the blue room. My room. To the right is the cold, lonely green room.' Her head was cocked, the half-smile making a comeback. She spoke softly; their fingers entwined.

'We both have life partners,' he said, his note doleful.

'Life *is* complicated, isn't it?'

Dominic drew her close to him, kissed her passionately before drawing away, letting her fingers slowly slip through his.

He turned to the right.

'Sweet dreams,' she said, disappearing into her own room.

CHAPTER 16: SURVEILLANCE

Birdsong, distant singing, and bright sunlight filtered through the cracks in the curtains, with dust motes dancing in the light heralding a bright new day. It struck Dominic that dark tumescent clouds, claps of thunder, snakes of lightning would be more fitting. He had tossed and turned, alarmed by the news about his sons, the hovering threats, the unreported violation of sweet Ellie. And his conscience was troubled. First his failures over Ellie's plight. And last night a simple choice – left or right. He could not summon the gumption to go with natural impulses: his craving, the urgent need for love, the animal sexual desire. His head had ruled the day, subjugating his lust. He would become proud of that decisive moment, he hoped. But in the meantime, he was assailed by guilty feelings of regret, unrequited longing. He felt confused, conflicted, conquered. The singing grew closer, then relented. There was a quiet knock at the door. It swung open, and Stephanie breezed in.

'Morning, lover.'

He sat up, quickly pulled his fingers through his hair, beamed his welcome. She came to his bedside, touched his shoulder lightly, bent down and pressed her lips to his forehead, affectionately brushing a loose strand of hair back. Her mood was light. He watched her intently, transfixed by her beauty as she went to the window and drew back the curtains. The sunlight flooded in, and he gasped as it shone through, silhouetting her. As she turned towards him her thin nightdress was transparent, rendering redundant any modesty it afforded.

'Steph…' he breathed.

She smiled, paused for a moment and in one languid motion pulled her nightie over her head; her gorgeous hazel gaze found his wide eyes and locked on. She cocked her head to one side – that endearing, tantalising habit of hers – and slipped in beside him. All his doubts and misgivings were gone in an instant as the consummation of their love engulfed them; family woes and business traumas cast aside by more immediate carnal pleasures.

Dominic sat alongside Stephanie at the granite-topped breakfast bar, his natural sunny disposition restored. He was glowing inside, was determined to put back the inevitable guilt he supposed was just around the corner. They had not turned the television or the radio on, instead opting for Beethoven in the background as they ate breakfast. Stephanie had insisted on cooking him poached eggs on toast with crispy bacon and ripe avocado; he was surprised at her skill in the kitchen. But why should he be? She seemed expert at anything she turned her mind to, whether in the kitchen or the political arena. Or the bedroom. She also seemed unhurried about allowing the realities of the real world to invade their stolen time of self-indulgence and respite. But she also chattered fondly about Rebecca and wanted to know more about Rosa. *I'd get on well with her, I like a feisty lady. The four of us should meet for dinner sometime.* Dominic shuddered at the thought. The notion that one might love two people simultaneously did not seem strange or fickle or disloyal to her. And he was swept away by her alternative liberal view of the world, his conservative worldview placed on hold.

But depressing reality was about to reassert itself as Stephanie sauntered down the hallway, returning with newspapers, and Dominic switched on his phone. *Ping.*

Rosa
Got here safely – thanks for asking!
Ellie looks terrible, Juan no better.
I look after them. Speak tomorrow. Hope
your darts evening went well.

Dominic
Sorry – late night. Send him my love. Speak
later. Take care. Love you.
Dominic
Missing you! X

He felt instantly guilty, full of remorse. Should he tell Rosa? Confess? He would call her later. He had so many questions. *Ping.* Breaking news.

> ***Jinks*** *calls for nationwide protests...*
> *A press statement has called on the government to*
> *change course, restore freedoms of speech, cancel*
> *taxation raids on the middle earners, halt*
> *constitutional reforms. He urges restraint and*
> *calls for the government to show leadership*
> *and compassion.*

> ***SNPS Accused of Heavy-Handedness.***
> *The rapidly expanding new state police force*
> *was deployed on the streets of London and*
> *Leicester last night. In an apparent hardening of*
> *tactics a zero-tolerance approach appeared*
> *targeted at PAD – the self-proclaimed*
> *pacifist group of the professional and*
> *managerial classes. Pro-government groups*
> *escaped unscathed. One hundred and twenty-five*
> *protesters arrested, scores admitted to hospitals,*
> *most with head wounds. Three fatalities reported.*

And Stephanie drew his attention to an article in the *Times*, featuring Dominic himself. In the *Times*! It had been awarded a half-page spread, providing a pen portrait of the celebrity chef: his working-class roots and lifelong support of the Labour Party. It reported the death of his father in the eighties from pneumoconiosis, the demise of his mining village in the Thatcher era. It traced Dominic's career and emergence as a celebrity chef with a popular fan base.

'Clever boy,' said Stephanie. 'You draw the distinction between the social democracy of Blair and Brown, and the emerging horrors of the Tobin and Connell brand of socialism. Quite the intellectual, aren't you?'

'Hardly. I just believe in the socialist cause. I've seen first-hand the cruelty of the Tories of the 1980s and the modern incarnation has been no better. As for Tobin and Connell and their revolution, they lied about their intentions. I'm so disappointed. Disgusted. Perhaps I'm naïve. Even my own son could see it – predicted all this happening. Maybe I should become a politician, introduce the novel concept of someone who does what he says he will do. Is that so unimaginable?'

'Well, to be honest, yes. You'd never make a politician. You're much too honest.'

'Back to mocking, are we?'

'A compliment, surely? And your transparent honesty is exactly why you're much loved by the hordes of middle-aged ladies. That and your swarthy good looks, your charm. And your enthusiasm for food and wine, of course.'

'Very flattering.'

'Well, I love you, and when are we next going to have a darts match, my lover?'

'*Enough!*'

'Surely not?'

Dominic re-read the article which also featured the re-education centre, his son's plight. It posed the questions he had raised and demanded answers. But of his description of the events at Chequers, the antics of government ministers and their guests, the attack on Ellie – nothing. Much too sensitive. Uncorroborated. Bill did not count, apparently. A legal quagmire. But their opinion page led on the escalation of violence, supporting the calls for restraint, calm, peace by religious leaders of all denominations. It commented on the bravery and leadership of Norris Jinks...

Dominic made a phone call while Stephanie busied herself preparing for her day ahead; she was opaque as to her plans, cryptic. *Terribly dull*, was about all he could get out of her. He was seeing her in a new light and that was not just the sex. First, there was her lesbian relationship with Rebecca – he had never suspected either of such an orientation, not that it bothered him. Not much anyway. And her liberal perspectives on relationships added another layer of intrigue. Her values seemed as flexible as a sapling, bending one way and then another. And now he had learnt of her having contacts in high places: Jinks. And who was Seb? What was that all about? And how come she had insights into government intentions? Intuition? Jinks? Suddenly her movements, how she might spend her time, seemed to matter. But she was not forthcoming. Sighing, he reached for his mobile. There was a call he needed to make.

'I'll see you in your office... Don't care about your bloody meetings... Yes, it's important – you owe me an explanation, a huge apology... I'm beyond angry. Be there. One hour.'

*

Dominic reached Brandon's domain first and awaited his partner's arrival. He took in his surroundings, whereas normally he could not wait to get back to his own territory. It was a traditional office: leather-inlaid mahogany desk, dark wooden bookcases, decanters of whisky, two squashy chairs with threadbare arms. Box files lay higgledy-piggledy, used mugs were scattered about, as were old newspapers, business magazines. The frayed carpet was a faded red, the whole office in need of more than a lick of paint. Shabby, untidy, unkempt. For the first time it struck him there were no pictures, no family photographs, just a promotional photograph of Dominic in his chef's whites advertising the Diamond Delicacies programme.

He went and sat on the business side of the desk and swivelled in the chair, trying it on for size – not a good fit. Opening the desk drawers revealed the ephemera of years of office work: old papers, previous years' diaries, a soft cuddly toy, photographs – presumably of old business contacts no longer regarded. Delving further he pulled out a file of papers: invoices, payment demands. Also a corkscrew, a glass tumbler, a half-bottle of whisky, pens, paper clips, printing paper and accounting statements. Dominic could just about make out a profit and loss statement, especially one with lots of red ink. It seemed things were as problematic as Brandon made out.

His thoughts were interrupted by a sharp rapping on the door. With barely a pause a stranger strode in, and Dominic's heart missed a beat as he took in the grey tunic uniform and the red M badge, the crimson epaulettes. He was tall and slim, wore wire-framed glasses and an air of arrogant authority, short black hair slicked over, cap in hand. He declined to say who he was.

'What do you want?'

'Checking who's here. I'll have a word with *you* later.' He paused and threw a dark look before closing the door quietly behind him. That sounded ominous, vaguely threatening. Most unsettling. *Ping.*

Brandon
Meet me in the usual coffee shop.

Dom
We agreed to meet here.

Brandon
Will explain. Please!

Bloody man, now *he* was being mysterious. What is it with people? He sighed and grabbed his coat, making for the exit. As he reached the reception area, he was assailed by the uniform.

'Where are you going, sir?'

'I'm sorry, what's it to you? And who are you? Not sure I caught your name.'

'Sergeant of State Security Harrison.'

Dominic noted the absence of the 'sir' this time. The previous politeness had seemed forced, this curt manner more authentic.

'Do excuse me,' said Dominic, as he made to pass by. He was stopped by a firm hand on the chest.

'I asked you a question. *Sir.*' Harrison's mouth tightened, cold eyes portending threat. It struck Dominic that violence was always an option for the man, perhaps a preferred option. He seemed to relish confrontation every bit as much as Dominic eschewed it.

'If you must know, I'm going for a coffee.' He was shaken by the exchange and his cheeks flushed instantly. Harrison slowly stood to one side and allowed him to pass. Dominic could feel Harrison's eyes burning into his back as he hurried down the street. As he reached the coffee shop he glanced around urgently, scanning faces. Pushing through a group of students he found Brandon at a corner table.

'What's going on? Who the hell is Harrison and why all the cloak and dagger stuff? And you owe me—'

'Surveillance by state security. That's what's going on. You've heard of the SNPS, I assume? You're under the microscope, my friend. Labelled a troublemaker. Your high profile's not doing you any favours. And if I were you, I'd stop running to the press. What were you thinking of, Dom? First the fracas, then the TV interview and now your name's splashed all over the newspapers...'

'So what would you have me do? What the hell are you doing about our business, about the intimidation, about, about...? And as for your fracas, I was...what are you wearing?' He pointed at the offending article. A badge with a large red M.

'Insurance policy. You should get one. You could do with currying some socialist favour. You've heard of Mobilisation?'

He nodded.

'Mobilisation's eyes and ears?'

Another nod.

'Harrison is our very own Mobilisation eye and I have every reason to believe there are ears planted in our office, kitchen and restaurant.'

'Which is why you wanted to meet here?'

'Sharp as ever, Dom. Take a little friendly advice from a dear old friend.'

'Who might that be?'

'Get your badge, assume you're being watched and listened to, even at home. *Especially* at home,' Brandon said in a hoarse, half-whispered voice, leaning forwards conspiratorially.

Dominic was so stunned he forgot to demand Brandon's apology, failed to tell him about his Chequers experience. *Ping.*

> **Breaking News – Constitutional Crisis Brewing**
> *The BBC has information that suggests the*
> *Palace is dragging its feet over the sanctioning*
> *of royal assent to the Parliament Bill. This*
> *is the last step prior to making a bill an Act of*
> *Parliament. The last time the monarch refused*
> *to grant the royal assent was in 1707.*

Dominic was lost in thought as he made his way down Oxford Street and on towards Trafalgar Square to meet Bill for a beer. His sous chef had taken time off work, so shaken, battered and bruised was he after their shared experience at Chequers. Though Bill was bold, even brave to the point of foolhardiness, it belied a fragile emotional state, and recently he'd descended into a cloud of depression. Dominic pulled the collar of his coat up to ward off the evening chill, reached for his fake glasses and donned a flat cap. He glanced around. Was he being followed? Just being paranoid, he remonstrated with himself.

As he entered the periphery of Trafalgar Square, angry scenes seemed to be developing. These were so commonplace these days he had not taken particular notice of the growing hubbub. But there was no ignoring it now. He paused, better to take in the scenes, to plot a route away from trouble. What he saw were factions of rival mobs in pitched battle surrounding hundreds of people assembled to hear a speech. Even with a loudhailer the orator was struggling to be heard. He was witnessing a political rally; the speaker was Norris Jinks, his supporters waving Tory banners, PAD flags and placards depicting doves. But the black-shirted activists, mostly sporting short, cropped hair or shaven heads, military insignia, and tattoos, waved clubs and knives, threw bricks and insults, foul, abusive language. The red shirts with the M as their emblem did similarly. The angry scenes were building in intensity, the mood ugly, intimidating. And then a shot rang out. The mayhem seemed to pause in freeze-frame momentarily, before fast-forwarding to a crescendo of screaming, shouting and panic. Blood was shed. More shots rang out. Bodies fell. A column of mounted police hove into view and charged. Not at the extremist groups, but towards the main stage. There was little doubting who their target was, but too late. He had been spirited away. Dominic watched in horror as dozens fell, soon trampled underfoot by charging horses and those merely trying to escape the onslaught; PAD demonstrators were assailed by red shirts. Alarm and confusion reigned. And piling in behind the horses were legions of SNPS, wielding wooden truncheons and handguns indiscriminately. Dominic turned around and made good his escape. A beer with Bill could wait.

CHAPTER 17: DESTINATION DAY -4, 08.15

2027

The night had been punctuated by cries from tortured souls. His own dreams had been kinder for once, but confusing as they mashed disparate parts of his life experiences: pleasures and crises, trauma, and elation. Juan and Albert were mostly young children, happily playing at the beach one moment, squabbling over something inconsequential the next. He kept the more recent images of both his sons at bay as best he could. And then there was Rosa, his beloved Spanish wife, the larger-than-life personality whose conflicting character traits defied pigeon-holing: one moment the doting mother, the next the intelligent professional and then his volatile, emotional wife given to histrionics.

And suddenly he was transported back to happier times with Rosa, pre-children. Idyllic days spent in the Spanish sunshine. Strolling hand in hand, lapping up the atmosphere as they meandered through the multi-generational family gatherings in the grassy, sandy areas behind the beach at Empúries in the dappled shade of the olive trees. Elaborate picnics that tended to be all-day affairs with grandparents and great-grandparents; the children playing in the shallow waters at the edge of the beach, overseen by young mothers chattering noisily, many puffing away on cigarettes. They sat alone, very much in love and looked on at the happy family gatherings, enjoying a glass of cava kindly offered by the nearest group. There always seemed to be a bottle of cava and a few beers at the ready to wash down the anchovies – the inevitable prelude to pan con tomate, cured Spanish ham and spicy sausages, Manchego cheese, grapes…

'Salud, señor,' they offered, as they hauled themselves up, intent on picking their way through the noisy gathering on their way to L'Escala, Rosa chatting animatedly about her desire for children: *at least three, maybe four.*

Dominic loved the family values and culture of Spanish people and hoped they would replicate that wherever home might eventually be.

His mind randomly alighted on tragedy, his sons, close friends, then the sensuous guilty pleasures of the enigmatic Stephanie who had led him astray. He had been happy to stray at the time – no thought to the repercussions. But the guilty baggage weighed heavily now. His times with Stephanie seemed to represent another dimension altogether and the images and experiences lingered, failing to dim. As they were relived, pangs of remorse tortured him. He tried in vain to avoid his mind snagging on it all. Even now, he recognised the tingling sensation in his loins – even in such straitened circumstances. His longing and guilt were twisted together, tight as barbed wire. Rosa melding into Stephanie, Stephanie into Rosa. Rebecca was no longer part of that mix, now a sibling-like character of enormous mental strength to whom he owed so much. And then there were the images of Juan and Albert that would no longer hold in the background, returning with a jolt to haunt him. And those of his friends. As he recalled the horrors he had personally witnessed, the obscenities committed, a spasm of fear swept through Dominic's body. He broke into a cold sweat, then let out a muffled cry of anguish, tears flowing freely, shoulders heaving as his body was racked with deep sobs. Celia shuffled over and pulled his head into the crook of her neck. She held him tight, stroking his head, shushing him like a baby. And he cried even more at the act of kindness, of love in the middle of their shared hell. There was only one means of escape from all the torment…soon now.

The sound of boots alerted Dominic to the dawning of a new day. His weeping abated as he heard the keys jangling, the door scraping open. The arrival of Pock and Shorty. Frightened eyes locked onto the guards; there was whimpering from an older lady in the far corner, fevered groans from a man close to her. They all shrank back as if trying to disappear into the walls. Meagre rations were slung into the middle of the floor.

'Tom Handley and Jimmy Bell. *Time*,' said Pock. He seemed jubilant. Shorty hurried them up, wielding his baton, expletives of encouragement tumbling from his foul mouth. Jimmy stared wide-eyed, his body shaking violently.

He struggled to his feet.

Tom Handley shrank away from the guards, resisted their call, was roughly manhandled up by Shorty. The front of Tom's trousers suddenly darkened, the damp patch spreading. Sharon Briggs looked up mournfully, a shadow of confusion passing over her features. As they dragged Tom and Jimmy out of the cell, Pock half-turned and threw his words in Sharon's direction. 'Your lucky day. Turns out you're not wanted just yet.' The guards' faces broke into rictus grins, uttering a vulgar commentary, slamming the cell door behind them.

All eyes were on Sharon.

She quivered.

One or two reached out to her, but she could not speak.

All of a sudden, she stood and dashed to the bucket in the corner, pulling her pants down and sitting just in time as liquid bowels emptied.

CHAPTER 18: ABDICATION?

2026

As the months slipped by, a new year dawned. But 2026 brought little change. Dominic's empire, once his pride and joy, was now depressing. Harrison and his cronies constantly bullied and provoked, scribbling notes in a small black book; the menace was morale-sapping. During his break, as the kitchen porter read about the night's riots, the excesses of the SNPS, he was quizzed as to his thoughts. Could he not see the lengths to which the Tory press were going just to protect the rich establishment? *It's comrades like you we're fighting for. Where's your badge?* They strutted around, getting in the way: bored, twitchy, taking every opportunity to hector and intimidate. Gina stood up to one of the bullies one day and was roughly pushed against a wall and held there while eyes feasted on her. She pushed back and received a sharp slap.

'Do that again, *please* do that again...' he said, his face thrust inches away, spittle splashing her.

'That's enough,' said Dominic. His words were pleading and lacked authority. Ignored.

'We'll report you to the police,' said the young kitchen porter, which was met with derision.

Dominic and Brandon had implored them to stay away from the restaurant when in service, but they seemed to delight in confounding such requests. Customers were clearly uncomfortable as the SNPS presence cast a pall, destroying any atmosphere. Meanwhile, the business seemed to be in a death spiral; debts were mounting, revenues declining as customer numbers dropped.

Dominic set off to meet Rosa at St Pancras station, into which her Eurostar train would roll in the next hour. He had left work early, under the watchful eye of Harrison, relieved to escape. He was appalled at how the creative, professional atmosphere had been rendered toxic by Harrison and his fellow tormenters. His mind was in turmoil. But he looked forward to seeing Rosa, hearing the news of their son and his girlfriend. He had missed her these last ten days, but he also felt remorse. Yes, their marriage was tempestuous but that was Rosa; her Latin blood, her passionate nature had always been her attraction and remained so. He loved her and always had. She could be somewhat trying, though; he smiled wryly to himself. But why oh why had he betrayed her? Bloody Stephanie and her wiles. But that did not cut it either. He could not cast aside the longing to see Stephanie again or promise himself that he would not repeat his act of betrayal. And he wore his guilt like a hair shirt. How could he harbour such thoughts about a woman other than the wife he loved, had never stopped loving, would never leave? He did not understand himself. *Ping*. He pulled his mobile out, pleased to have his thoughts diverted.

Breaking News: Monarchy
The constitutional crisis mounts as the Palace
fail to give the Queen's agreement to rubber stamp
the declaration of a state of emergency. This
follows hard on the heels of the delay in granting
royal assent to the Parliament Bill.

Political Broadcast
The PM will make an urgent statement to the nation at
18.00 from Downing Street.

At last, Rosa emerged from the throng, and he rushed to embrace her. Grabbing her bags, he guided her away from the packed concourse and they bundled into a taxi. She seemed tired, deflated even. They decided to get home, pour a large glass of wine and then she could bring him up to speed with her news. The traffic clogged much of their route and a demonstration had forced a diversion but eventually they were sipping Rioja. She seemed reticent to share her experiences. The journey home had clearly sapped her energy; she was subdued, restrained even. Their phones had been pinging furiously but were ignored. Slowly the essence of the story was pieced together.

'I worry 'bout them. Ellie's been deserted by her family, who've been subjected to harassment. Her dad works in the civil service. He threatened, bullied. He's no cojones either.' Dominic winced, but said nothing. 'Her mum's the stronger one. Always the way.' Rosa looked daggers at him. 'She was in touch every day and has sent money. I think she's going to see Ellie next week. Poor child's not well. Not well at all. The bruises are one thing – she showed me. But she's disturbed mentally. How could you not be, poor lamb.'

'And our Juan?'

'Says he was beaten up. Some of the things happening on campus are unbelievable. Student kangaroo courts, punishments, gang battles…he has such a gentle nature—'

'To a point, but we know he can also be aggressive, too fast with his fists when riled.'

'True. And he was unmercifully targeted. Your fault. And Albert's. That's how he sees it. But I check with university. They tell a different tale. He reacted to the provocation with his fists, put some bully in hospital they say. He's been expelled. It brought all that unpleasant incident at school back to me. We need to get to him, calm him down. But he refuses to come home. He's found a part-time job in a bar and has become bitter, angry. Ellie tells me he's opted into the FF, which is the real reason for being in France. He's been going to a training camp. She expects him to head back to England soon and worries what he might be planning.'

'That's more than worrying. He'll just get himself into trouble, put himself in harm's way.'

'And what are you going to do about it, Dom?'

'I'll keep trying to ring him. What else can we do? If he won't listen to you…'

'I know, but—'

'I've tried ringing him. I'll try again.'

'Juan's thrown his phone away. He's convinced it's been bugged. And he's not ready to speak to you yet. I suppose at least he's trying to make his mark, Dominic,' Rosa said, her eyebrows knitting together in a frown, her dark eyes narrowing.

They fell into silence, Rosa darkly brooding, while Dominic racked his brains in vain as to where they could go to next on this. He supposed they just had to be patient. Changing the subject he tried to fill her in on what was happening at work, but she reacted angrily. How could he talk about Brandon and money and food when their family was falling apart at the seams? Rosa topped her glass up and huffily left him to his own thoughts as she headed for a long soak. Dominic sighed and turned on his phone to scan the headlines. Soon he was open-mouthed in disbelief:

Royal family to relocate to Canada as PM declares state of emergency.

He reached for the unopened post and cast aside the circulars and leaflets, appeals for money, bills. He slit the envelope of an official-looking letter. As his eyes took in the heading his heartbeat quickened and he flushed instantly. *Eviction Notice.* His chest constricted. He had to read the document three times before he could take it in. They were being evicted from their house with one month's notice. Their own home. It was all part of the government's plans to redistribute wealth and end the obscenity of rich couples living in large, expensive homes that could house poor families. All in the name of social justice and equality: social re-engineering. They were to be re-housed to a two-bedroom flat in a tower block. There was no appeal process. On an impulse he rapped on the bathroom door and shouted that he had to go out and might be late. Rosa seemed disinterested.

Rebecca opened the door to his urgent knocking, welcoming him with a chaste peck on the cheek. She did not seem surprised at him calling. He followed Rebecca into the lounge where Stephanie met him warmly, kissing him lightly on the lips. He held her at arm's length, kept hold of both of her hands and sought the words that might convey his thoughts, his brow furrowing. He had not known where else to go. But she seemed to be in the know, possibly influential in some circles. Perhaps she could help him unravel the knots.

'Whatever's wrong, dear Dom? I can see we have our work cut out this evening, Becks. We have a stressed, ailing celeb in our midst. A gentleman in need of succour. Well, you've come to the right girls, Dominic Diamond,' she said, that half-smile firmly in place. 'We'll do our best, won't we, Becks?'

'You've never failed for the want of trying,' said Rebecca, smiling openly. She tucked her legs under her as she opted for the far corner of the settee: more a spectator than a participant.

'Not tonight please. I'm in trouble.'

'Oh dear. I'm afraid the whole world's in trouble, courtesy of our Marxist masters. What gives?' said Stephanie.

'How can they do this?' he said, showing them the eviction notice. 'They can't, can they? I'll speak with a solicitor tomorrow but, but...'

113

Rebecca leant forwards and offered her thoughts. 'The government can do pretty much what it likes. A state of emergency means they can suspend whatever laws they don't like, create new powers. You obviously didn't see the PM's broadcast. Chilling. Bank accounts are to be frozen, and a further tranche of wealth taxes will remove twenty percent of all balances over ten thousand pounds. Can you believe it? The justification? Redistribution to the poorest in society, the ending of unemployment and homelessness. The reality? The insanely rich have already moved their accounts or fled the country, so it will hit the professional and management classes. The government is broke. Bust.'

Dominic frowned. 'I didn't think they could do this without royal assent. And what do you make of the royal family heading to Canada? The country will be up in arms. The Queen's untouchable, loved, revered. There'll be civil war, the way we're going.'

'A republic will no doubt be announced in the next week or so; Tobin will become president and Connell the leader of the upper house. They promised a revolution, but no one realised they really meant it! You mark my words, GB will be a single-party state very soon,' said Rebecca. She spoke quietly with an authoritative air. Not for the first time it struck Dominic that these two were more than met the eye. He had always accepted Stephanie as she presented herself: carefree, rich, and well-educated; and latterly well-connected and even insightful occasionally. But he knew little of her background, nor of Rebecca's, come to think of it. He had known Rebecca during their brief fling but had never met any of her circle of friends and had known precious little about her or what she did for a living. He had been perfectly content to live for the moment, in fact that had suited him very well.

'How can you know? And…how come you two are so well-informed?'

'We're just two good-time girls with the good fortune to be born into wealthy families, imbued with privilege. All that our socialist government loathes – wealth, private education, elitist roots,' said Stephanie lightly, with a shrug.

'There's more to it than that. Are *you* being evicted?'

A shake of the head.

'I thought not. Why not? And wealth taxes?'

'All random, indiscriminate actions of a depraved government,' said Stephanie.

'But how come you know so much, yet by your own admission you represent everything the socialists hate. Why aren't they coming after you?'

The women exchanged brief glances, knowing eyes communicating.

'We're probably next on some faceless civil servant's list. Who knows?'

Rebecca nodded her agreement and grimaced at Dominic. Her reaction seemed to convey a message but what was it? He decided not to press further. He made a mental note to engineer a private conversation with her. For now, he had enough to worry about, what with losing his house, a large slice of his savings, in all probability his business. How could they simply raid people's bank accounts? That amounted to governmental theft in his eyes, dressed up as taxation justified in the cause of equality.

'And what are you going to do about it, Dom?' asked Stephanie. 'Seb?' she said, her eyebrows and tone conveying the question.

He had no idea. But it was a thought.

'Whisky?' asked Rebecca.

'No. I'd better get back.'

'Oh, do you have to? Not time for a game of...' It was almost a relief that Stephanie had resorted to type, back to tantalising and teasing – now witnessed by Rebecca, who sat quietly.

'Rosa is home. I've not even told her about this yet. She'll go ape.'

'You need to hurry, then. You don't want to break the curfew at the very first time of asking. Let's meet for a drink tomorrow evening. Nags Head in Hampstead?'

CHAPTER 19: REVELATION

The day ebbed all too slowly: a noxious cocktail of Brandon's gloomy predictions, bullying and intimidation from Harrison. Trade was slow, staff morale in the doldrums having been informed their wages would be cut by twenty-five percent; Brandon's and Dominic's were to be halved. They all harboured concerns for their families' well-being as food shortages and inflation took hold. It was difficult to understand the fervour and passionate support the government aroused in mass rallies attended by red-shirted supporters. Dominic supposed it was the promised financial bounty from the rich, the rhetoric driving many to frenzied support. It also smacked of being organised – senior figures surrounding themselves with their chosen backers, disregarding and excluding misguided rebels. And any blame for the malaise of the country was laid at the door of the mainstream media's lies, the rebellious Tories, the rich elitists. Government pointed to Jinks inciting violence by mutinous factions, a convenient scapegoat given to florid language.

During an afternoon break, Dominic was languishing in Brandon's office, not paying much attention to the tendered platitudes – mostly gloom-laden morsels. He declined the proffered whisky, opting for tea. *Ping.* What now?

Breaking News: Enablement Act
Government announces the passing of The People's Enablement Act as one of their emergency measures. It empowers The Leader to enact whatever laws he wishes without reference to parliament.

Proroguing of Parliament
Also announced was the suspension of

*parliament together with legal instruments to
render impossible any legal challenge.*

President Tobin
*As expected, Thomas Tobin anointed President
of Great Britain; Jane Connell becoming The
Leader of the Upper House – the executive
of twenty-four.*

Government Regrets: Abdication of Monarch
*A government statement expressing regret at the
abdication of the Queen and the fleeing of the
royal family will be met with derision in many
quarters. 'The height of hypocrisy' was the immediate
response of the leader of the opposition, Norris Jinks.*

Leader Statement Announced for 18.00
*It is understood that The Leader, Jane Connell, will
be making a statement to the nation this evening
from Downing Street.*

Settling into a corner of the Nags Head, Dominic distractedly pulled at his pint of bitter. An unusual choice for him but it had been a long day, a trying day; his thirst needed slaking. Looking around him, he noted the pub was quiet, a recent phenomenon. In the good old days London pubs had throbbed with after-office trade spilling onto the pavements. It seemed that Rebecca's prophecies (or were they Stephanie's?) were all falling into place. All the revolutionary building blocks stacking nicely, like some tragic Jenga construction. He had read somewhere that Hitler had used an Enabling Act of 1933…perhaps Tobin's inspiration for the modern incarnation. The thought that similar horrors to Nazi Germany might develop in today's GB was unthinkable. And it had taken more than a decade back then to dislodge enough bricks until the whole edifice crashed. He pulled himself up short. He must not let his imagination run riot. Stephanie soon arrived to distract him.

'How was your day?' asked Dominic, having returned from the bar with her gin and tonic.

'Tedious,' she said, waving a hand dismissively. 'Have you decided what you're going to do about your eviction, dear Dom?'

'Move,' he said. 'What else can I do?'

'Talk to Seb again. Oh, do say you will,' she said, taking his hand.

'How could he help? He just wants to lure me into trouble. I'm in enough already what with my youngest son being drawn towards the FF, which just spells danger to me. He won't return my calls either. Albert is…well, you know. And I'm perennially in trouble with Rosa… Can't do right for doing wrong.'

'You poor darling. Times are hard. You really do sound down in the dumps. I'll have to see what I can do about cheering you up later,' she said. 'But first let me get you another beer.'

When she returned their attention was drawn to the TV in the far corner, now blaring loudly, the juke box having been abruptly switched off. They went over to join the handful of other early-evening drinkers and were soon spellbound by Jane Connell's performance. The rhetoric flowed, the sanctimonious outrage at the excesses of the rich and privileged at full volume. In her sights were two primary targets: the mainstream media and the Tory party. In a bravura performance she worked herself into a rage. She had seemingly extricated herself from her chrysalis of good-humoured, avuncular bonhomie to emerge a bombastic guardian of the socialist faith. In the name of *The People* and social justice, the violence perpetrated by the saboteur Tories, the incitement to bloodshed of their leader, Norris Jinks, and the bias of the media, particularly the BBC, could no longer be ignored. The Tories had been formally classified as a terrorist group; members had two weeks to rip up their membership cards or face the full fury of the law. *We know who you are, where you live and work.* Norris Jinks was declared an enemy of the state with a warrant issued for his arrest. The statement drew gasps from some early drinkers, a few cheers, while two old timers drank on in silent apathy. She went on to announce that the BBC's governing body had been sacked. The government had assumed direct control with immediate effect. Tight censorship laws were to be enacted and media moguls were warned: toe the line or face prosecution. And she advised social media platforms that their onslaught of fake news could not continue; the government had invested in a British equivalent that would supplant Twitter, Facebook, WhatsApp and all the others if they failed to desist. Censorship rules would apply to their global platforms and if they failed to comply they would be switched off. Dominic noticed the absence of any indication as to how the threats might be carried out.

At last The Leader paused for breath, took a sip of water and struck a quieter note. She announced the new measures of redistribution with pride: eviction of the rich from their big houses to make way for the poor; a raft of wealth taxes, some of which would be made available in the form of monetary dividends to the bottom ten percent of earners. She was vague as to the details, but the crowds of socialist supporters assembled as her audience in Downing Street cheered vociferously, waving red flags in celebration.

As they returned to their corner of the dingy pub, it appeared they had company. Dominic groaned internally, shooting a disapproving glance at Stephanie. Seb was quite a sight. A large man with an overflowing beer gut, torn jeans, a flowery shirt, and paisley neckerchief. It was an odd ensemble for anyone, but on a man well into his fifties with a red goatee beard, it was quite incongruous.

'Just popped in. Not got long. Need to keep on the move, you know how it is.' He looked around furtively, leant forwards and bent low over the table. 'Stuff to do, reputations to shred, sacrificial lambs to slay, stars to elevate...'

'What's he talking about, Stephanie?' Dominic had meant that as a stage whisper, but Seb answered, 'Are you up for it then, my friend? The delectable Stephanie here tells me you could be...'

'You're incorrigible, Seb. You know perfectly well I told you nothing of the sort. And you should be a bit more considerate. Dear Dom's had quite a week: family rifts, business in freefall, revelations on the carnal side...'

'*Steph*! Let me put a stop to this. An end. Once and for all. I will *not* be joining your... *No way*. Not now, not *ever*.'

Seb looked at him, grinned, knocked back his whisky chaser and stood. 'You'll think about it, then. Good call,' he said, with which he bent down and kissed Stephanie hungrily. 'See you guys soon.'

Stephanie looked at Dominic and shrugged.

'What can you do? The man's an enigma wrapped in a mystery spouting riddles.'

Dominic shook his head and said he had to leave.

As he flagged a taxi, on an impulse he asked the driver to wait a minute. Stephanie had emerged and was also hopping into a black cab. Dominic asked his cabbie to follow hers. He looked at Dominic in disbelief, grinned and gunned the engine, smirked, and began whistling: a story for his fellow cabbies over a mug of tea later, no doubt. After twenty minutes his taxi drew to a halt as Stephanie hopped out and headed for a heavily guarded gate.

'Where are we?' he muttered, almost to himself.

'The Labour NEC headquarters, mate.'

Dominic paid his cabbie and ambled down the street, hands in pockets, hat pulled forwards. His eyes never left Stephanie, who seemed to be recognised and was quickly through the security checks of state policemen in their grey tunics. He crossed the street and watched her disappear inside. He was nonplussed. Next moment, he was aware of someone hooking an arm through his.

'What are you doing here?' Rebecca whispered urgently in his ear. 'You need to be more careful. Come on, let's find somewhere quiet. Away from prying eyes.' She glanced around before darting down a side street, turned left into the next and then immediately right. They slowed their pace, the better to blend in with the shoppers. Drawing to a halt, she dragged him into a ladies' fashion shop. Grabbing a garish blouse from the rack, she grasped his hand and pulled him towards the dressing rooms. Nodding to one of the staff, they strode into a large room in which were four curtained cubicles. Ignoring an indignant elderly lady in a state of half dress, she dumped the blouse unceremoniously on a chair in the outer area and pushed open an emergency door. They found themselves in a dark alley. She put a finger to her lips. They stood stock-still in the shadows, stayed quiet, watched, and listened.

Nothing.

Safe to move on.

A few more twists and turns and they pushed into a pub, the Headless Lady. She nodded at the barman, who flicked his head towards a back room. A bottle of wine and two glasses were passed through.

'Rebecca, what on earth...'

'You're flirting with danger. There's eyes on you. I don't think they're about to "disappear" you, but you can't be sure. And going to the heart of our socialist maniacs' inner sanctum defies sanity,' she said. She turned her blue eyes on him and squeezed his hand. 'We can't have our Stephanie's favourite celeb damaged, now can we? She'd never forgive me. You're quite her favourite plaything at the moment.'

'Rebecca,' he began in his sternest voice.

'Dom,' she quickly re-joined, looking earnestly at him.

'You two really are the most intriguing, annoying, mischievous...'

'Stephanie would be so heartened to hear you say that. But leave me out of it. I'm not like her. You and me go back, Dom, if you haven't forgotten—'

'Never. How could I?... I didn't even know it was the NEC headquarters until my cabbie told me. And she was recognised, breezed through security. Don't you find that strange?'

'Not a bit of it. She was only popping in for a spot of supper with her uncle.'

CHAPTER 20: RELOCATION

As they struggled down the front path of their Notting Hill town house others were making the opposite journey. Dominic looked on in dismay as they were bustled by a young, tattoo-embellished couple with two unruly kids. An elderly smartly dressed couple looked sheepish and stopped to exchange a few awkward words with Rosa. They recognised the man they knew as Dominic Diamond and mumbled their admiration before moving on, seemingly embarrassed. A car screeched to a halt and a family poured out and ran up the drive; loud, ebullient, and jubilant. There was no sensitivity or apparent recognition of the plight of Dominic and Rosa, no slack cut. Stepping to one side they watched the new residents pile into their house; the children could be heard running from room to room exploring. Rosa turned dead eyes on Dominic, sighed deeply and shuffled down the drive clutching her box of personal possessions. To see Rosa in such a state was painful, her zest for life extinguished. They were allowed to take with them only the personal things needed for daily use and work in line with the teachings of Marx. He had looked it up and the phrase stuck in his craw and popped into his mind now: nothing in society will belong to anyone except the things for which the person has immediate use, for either his needs, his pleasures, or his daily work... It was left for the new residents to discover and enjoy the B&O stereo system, the plasma television, the full wine racks, their expensive furniture, fresh bean coffee machine and mod-con kitchen appliances...

Having rented a man-with-a-van to transport their belongings, all overseen by a Mobilisation activist, they set off to find their new abode: a block of flats in Hackney. Progress was slow in the heavy traffic but as the van drew to a halt Rosa looked around mournfully at their new surroundings. The tower block was one of four, in the middle of which was an area of littered greenery, behind that a pub, a shop and a boarded-up café. Graffiti covered one side of their block and the café front, children ran around the green, arguing over the use of the two swings and the roundabout that still worked; the seesaw lay in pieces on a muddy patch; the paddling pool had been filled with sand, which the local cats obviously favoured. Feral dogs roamed, sniffed, and snarled. The whole area had been created in a building frenzy in the 1960s, once proudly proclaimed for its architectural merit and creation of community. That dream had long since died. Dominic reached out to Rosa and pulled her into an embrace; her shoulders heaved. How he wished she could summon up her reserves of spirit. How he wished she would threaten to *keeeel* someone. Instead she was monosyllabic, tearful, and morose.

'It'll be alright, mark my words. At least we have each other, don't we? They can't break us, Rosa.' Her tears soaked into his jumper until at last her body stopped shaking. While leaving the van man to guard their chattels he took her hand, and they entered the building.

'Name?' barked the lady on reception.

It was an old makeshift reception area, which had seen better days. Pretty much like the lady manning it. She was elderly and had a lean face with a sharp nose and beady eyes. She exuded cold hostility, but he supposed she had a job to do.

'Good morning, good morning,' he said, mustering forced cheerfulness. He noticed the red M. She glared at him and tapped her pen on the notebook in front of her.

'*Name?*'

'Green, Dominic and Rosa.'

She ticked the sheet in front of her. 'Eleventh floor, flat 1107. Keys. Lift's over there. You're the lucky ones, two bedrooms. Sign here,' she said, turning the sheet towards them.

Lucky! His heart sank as he opened the door, pushing back a pile of debris: circulars, local newspapers, old bills by the look of them. The flat was tired, in need of a clean. Furniture was basic and drab, the leather-look sofa snagged on the arm, foam poking through. A small television sat in the corner; thin curtains hung at the windows, a two-bar electric fire on a hearth that someone had built in stone, a surprising addition. Someone had once loved it, tried to put their own stamp on the place. Dominic guessed that had been a long time ago. Rosa meandered disconsolately from room to room, the inspection not taking long. The entire flat was in keeping with her mood: grey, cheerless, depressed.

As they emerged from the lift, they were accosted by the Mobilisation lady and told they were required to sign in and out. Failure to do so would result in them being reported, she did not say to whom, any repetition rendering them liable to eviction. They found the local pub on the estate but chose not to stay. After piling into a cab they went into the city and found a pub with more life, background music, chattering groups of drinkers. Settling into a corner they sipped their drinks. Dominic tried to lift Rosa's spirits, pointing to one upside at least: their mortgage had been cancelled and the rent was a fraction of the mortgage payments they were freed from. Government had made a desultory final payment, emergency legislation defining a token price. They were not the only ones losing out here. Ownership of the town house was now invested in *The People*, the state the custodians. All payments made had been lost, no compensation other than the flat that had been regarded as perfectly adequate to meet their needs. They should be grateful.

'A silver lining…the rent,' suggested Dominic.

Rosa cast him a withering look. After a couple of drinks and a snatched meal he joined her under her blanket of depression as they made their way back to Hackney.

'I go back to Brittany tomorrow, then Spain,' she announced.

'Have you spoken with Juan? When did you make these arrangements? How long—'

'Don't know how long. No answer from either Juan or Ellie. I worried. He was in a state. Shouldn't have left him…must find him.'

'I thought Ellie had said he was returning to the UK… GB?'

'Don't suppose you've…?'

He shook his head.

'I spoke with some of his mates, and they haven't heard from him either. He must still be over there.'

'I'll come with you.'

'*No.*'

'Rosa, you're scaring me. What are you saying?'

She turned on him, her temper flaring. She suddenly became animated: flailing arms punctuating the air. 'I've had it with this place, Dominic. We don't know where either of our sons are. I'm sure they're in danger, feel it in my bones. I'll find Juan and persuade him to join me in Spain. Ellie too. Why not? My papa's not been very well. I've not seen him for too long. Mama too. And some Spanish sunshine will do me almost as much good as getting out of this place…and anyway I need to spend time in Barcelona. We're expanding the office base there. The decision's been made. It will become our new HQ – chosen over Paris. I may well relocate there too…under some pressure from colleagues to do so and to be honest the prospect's appealing.'

'Then I'm joining you.'

'*No*! On the work front we need to develop the strategy further. There's lots to do. On the family front I'll find Juan, you find Albert. You got us into this mess, now get us out of it. Away from this dump. Then I'll come back. Or you can join me there. Maybe. If we can reunite the family…if you and I can find a way back somehow.'

Dominic felt sick to his stomach and was stricken with an immediate tension headache. He pleaded for her to be reasonable, to acknowledge they were powerless to fight the authorities. But she sneered at him, castigating his weakness.

It was late afternoon the following day when Dominic said a sad farewell to a frosty Rosa. She climbed into a cab, would not countenance him taking her to the airport. *Enjoy your darts*, she told him. But he had other plans first – an unfinished conversation.

They had arranged to meet at her place in Mayfair where they could speak without fear of being overheard. Stepping over the threshold, Dominic was relieved to leave the cold London evening and constant drizzle behind him, instantly warmed by a welcoming smile. She took his coat and hung it up to dry. He admired the painting of Hope Cove, and then paused briefly in front of the mirror in the hallway to run his hand through his hair, pulled his jumper straight and checked that his shirt collar was tucked inside the crew neck, just showing as he liked it. Looking up, he saw Rebecca smile knowingly before leading him into the lounge.

'Love that painting. As you said a few weeks ago, we go back. They were wonderful days, Rebecca.'

'But firmly in the past,' she said quietly. 'We've both moved on.'

'Yes. But I'll never forget…'

'Nor me… But you said you had something you wanted to sort out?… I hate to see you so anxious. Anything I can do to help?'

'You could give me some answers,' he said.

'Do you want to wait for Stephanie? She's not likely to be back until gone seven o'clock though,' Rebecca said. She offered him a drink, but he declined, so she poured herself a glass of wine before plopping down on the sofa, curling her legs beneath her.

'No. I wanted to speak with you...about that merry dance you led me the other night. What was going on? What were you up to? And Stephanie?' asked Dominic.

'All I did was come to your aid,' she said. Her smile had evaporated, the sparkle in her eyes replaced by flint steeliness.

'Were you following *me*? Or Stephanie? Why either of us?'

'I just happened by, that's all.'

He looked doubtful. She got up and refilled her glass. She held the bottle up to Dominic, who shook his head.

'That it? Why don't we watch a film or something? What do you say?'

'What was Stephanie doing at Labour's HQ?'

'NEC actually.'

'And does she really have an uncle there? Who is he? Who is *she*? I'm even beginning to wonder who you are too. What *do* you do? Who do you work for? Who does Steph work for? That will do for starters. Oh, and why me? Why is an ageing, humble chef the subject of outrageous flirting by two beautiful women? And...'

She looked down with knitted eyebrows, studying her glass, swirling the contents.

'Stephanie's the flirt...not me! I've told you. That's in the past. I will always remember you fondly, will always be grateful to you for saving me...but our relationship is consigned to history. I hope we can be friends though, Dom. As for Steph – you'll have to ask her. Good luck with that, by the way. But with your looks...false modesty doesn't suit you, by the way. She seems quite serious about her relationship with you, although one can never tell what she's up to. A schemer is our Stephanie, always a plan, always a game to be played out. You may have noticed. Impossibly beautiful but...quite the social butterfly; finds it impossible to be monogamous too, eclectic tastes. What I *can* tell you is you need to be careful.' She leant forwards and grabbed his hand. 'You should assume you're being followed. Someone's out there right now, reporting back your whereabouts. Best to assume that.'

'But why?' Dominic said.

'Oh, come on. Your track record's hardly exemplary. And look at what Albert's done, where he is. Juan too. And you keep appearing in the press. They despise opponents, especially former supporters. They're on high alert for troublemakers – you know that.'

'But I'm Labour through and through.'

'That's not how it looks from their end of the telescope. You're a popular, wealthy, recalcitrant public figure. You were a star with a popular following. They must see you as some sort of turncoat now. That might explain quite a lot, might it not?'

'Enough for people to throw rocks and abuse at me?'

'Activists doing what they're told. You're high profile. Your sons are viewed as unruly, defiant, rabble rousers. The expanding SNPS must find something to do, people to track, victims to bully, fear and intimidation is their stock in trade. And the odds are they know you're coming under pressure to sign up to the resistance.'

'How?'

Rebecca sat back and simply raised her eyebrows.

At that moment, the front door opened, and a cheery hello signalled Stephanie's arrival. Rebecca leant forwards and urged Dominic not to say anything about the other evening. *Not safe to.* He frowned, but silently nodded his acquiescence. Rebecca kissed him lightly on the cheek and squeezed his hand.

Rebecca joined Dominic and Stephanie for dinner in a small Italian restaurant. Dominic found it all very strange that the three of them should spend an evening together at Stephanie's behest. And what Steph wants… The wine flowed but the conversation became stilted. Stephanie seemed oblivious as she chatted on. But the flirting was more restrained, and her mood changed, becoming serious as Rebecca surprised Dominic by speaking of the emergence of a violent, extremist strand of the resistance – seemingly taking on the earlier conversation. She spoke of a new phase in the troubles, a rebellion.

'You heard of the attack the other night on the SNPS barracks? A successful operation ended in disaster,' said Rebecca.

'I heard about the deaths. Tragic,' said Dominic.

'Yes, but I'm talking about the capture of two of the so-called terrorists from FF. The BBC's silent on this now it's controlled by government. It can only be a matter of time before they crack under torture. A whole cell will be blown.'

'You seem well-informed, Becks,' said Stephanie, raising an eyebrow in her direction.

'Is this anything to do with Seb?' asked Dominic, looking from Rebecca to Stephanie.

'I wouldn't have thought so, not his bag at all. His activities may be affiliated but he will have no idea about the FF. I keep telling you that all he does is arrange for celebs and popular public figures to tell their stories. To propagate the truth in the face of all the propaganda. You really should,' said Stephanie.

'Don't go there again. I've told you; I'm not interested.'

Rebecca had fallen silent, pensive. She picked her glass up and lifted it to her lips, paused, placed it down again. She wore a frown. And she was no longer forthcoming. Had she said too much? And to whom? To him or to her partner? How did she know these details? He was sure it had not been reported on national television or in the papers. He would check that out. And he must ask her more about her relationship with Stephanie, as difficult as that might be to broach.

'How can you know that Seb's not mixed up with FF, Steph? After all, he would hardly advertise that fact would he?' asked Dominic, after a while.

'Oh, I know Seb pretty well. I have other friends too. I keep my ear to the ground. After all, what else do I have to do?' she said, as she became lighter in tone, playful in an attempt to change direction, reset the mood. But it failed. Her responses to his ongoing questions were superficial and non-committal, as were Rebecca's, and he soon wearied of it.

After signing out of the building, receiving a gruff response to his cheery good morning, he stepped out of the front door, bracing himself against the wind and rain, which deluged the morning commuters. He wore a small backpack and held an umbrella aloft. Taking his normal route, he hopped onto the underground at Hackney Central. Was he being followed? Rebecca's words came back to him. He willed himself to act normally, did not try to spot anyone, assumed they were good at what they did. But he hoped they had become complacent as he set off on his normal route: Hackney Central to Highbury & Islington, change onto the Victoria line until Oxford Circus, then a walk to his restaurant. He had taken to repeating the same route daily, always at the same time, never varying. A man of ingrained habit. Until today.

He took the opportunity to place himself in the middle of a scrum that pushed their way off at the first busy stop, Highbury & Islington. Fear bubbled to the surface. Dominic did not look behind him but walked briskly, his heart beating rapidly, his hands moist. He found a gents' toilet and a spare cubicle where he sat quietly for fifteen minutes. When he emerged, he sported a moustache, a pair of wire-framed spectacles, a thick woolly jumper, and denims. The clothes they replaced were in the backpack, which was strapped tightly around his midriff beneath the jumper, Dominic now positively rotund. He took a Tube to King's Cross, spent another twenty minutes in another toilet. He sipped a flat white on a concourse café and put his head into a red top tabloid newspaper – wasted more time, his heart racing whenever someone came near. He struggled to concentrate on any of the reports but took in the headlines about yet another attack on a SNPS barracks in King's Cross; two explosions, gunfire exchanged, three rebels and national state security officers left dead.

His hand went to the pocket for his mobile but of course he had left that behind. They might be tracking him, he assumed. Perhaps he was being ridiculous, but he thought it better to err on the side of caution. He wanted to ring Rosa but that would have to wait.

Time to move on. A Northern line Tube to Bank, finally the Central line to Stratford back in the East End. Had he done enough to lose any tag? He hoped so. This was all alien to his nature, and he knew he was ill equipped for subterfuge. His armpits were leaking, his brow was pitted with beads of perspiration, his head throbbed, and he felt sick to his stomach. Dominic pulled on a cap as the lightening grey sky and torrential rain gave way to a persistent drizzle. He looked around the litter-strewn streets, taking in the surroundings, scanning for possible eyes on him – without making it obvious, he hoped. Two homeless characters seemed to be pulling themselves out of their slumbers; one of them reached for a bottle and swigged heartily, the other coughed on a cigarette and spat on the pavement. They seemed invisible to the pedestrians striding past them, ignoring the plight of two characters who had evidently fallen off the social radar. So much for having eradicated homelessness. A black guy on crutches offered Dominic *The Big Issue*, looking for a donation in return. Dominic absent-mindedly handed over some coins, declining the magazine. Morning shoppers bustled by, scurrying to find shelter. Dominic slipped into a dingy building and spotted the name he was after on the board in an unmanned reception area that was run down and grimy. Jo Holcombe's office was on the third floor. He opted for the stairs, first taking five minutes in a toilet on the half-landing. He composed himself, ordered his mind. His heart was racing, and he could hear the blood pulsing in his ears.

Sharp knock.

The door was opened by a slim black lady, Jo Holcombe, a lone-shark private detective. Surveying the small office, he was surprised. He had expected seedy, unkempt, down at heel, but it was smart, orderly, and comfortable. There was a faint smell of fresh paint and it had obviously been renovated recently: light grey walls, a slightly darker shade for the woodwork. Modern black blinds were at the window and there were plant pots with cacti of varying sizes on the coffee table and windowsill with a large specimen on the floor. A few pictures adorned the walls, but there were no photographs. The office desk and filing cabinets were modern, light oak-effect. Jo offered him coffee. *Just a dash of milk, no sugar.* Returning from the small kitchenette linked to the main room she poured his coffee and engaged in small talk, perhaps sensing he was on edge. But she soon got down to matters; quizzed him closely, gently challenged his motivations. After a while she sat back and seemed content to consider the assignment, proceeding to set out her terms. Dominic blanched but nodded his assent. Jo shook his hand, accepted the commission, and took the brown envelope with a smile. She was easy to talk to, which was a relief. The meeting took less than an hour and it felt good to have a plan, to have taken the initiative. He hoped Rosa would see it as an indication that he had rediscovered his cojones.

CHAPTER 21: HARTLEY

Red Hair had been assigned to kitchen duties after the latest in a series of confrontations and the inevitable periods of isolation that followed. He seemed to be attempting to knuckle down to an apprenticeship with a view to becoming a chef once released. He was closely observed, and his behaviour improved as his rebellious ways and outbursts fell away. Whether this was because he had seen the light, or due to his drug therapy or coercion, was impossible to know. But he had changed; he was withdrawn rather than mouthy, morose rather than ebullient, content to gaze blankly at nothing in particular. As a commis chef he was largely involved with basic duties: vegetable and salad preparation, boiling and shelling eggs, sandwich making, cutting, slicing, dicing, stints in the pot wash area. Albert had opted for a similar route and gradually the two had struck up a silent camaraderie. They had maybe not only learnt from their own experiences but had noted other cadets who had fallen foul of their emotions, too free with their views. Any slight led to the visitation of the white coats carrying their ubiquitous black medical bags. To harbour views was natural, to voice them dangerous. Albert had been escorted to the ICU on one occasion, of which he had no recollection he had admitted to Red Hair one day in a whispered exchange in the showers. Since then, both cadets had steered clear of trouble, charted a safer path, perhaps dropping below the radar.

Albert was told to fetch cheese from the walk-in dairy fridge located at the back of the kitchens, close to the cavernous stores. As he reached the back of the fridge, he selected the two blocks of Cheddar and a wheel of Cheshire, turned, and found himself face to face with Chef Whittaker.

'Albert, listen to me.'

Albert's eyes opened in surprise, and he shook his head: *too dangerous to talk, go away.*

'It's okay. We're in a dead spot. I just want you to know. Wanted to make contact. I've friends on the outside. I'm not one of *them*. Our time will come. Work here. Keep your head down, work hard. I'll keep you posted.'

Albert nodded and scurried past him, depressed the internal handle to open the door and headed back to the kitchens. As he approached the prep area four SNPS officers burst past him, followed by two white coats. Turning around he watched in stunned silence as they headed to the rubbish area. A single shot rang out, the first time one had been heard in recent months, and the whole kitchen brigade shrank back into a corner of the kitchen, Albert amongst them. *An escape attempt*, someone dared whisper. Another six officers burst in, two of whom stayed with the kitchen staff and apprentices, herding them into a tight group with rifles at the ready. Moments later, two white coats emerged from the bin area gripping an arm each of their captured cadet, whose feet dragged behind him. There was no sign of blood, no visual injuries, a syringe most likely to be the cause of him being unconscious. The kitchen staff watched on, shock registering on their features as the red-headed cadet disappeared through the doors, presumably bound for ICU.

CHAPTER 22: NEWS

It was early evening and he and Rosa had exchanged a few terse messages. No news of Juan or Ellie. A local had suggested they had returned to England. Dominic implored her to come home. She reminded him that their home had been sequestered. They were ruined. Why did he just meekly accept his lot? And she was adamant that she needed to see her mama and papa, rediscover bright sunshine and a civilised life. He sighed and was wondering what to do with his evening when there was a knock on his door. Strange. Neighbours kept themselves to themselves and being on the eleventh floor... He pulled the door open. A red-faced caller was propping himself up against the door jam, breathing heavily, sweating profusely, swearing obscenely. He collapsed in the chair and Dominic handed him a glass of water, taking in the wild grey hair, the braces, the knotted tie that had been pulled down and hung askew. He looked like some mad professor.

'What a place. Lift out of action,' said Brandon.

'What on earth brings you here? Did you sign in?' As he recovered his breath, he wanted a whisky but accepted a coffee and a biscuit instead. No, he had not signed in. He had waited until the old bat was not looking and then had set about the eleven floors.

'I bring good news, Dominic.'

Dominic was immediately on his guard.

A new assignment. A series of short programmes to bring his cuisine to his loyal followers – lighten their lives, bring some sparkle into a drab world. He would be interviewed while preparing his food. Nothing serious. Just his own background and experiences. BBC? No! We need to embrace modern media channels. Social media video clips in bite-sized pieces. Dominic was wary but nonetheless intrigued. And it sounded like a break from the humdrum of the restaurant, the intimidation of Harrison.

'The business is close to folding, Dominic. My friend, we are in the brown and sticky.'

'It's dire, isn't it?'

'You're the optimist, remember? But I have a plan.'

'We're doomed then. You and your scams. And if it's going back to Chequers—'

'No worries. Nothing like that. I'm terribly sorry about that, although the cash came in very handy. We needed an injection and…' Dominic scowled, and his partner stopped himself from extolling the virtues of a disastrous project.

It turned out the government was intent on opening a series of soup kitchens and cafeterias to feed the homeless and the destitute. Diamond's had already suspended its lavish menus for the affluent in favour of traditional British fare but would now downgrade further to offer cafeteria food. They would also prepare food packs for charitable organisations, for which the government would pay a fee; the business could then limp along until the economy turned a corner. Then Diamond's could be resurrected. And it would get Harrison off their backs. And the activists might stop hurling rocks at Dominic, who at first registered his shock, then his refusal to countenance the change. But Brandon was insistent. It was their only chance. What else could they do? Perhaps they should just close the business, mothball it. But that did not appeal either. Dominic eventually accepted the change on condition it was temporary; that Brandon would use his business skills and entrepreneurism to find a path to renewal and resurrection for Diamond's.

Having seen Brandon out, he made another coffee and caught up with the news: more of the same except the spiral of violence now seemed to increasingly involve guns and knives. Deaths were all too frequent. And the government's state security police force had rapidly expanded, their remit becoming ever wider. The army were occasionally called in but usually the SNPS brought rioting factions to heel using a degree of force few could recall outside Ulster. Dominic flicked between the BBC news and satellite channels. The differences in reporting were more than nuanced. While the BBC spoke solely of terrorist factions undermining peace, Sky News was more even-handed: red-shirted Mobilisation activists condemned as readily as the FF forces and black-shirted far-right extremists. The SNPS also came in for strong criticism, although the BBC proclaimed their bravery in protecting *The People*. *Ping*.

Stephanie

Hi lover. Did you see this video clip?

Dominic clicked on the link and watched a short video of the famous actress Samantha Hathaway being interviewed. The questions were interspersed with snippets from her films and glamour photographs. She had tens of thousands of followers and was something of a style guru. He fast-forwarded but got the gist of it. Members of her family were being persecuted for her outspoken defence of free speech and her criticism of the onset of totalitarianism. It was an emotional clip that immediately attracted thousands of "likes". *Ping.*

Stephanie

And this one?

This time it was the naturalist Lawrence Smith. The theme was similar, but he spoke of his brother having been sent away to a rehabilitation centre somewhere in the Pennines. Dominic's attention was piqued. It was followed by two others. He sat and mused. It was not too difficult to see what she was doing. If actors and television personalities could speak out, why not a celebrity chef? He chose not to reply.

He scrolled down his mobile and opened a news feed. Not the BBC. An uptick in influenza, the imminent threat of Storm Benjamin rolling in from the west... But it was the political news that captured the headlines:

Palace Statement Due

The Palace, speaking from their new base in Montreal, announced that Her Majesty would broadcast to the nation later that evening at 21.00. Meanwhile a short statement has sought to reassure the public that the royal family would not desert the British people.

Jinks in Contact with the Queen?

Rumours abound that the former leader of the opposition, Norris Jinks is in contact with the Queen. It is thought that the royal family would lend their support for the resistance to the Marxist revolution underway. It seems likely they will repudiate the Marxist creed and declare illegal the formation

of a republic. Freedoms would be restored, law and order
would return and parliamentary democracy would once
again be the hallmark of a civilised, free, democratic,
parliamentary monarchy in Britain.

Resistance Becoming More Extreme
The FF is thought to have the backing of the government-proclaimed
terrorist, Norris Jinks, and be attracting funds from
the USA and Canadian governments. Jinks is leading a call to
normal, everyday British people to resist the new regime. The
government of GB is likely to see this as an explicit call to arms.

EU Crisis
The EU is also thought to be about to raise the stakes in the face of
violations of EU law and the flouting of the founding principles of the
European Union which embrace fundamental values of respect
for human dignity and human rights, freedom, democracy, equality
and the rule of law. It has sought to apply pressure on the British
government to restore democracy and end unrest and violence.
The expulsion of GB from the EU now seems likely following the
closure of British borders, primarily to stem the flow of emigration
and retain citizens as the numbers of tourists and migrants slow to
a trickle. The EU has also pressed the British government to resume
its payments, which appear to have halted.

It just seemed to be one thing after another. And then it struck him with a jolt. Rosa. How could she get back now? His heart sank, although he knew that currently she gave no appearance of even wanting to. *Ping.*

Stephanie
Meet me later. I have news for you
about Juan. And Albert. My place in an hour.
Stay over.

Dominic
What news?

Stephanie

Come over.

Stephanie hustled him inside – out of the strengthening wind and swirling rain. He shrugged his coat off, draping it over a radiator, and they settled themselves in her lounge to the sound of Brahms in the background. It was toasty warm, and she opened a bottle of Nuits-Saint-Georges, splashing the mildly fragrant red wine into large glasses. She sat opposite him. He looked at her, noticing she seemed serious tonight.

'You said you had news about my lads, Stephanie,' he said.

'We understand Juan's no longer in France. He slipped back into England having come over in a small craft which landed on the South coast.'

'Great. Where is he?… But how do you know? Who's *we?*'

'I'm not certain where he is now but I'm fairly sure I know where he's headed. A camp in the Northern Pennines, near Alston in Cumbria. That's where we think Albert is,' she said. She spoke slowly, watching him carefully.

Dominic sat back and tried to take the information in. He rose to his feet, picked his glass up and took a deep draught. Glaring at Stephanie he demanded to know how she knew. What was going on? He paced around the room as she delivered one generalisation after another. He fumed and came close to losing his temper. But the best he could get from her was that she had good friends, knew influential people.

'*Who?*'

'What I *can* tell you is that Albert's still locked up and Juan is heading north. It's obvious what he's got planned, isn't it?'

'You reckon he's going to walk in and demand the release of his brother? Don't be bloody ridiculous. And you don't know Juan. He's thoughtful, intelligent, not usually given to outpourings of emotion or precipitate actions. Unless he's provoked that is,' he added, recalling the incidents at school and the reports from his university. 'No, he's the chess player of the family…he's…he's…'

'Juan's joined FF. He got his training in France. Several camps have been established in remote areas. Apparently, he's become a crack shot—'

'He used to be a member of a rifle club actually.'

'There you go. He will also have learnt about explosives, navigation, surveillance. Dominic, you must realise we are close to civil war. A network of resistance cells has sprung up around the country and Jinks is finding financial support from influential people in the USA, Canada and on the continent. Do you think France or Germany want a Marxist regime on their doorstep? Lots of young people, brave young people like your Juan, are intent on doing their bit. Oh, I know that sounds corny but many of them are motivated by crimes against their families or friends. Juan may have thought deeply about this, but he wants revenge for his brother and the way you've been treated. He's a brave lad.'

Dominic put his head in his hands and rocked back and forth. 'So many questions, so few answers. Are you telling me he's part of a resistance group determined to storm the camp?'

'Who knows? But they seem to be intent on discovering what's going on. These groups are disparate currently, but Jinks is creating a network with a single chain of command. A federation of resistance groupings, if you will.'

'You're part of this, aren't you?'

She smiled demurely, poured more wine, and turned the television on. Time for the promised broadcast. A statement by the monarch. All attempts to get her to say more were deflected. Sighing deeply, he settled back, Stephanie curled up with him, pulling his arm round her. He seemed powerless to resist. Images appeared of Buckingham Palace, the Houses of Parliament, a state banquet for the President of the USA, a royal wedding, the Black Rod procession that precedes the State Opening of Parliament and the Queen's speech, capturing the pomp and glory of the British monarchy and the treasured parliamentary democracy. They were watching ITV. The BBC had refused to broadcast. Then the cameras cut to a fireside scene, log fire burning, and Her Majesty the Queen sat with two of her corgis at her feet.

Then the screen went blank.

CHAPTER 23: PODCAST

Emerging at Oxford Circus he opted for a walk on a bright morning. Dominic headed towards an address in Marylebone. Winter was giving way to spring as the clouds parted, watery rays of sunshine casting a golden hue to the damp streets of London. He chose a route behind Oxford Street that would take him into Cavendish Square Gardens. With plenty of time before his appointment, Dominic sauntered. He enjoyed the birdsong, the flowering snowdrops and daffodils and the crocuses bathing in the sunshine as they opened to create a colourful spectacle across the lawned area in amongst the trees. Finding a bench, he recalled how Rosa had always told him to pay more attention to people around him and appreciate the simple delights of the natural world. So Dominic tried to set aside his troubled mind as he took in the surroundings, savouring the gentle warmth of the sun's rays. He smiled at a young mother pushing a buggy while shushing her crying baby, watched an elderly couple with an awkward gait link arms and chat, two young teenagers kicking a football around, all enjoying a perfect spring day. The birds were relishing the release from winter's grip and there was that distinctive, strident call. Much louder than the blackbirds and robins: a mistle thrush possibly. Casting his eyes to the top of the tree, he saw the brown-spotted white belly. It must be a mistle thrush. Rosa would have told him in an instant.

Rosa. And quickly his mind became impaled on the troubles his family was enduring. What a mess. How could he pull them back together? It just seemed impossible. Whatever he tried fell apart. Whatever he said was not good enough, provoked derision. A rapprochement with her was the key to end this misery. And the key to that was the release of Albert and the rescue of Juan from the clutches of extremists. And there his logic snagged on the nail of "how" and suddenly he was replaying last night's short conversation. She had at first sounded lighter in spirit, no doubt imbued by Spanish sunshine, Rioja, parental attention, positive professional agendas. But her mood soured when he tried to persuade her to return home. She had put feelers out for Juan and Ellie but had heard nothing. She was struggling to understand what was happening to her family or why. Who could blame her? But mostly she was angry. Angry with Dominic, angry with their harsh treatment, angry with the world. Dominic chose not to tell her about Juan having returned to GB. After all, he could not be certain. All he had to go on was the confident assertions of Stephanie and he had no intention of talking about *her* to Rosa. There was no proof, no one had met or seen Juan, he had not heard from him. He did not know if he could believe Stephanie, although he could not imagine why she might want to mislead him either. The conversation had ended tersely despite Dominic's declaration of love. *Sort it all out and I come home. Find our boys, I come home.*

He looked at his watch. Plenty of time yet. And as his eyes alighted on a young woman on the far bench tilting her head back to allow the sun's rays access to her pretty features, he thought of Stephanie, a shiver immediately coursing through him. She seemed to threaten his equilibrium, representing something of a wrecking ball for his marriage. But he simply could not escape the memory of that bright sunny morning. Standing in front of that window: translucent, provocative, seductive, her exquisite figure ingrained on his retina. He doubted that vision would ever desert him. Perhaps he didn't want it to. But he did not understand her. Which of her many faces was the real Stephanie? The socialite butterfly given to frivolous superficiality or the sophisticated intelligent woman who occasionally emerged? And what about her high-powered contacts? They seemed to bring credence to occasional political commentary, but she was contradictory in her attitudes, her opinions, her actions. Was she really Tobin's niece? If so, why the name-dropping of Jinks and the open anti-Marxist narrative? How could he trust what she had to say when she was so vague about the provenance of her intelligence, offering no rationale for her assertions? That he was asking such questions seemed confirmation of the absence of trust and yet he was still drawn to her. And come to that, why was Rebecca also opaque as to the source of her insights? His head hurt trying to fathom it all out.

Dominic decided he should press on and began to amble on his way. He remonstrated with himself as to why his thoughts so readily drifted back to

Stephanie and Rebecca. Well, that's easy to answer, he told himself, mumbling aloud, to the apparent consternation of a passing couple who scurried on quickly. Rosa had been so impossibly unreasonable that Stephanie had become his escape valve, his release from domestic torture. And Rebecca being around was simply an added bonus. Oh yes, they had connected, and he felt that at least their friendship would endure. On the other hand he was not sure how he could trust his own thought processes these days.

He was shown into a large, spotlessly clean, well-equipped kitchen in a flat just off Gloucester Place. Extra lighting had been set up to illuminate the main cooking area and there were PCs on the breakfast bar. The contract had been signed by Brandon and now countersigned by Dominic. The commitment was to film a series of six live podcasts as part of a series: *Meet the Man Behind the Talent*, the idea being to showcase the skills of celebrities, interspersed with questions about their lives. Actors, musicians, authors, scientists had all been signed up and video clips and podcasts streamed. He may have seen some? He had.

Having changed into his chef's whites he met his interviewer, a young woman. Samantha. *Call me Sam.* She seemed confident and had a pleasing, open manner. He sensed they would get on well. Sam stressed that the idea was for it to be impromptu. Not a glossy broadcast but rather an informal, relaxed, conversation. She outlined the area of questioning: his background, interests, and passions. Dominic set to and prepared the food that would be featured: Diamond Delights, dishes that could easily be prepared at home at low cost but with a professional touch. Today it was to be a red wine sauce for serving with the humble lamb chop.

After an hour, he was ready to go.

Thumbs up.

They were live.

Samantha welcomed Dominic and promised the viewers Diamond Delights. The chef working in the background was soon centre stage.

'Today I'll be showing you how to make a superb red wine reduction sauce that you might find on a restaurant menu. Sounds complicated? Not a bit of it. Have faith, it's easy. First, we take a selection of root vegetables: carrots, swede, parsnips, onions... Time to enjoy a glass of wine meanwhile. Cheers...'

'Tell us about your upbringing, Dominic,' asked Samantha, out of shot.

'A humble background. I'm a northerner born in a mining community. My dad was a miner, his before him. We had little money, but I remember a close, happy community during my childhood until…'

'Until?'

'Well, it's all a long time ago. My dad became ill and in the eighties the mines were all closed. We were embroiled in the miners' strike. A difficult time… Now let's take a look at the root vegetables. Yes, nice and brown, charred,' he said, turning the pan so the viewers would see. 'Now for some stock and red wine. I use one part stock to three parts wine. Allow to simmer and reduce…'

'Your dad died of a mining disease, didn't he?'

'Pneumoconiosis. I couldn't believe that my dad was taken from us and of course that was when all the mines were being closed down, which destroyed our village. Tragic. It all seemed so unnecessary.'

'Did that affect your political views?'

'I suppose so. It's impossible to live through such times without it leaving its mark. I've always voted Labour, could never bring myself to do otherwise.'

'So, you voted Labour at the last election? Would you describe yourself as a socialist?'

'Yes, but my family have always been staunch royalists too. Love of Queen and country and all that but I'd rather not talk about such things. Food's my bag.'

'Where's your eldest son, Dominic?'

'I'm sure listeners won't be interested…'

'But they are. You have a fan base tuned in to witness your skills *and* to hear about the man behind the chef's whites, the tall hat, the swarthy handsome exterior…'

Dominic scowled at her.

'Albert's been convicted of assaulting a policeman, hasn't he?' she persisted. His scowl morphed into a glare of disapproval. Samantha simply smiled sweetly and pressed him. He eventually conceded the point, but insisted it was a trumped-up charge.

And then his emotions took over. 'I don't understand why he was so harshly treated. Why does he deserve three months in a so-called rehabilitation centre? Why has he not been released after all this time? Where is this institution? What does it do? Why will no one tell his parents of his whereabouts and well-being?' Emotions and words poured out of him; his face flushed. His indignation was palpable, his pain obvious. The podcast had moved from being a gentle, low-key cookery demonstration to one of human drama. The apparent disinterest of the system, the judiciary, the government, was shocking. Samantha reminded viewers of other similar stories. This was happening all over the country. She also spoke of people disappearing having been visited by SNPS officials, often in the early hours of a morning.

Dominic finished his cookery demonstration in a daze, but even on autopilot his natural enthusiasm for food and wine still surfaced. As he put the finishing touches to his demonstration, Samantha pressed him further on the circumstances of both Albert and Juan, but he clammed up. At last they received the finger across the throat signal that the session was over. Dominic threw the pans into the sink, removed his apron, and slung it towards Samantha.

Having changed back into civvies he attempted to calm down, restore some equanimity. Grabbing his coat, he headed for the door. He stopped short as he caught sight of the contract's manager with Brandon. He made a beeline for them. 'I want a word with you, Brandon. You've stitched me up...'

'Now don't start, Dom. You were great, a real star. Don't you think so, chaps?' he said, twanging his red braces then running bony fingers through his grey straggly hair. He stood and offered his hand in congratulations. It was not taken. Then, Dominic's mouth opened wide, as an unmistakable giant form with a red goatee beard emerged from the toilet and made straight for him.

'Gentle start. Build the suspense. Just the ticket. Good for you but next time a bit more drama. Blood and guts; aim for the sympathy vote. Impact. More viewers, headlines. Get the picture? Good!' he boomed.

Seb.

Brandon and Seb. He had fallen for it. How naïve could he be?

Dominic raised his hands, let out a huge sigh of exasperation and pushed his partner back down into his chair. He turned on his heels, strode to the door, stopped short, swivelled and exploded, 'Never again. You've tricked me into this. That's it. I'm done. We're finished, Brandon. As for your resistance fun and games, Seb, you can...you can...you know what you can do with it.'

He slammed the door behind him.

CHAPTER 24: DESTINATION DAY -3

2027

A grim routine had established itself. A handful of prisoners were served special meals each evening, the prelude to the long walk to oblivion. Normal rations were meagre: water, stale bread, mouldy lumps of cheese and the occasional watery soup with floating gristle masquerading as meat. *Don't need to worry about your five-a-day*, Shorty said, laughing. But one of the guards seemed uncomfortable with his role. A young man short in stature with a morose, quiet demeanour that earnt him the nickname of Happy. He never raised his voice, never struck anyone, was always strangely polite and as respectful as the circumstances allowed. Dominic watched him call the names one evening. He did so quietly, his eyes never meeting the condemned. He seemed apologetic and visibly winced when Pock struck one of the inmates with little pretext. Simon would have cited him as the embodiment of the decency that is within all human beings. But he was no longer here to comment.

Four out, four in today. Three of the newcomers were young men, one a middle-aged lady. They all seemed defiant, strong. Rupert took a spot next to Dominic.

'FF?' asked Dominic quietly.

'Yeah. Bloody unfortunate to get caught right at the eleventh hour. Nearly there,' said Rupert, pulling a hand through his bushy hair. He spoke with preternatural confidence. 'Can't last much longer...then they'll get their comeuppance, mark my words.'

'Americans?' asked Dominic.

'And Kiwis and sheilas; Indians, Canucks too. Multi-national really. British army, SAS, you name it.'

'How soon—'

'Soon,' Rupert said, and shrugged before adding, 'Probably not soon enough.'

'No.'

'Aren't you that celebrity chef bloke?' asked the middle-aged woman.

Dominic nodded and shrugged.

'Bloody inspiration, you are,' she said, in a cockney accent.

'Not a fighter, I'm afraid...'

'Wish my old man had your balls...bloody useless fat slob. Sits on his arse all day, kow-tows to the bullies, wears his M, does bugger all. Least he'll survive, I s'pose. All he was interested in was where his next meal and his next lay was coming from. Not from me, I told him in no uncertain words. And he ain't getting it anywhere else without paying for it, you can be sure of that...'

The newbies were a breath of fresh air, soon raising a few weak smiles. One of the women even broke into a chuckle. It became clear they had all been active in FF resistance since the start. They had enjoyed a decent run but acknowledged it was bound to end up here. They related some of their victories, the narrow escapes. Suddenly, the flat air of dejection in the cell was no longer uniform, becoming more turbulent; a high-pressure system meeting the deep low, bound to produce lightning strikes and thunder. They even raised a few hopes that the troops would arrive in time.

Celia nudged Dominic's arm, whispered in his ear, 'She's right. You were an inspiration. Don't run yourself down so.' He met her eyes and the blueness seemed to sparkle briefly, just a flash of sapphire light reminiscent of another time, before dimming again. The exchange petered out and Dominic turned the news over in his mind, briefly allowing a scintilla of hope to invade his philosophical sense of the inevitable. But it did not pass muster. He knew any liberation would be too late. But there was solace in knowing that it was likely to come to pass. Then his reverie was broken by the ominous sound of boots which preceded the turning of keys in the locks, creaking and groaning of the steel door, inane chatter of the guards. This time it was Shorty and Happy – an incongruous pairing.

Shorty led with his baton, following up with a verbal assault. 'What's all this noise from you bunch of traitorous bastards? Christ, it stinks in here. Bloody animals.'

'Name?' said one of Rupert's colleagues, a virtual pencil poised to make an entry into an imaginary notebook. A hush fell on the room as all eyes turned to the guards. Any sign of spirit usually led to a brutal quashing with boots,

AK-47s, batons. Whichever took their fancy. But Happy looked uncomfortable as Shorty approached the lad.

'Come on, not all day. Name, rank. Day of reckoning approaching…any time now…' But he was predictably stilled by a blow to the head, followed by another to the midriff.

'Last chance to make your choice…just hours away…' said Rupert from behind Shorty.

'Which cocky bastard said that?' he said, swivelling round. Unsure of who it was he struck out at two of the prisoners: Dominic catching one glancing blow, Rupert taking the full force of another.

'Got your card marked…one *cruel bastard* you are…' said the cockney lady from the far corner.

'Easy…' said Happy. He spoke softly, his voice pleading. It was not clear to whom he offered the plea – Shorty or the prisoners.

The confrontation resulted in gratuitous blows seasoned with expletives. Food was withdrawn, even for the names Shorty took pleasure in reading aloud. Six for tomorrow. They seemed to be speeding things up. That might lend some credence to the news delivered by the newbies but would not help the chosen six.

CHAPTER 25: SCARECROW

2026

Dominic's mood was dark as he made his way back to Hackney. He had been duped, taken for a mug. As the Tube trundled on, he picked up a cast-aside *Evening Standard*. He was too preoccupied to read the detail but picked out the depressing story headlines.

Higginbotham Dead!
Shadow Chancellor found dead in a hotel bedroom in Luton. The police say that no foul play is suspected. He died of a massive heart attack. Geraldine, his wife of twenty-two years, is said to be under sedation. His son insisted there was no history of heart disease and demanded that ministers account for his movements and ultimate demise: 'The last time he was seen was in Downing Street for his appointment with Jane Connell. We have no family or friends in Luton. Why would he be there?' A government spokesperson responded by saying, 'Our hearts go out to Thomas Higginbotham's family. We offer our sincere condolences.'

Samantha Hathaway Disappears
The actress has 'disappeared' according to her partner. No one can account for her whereabouts. This seems to follow reports of early morning raids in major cities conducted by SNPS officers, who are accused of brutish, bullying behaviour. Most have not been seen since.

Government officials defended the hard-working, patriotic
SNPS, saying they would continue to purge enemies of the
state, dismissing so-called 'disappearances' as fake news.

That reminded Dominic. Bill. He had not heard from him for ages.

Dominic
Hi Bill. Not heard from you. How
are you? Been meaning to call, will
ring later. Cheers mate.

The sunshine of the day had given way to early evening drizzle and the gathering clouds seemed to portend more rain. As the mercury dropped, it could even be cold enough for snow. He would use the evening to catch up with a few domestic chores, then ring Stephanie. *No!* he remonstrated with himself. Rather, he would contact Rosa again. He needed to persuade her to come home. Perhaps he should just catch a plane and join her in the sunshine. Brandon and the business were now history. Why hang around here? Except that travel restrictions made flights out of the country hard to come by, borders effectively closed. Another avenue closed down.

He strode out purposefully, pulling his coat tighter around him as the drizzle gave way to sleet. Close to their humble flat: home. Sighing, he turned the corner and abruptly halted on encountering a crowd. More protesters perhaps? But there was near silence. No chanting or banners or thrown missiles. No quasi-military groups. No thugs. As he drew closer, he saw ashen faces, a middle-aged lady vomiting into the gutter with a comforting hand placed on the small of her back. A young woman was weeping; another couple embraced. People appeared to be traumatised. Many were crying; mothers pulled their children's faces into their bodies; many clasped a hand to their mouths in shocked disbelief.

And then a police van drew alongside, and the crowd parted as SNPS thugs approached from behind, shouting at them to stand back, pushing aside slow movers. They carried their ubiquitous clubs; some had notches on the handle. He shuddered to think what that might signify. As a pathway opened, Dominic gasped at the sight ahead of him.

Hanging from a lamppost was a scarecrow.

It then hit him. Hard.

It was a corpse.

Hung by the neck, head leaning at an unnatural angle, a broom handle threaded through both arms of its coat. For all the world it looked like a scarecrow.

Pinned to the corpse's back was a large red T; the words, *The People's Enemy*, emblazoned his chest and a black, floppy, conical-shaped straw scarecrow hat was perched on his head. An elderly man and woman knelt at the feet of the body wailing, tears flowing, their frail bodies shaking uncontrollably. They looked up and the screaming became shrill; they clasped and sobbed into each other. Mother and father? Probably.

Their son was unceremoniously cut down, loaded into the back of the van like a carcass, a side of beef thrown into a butcher's vehicle. The elderly couple were cruelly brushed aside. The van sped away leaving them staring after it. A few people attempted to provide solace and a neighbour helped support them as they slowly shuffled down the street, a pathetic, heart-rending sight. Slowly, the crowd dispersed, mumbling incredulously.

Dominic poured a large whisky, plopping in ice. He sat down heavily in his threadbare chair, in the dark, trembling. The whisky was quickly despatched and followed by another large measure of the amber nectar. He took a slug and reached for his mobile, began to punch in Rosa's number, but changed his mind. Not a good idea at the moment. He would not cope with Rosa's disdain on top of everything else. Not tonight. He impulsively rang a different one. No answer, so he tried a landline.

'Hello? Oh, hi, Dom. Steph's not here... Are you alright?... Dom, are you there?'

'Yeah. Sorry. Bit shaken up. Steph not there you say?'

'What's wrong? You sound odd. Can I help? Come over.'

He held his mobile away from his mouth as a jumble of thoughts hurtled through his mind like colliding subatomic particles in the Large Hadron Collider.

'Talk to me, Dom. Hell. What on earth's wrong?'

'... No, I don't think I will. Not tonight. See you...' He hit the red phone.

Dominic took another swig, then threw the rest away. He needed a clear head. He simply had to contact Rosa. But first Bill. He called his mobile. No reply, so he left a message. He called his home. Mary answered. *Terrible news, Dominic.* It took some coaxing, but he eventually pieced together what she was saying as the words ebbed and flowed in confusion. They had been woken in the early hours; the front door had been caved in and men had swarmed through shouting and banging. As Mary looked on, Bill had ventured into the hallway where he was assaulted, cuffed, and taken away. It had taken only a few terrifying minutes but seemed to her to happen in slow motion. As the van into which he had been thrown took off, neighbours cautiously crept out of their homes to gawp. He was apparently helping the police with their enquiries, they later told her. The SNPS or the police? *SNPS*. Dominic's stomach lurched. Bill was required to answer questions in connection with his conduct towards security police and officials at Chequers. He needed to account for allegations of aggressive and threatening behaviour. Mary had neither seen nor heard of him since. She had made enquiries at the police station, but they could not help. She had tried to speak with SNPS staff, but to no avail. They claimed they had no record of Bill having been arrested. It had been two weeks now. Her MP was no use. He had gone to ground: a Tory.

Dominic was shaking with shock, fear, and a growing anger. Where was Bill? After what he had seen today the omens did not seem good. How could this possibly be happening? He could not speak to Rosa in this state and reached for the whisky again in need of something to calm his nerves. But he simply had to speak with someone – he craved company and reassurance. If only someone could tell him what to do, help him to rewind. He reached for his mobile.

Dominic

Need to speak with you, Steph. You ok?
Terrible thing happened today. Simply
awful. Need to hear your voice. Please ring.

Dominic

X

He hoped for an immediate response but hoped in vain, so he set about various chores in a distracted, haphazard manner. He put some Beethoven on, then turned it off – not in the mood. He switched on the television but couldn't stomach the murder mystery drama being shown. He had seen enough murder to last a lifetime. What he needed was Rosa. And Juan. And Albert. But he had no idea where his boys were, and he could not see Rosa. Her obstinacy and the draconian new laws stood in the way. It would probably be easier to change the laws than his wife's mind. Stephanie would provide succour, but still no answer there either. The doorbell rang. He cursed. Who the hell is that?

'*Rebecca!*'

'You sounded in need of help,' she said, pushing her way in.

'How did you get past the dragon?'

'Slipped in when she was arguing with someone. You look terrible. What on earth's the matter?'

'Well…'

He told her the story of the scarecrow killing and the callous actions of the SNPS. Her eyes gained an intensity, a steeliness, as she closely questioned him about the details. She admitted she had heard of a few such instances, feared this was a new form of terror being unleashed by unscrupulous forces determined to cow the British public into submission. But when he told her about Bill and Chequers the questioning became rapid fire. He had not intended to mention anything about Chequers, the banquet, Ellie, the row with the security officials. But she dragged it out of him – at first drip by drip and then in a torrent. The telling of the story to someone other than Rosa was a relief, almost therapeutic.

'Have you told Stephanie about all this?'

'I don't think so… I may have mentioned it…don't know. Why?'

'And Bill's disappeared?'

'According to his wife. I've not heard from him either, hasn't answered my calls.'

'Okay, we need to get you somewhere safe. I'll make a couple of calls. Then…'

'What're you talking about? Safe from whom?'

'If they've snatched Bill it can only be a matter of time before they come for you. And your podcast won't have helped. You've become a thorn in their side. Think about whether you've told Stephanie about this. It might be important. You could be in danger.'

Dominic refused to be panicked into a snap decision, found it hard to believe he was in imminent danger, but in the end yielded to the extent that they would stay the night elsewhere. Just in time to beat the curfew, they registered at a budget hotel as a couple under false names. The national identity scheme was not yet in place and all hotels were required to do was register guests and file their records with the SNPS. So it was that Dominic and Rebecca became

Mr and Mrs Richardson staying in room thirty-three on the second floor of a seedy hotel in the East End of London.

The chair and drawer unit were wedged against the door. They had a double bed in their pocket-handkerchief-sized bedroom and a washbasin in the corner. A tiny toilet and shower cubicle constituted their so-called bathroom: stained once-white sanitary ware, chipped tiles, old-fashioned, ripped linoleum with cigarette burns. Their bed sat on a central green carpet – worn, stained, dusty. Somewhere above them a bed creaked and groaned. He remained fully clothed, set a line of cushions and coats down the centre of the bed, a demarcation line as they settled down to grab some sleep.

'We need to get you somewhere safe tomorrow, Dom.'

The thin mattress, clanging, creaking beds to the left and above, drunken shouts, crazed laughter all conspired with troubled thoughts to ensure a night spent tossing and turning – his mind unable to let go of what he had witnessed. Coming to, he found breached demarcation lines and his head in the crook of her neck. Nightmares of scarecrows and disappearances, Albert and Juan beaten by thugs. He yearned for Rosa, had moaned, and shouted in his sleep and shed tears. Rebecca had comforted him, mopped his fevered brow, dried his tears: a sisterly act, lovingly given in a world seemingly devoid of kindness, which broke his heart. She gently kissed his forehead.

'You need to make your decision very soon, Dominic,' she had said as she left. 'Stuff is happening to you and yours. What are you going to do about it? You challenged my trustworthiness recently. You have to decide for yourself who you *are* going to trust. And I can't tell you what I do for a living, I'm afraid; sworn to secrecy. But I'm on the side of the angels, Dom. But our Stephanie? Think on.'

She closed the door behind her.

CHAPTER 26: AMBIGUITY

As he reached Oxford Circus, he received a call: Jo Holcombe. Could he meet her this afternoon, not in Stratford but on Hampstead Heath? Why? *Make sure you're not followed, will explain later.* Curious. She was self-assured and composed on their previous meetings, but now on edge.

He spotted her on a bench in a quiet spot looking down a large grassy slope to the ponds where people gathered. When he reached her, she motioned for him to sit down, no handshake. She glanced around and it was then he noticed the left side of her face was swollen with abrasions running from forehead to chin; her eye was half closed. Dominic expressed concern. *I'm okay, thanks. We need to be fairly brief.* She insisted he listen while she reported her findings. Yes, she would tell him how her facial injuries came about. *Bear with me.*

'I've been in this business ten years and before that worked in surveillance, having been extensively trained. You have to believe me. I've worked on dangerous assignments tracking terrorist suspects and always emerged unscathed. I'm no novice at this game.'

'Never thought you were, Jo.'

'Your two ladies are interesting characters. How well do you know them?'

Dominic coloured and indicated he knew them as customers who had become friends. He described how their friendship had blossomed. Jo pressed him. *How well, Dom?* Yes, he had known Stephanie closely. Once. Jo appeared to understand.

'And Rebecca?'

'We met years ago and then lost touch… She's kind, attentive even. I'm fond of her. I once helped her when she was in trouble, and she seems to think she owes me.'

He fidgeted and ran his hand round his chiselled, stubbled chin.

'In truth, I don't *really* know either of them, not deep down. They're friends, and Stephanie's an outrageous flirt, always teasing. We get on. She likes to embarrass me. Our main common interest is in fine food and wine; we've visited a few restaurants. But I really don't *know* either of them. Stephanie's elusive. Who she really is and what she does I've no idea. Rebecca's more open, but I've come to realise that I never knew what she actually did for a living and when I ask her now, she's vague. Who knows how she spends her days either. I'm rather hoping you might tell me... They're supposed to be partners but how close are the two of them really?'

'Yes, I understand that, but you can help with background information... Let me turn to Stephanie first. I've enclosed all the details of my surveillance in here,' she said, handing him a large, padded envelope. 'Dates, times, venues, together with observation details and photographs. The first few occasions were uneventful. Shopping trips and lunches with friends, coffee mornings, that sort of thing. Then it changed. It became more difficult. In short, I was rumbled and intercepted and warned off by two heavies. They were full of brutish intimidation but nothing I've not encountered before. All in a day's work.'

'Your face?'

Jo took a sip from a bottle of mineral water extricated from a bag. Continuing, she said, 'No. But on that same day, I followed Rebecca – and lost her. It happens. I was in a narrow back street, and she must have sensed something. Suddenly I was grabbed from behind. The left side of my face was slammed hard against a brick wall and held there. I was left in no doubt as to what would befall me if caught again.'

'Rebecca? I don't believe it. She's such a sweet person, heart of gold.' The recollection of her comforting him, cradling him in her arms; an oasis of kindness in a desert of human cruelty.

'I never saw her face, but it was a female voice. It could have been one of her minders, I suppose, but I'm not sure it makes much difference. Now, have a look at this photograph...'

'Well, that's certainly Rebecca.'

'Look at the building she's entering,' said Jo, leaning forwards. Dominic studied it but was none the wiser. He looked at her with a puzzled expression.

'It's Thames House on Millbank. The home of MI5.'

'MI5? Rebecca? I don't believe it. You're saying, she works for the government?'

'Apparently. Anyway, it had been a bad day. After that I was more careful, bringing in my own helpers, a tag team of experienced, skilled practitioners with real expertise in this area.'

'Sounds expensive,' said Dominic, his forehead creasing.

'We'll come back to that,' she said.

He winced.

'Getting back to Stephanie... On one occasion, we followed her to her uncle's residence. *Thomas Tobin*. I've researched her background and whilst much of it's unclear, I've confirmed she really is Tobin's niece. That raises some interesting questions. More recently we followed her to a remote area on the Kent coast. That was tricky, but we pulled it off. What we've learnt about your Stephanie is that when her minders aren't around, her movements are innocent, as far as we can tell. But when she's heading to see her uncle or his advisers... Please let me continue. Bear with me. What her agenda might be, and her various associates all build an abstruse, intriguing picture. She has extensive contacts with the government beyond her family ties. Now park that and we'll return soon...'

Jo suddenly stopped as a couple ambled towards them. Her right hand reached into her pocket; her eyes narrowed as she watched them intently. But they continued past, holding hands. Just a young couple out for a stroll.

'Okay,' she said, letting a tiny stream of air escape pursed lips. Her right hand joined the other in her lap. They exchanged glances. Dominic raised his eyebrows, his eyes glancing down to her pockets. She ignored the question.

'So, Kent. Cutting a long story short, we observed a meeting on a motor launch. The details are in there,' she said, patting the envelope. 'This vessel is normally only operated by the military. Fast and highly manoeuvrable. There aren't many others that would catch it in a chase. Stephanie was taken out to this and met with none other than Norris Jinks...'

'Jinks? He's in Canada, isn't he? Or is it the USA?'

'Take a look for yourself,' she said, flashing a blown-up photograph of Jinks with four others.

'Who are they?'

'Neil Foster was ex-MI5, and we think formerly SAS; Serena Murphy's a member of the USA intelligence services; Rupert Twigg was the chairman of the Conservative Party; and Leonard Staveley is the putative head of the resistance group, FF – Freedom Fighters.'

'I don't see Stephanie.'

'She's out of shot but we have these...' Photographs of Stephanie on shore, Stephanie stepping onto a small boat, Stephanie boarding the motor launch.

'Wow. What has Steph to do with all this? Which side is she actually on?'

'*Good* question!' said Jo. 'What we do know for certain is that these are two dangerous ladies mixing in powerful company, whatever the façade. Talk to me, Dominic. What's going through your mind?'

He got up and paced around, ruffling his hair. Sitting back down he opened his mouth as if to speak, but he jumped to his feet again and circled the bench. Jo let him meander. He stopped in front of a now more composed Jo. He played with his wedding ring and distractedly rubbed the end of his truncated finger before sitting back down heavily.

'I'm confused. What you seem to be saying is that Rebecca works for MI5. For the government. Stephanie is the niece of Tobin and has strong active contacts with both Labour activists and with Jinks, the American secret services, and the FF. Is Stephanie playing both ends against the middle? Why? At least we know which side Rebecca's batting for, I suppose.'

'I'm not sure we do yet,' said Jo. 'She could be part of a group of MI5 officers who've gone rogue. And anyway, is MI5 loyal to Queen and country or government? After all, MI5 is part of the establishment which takes a long-term view of the safety of our country and its citizens. These days they liaise closely with MI6. I doubt either organisation will be thrilled at the ingraining of Marxism, the overthrow of the monarchy and the current mayhem.'

'See what you mean. Oh, God. What now? I can't afford such an intensive investigation, Jo. You know what's happened to my family of late, lost my house, my business, wealth taxes...'

'It won't cost you a penny. This is now *personal*,' she said through clenched teeth.

'Rebecca you mean? Payback?'

'A bit more serious than that...' Jo paused and sighed deeply before explaining that she and her partner had received an early morning visit from the SNPS. Oliver had been taken away for questioning. That was a week ago. She had not seen or heard from him since.

'He might be languishing in some cell somewhere; he might have been transferred to one of their so-called rehab centres. He could even be dead, God forbid.' She told him that she had shed all her tears. Now she felt compelled to find out what was going on.

'I don't know what to say, Jo. I'm *so* sorry. If it had not been for me coming to you...'

'I don't give up easily and I'm not about to be pushed around by thugs and your smart-arsed ladies. Ha, *ladies*! All I ask is that you tell me everything. Trust me.'

Dominic readily told her all he knew: the pressure to join the resistance; the podcast; his worries that others who had featured in such broadcasts had disappeared; Chequers and Bill and Ellie. It poured out of him, a burden shared. He told of his horror at stumbling upon a *scarecrow* hanging and of Rebecca's insistence he hole up in a safe house that she'd arrange. Jo listened intently, asking probing questions, encouraging him. He also spoke of his distress at the gaping rift with Rosa under the tension of their missing boys.

'Rebecca's right about one thing. You need to move to somewhere safe. Me too. I've already done that. You could join me. It's a three-bedroomed terraced house, so enough room. But you have some decisions to make, Dominic. And you need to get this right. Your life could very well depend upon it. Who do you trust – Stephanie or Rebecca? Or neither?'

Images of Steph and Rebecca flashed through his mind. Surely Rebecca's compassion meant more than Stephanie's flirtatious teasing? Surely it was more reliable? But then he recalled the hard edge of Rebecca's character at times.

'Which safe house do you opt for? Rebecca's or mine or do you want to go solo?'

CHAPTER 27: HOXTON

Dominic attended to his appearance, first with the help of a blonde wig, a red one as an alternative, plain glass spectacles with tortoise shell frames. He bought a range of clothes from a second-hand shop: torn jeans, which he abhorred normally, heavy corduroy trousers, tee shirts, shabby woolly jumpers, hoody tops… He decided to cash in most of his current account in a branch in Highgate, chosen at random. He switched location services off on his mobile, took the SIM card out and turned the device off. Hopefully, a belt and braces approach would stand him in good stead, although he made a mental note to check such procedures with Jo. And then he remembered that she had told him to throw it away. He donned his new garb, and his blonde head bobbed through various Tube stations and atop buses as he took a circuitous route, casually slipping his mobile into a bin. He thought he had seen a follower earlier but could not be sure. He was spooked, on tenterhooks. Dodging into shops, using toilets to hold up in, finding back entrances, and he would pause at a bus stop until hopping on at the last moment, dashing into Tube trains just as the doors began to close. Holing up in the back of a coffee shop in Highgate he drank his cappuccino dusted with chocolate – seemed more in keeping with his dishevelled, ageing hippy appearance as he strove to get in character.

As he emerged from the bank with his cash in a backpack, he was approached by two men: one young with close cropped hair and facial studs, the other pugnacious and portly, forbidding. His heart thudded, he could hear his own blood pulsing, palms moistening. But they simply wanted to know where the Tube station was. Tourists. Few of those to be seen these days. Were they who they purported to be? He watched them saunter off and slowly the chilling shivers of apprehension subsided. *Get a grip, Dom.* But he resolved not to darken that bank's doorstep again.

On an impulse he took a cab to Hoxton, unsure as to whether this was foolish. Had he panicked? No place for that now. Alighting several streets away, he took care he was not being followed. She had been helpful in explaining the basics, but it seemed mainly common sense. At the end of the street he delayed at a bus stop. Good cover. The street was all quiet, bar an elderly man scurrying along with his newspaper, pulling deeply on a cigarette. A sulky teenager leant against the stop, thudding music leaking from his buds. At last Dominic decided it was clear and he headed to number seventy-five, checking for the candle. Yes, it sat alight on the front windowsill. All clear. One loud rap, two taps, a final loud knock. He heard footsteps, then bolts being slid back, a key clunking in a lock. The door opened on a chain, was shut briefly, then opened to admit him and relocked quickly.

'Hello, Dominic. Good to see you've made your decision. Phone?'

'As instructed, ditched. A pay as you go and SIM cards from different shops. All off.'

'Let me show you to your bedroom and bathroom on the top floor. You should be comfortable there. I'm on the first floor. Bolts on all bedrooms, new and substantial. Window locks too. If you need to get out quickly there's a fire escape ladder from your window.'

'And you?'

'Don't worry about me. I have security and means of self-protection. If we observe our own protocols we shouldn't need all this, but best to be prepared.'

She showed him the ground floor lounge, kitchen, and dining area. It was old fashioned but clean, fully furnished. The back door was bolted top and bottom, large functional devices not chosen for interior design. A hefty key was turned in the lock and the door opened onto a small garden, a fence at the bottom. Jo pointed to a gate in the corner, which led into a neighbour's garden with a side passage to the street. No one living there, she pointed out. Almost derelict. Clearly an exit route in extremis, but one that good tradecraft would prevent being necessary, she insisted. The landline had been disconnected; the Wi-Fi hub disposed of. They should be careful to avoid the internet or switching on mobiles when at home. If they needed access, then best to find an internet café away from Hoxton. If they used their mobiles, then the SIM card and phone should be dumped separately and replaced; always take the SIM card out of the phone. She waved a bag of cheap, used mobiles that had all been wiped, data extirpated. Download WhatsApp only, still thought to be securely encrypted, other social media less so. Use it once and...yes, he got the message.

That evening they sat together in the lounge and shared a bottle of wine and a takeaway.

'We aren't being a bit paranoid about all this, are we? Getting it out of perspective?' said Dominic.

'Have you heard from Bill?'

'No.'

'Any reports on any reappearances? Samantha Hathaway? Lawrence Smith?'

'Lawrence Smith as well?'

'Reported yesterday. In fact, all of the celebs your Stephanie introduced to Seb have now disappeared. Lawrence had become outspoken about the erosion of civil liberties. He was unbelievably more irate about that than *scarecrow* hangings and disappearances, despite two members of his wider family having been disappeared; the BBC becoming the mouthpiece of government, the muzzling of the press, closure of several national newspapers, wide-ranging censorship, border controls all seemed to exercise him more. The irony is that Lawrence, for all his popularity, was one of the left-leaning, metropolitan, ultra-liberals crying out for a left-wing government. Samantha was a bit of a luvvie too but talented, much loved. What about you, Dom? May I call you Dom? What are your plans?'

'I'm intent on rising to Rosa's demands, to find my *cojones* as Rosa puts it; take control of my life. I'll sit back and suffer in silence no longer. Better to go out trying to *do* something than waiting to be caught, disappeared or worse. I've had it being the victim. If you give in to a bully...'

'Indeed. Sounds good. But how?'

'Mm. Not worked all that out yet. I know what I'm *not* going to do. Brandon, work, Stephanie, Seb – steering clear of all of them.'

'Rebecca?'

'Not sure, Jo. What do you think? We were friends...still are, I think. I just feel in my guts that she's okay. Her contacts and knowledge could be useful. And if she works for MI5, presumably her skills as well. But I can't trust her completely. I think I'll make contact as clandestinely as I can without betraying my location or my work with you.'

'You need to be careful but...' She raised her eyebrows and looked at him quizzically. 'Are you sure you want to court danger? Risk everything? The people we're dealing—'

'I know they're dangerous. But what else can I do? Most of all I want to find a way of getting to Rosa. I've no idea how, given travel restrictions, and anyway it's not safe for her to be home with me. But we need to speak – she needs to know I'm doing everything in my power to find our boys.'

'And that's where I suggest we start, Dom. Albert and Juan. And the best route to them might just be Rebecca. From what you say she feels a debt towards you and her MI5 contacts may be useful… But why's she still living with Stephanie? Is their relationship a charade? Perhaps she wants to stay close to Stephanie for covert reasons? It seems to suit both of them for the time being. But I doubt either trusts the other.'

'Some basis for a relationship,' said Dominic. But as soon as the words were out of his mouth, he felt the hypocrisy reverberate in his guts. Rosa had trusted him, and he loved her, but that had not stopped him from transgressing…from being happily seduced. He lapsed into silence as the thought struck him; his head told him he had been foolish and should regret it. But did he *really*? His heart told him something entirely different.

After a while, Dominic leant forwards and told Jo he was going to contact Rosa and Rebecca. Tomorrow. No time to lose. Jo looked anxious and asked how he proposed to do that. He would find different internet cafés, make up a number of Hotmail addresses and try both WhatsApp and email to contact them. What was he going to say? He wasn't entirely sure but needed to signal his love for Rosa, his refusal to give up on her, his determination to find their boys.

'And Rebecca?'

'See if she can help me. Stephanie led me to believe that she knew where Juan was and what he was up to. If she does, surely Rebecca might? Or may be able to find out from Steph. Or perhaps Steph found out from Rebecca? I don't know. But I do know I want her help, and yours, to contact PAD. I'd like to contribute but need to sort out security somehow. And I'd like to make a series of video clips – have them launched. I'm not yet sure how to go about this, but I intend to make some waves. Stop pussy footing around.'

'If that means working with Seb you need to be careful, Dom. Promise me you'll sleep on it. Let's talk in the morning. I can help with some of this. I've scores to settle as well,' she said, as a silent tear slid down her cheek. Dominic reached out to her, trying to offer comfort.

'Please don't,' she said. 'Any sympathy will open the floodgates again. Listen, I'm whacked. I'm off to bed. Remember to check the front and back doors, lock your bedroom too. Goodnight.'

*

CHAPTER 28: UNDERCOVER

Dominic woke early and set about preparing breakfast. He laid the table, squeezed fresh oranges, brewed coffee, and prepared the ingredients for pancakes; he reached for the Greek yogurt and assembled fresh fruit to accompany them: bananas. No strawberries or raspberries or pineapple in the shops. They would have to do without maple syrup too. He sliced granary bread ready for toasting, to be served with marmalade or honey. The radio played softly, the news a mix of upbeat government messages. No mention of scarecrows or disappearances or mysterious deaths. No news of an economy in freefall, declining markets, rampaging inflation, empty supermarket shelves. The manipulation was depressing.

Jo was tardy, eventually emerging at around 08.30, dressed as if for the office, eschewing disguise, trusting of her tradecraft. As they ate breakfast, she took him through the security protocols again: a location for leaving messages should the need arise. *Dead letter box?* Yes, if you like. Yes, just as in Le Carré books, smiling with him. A rare moment of light relief. She told him where the alley was, which cobble was loose: count twelve cobbles from the tarmac road at the Shoreditch end, and three cobbles in from the left-hand side. Yes, he understood. How would they know to check? A chalk mark at the end of their road in Hoxton. They agreed the precise location and the mark to be used, an arrow pointing skywards meant check the cobble. An arrow pointing downwards signified danger: go to ground, find another safe location, lie low. If the intended recipient did not respond to a message, then in extremis they could use WhatsApp to check all was well. They both designated a particular mobile, which was then secreted under a floorboard in the unused bedroom, SIM cards placed in a plastic bag alongside; the numbers were ingrained in their memories. Remember that if there is any danger or cause for concern – remove the candle in the window.

'Are you sure we aren't overdoing this, Jo?'

'How much more evidence do you need? What with—'

'Yup, I get it. Oliver, Bill, Juan, Albert...'

'I should go now, Dom. I want to set up for you to do your video clips and find a way of posting. I know someone who should be able to help. I'm also meeting a friend who's one of the leaders of PAD. They're crying out for known faces brave enough to speak out.'

Having watched for the best part of an hour, he emerged from the shadows and entered the internet café. Most of the customers appeared to be students: rowdy, playful, spirited. One of the lads was full of banter, most directed at a pretty girl with auburn hair. They flirted remorselessly. Dominic allowed himself a brief smile. Good to see that young people still managed to rise above the crisis surrounding them.

Dominic found a spot in the corner, placed his backpack on the floor between his feet, pushed his hoody back and set about his task quietly, unobtrusively. First an email to Rosa. How to compose it? Several attempts were dismissed with sighs of exasperation. Eventually he settled on an approach he hoped would have impact, tug on the heart strings, transmit his resolve. Dominic vowed to find their boys and could not countenance much more time away from her. *I miss you, love you, life's worthless without you.* He sat back and read it again. Clumsy perhaps, but he hoped it conveyed sincerity. He also spoke of his flight from their Hackney flat. He said he was somewhere safe. *I'm being followed. Bill's disappeared. Too much happening to tell you all about it.* Finally, he hit the send button, exited the application, and finished the remnants of his coffee. Sitting back, he allowed himself a sigh of relief. His shoulders relaxed, some of the tension leaching.

Tap on his shoulder.

He turned around sharply. Adrenalin surged. He gasped for breath, almost paralysed by shock, flushing instantly.

'Not sure about the blonde mullet,' she said, having watched his reaction with apparent amusement. She bent down to kiss him on the cheek.

'Stephanie. What...how...'

'I just happened by, Dom. Aren't you pleased to see me? Let's go somewhere quieter. A bit more stylish, more comfortable. This is *so* seedy.

I know just the place. Come on.'

It must be a trick; his head screamed objections. His heart hammered. A trap. Get out. Fast. Get safe. But his legs were unwilling. He could not believe she meant him harm. And he had so many questions. Succumbing, he let her lead him out of the café, her arm linking through his.

They entered a five-star hotel, all plush carpets, shining brass, marble, sweeping staircases. She shushed his protestations, found a quiet area, ordered glasses of chardonnay and smoked salmon sandwiches. Dominic insisted on a table adjacent to a nearby exit, his back to the wall.

'My, my, we're jumpy, aren't we? Whatever's wrong? Where's my happy celebrity chef oozing positivity – been missing me?'

It took Dominic a while before his jitters eased, the wine helping. Stephanie chattered away inconsequentially, irrelevant small talk. He pondered how to challenge her, how to phrase his questions, then blurted out, 'I know you're Tobin's niece with contacts across government. Irrefutable proof. But you also met with Jinks and foreign security services, resistance and God knows who else. What's your game?'

'How frightfully clever of you,' she said, the Mona Lisa smile making a return.

He pressed her.

'We can't choose our family, but we can choose our friends. Who was it that brought you news of Juan? What are you saying, dear Dom? You're not impugning my honour, are you? Surely not? Not after the blossoming of our relationship and that seems *sooo* long ago... What are you doing this afternoon? We can top up our wine, you can get rid of that awful wig and let the afternoon take us where it will. What do you say?'

'Stephanie...please.'

'What? I thought we had a thing going on?'

'Yes...*no*! Oh I don't know. It felt special. But also...a betrayal. I just don't know—'

'You poor tortured soul,' she said, reaching for his hand.

'*No*! Stop it. I always feel you're playing with me. Is that what you do, Steph? Treat people as your playthings, for manipulation and amusement – a kitten toying with her quarry before the kill? Can't you answer my questions? Who are you? Where are your loyalties? Can I trust you? How did you find me?'

'Questions, questions. So insulting,' she said with a pout.

'One last attempt. You tried to persuade me to join Seb and his merry band. You were almost certainly implicated in tricking me into that podcast. Don't deny it. You introduced Seb to Lawrence Smith and Samantha Hathaway. Both have been disappeared. Trying to bump me off too, Stephanie?'

'Well, well. So, I'm knocking off celebs now? And the *scarecrow* killings – three more last night by the way – is that all me too? Can you really believe I would mean you harm? We were *lovers*, Dom.' She looked at him intently, serious for once. 'Look, all you need to know is that I'm no apologist for the Marxist regime; the intimidation, violence…it appals me. We all have to stand up to it in our own way. I have contacts, family in that regime. Why would I *not* use them? And do you honestly think your private detective and her tag team would have got near Jinks had we not wanted them to? I trust she got good shots with the telephoto lens? Put the evidence to good effect but keep my mug out of it, if you would be so kind. You could get me shot. See how I put myself out on a limb for you, Dom. And you have the gall to question my motives, my actions, my loyalties. I may be unconventional but… Enough. I've said more than is wise. You and your clever colleague must reach your own conclusions. See you soon.'

She got up and threw him a caustic look. He had never seen a haughty side to her before, never penetrated her layer of self-assurance, let alone provoked a reaction. She suddenly seemed genuine. Human. No Mona Lisa antics, no teasing. Tense body language, dead eyes. He watched her walk to the desk, her gait purposeful, brisk. She produced her card, settled the bill. Business-like, short, and sharp. Striding to the exit she stopped for a moment, spun round, and threw him a quizzical glare, then turned on her heels. Dominic stood at the window as she marched down the street. Her body language and high tempo bristled resentment, hurt. And then she slowed, paused, and had time for an old lady with silver hair and a walking stick. It suddenly struck him that he had not witnessed empathy from Stephanie before as she escorted the old lady across the road. Watching intently he saw her chat briefly as they seemed to share a light moment. Stephanie waved her goodbyes, and the pensioner waved her stick cheerily as she made her way into a shop.

Dominic thought for a moment but could not unravel the conflicting strands of logic and emotion surging through him. Most of all he was confused. But he must not allow Stephanie's appearance to distract him from his purpose. He reached for his bag.

He later emerged from the gents' bathroom ginger-headed wearing corduroys, a flowery shirt, trainers, and a cagoule. He found another internet café in a different area and was extra careful. He did not think he was being followed. But then he was confident he was without company this morning until Stephanie breezed in. How did she do it? This time it was Rebecca he contacted, and she responded quickly. They met and she gave him contacts for PAD. *Leave it a day or two, let me introduce you. Are you sure you want to do this?* He was. She had no news of Juan but would investigate. Of Albert, all she knew was that Hartley Camp was in turmoil. Two guards had been accused of spying.

'How do you know all this?'

'I can't say, not yet. Trust me.'

'And what about your relationship with Stephanie?' asked Dominic.

'No change. Steph's all sweetness and light, back home now. Everything's normal.'

'Normal? You both flirt with other men. And women. And yet...'

'I've told you before – I'm no flirt. Don't conflate me with Steph. You really don't understand her either, do you?'

'Nor you.'

'Steph's a complicated, social animal. As for me... What matters is that you're careful. The advice remains the same. Be wary. Lie low.'

'Ahh...' He told her about his encounter earlier, of his dismay at her finding him. He held back her monologue, her angry account of herself. He needed to think that through, make sense of it – if that was possible. Jo might help. Yes, Jo was the answer.

He checked the wall at the end of the street. No chalk marks. As he strolled past their safe house the candle flickered. A relief. Enough drama for one day. He used the knocking code. After letting him in she headed back to the lounge where he joined her. Dominic found her sitting in the gloom, rocking back and forth, arms crossed. He turned a lamp on and noticed tears streaming over yellowing bruises.

'Whatever's wrong? Are you okay? Sorry, stupid question.'

'More *scarecrows* last night,' she said, in a whisper expressed between sobs.

'So I hear. But... What is it?'

'My partner, Oliver...'

'One of...oh, my *God*! You mean he was one of the...?'

She nodded and the tears flowed freely. She ran out of the room, and he

166

heard water running. As he ventured into the kitchen, she was drying her face. Jo turned to him, distraught, shoulders shaking. He pulled her into his chest, consoled her as best he could; the breached dam drenched his shirt. He held her tight until the spate slowed.

'Come on. I've brewed some tea. Something stronger later.'

He led her back into the lounge and sat opposite her.

'I'm so sorry, Jo. This evil, corrupt...'

'That's not all, Dom. Brace yourself—'

'No! *No*! Not—'

'Not that bad... It's Bill,' she said in a quavering voice. 'I'm so sorry, Dominic, words can't describe what's happening. Impossible to comprehend...'

Dominic stared at her, dumbfounded. His friend, his sous chef. They had worked alongside each other for years. Now dead. Brutally killed by thugs given a licence by a malevolent regime. He knew Bill's kids, Jake, and Vicky. Young teenagers now. He and Rosa had spent lively evenings with Bill and Mary. He had shared many a pint of beer with Bill after work, many a lewd story. He was always good company. And together they had endured the Chequers experience. Bill had come to his defence, tried to intervene for sweet Ellie. He had acted bravely and been assaulted in response. Dominic shook with emotion. But shock and dismay soon gave way to anger.

He vowed revenge for his friend.

Later that evening, he poured himself a large Scotch on the rocks, a glass of Cabernet Sauvignon for Jo. As they slowly recovered some degree of equanimity they caught up with each other's day. Jo was shocked at the news he related. How on earth had Stephanie found him? Had their security been compromised? They might have to find another place. Jo would instigate that just in case: a contingency. Trusted colleagues would arrange it. And then he told Jo what Stephanie had said about her luring them to Jinks, allowing them to witness the meeting, take photographs.

'Did you believe her?'

'Yes, absolutely. How otherwise would she have known we knew? I saw a side of her I've never before witnessed. Honestly, Jo, I've never believed her more. And her account would make sense, wouldn't it? It casts her in a different light. Potentially.'

Jo also revealed the progress she had made in her day. Contacts with some of the leaders in PAD secured, one of whom was the same as the contact

Rebecca had offered. And she provided a location where he could go to have his video clips recorded.

'But we can do better than that,' she said earnestly. 'Have you heard of NFN?'

'I don't think so, no.'

'*Not Fake News* – a news streaming service. Like-minded professional reporters committed to broadcasting the news. Real news. Not propaganda. Uncensored.'

'Sounds dangerous. Why does the government allow it?'

'Don't worry. They cover their digital tracks, essential they do. The guy's an IT expert, something of a guru. Completely trustworthy. And you said you wanted to...'

'I do. Are you sure he's dependable?'

'Oh, yes. I have sensitive information which compromises him. He wouldn't want certain people to have sight of that. I don't want to do that and don't expect to have to.' She had used him many times. 'All you need do is get there undetected then say your piece.'

The rest of the evening was spent sipping their drinks, glasses recharged a few times, watching some of the video clips from the streamed NFN service. The content was dispiriting, the drama compelling, the human misery appalling. Most of the interviewees were incognito, questioned with their backs to the webcam, their voices disguised. Dominic wearily made his way to bed after Jo insisted she would be alright. He felt a weight of sadness at Jo's loss, just as he bore Bill's fate heavily but with a determination to channel the anger into action.

No turning back now.

CHAPTER 29: HARTLEY

All sense of time had long since been lost in the absence of watches and clocks and diaries. Some attempted to keep tally: marking walls or floors, counting off the days and weeks. But those weeks never turned into months let alone years as the practice was always found and snuffed out, with perpetrators referred for therapy. The months and years passing by were *sensed*, however, as cadet numbers swelled. Albert had learnt to curtail natural instincts, to conceal his emotions and draw a veil over opinions in exchange for a weekly phone call. But then that was cancelled, and his promised release failed to materialise. External communication was no longer allowed for any cadet. All releases, early or otherwise, ceased. Officers and staff seemed twitchy and were also denied leave, confined to camp. There was no occurrence inside Hartley that explained the changes; inmates could only speculate privately as to what had happened in the outside world to trigger the ban. All the young men could do was abide by the monotony of the strict regime – aliens inhabiting a false world. Even their weather was false – the same warm sunshine every day. Rain or mist would have been welcomed. A storm. *Anything* natural would be welcome. Anything free. They all knew that their tea was laced with bromide to depress their sexual urges, their food with drug compounds to depress their natural personalities.

But the end-of-day leisure period was still permitted – and embraced by most. It was a release from the re-education propaganda sessions of mindlessly intoning the learnings of Marx and Engels, the obligatory renditions of "The Red Flag" and their work in the kitchens or laundry or workshops. The one freedom, their one privilege, was in being allowed a choice as to how to spend their time-limited leisure period. Matthew 2225 extended his arm as he entered the reception area. *Beep.* Having changed, he walked silently to the gym for a cardiovascular workout in a large pod within the gym, where another fifty-plus cadets were toiling away. He could access treadmills, rowing machines, spin bikes and SkiErg machines. He took his place in the queue to wait for one of the twenty treadmills to become available, his eyes drawn to a virtual tropical paradise: a necklace of tiny islands fringed with fine white coral beaches, dense tropical forests reaching down to the shoreline. Islands were set in a flat, turquoise sea fading to the dark blue depths. The sight and sounds of birds mixed with the odours of exotic flowers, permeating the senses so cadets were able to transport themselves to Bali or the Maldives, the Seychelles, perhaps Sri Lanka or maybe Phuket in the Andaman Sea. A green turtle bobbed to the surface and then dived to feed on underwater grasses in the shallows, at the far end of one of the islands that had come into sharp focus. Manta rays glided through the crystal-clear waters. They could also make out black parrots, blue-footed boobies, scarlet macaws, parakeets, bald eagles, blue pigeons, kingfishers from different parts of the world.

Albert took to the equipment with enthusiasm, worked hard, ran hard, pedalled hard, rowed hard, skied hard. As did most of those around him. The absence of officers and white coats was a relief, but all would understand that surveillance remained high, that the syringes were never far away should they stray from permitted activities or breach fundamental principles.

Albert was beeped into the kitchen areas, changed into his chef's whites, and allocated his duties. He was performing the role of commis chef assisting three chefs preparing the main courses for that day's lunch: cottage pie, chicken fricassee, beef casserole with carrots and stuffed peppers. He had established himself as being competent and set to his tasks in meditative silence. The kitchen wasn't the same without Red Hair, who had disappeared with a small number of others. Most assumed they had been isolated as bad influencers and were being subjected to intense re-education programmes and social conditioning. One of the men in black had let slip the special programmes and used the term. Who knows what that might be proxy for. *They'll be using psychotropics to change brain function*, whispered Blondie, a lanky youth who had been a medical student. He and Albert were neighbours in their sleep pod and were working on their near-silent relationship.

When Albert was asked to retrieve some herbs from the walk-in fridge, the door closed behind him and he was joined by Chef Whittaker.

'The time's approaching. You are up for it, aren't you?'

Albert looked at him blankly and shrank back.

'Albert? What's up?' said Whittaker, reaching out to shake Albert – an attempt to break his torpor.

'Oh… Don't know. What?'

'Are you up for it? It's nearly time,' the chef repeated.

'Not sure… Red Hair…' said Albert.

'He was a loner. This is a co-ordinated plan to spring not only you but others.'

'Why me?'

'Your father seems to have influence…you've acquired quite a PR value, Albert.'

'But…'

'No time to debate. Yes or no? Can't see the downside.'

'Apart from getting myself killed, you mean…but yeah, why not. When?'

'Soon. Stay calm, stay quiet, keep yourself out of trouble.'

CHAPTER 30: NFN

Dominic nursed his mug of coffee while transfixed by the interview taking place live from the glass pod and transmitted from ceiling speakers in the waiting area. Ronald Dicks, the heavily built interviewer, made no attempt to disguise himself. His guest did. As she was interviewed with her back to the camera, she made eye contact with Dominic through the acoustic glass partition. "Jenny" was a diminutive young Asian woman, an aspiring actress just out of drama school. Her hands fidgeted in her lap, she crossed and uncrossed her legs. She spoke with a wavering voice, urgently – conveying a nervous determination to tell her story.

'Viewers will respect your courage, Jenny. We thank you for speaking out on NFN.'

'We have to. What's happening is wicked and immoral. Our liberties have disappeared, our people are subjected to terror. If my story persuades just one person to repel this regime and protest then it will be worth it. And what can they do to me now? I've lost pretty much everything. But I'm not prepared to lose my self-respect. I won't be cowed...'

'Tell us...tell us about your family.'

'I've got no script, not even thought about how to present...but here goes. My mum's Chinese, born in Shanghai. She met my dad on holiday in England. He was a preacher, born and bred in London. She never went back, they married and, well, I'm the product of their love. Mum especially valued the liberal freedoms we all used to take for granted in this country. Where she came from, oppression and control was the norm. Much as we are having to... well, you know. They worked hard, paid their way in life, were active members of the community. My dad was passionate about the plight of homeless people, child poverty, inequalities...all the things this government supposedly stands for. He was a firebrand in the church – perhaps I got my passion for the stage from his pulpit dramas…' She paused, her head drooped, and a sad smile crossed her features. Only visible to Dominic. He was enraptured by her charm, her intensity, and moved by her depth of sadness. Ronald was quiet, allowing the silence to speak volumes. She lifted her head; her eyes locked on Dominic's, and she nodded her recognition before continuing.

'They brought me up to believe I should follow my dream. I always wanted to be an actress: school plays, amateur dramatics, that sort of thing. My mum and dad were amazing, so supportive, and I did pretty well and got a scholarship to drama school. I absolutely loved it. Then it was closed down.'

'SNPS?'

'Wielding their clubs, breaking heads. Bullies, vile psychopaths.'

'Why did they raid your school?' asked Ronald. Gently.

'We were just a bunch of kids, budding luvvies if you like. We embraced freedom of speech, naturally opposing anything smacking of authoritarianism, liked to demonstrate…'

'Were you hurt?'

'I ran but my friend, Tamsin… She was disabled, you see. Part of her leg had been amputated when young. She couldn't go fast enough and…' Jenny stopped, shoulders heaving. Stifled sobs took hold as Jenny fought to retain control of her emotions. Ronald let the silence endure. She slowly recovered her poise to resume.

'They caught her, hit her. Hard. Kicked her. Nothing we could do…'

'Where is Tamsin now?'

'She's…she's at home. She can't talk, she can't eat solids. Tamsin's fed… fed…through a tube. Her mum cares for her. Her life has effectively ended. All because…'

'But your story doesn't end there, does it?'

'My dad spoke out about Tamsin, made accusations from the pulpit and in public. Not just about Tamsin but others too. Then one night they came. It was early in the morning. One minute the house was in silence as we slept, the next there was a crashing sound as the front door was smashed in, boots were running up the stairs, shouting and screaming at my mum and dad and me. They took him, they hit my mum.'

'And you?'

Silence.

'In your own time, Jenny. We can see how painful it is for you…'

'Two of them pushed me back into my bedroom and slammed the door shut. They were on the inside. I stood no chance. I struggled, but...'

'Did they—'

'Both of them... I... I...'

Jenny broke down and she was helped out of the booth. As she was led away, Ronald summarised the rest of her story for the viewer, told in chilling, hushed tones. Her dad has not been seen since. Like thousands across the country. All in the name of *The People*. Jenny will never have children. Her mum no longer speaks to anyone, has lost her mind. Just one family's suffering, he said simply.

He lapsed into contemplation for a moment.

The recording continued, the silence settling on Dominic like dust.

Finally, he leant forwards and spoke earnestly.

'How long are we to tolerate these deprivations of liberty? The calculating cruelty, callousness, criminality? How long before this happens to you and your family? Perhaps it already has? This is *Not Fake News*. This is happening daily. But take heart that Jenny and others like her have the courage to tell their stories. Our hearts go out to her, to her mum, to Tamsin... Resistance gathers daily. The international community's protest is gathering force. But the courage to denounce our Marxist government must come from within. From *The People*. That is happening: Tobin's and Connell's days are numbered. Will we see the restoration of a parliamentary democracy? The restoration of our monarch? This depends on *YOU... The People...* This is Ronald Dicks from NFN signing out for now.'

Dominic was soon joined by Ronald, an imposing bear of a man with a full beard but a soft voice. They chatted about the podcast he was about to make, checked that he understood what was involved, knew the potential risks of raising one's head above the parapet. *Already there, already dodging the bullets. Time to fight back.*

Ronald welcomed his viewers back and turned to his guest, the camera focusing on the presenter.

'Most of my interviewees prefer the cloak of anonymity in telling their stories for fear of reprisal, to guard the safety of their families. But I understand you're prepared to waive this protection.' Dominic nodded his affirmation off camera.

'Yes.'

'My new guest hardly needs an introduction, the famous celebrity chef Dominic Green aka Diamond. Today he shuns his chef's whites and the kitchen for more sober attire; his usual tasty morsels supplanted by an unpalatable but important offering: *Dominic's* story... Welcome, Dominic.'

'Thank you. Hello, everybody.' He sat stock-still, finding it impossible to stay the fluttering butterflies, and drew on his experience of exposure to the lens. Dominic rubbed his finger stump, played with his wedding ring, and took a deep breath.

'I must first of all ask you to explain why you are content to show your face.'

'I'm done with hiding, shrinking from the realities we all face. I've been targeted already. Beaten up. Threatened. But that's nothing to what they're doing to my family – they've torn us to shreds. Even that's nothing compared to what they've done to my friend Bill. He's been *disappeared*...only to turn up *scarecrowed*. So has a friend's partner. So have countless others. I've all too readily given in to intimidation, become a pliant victim, stood by as my family suffer... I've been weak. I only ever wanted to immerse myself in my passion for food. To support my family and provide for them. But there comes a time when you have to break out of your torpor. Fight for survival. As my Spanish wife, my beloved Rosa, has said, I need to find my *cojones*! I'm trying to... find my sons, be reunited with my wife...do my bit to rid us of this vile evil...' Dominic paused, ran a hand across his brow.

With Ronald's gentle but persistent questioning the whole story came out about Albert, Juan, Chequers and Bill. Then Dominic was asked to focus back on the Chequers experience.

'Were you not sworn to secrecy?'

'Yes.'

'Will you not be in breach of a legal contract?'

'I guess so.'

'Are you not putting yourself at risk of prosecution?'

'We were forced to sign, told it was like the Official Secrets Act. But it can't be right to stay silent in the face of depraved criminal activity. And as for prosecution...ha, it would never get to court. They wish me more harm than that. I'm under no illusion. My life's in peril. I've been stalked. I live in a secret location. Government agencies are seeking me out...'

'Who was raped, Dominic?'

'I... ' He stared blankly at Ronald, mulling over his response. The pause was allowed to stretch.

'I can't say. That's for her and her parents to decide what's best.'

'Do her parents know?'

'They're scared. Can't blame them. Who wouldn't be? Perhaps her father's under their direct control, being threatened...'

'The government. SNPS?'

'Of course.'

'Did you see the rapists? Can you identify them?' asked Ronald.

'The home secretary, the health minister and two others I didn't recognise.'

'Are you certain about this? Quite certain? It's a shocking claim.'

'Oh, yes! And it should shock people, it needs to. How can we allow these animals to rule us?'

Dominic put his head in his hands. But Ronald pressed him further. Why had he not reported the crime? *He had. They didn't believe him, claimed the girl wasn't even at Chequers. Lied. Threatened him. Hit Bill.* Why had he not called 999 or gone to the police station immediately? *Communication was banned, they weren't allowed to leave Chequers, effectively incarcerated.*

Jo had watched the podcast and complimented Dominic on his courage. It had already accumulated hundreds of thousands of hits. But she worried that it made him even more sought after, a target. Jo also told him that she had arranged for him to meet with two of the leaders of PAD at tomorrow's demonstration outside the Houses of Parliament. If he was still up for that? He was. He could speak as well if he were prepared to. *Definitely, let's do it.* His voice was strong, his determination steely, but he drummed his fingers on the coffee table, gulped. He reached for the whisky. Jo stayed his hand.

'Are you going to be okay, Dom? You really don't have to do this, you know. Everyone would understand if you chose to lie low. You've not even had time to mourn Bill. I know you were close and...'

'There'll be time enough for that in the future. If we get through this. We have to. I've just got Rosa's voice reverberating in my head: man up, find Albert and Juan and then I'll come back. I've got to do that; I can't fail her again. Nor the lads,' he said, grasping his whisky glass, draining the contents. His face had flushed, beads of perspiration gathering on his forehead.

'It's okay to be scared you know.'

'Well, that's a relief to hear.'

They exchanged weak smiles.

Suddenly a sharp rapping on the front door.

They sat up abruptly, instantly alert. A bubble of fear fizzed to the surface. His heart thudded. Jo reached inside her bag. Was that a small pistol she extricated? Slipping it into her jeans as she stood. Then the rapping resumed, this time their secret signal. Time to get out. As silently as they could, they pulled on shoes, grabbed mobile phones and SIM cards, coats. They made for the back door. Dominic opened it a crack. All seemed quiet. It was dark. They walked briskly up the path, through the secret gate into the garden of the deserted house. Still quiet. Then a crashing sound from behind froze them to the spot. Jo recovered quickly, pulling him into the protective shadows. Their visitors must have caved in the front door.

Edging along the perimeter of the garden they reached the side entry. All seemed quiet. It was pitch dark. Dominic grabbed Jo's hand as they moved forwards warily, all senses on alert.

Sounds from behind. SNPS thugs, presumably.

And then a clattering in their vicinity. Dominic's heart thudded; his pulse raced. He gasped for breath, almost paralysed by his own fear.

And relax – a meowing revealed the culprit as a spinning dustbin lid slowly clanged to a halt. But their pursuers would have heard that too. They quickened their pace, breaking into a trot as they penetrated the dark tunnel that was the passageway.

Nearly there.

Suddenly the blackness was filled with light.

Their path was blocked as a silhouetted figure appeared in front of them.

Instant recognition.

Jo raised her pistol just as he heard a familiar voice.

'In a hurry, Dominic?'

Stephanie!

'Move. Quickly,' said Jo, with asperity, directly facing her, blinking in the bright light. She brandished her Mauser, pointing it directly at Stephanie.

'Oh, let's not be dramatic. Where did you find *her*, Dom?'

'How did you find *us*?' asked Dominic, placing himself between the two women. Jo seemed about ready to explode, quite unlike her, but Stephanie at her most insufferable provoked reactions in even the most composed of people.

'Let's go back inside and have a nice cup of tea. Unless you have something stronger in your squalid abode? Yes, let's do that shall we? Come on. I'll persuade my heavies to leave us in peace, repair any damage. They get a tad carried away, but they mean well. We're all concerned for your safety. After all, we're on the

177

same side. That's right, isn't it?'

'Who knows?' said Dominic, letting an exasperated jet of air escape with his words. 'And if you're so concerned about our safety just leave us be. I don't need you, Steph.'

'Oh, Dom, that's so hurtful. You can't mean it.'

Jo pushed Dominic out of the way, raising her pistol slowly, threateningly. Stephanie's eyes registered momentary alarm but by the time she had compliantly raised her hands there was a shadow of a smile suggesting something half-way between complacency and conceit: provocative rather than conciliatory, mock surrender at best. Jo stared at her, fuming. A stand-off until a figure emerged from the shadows, disarming her in one swift, skilful movement. The two women faced each other, one glaring, the other donning a condescending half-smile. Dominic gently eased Jo back, offering her comfort. She recoiled. But he persisted and took firm hold of her hand. There seemed nothing to do other than head back in. Stephanie followed them, chattering inanely all the way as if on a stroll in the park on a sunny afternoon.

'No tea? No welcome? Oh, well, whisky will have to do,' she said, reaching for the bottle of malt and pouring generously. She settled back, crossed one leg over the other and surveyed the room. 'It's hardly the lap of luxury, you poor things. And who is this delightful creature? Aren't you going to introduce us?' The Mona Lisa look.

Jo glared but Dominic took centre stage.

'You will know perfectly well, this is Jo. You seem to know everything, Steph. How do you do it? Why are you stalking us? What harm do you plan? How do you live with yourself? When will…just what are you doing here? And how did you find us?'

Stephanie looked at him as his torrent of words dried up, sipped her whisky, and turned her head to one side. Once more the winsome coquette.

'I wanted to say hello, congratulate you on your video podcast thingy. It appears to have gone viral. Over a million hits. NFN are replaying it every hour, adding further clips from others claiming all manner of deprivations and dramas. Very emotional. You've made quite an impact, Dominic. You've done the cause a great deal of good. Seb will be pleased. And as for finding you, it really was terribly straightforward. You see, I work with professionals. Not amateur sleuths,' she said, smiling sweetly at Jo.

CHAPTER 31: SHOREDITCH

They risked remaining in Hoxton overnight, both opting to sleep in their clothes, alternating sleep with vigils. If Stephanie was working for the government then their cover was blown, and they could expect to be apprehended if they did not move quickly. On the other hand, if she was on the side of Jinks they would be alright, he had argued. Jo was less sure, but Dominic still struggled to believe Stephanie meant him any real harm, although he did not entirely trust his own judgement these days. He had crossed that line in trusting Rebecca. Probably. But he had not quite been able to get there with Stephanie. And after last night's antics his trust had regressed sharply.

Preparing for a busy day ahead, Jo suggested he arm himself, but Dominic refused the offer of a gun. They scared him. Words exploding over the airwaves was one thing, bullets quite another. Anyway, if he were stopped, the game would be up. Over and out, he had argued. It definitely will be if you are stopped without, had been Jo's rejoinder. True enough. Nonetheless, he resisted the option of violence.

They agreed to divide their efforts: Jo to execute their contingency plan by securing a new safehouse; Dominic's focus was the PAD demonstration on the main stage in Trafalgar Square. Speaking in such circumstances was a daunting prospect, but first he needed to get there safely, find his contact, agree security arrangements. An escape route had been promised. He would have to trust them and did so instinctively. Before setting off, they agreed a new dead letter box location and a suitable code. No cobbles this time. A coded message would be left. A chalk mark in the shape of a star set up two streets away would indicate it was safe to access the message. Or not. *All set?* All set.

Donning the ginger hippy look, he made his way to a white transport van parked in Bedford Street in Covent Garden; the intention was to hide in plain sight. He piled into the back and was pleased to see Rebecca there. Dominic was assured they had taken precautions; security staff were looking out for them right now. *Professionals.* That felt like a dig at Jo, the second such jibe in the last twenty-four hours. He let it go. Having been introduced to Gareth, a consultant anaesthesiologist at St Thomas', and Ruth, a solicitor, they slipped out of the van on receiving the signal. A crowd of PAD demonstrators engulfed them, as they made their way towards Trafalgar Square where groups were converging from all directions. SNPS forces were gathered in the side streets, numbers swelling by the minute, many clad in riot gear. They cut an intimidating sight. As they slowly advanced on Dominic's crowd, another PAD group converged to form an additional barrier between him and the SNPS. A gang of black-shirted anarchists simultaneously upped the tempo of remonstration, chanting obscenely, provoking remorselessly until an officer lashed out. The scene felt staged to Dominic. He was shepherded deep into the square and took refuge with a small group of organisers as the stage was being prepared. They all seemed calm, but Dominic was not used to confrontation, had avoided it all his life. Rebecca spoke quietly, reassuring him that many people had his back.

'MI5 agents?' asked Dominic.

She looked at him quizzically. *You need to prepare for the speech. Let's focus on the task in hand*, she had insisted, sidestepping the question. He knew she was right, but he would return to this later. Meanwhile, he needed to get his act together, make the most of the opportunity to demonstrate proactivity. Apparently the NFN clip had millions of hits, both surprising him and boosting his confidence. The government had also denounced the claims in a BBC news bulletin: in itself extraordinary given the increasing volume of protests, the disappearances, the atrocities. To single out one claim underlined the impact he was having, but the danger to his life felt clear and imminent. Demonstrators seemed excited as a wave of anticipation took hold; word of mouth had leaked news of the celebrity chef's key speaker slot. Meanwhile, Ruth's oratory was commanding the stage, drawing loud applause and cheers. She spoke of uprisings in Newcastle, Sheffield, Bristol, Oxford, and Cambridge; of the rejection of the totalitarian, Stalinist Marxism pursued by Tobin and Connell; called on all decent people to resist. *Make your voices heard.*

'Like *Dominic Diamond*,' she roared, provoking loud cheers, banner waving, chanting.

'A fearless man whose family has been persecuted. Like so many of yours. Brave enough to condemn the wicked antics of government ministers in the luxurious trappings of Chequers. Yes, *Chequers*! A government that claims to act for *The People*; a government that denounces poverty, decadence, and inequality, yet inhabits the grandeur of country palaces, wallowing in the very privilege they disparage. And government ministers who abuse their power, act criminally and *viciously gang rape a poor young girl...* Dominic is now hunted by SNPS thugs, yet is brave enough to appear before you today...*Dominic Diamond.*'

Shorn of his props, left in the safe keeping of Rebecca, he ascended the steps onto the main platform. He stared out at the masses in front of him, quite overwhelmed by the cacophony of noise that welcomed him. He felt humbled by the support, the contrast with how he had come to be regarded by those closest to him was refreshing and a little disorienting. And his own face stared back at him as the crowd waved his picture on hundreds of placards. He gazed around, astonished at the scene, speechless. He looked down at Rebecca and Ruth and Gareth, who smiled encouragement. Dominic gripped the microphone, prompting a fresh wave of cheering, drowning out the opposition emanating from red-shirted Mobilisation activists at the periphery. He stuttered and spoke awkwardly, but it did not seem to matter. Perhaps it underlined his humanity. He gradually found a rhythm, spoke of the atrocities, called for calm and stressed the need for peaceful demonstration. And then he became animated, emotional as he recollected *scarecrow* killings he had witnessed, recalled his friend Bill, then ostentatiously held aloft a Mobilisation banner and a badge, a red M. The crowd fell silent. The factions at the edges of Trafalgar Square became emboldened and the SNPS began to mass; an advance column of riot-gear-clad officers formed; visors lowered, clubs beating on their shields, guns at the ready.

'I was a Labour supporter...'

Boos rang out from some quarters, shuffling and muttering demonstrators signalled disappointment, dismay, disillusionment. The beating on shields increased in tempo and volume. Dominic surveyed the scene, understood the mood change, the growing danger. He silently let the banner flutter from his grasp, landing a few paces away from him. He quickly, urgently reached for and lit a blowtorch, which he held aloft, and then he strode over and set fire to the offending banner, subsequently tramping the ashes under his feet.

Boos transitioned into cheers, which reached a new crescendo, the relief palpable.

'I was advised to buy one of *these*,' he said, referring to his badge. 'As an insurance policy. This is what I say now, what *I* think of *Mobilisation, of the Marxists, of this despotic government*...their cruelty, their evil wickedness. They do *not* act in the interests of *The People...*'

He threw his badge on the ground and followed it by opening and pouring a carrier bag full of red M badges onto the smouldering ashes. The demonstrators roared their approval and suddenly red Ms were pouring onto the stage. Those towards the back turned and threw them in the faces of the red shirts, at the SNPS, shouting their approval of Dominic, their rejection of the government and their agencies of malevolence.

Dominic had hoped the theatricals might be well received but could not have imagined just how enthusiastically. Glancing down at Rebecca he noticed her urgently advancing up the stairs. He reached her at the edge of the stage just as the column of SNPS charged, mowing down demonstrators, cracking heads indiscriminately. The shouts gave way to cries of terror, outrage. Fighting broke out throughout the square, knives were drawn, machetes wielded. Then a shot rang out as the column broke through, nearing the platform. Rebecca grabbed Dominic's hand and ushered him off the stage, taking him into a crowd of heavies who encircled them, pushing their way towards their escape route.

But one of them was felled.

Shot.

The SNPS were close.

Dominic paused, knelt down. First aid was imperative as blood pumped out of his protector; his face ashen. Pain would soon kick in. He needed to apply pressure to stem the bleeding. As a first aider he was more used to knife accidents in the kitchen but knew what to do. Rebecca urged him to get going. Someone else will care for him.

No way.

'He'll die.'

He tore the guy's shirt off him, folded it into a pad, pressing firmly on the wound.

The sounds of the SNPS grew nearer. Time was running out. Another man fell. Mayhem was all around. There could be little doubt as to who their target was.

Suddenly, Gareth appeared and took charge. His medical training trumped Dominic's expertise.

He could leave the victim in expert hands.

*

Having restored his thin disguise, he now had to find his way home: a new home, wherever that may be. Rebecca offered to mind his back, using her small crack team of spotters. Dominic havered. But he needed her help, felt lonely, threatened.

'Which way, Dominic?'

His heart was still hammering in his chest, he was sweating profusely, and he felt sick. If he accepted her help he would be contravening the conventions he and Jo had meticulously agreed. What would she say? But Rebecca took charge, was gently reassuring, quietly insistent. He could certainly benefit from her expert tradecraft. He came to a sudden decision, a no-brainer. They made their way there with stealth, two watching their backs, two scouting ahead. All wore earpieces except him, spoke into their sleeves. Dominic trusted in them; he felt he had little choice. He was relieved to shelter under a protective umbrella, happy to shrug off the burden of responsibility and be reassured by their fastidious attention to detail.

At last they drew close, falling into the shadows, watching, and waiting a hundred yards or so away. He needed to check the signal. As they hunkered down, Dominic and Rebecca acted as a couple: the middle-aged, ginger-haired hippy and a young woman. The closeness was an immediate source of comfort. He squeezed her hand and she turned and smiled at him; it felt genuine.

She put her finger to her ear. All clear. They wandered down the street casually, hand in hand: a couple finding love in a troubled world. A chalked star indicated it was safe to access the dead letter box.

All good.

Dominic now told Rebecca where the message could be located. He trusted her. All in. No turning back now. The message was extricated from under the coving stone. It took an agonising ten minutes to decipher. The team watched with Rebecca alert, her eyes scanning their surroundings. Dominic's heart was racing, his eyebrows in furrowed concentration as beads of perspiration dripped from his forehead like raindrops coursing down a windowpane.

Done.

Shoreditch. Half a mile distant.

Rebecca urged the team to be extra vigilant. As they approached the end of the destination street her hand went to her ear, a flash of concern flitting across her features. She brought him to a sudden halt, taking refuge in a dark entry.

'What's wrong?' he whispered.

'Watchers.'

'Is the candle in the window?'

'Negative. We need to get you out of here…'

'Jo must be in danger. Chalk mark clear, candle not displayed.'

'She may have spotted them too; she might not be in the house.'

'But we don't know. I can't leave.'

He trembled and he was now sweating profusely, could smell his own fear. But he would not desert Jo as he had poor Tim, all those years ago. And the thought strengthened his resolve.

Rebecca looked sharply at him, eyes narrowing, but then squeezed his arm and spoke quietly, urgently into her sleeve. One of her team was instructed to scout the back entrance. Three minutes later the word came. All clear. Lights on. Someone's home. More instructions issued and received. A plan had been hatched.

Rebecca and Dominic made their way stealthily around the back, all senses on full alert.

Still all clear.

The message came in: three figures in the house. Jo had company. As likely as not SNPS. Dominic was instructed to stay back. He did so gratefully, he hoped not cowardly. He was scared but he felt indebted to Jo, committed to her. His whispered words tumbled out haphazardly, but Rebecca nodded her understanding.

Dominic watched from his vantage point as Rebecca and Arty made their way towards the rear door. Arty wielded his tools, secured entry, slipped in.

Rebecca followed on a signal.

Then silence.

Two minutes passed. It seemed much longer. Nothing happened.

Then it kicked off: a feral scream that chilled his blood.

Shots rang out. One…two…three…four. Dominic felt shivers of spine-tingling apprehension surging through his veins, could hear his heart hammering in his chest. Then all quiet again. Tension levels were high grade. A shaft of light briefly illuminated the patio. A figure appeared and urgently beckoned Dominic in. He crept forward in a half crouch. One of the SNPS officers lay in the hall in a crimson puddle, his life ebbing: eyes dulled. Another prostrate figure lay in the lounge. Rebecca was tending Jo, and on realisation that she was stricken, panic bubbled in his throat.

'Just a flesh wound. Nothing too serious,' said Rebecca to Jo. 'It needs cleaning out, a stitch or two. We can sort that out, no problem.'

'What about the watchers outside?' asked Dominic, in a raised voice. He did not realise he was shouting until he was told to quieten down. Jo offered him comforting reassurances, which he gratefully received but they seemed the wrong way round. *Get a grip, man.* First aid was administered, and Dominic took over the ministrations to Jo, pulling a blanket round her as she shivered from the shock.

'A cup of sweet tea perhaps?' said Dominic.

'No time for that,' said Rebecca. 'Kill those lights,' she instructed, shaking her head in disbelief.

'Sorry, ma'am,' mumbled Arty.

'What about the goons outside?' asked Dominic, his brain kicking back in, overriding his shock.

'Dealt with,' said Rebecca.

Moments later, her other team members were at the front door. They pulled in two inert bodies, dumping them in the hall: knocked out, still breathing. Rebecca spoke rapidly to her team: Arty, Bridgit, Sandeep, Stefan. Then she turned to Jo and Dominic.

'We need to move fast. They're likely to have called it in. Just trust in me, do *exactly* as I say…'

They both nodded.

'Good…a safe house has been located overnight and then we'll move to a rural location until all this dies down…'

'I'm not backing out now, not running. Can't. Albert… Rosa…'

'No time for discussion. We talk later. Meantime just do as I say.'

Rebecca was firmly in charge. Steeliness, expertise, leadership all on display. She would brook no argument. They acquiesced, placing themselves in her care.

CHAPTER 32: HEROIC

He woke in the third house in as many days, this time with minders in residence. He and Jo had two bedrooms on the top floor, sharing a bathroom. That would call for some choreographing, but it seemed a trivial anxiety in the midst of everything else. He felt terrible and gazed distractedly into the bathroom mirror, taking in his appearance – stubbled chin, rheumy eyes. And his stomach gurgled a soundtrack of discontent as his head throbbed. How had it come to all this? The experiences, the terror of yesterday's demonstration and last night's drama had haunted him, denying him the good night's sleep his body craved. Sighing, he set about shaving with the kit provided by their protectors. Protectors or jailers? He tried to dismiss the doubts, needing to recover his sunny disposition, get a grip. He reminded himself that Rebecca's protection had allowed him to escape capture. But now he was hunted and felt vulnerable. A long, hot shower helped a little; he emerged later with a towel around his waist and a fragile quest for positivity. Jo was waiting patiently in the corridor with her dressing gown held tightly at her neck, clutching a towel. She muttered a good morning, flashed a fleeting smile, but her eyes told him off for taking so long. *Sorry, Jo.*

He made her as healthy a breakfast as the available groceries would allow by way of apology and they settled down to reflect on the cards dealt to them. But Jo's mood was dark; she was monosyllabic as grief consumed her. He understood and tried to respect her need for space and internal reflection. He had parked his own grief for Bill, but everyone handled these things differently. And being shot was hardly likely to help either. Added to which she was disconsolate at the thwarting of her professional skills, first by Stephanie and now the SNPS.

Having cleared the breakfast things and busied himself with various chores, he sat back down with Jo, who had not moved. She needed time but they did not have that luxury. They had to work out where to from here, and he hoped her strong character would shine through.

'Are you okay about all this? Taking refuge under Rebecca's wing?' asked Dominic. He asked gently, scanning her for a reaction. Had he made a serious error of judgement? He recognised that he had been on his knees emotionally and physically. And scared. Perhaps it had been a moment of weakness. Had he been too ready to accept the extended hand of help?

'It's done now. And all my best attempts have failed. I've got to face up to that. You obviously trust Rebecca. We'll find out very soon, I guess.'

'Surely you don't think...'

'Let's see if we're still around tomorrow... We should tune into the news with NFN, I suppose.'

'If we must...'

Rebecca's team had provided for most of their basic needs: toiletries, shaving kit, food. And a couple of bottles of wine, a bottle of whisky he was pleased to see. And a PC. The Wi-Fi had been disabled; 4G was good and they were assured it posed no security risk: special measures installed. MI5 at work? He hoped so.

They watched the podcast from last night. It seemed the dangers that GB now represented was a major focus internationally. The Europeans and Americans were desperate for the Marxist contagion to be snuffed out. Brussels reported that the British contributions had ceased, criticising the government for their abuse of the principles underpinning the EU: of open borders, freedom of the movement of goods, capital, and people. The inference was that expulsion was inevitable unless change was rapidly forthcoming. The French president was blunter, calling for GB's ejection. The American president was even more damning, spelling out in plain language that GB was becoming an international pariah state. The USA was cutting all trade links, imposing sanctions; it berated Tobin and Connell for the erosion of the parliamentary democratic model of government, the ostracisation of the royal family, the absurd branding of Norris Jinks as a terrorist, the assault on individual freedoms and basic human rights. The statement finished on a hostile note with thinly veiled threats of military intervention.

'Wow! She didn't pull her punches...'

'Unlike the Eurocrats of Brussels,' said Rebecca, joining them. 'How's the wound, Jo? Feeling a bit groggy today?'

'I'm fine.'

Jo spoke quietly and cast Rebecca a wary look.

'I've bad news for you. Sorry. One of your team was feeding information to Stephanie. It seems she's been doing this from early doors. Whether she was also informing the SNPS or whether they knew of your whereabouts courtesy of Stephanie, or just found you from their own efforts, we don't know.'

'Who the hell was it?' Her fury quickly replaced her lassitude.

Dominic tried to reassure her. 'Don't blame yourself. The state permeates every walk of life these days, incentivising people to snitch.' Mobilisation eyes and ears were everywhere. But Jo was not up for being placated.

'Amelia...' said Rebecca.

'Take me to her.'

'She's been dealt with.'

'And Stephanie?' demanded Jo. A quiet forbidding rage seemed to grow from within, bubbling to the surface, just about held under control.

'Let's not go there.'

'Yes, let's.' The sentiment was blunt, the tone caustic.

'Hey, don't get all aggressive with me. Having saved your skin, you should be grateful. We should focus on our current plight and the next steps,' said Rebecca.

'Really? Saved for good...or for some other purpose by you lot playing cat and mouse, capture suspended for some greater purpose? What's your game? And Stephanie's? Lovers or enemies or partners in crime, eh? You still owe me an explanation...'

'Not now.'

Dominic turned from one to the other as if watching a game at Wimbledon, a sharp rally at close quarters by two unyielding competitors.

'And when are *you* going to pipe up?' asked Jo of Dominic; dander up and turning her fire on a recalcitrant ball boy.

'Err...can't believe Stephanie would...could possibly...'

'Oh, for God's sake man! One poke and she has you still at the doe-eyed little boy stage even after all...after all this...bloody grow up.' The eruption was violent, magma and debris raining down on him. Dominic stared at her. A Jo he had not seen before. The explosion was of Rosa proportions.

'Jo...' said Dominic. She waved her hand. Dismissed. But he ploughed on, turning his focus on Rebecca. 'We do need to know where we stand with you, Rebecca. You've done a lot, risked much, but our lives are on the line here. We want to believe in you, we want to trust you, but you have to level with us.'

Rebecca looked at them warily and seemed to be weighing up her options. Or perhaps just working out how much to share, calculating the minimum she might get away with.

'*Okay*. Perhaps it's time...'

'Really? Are the lesbian play-acts to be cast aside too?' said Dominic. The tone was strong, but the voice wavered. He sighed internally. Not made for conflict.

Rebecca sat back and folded her arms. Silence stretched out, a pause in hostilities was welcome but he had ill-judged the intervention. She seemed to be clamming up again. Dominic breathed deeply, wiping moist hands on his trousers. Rebecca scowled at him. Jo looked heavenwards.

'What about Jinks?' asked Jo, changing tack.

'Okay, okay. We've opened a backchannel to him, the message that Stephanie may not be a trustworthy source conveyed. Mind you, I'm not sure how he'll respond. It seems our Norris was another in a long line of boys under her spell.'

Dominic coloured, suddenly finding his hands worthy of close scrutiny as the two of them looked in his direction.

'MI5?' asked Jo. 'There was that picture of Jinks on the boat with Neil Foster: ex-MI5 and formerly SAS?'

'Yes?'

'As well as Rupert Twigg, the chairman of the Conservative Party, and Leonard Staveley, the head of FF, there was also a certain Serena Murphy...'

'Your point being?' said Rebecca.

'Oh, for goodness' sake. It's like pulling hen's teeth.'

'Humour me.'

'*Please*,' said Dominic.

Rebecca ignored him; Jo cast a scathing squint.

'Serena Murphy's a member of the USA intelligence services. If she was with Jinks, then any backchannel would be through her. It seems obvious that the only route back to GB and any rescue mission will be led by the Americans.'

'Supposition – but okay. Your point?' said Rebecca.

'Are you being deliberately obtuse?'

'Not sure I get it either, Jo, to be fair,' said Dominic.

Again ignored.

'Serena equals CIA, which equals connivance with MI6...not MI5 if effective liaison and rescue missions are afoot. *But* you're in MI5.' Turning to Dominic she further explained as if to a child, 'MI5 is all about domestic intelligence, MI6 foreign intelligence; FBI and CIA are the equivalents in the USA.'

'I've never claimed to be in either. Anyways, the two reputedly co-operate rather better these days. So they say. But who knows?' said Rebecca, flashing a smile at her assailant.

'And you're calling this levelling with us. *Really?* You're just spinning us another yarn, aren't you?' said Jo.

Rebecca sighed. 'You *have* to trust me. You've no one else to turn to. Christ knows I could have done you harm on numerous occasions had I been so minded. You know that. *Dominic* knows that. That's why he trusts me instinctively...' She stopped and looked at Dominic, who nodded silently, bowing his head, not daring to look at Jo.

'But give us good solid reasons to entrust you with our lives, Rebecca. Something more than gut reaction. Oh, there've been occasions you've been, well, kind, shown compassion in the midst of... I *do* believe in you. But people tell me I'm too optimistic, too trusting, gullible even. Give us more. Really level with us. Jo deserves that. *Please*, Rebecca,' said Dominic quietly. His plea sounded weak to his own ears, but it was heartfelt.

For a brief moment Rebecca's blue eyes softened.

'You forget the tip-offs, the rescues. Last night! How can you dismiss that as clear evidence? If you want hard and fast that's where you might look, Dominic. But you have to make your own minds up. Frankly, I'm sick and tired of all this. We've been here before. As to intelligence services...all I'll say is that you can be confident the British and American services are in touch; plans are afoot. I can't say more than that and it's not fair of you to ask me to do so.'

Jo nodded and sat back. Had Rebecca's outburst convinced her? It had Dominic. It all made eminently good sense to him.

'And what about Stephanie?' asked Dominic.

'Status quo.'

'You're still *living* together? After all this? Won't she smell a rat with Amelia's disappearance?'

'I'm biding my time. She trusts me every bit as much as I trust her...' Rebecca said.

'And you still share the same bed? How...'

'Nothing to set your pulse racing, Dom. Mostly bed socks, bedtime reading, Bovril...' said Rebecca, smiling softly, the injection of weak humour to ease the tension perhaps. 'She has her people follow me. I reciprocate. And as for Amelia, she'll have been reporting to the head of Steph's team. Our Stephanie never bloodies her hands – she leaves the details to others.'

'Sounds a bloody dangerous game to me,' said Dominic.

Rebecca stared back at him with fathomless eyes. They seemed to have run out of words, exhausted their appetite for attack and parry and counterattack. And Dominic at least was convinced that true words had been spoken. He knew that Jo was hurting, but he was fairly confident she would acknowledge the lengths to which Rebecca had gone to secure their safety, that their causes were aligned even if there was much they still did not understand.

'Let's catch up with the news,' said Jo, composure restored.

They discussed the NFN news clips. Rebecca was confident the Americans and Jinks would mount a rescue. She insisted that the FF leader's hand could also be detected in the synchronised resistance attacks on the SNPS and the support of PAD demonstrations. She was vehement in her insistence that the reality peddled by Tobin and Connell was not the experience of most in the country. But the BBC told a wholly different story. They watched in stunned silence at the replaying of three Mobilisation rallies held at Wembley and the Olympic Stadium in London and Old Trafford in Manchester. All held on the same day, neatly choreographed. A sea of grey and red as Mobilisation activists marched in their red shirts, holding flags proclaiming the new era's adopted slogan: *equality, freedom, justice*. The SNPS paraded in their grey tunics with red flags on their lapels, bright red Ms sown into the left breast of uniforms, baseball-style red caps, the M on the front, this time in black. Thunderous applause, flag waving, cheering of tens of thousands that crammed the stadia and those outside thronging the streets, red Ms proudly displayed in welcoming the forces. Banners in the stadiums variously proclaiming class warfare, *the rise of the proletariat, the end of capitalism*. Loud martial music with renditions of "The Red Flag" sung gustily before each speech. Ranks of police also marched, interspersed with the SNPS and units of the military, Mobilisation activists bringing up the rear. Gun salutes resounded from the Tower of London and Hyde Park, shown on large screens: the traditional twenty-one guns at both venues followed by a pause, and then another twenty, defying the convention that only salutes from the Royal Parks should fire the extra salvos. But this now marked the assent of the Marxist Labour Party to power on 20th November 2019. It also seemed to underline the passing of the royal family in GB. In Wembley, Connell delivered an impassioned, rousing speech; Tobin at the Olympic Stadium; Carstairs, an orator of note rising quickly through the ranks, took centre stage at Old Trafford. Keynote speeches arrogated to the government social injustices righted, homelessness and poverty eradicated, the fair distribution of wealth. Assembled crowds whipped into a frenzy took the claims at face value. The police on horseback put on a display at Wembley, the Household Cavalry at the Olympic Stadium, and the Light Dragoons at Old Trafford...

'Unbelievable,' said Dominic.

'I've had enough of this bilge,' Jo said, turning to her PC for the various NFN podcasts.

'Oh, look. You feature again, Dom. Crikey...'

She turned the PC towards him, Rebecca looking over their shoulders. Together they watched footage of the demonstration in Trafalgar Square; of Dominic's speech; of the denunciation of Mobilisation and the casting aside of the red Ms. And then of the SNPS charge, and the attempt to apprehend Dominic; knives wielded, machetes too, a gruesome image of a severed limb; shots rang out and people collapsed, blood spilt as Dominic knelt to attend to the felling of a security guard. The camera swung to the charging SNPS officers in full riot gear, visors down, batons drawn. A snatch squad with a clear objective: Dominic Diamond. Some brandished guns, shots resounding. Still Dominic knelt and attended his wounded charge. The camera swung from Dominic's attentions to the advancing guards: back and forth. The reporter pointed out the selfless act to save a fellow human being, portraying him as heroic. Then Gareth relieved Dominic but he had not known then what he now witnessed: the consultant anaesthesiologist had been attacked, beaten with a club, taken into custody.

He stared open-mouthed, dumbfounded.

'Hundreds of thousands of hits, Dom. And your own podcast streamed millions of times. Here. Look here,' Jo said. Her voice was now energised. Clips were shown of SNPS officers being showered with red Ms from angry crowds in all the major cities throughout GB. It was becoming as much a symbol of freedom and peace as the dove; it was even compared to the defiance of the Churchillian V. A symbolic demonstration of opposition taken up across the country. He flashed a weak smile, rubbing his truncated finger.

'Are you okay? You should be proud. Why the glum face?' she asked.

'Where'd you want me to start? Life's reduced to survival. It's tribal warfare. And what am I to be so proud of? It's supposed to be all about one thing: my family. Oh, I know that's selfish. Weak. Inadequate. And I'm also picking up the cudgels for people like Bill and Ellie and your Oliver. But I'm no closer to Albert or Juan or Rosa. I've not spoken to Rosa for ages. I *need* to speak to her. Can't you help, Rebecca? We've no phones left, can no longer risk internet cafés. We just slink here, scuttling around like rats in a sewer...'

'I must press on, guys. Sorry,' said Rebecca, looking down at them. 'I'll see what I can do on the comms front, Dom. I'll sort something out. As to your lads, let me enquire again. Stephanie also volunteered intelligence about some rescue plan for Albert. Juan is thought to be involved in that, although it sounded like idle speculation to me. No details to latch onto, but that's Steph for you. It might be a smokescreen. Hang in there. And stay put. It's getting more and more dangerous for you. Please, just lie low. I must get on. See you later.'

Dominic looked up at her with hangdog eyes; an errant, silent tear slid down the side of his nose.

'We'll get you through this, cheer up. I'll definitely sort the comms issue out. Promise,' she said, with which she squeezed his arm, bent down and kissed him lightly on his cheek.

'And you both really can trust me. I'd never sell you out, Dom.'

CHAPTER 33: FLIGHT

Dominic had grabbed a few hours' rest until roused gently by Rebecca, one of her team members waking Jo with a rap on her door at the witching hour, an hour past midnight. Curfew was to be breached to take advantage of the cover of darkness. Over the last few days watchers had been seen in the area along with too many SNPS search patrols. It was only a matter of time before the dreaded early morning knock, the heavy boots on the stairs: the prelude to disappearances, beatings, trumped-up charges, correction centres. Even *scarecrowing*. And Dominic was scoring too many hits; his actions replicated by FF groups and PAD at demonstrations throughout the country. The government had put a reward on his head and in these straitened times that was likely to prove too much to resist for too many. Government ministers denounced his actions as those of a terrorist, an enemy of the state: a traitor. The facts were bent into a shape more conducive to the propaganda of Connell as her oratory whipped government supporters into a frenzy at the various rallies attended by loyal, baying activists. The message resonated with many who were benefiting from the redistribution of wealth: crude measures designed to curry favour with the poor and disadvantaged but resulting in the leaching of support from the middle classes and the left-wing-inclined intelligentsia.

Few streetlights remained in London these days, which was helping them, as was the cloud cover. Perhaps the Gods were with them, and Dominic muttered a private prayer to his. The route had been carefully planned, scouts to the front and the rear, earpieces worn. The modus operandi was becoming familiar. They took two hours to navigate the streets and alleys of Shoreditch and Whitechapel, occasionally hunkering down; a grandstand view as a SNPS snatch squad hammered down a victim's door, emerging minutes later with their victim. The wielding of the ubiquitous club snuffed out any remnants of protest as his bloodied and bowed body was unceremoniously bundled into the waiting van, leaving his wife and daughter wailing on the doorstep. Heart-breaking. Pressing on they reached the Thames just under Tower Bridge next to the Tower Hotel, long since transformed into a hospice for the down and outs.

Rebecca signalled them forwards.

'She's got to be kidding,' exclaimed Jo, spotting the waiting canoes.

'It's too obvious. Someone will see us...' whispered Dominic sharply, in Rebecca's ear.

'Audacious I grant you but trust us. It'll work. We stay close to the bridge; the shadows provide cover. Look around you. No one.'

It seemed churlish to point to the drunk slurping from a bottle, but if he was undercover it was a hell of an act. All was quiet – even the lights on Tower Bridge were sparse and there was no river traffic. Nothing was crossing the bridge either.

'Come on, Jo. I'm sure it'll be fine.' Mr Micawber made a fleeting return. But he wished he could quell those butterflies. And his bowels churned too, pelvic muscles flexing defensively.

They breathed in deeply, ventured forwards and stepped gingerly into their respective canoes. Two team members were in each, both armed. Rebecca scouted ahead with two others. All good. Time to go.

Suddenly Rebecca waved her arm; take cover.

Then Dominic heard it. The deep throb of an engine. A river-patrol. Their minders pulled their canoes deeper into the shadows. Fear beat wildly in Dominic's heart, his hands growing clammy despite the chill of the night. Then a pool of light illuminated the river. A searchlight. Had they been set up? Had someone informed on them? He refused to believe Rebecca had led them into a trap. She would not do that. The launch drew closer. It was inevitable they would be seen. This was it. The game was up. No more than twenty feet or so away now although the light shone upriver, away from them. A hiss of static, followed by muffled voices. What now? Had they been spotted by someone on the banks? Their guards had their guns at the ready; he heard safety catches being slipped off. Is this what it had come to? A gun battle on the Thames? The point at which his luck finally ran out.

Suddenly the motors roared, and the launch sped under the main span of Tower Bridge. Summoned to an urgent matter perhaps. Rebecca signalled for them to stay still, duck down. Soon another police launch hove into view, speeding after the first patrol boat.

Another two minutes of tense inactivity followed. Safety catches had been restored; guns relaxed. Dominic concentrated intently trying to pick up any tell-tale sign that danger approached and muttered a silent prayer. A religious man whose belief had been shaken by recent events, now returning to pray for divine protection; give God a final chance to prove Himself. At last they moved on and made the far bank safely, navigating the landing and subsequently scuttling their canoes. Was that strictly necessary? Apparently so, as he watched the last disappear under the inky surface.

Rebecca scampered off with two of her team, soon returning to guide Dominic and Jo to a waiting car. An electric car. Black. Fully charged? Of course. At least it had the merits of silence as they picked their way through the back streets of south London, steering clear of the main arterial routes, no headlights. This seemed a risky mode of transport. A bold breaching of curfew but after less than an hour they glided into a back street near Orpington and turned into a garage. The doors were closed. This was where they were to hole up until first light before resuming their journey. Nerves were frayed, adrenalin still pumped, and minds were alert, making sleep nigh on impossible. But at least it felt a little safer, the respite providing a strand of comfort.

They waited until mid-morning, settling for a coffee from a flask that one of Rebecca's minders had brought with them. And chocolate biscuits, a rare treat. Natural needs were catered for by a squalid, barely functioning toilet in the corner and a grimy hand basin. At last it was time to move on and they piled into the car. This part of southwest London was less targeted by SNPS, but there were no guarantees, so alert levels remained high, tension saturating Dominic's whole being, causing a banging headache. But this part of the journey passed without incident, and they eventually drew up at their new destination near Plumpton, a small village on the edge of the South Downs.

Their ancient cottage was in a rural area beyond the village, surrounded by fields and trees. A derelict chapel stood adjacent, and piles of stone amidst the foliage suggested the site of a hamlet in years gone by. Dominic and Jo were assured of the safety of their new temporary abode but asked to stay within the confines of the house and the rear garden, which looked up the South Downs Scarp.

Alongside the old church, a smattering of yellow primroses adorned the hillside, resembling scattered confetti blown on the wind. A skein of geese flew in formation, honking their progress noisily. Sighting a scarecrow in the neighbouring field brought a momentary jolt of terror but it was just doing its job, albeit ineffectively as a jackdaw perched on the straw hat, others pecking at its feet. Rebecca soon joined Dominic and Jo and sat on the remnants of a dilapidated stone wall, the demarcation between terrace and a cottage garden, now melding into one overgrown tumble of brambles and weeds. She brought news. PC all set up. No Wi-Fi. *Is 4G any good in this remote location?* It is. A consideration in identifying this as a safe house, they were assured.

CHAPTER 34: ROSA

Rebecca followed them into the lounge and fiddled with her PC. She told Dominic he needed to watch. 'Look at this clip. It's a podcast to be released at prime time, a special preview for you.'

'What now?'

'*Rosa.*'

'Oh, God. It's not...'

'No,' she said, blue eyes sparkling.

'I'll leave you to watch alone, Dom,' said Jo, reaching for his hand.

'Please don't. Come on, let's watch it together. You too, Rebecca. And thank you. I'm sorry about...' Dominic looked encouragingly towards Jo, hoping she would join him in apology, but her expression was blank.

Dominic and Jo perched on a small sofa. *Ready?* Ready. The podcast began with a familiar, melodic voice: Ronald of NFN, as avuncular and charming as ever in his casual, slightly dishevelled attire. It was to be another in the series about known figures with real news to relay: Rosa a celebrity by association. And there she was. Dominic's heart lurched. It had been much too long. It brought into sharp focus just how much he missed her; he struggled to function properly, misfiring all too frequently. Where was she speaking from? And why? What news was she about to impart? Oh my goodness, what's happened? He looked at Rebecca, his angst transmitting to her as she tried to reassure him. 'It's okay, Dom. Really.'

And then he took in the other two women sitting with her: Ellie, and presumably Ellie's mum, Geraldine.

And suddenly he knew.

Rosa, the human dynamo, had brought them together by sheer force of personality.

The Chequers claims by Dominic were reprised; particulars were confirmed to the best of Rosa's knowledge, a few details added. At last the lens focused on Ellie, whose hands were held firmly by the women who flanked her. She seemed frail, thinner than he recalled. Her voice was weak, the wavering conveying her nerves.

'How are you?' asked Ronald gently.

'I'm fine.'

'We're all so sorry. Are you recovering? Can you tell us what you feel?'

'Shame, deep shame.' Ellie pulled her hands free of her protectors. She covered her face with them, as if hiding from the world. Her mum offered gentle reassurance. Rosa placed a protective arm around her shoulders. Gradually, she recovered some self-control to focus on Ronald. Her eyes were wide, they seemed to be imploring him...but to do what? Who could guess at her suffering let alone what was flying through her mind?

'I meant what do you think of the men who...'

'*Mierda!*' interrupted Rosa with force. '*My Goddd* the poor girl's been through so much. But when I catch up with these...these *bastards*... I'll...'

'Ellie, did Dominic, your boyfriend's dad – the celebrity chef Dominic Diamond – try to intervene? Or his colleague, Bill? Were you aware of any of that?'

'Not really except for a scuffle but there was so much laughter... Why did they think it was funny? Why were they *laughing*? I don't understand. Why wouldn't they stop? My fault I realise...'

'It's many things, Ellie, but it was most certainly *not* your fault. The shame is with these men. You did *nothing* wrong.' Ronald spoke quietly in soothing tones and leant forwards as if to reach out to her. Ellie shrank back, her eyes brimming and spilling. She wiped tears away with a flourish of her sleeve, suddenly angry.

'I should never have put myself in danger. I was stupid, naïve, crazy,' she blurted out, her anger directed inwardly. Then she was suddenly plaintive. 'But honestly, I'd no idea. Who could have thought...who could possibly do such things...why...' She crumpled.

It was clear that she could not go on and her mum helped Ellie out. Just before Geraldine disappeared off camera she said to Rosa, 'Tell them. Please tell them.'

'Rosa, let Ellie know how brave we all think she is, how much we appreciate her telling her story if you will. A harrowing experience, traumatic to hear, shocking to see her pain. Our hearts go out to her… But do you have something else to tell our listeners? What was Geraldine referring to?'

Rosa dried her eyes and snorted into a handkerchief.

Dominic allowed himself the briefest glimmer of a smile. Ever the loud, vibrant Latin temperament; whatever Rosa did she did noisily, dramatically.

'Honest to *Goddds*, I can't *belieeeve* this. What's happening to this world? Why can't people just live and let live? The evil…'

'Please tell us what Ellie's mum wanted you to say,' Ronald said.

'At first her mum and dad couldn't believe what had happened, couldn't comprehend. They felt all the emotions: shame, anger, guilt, shock. Geraldine wanted me to tell you they quickly became sorry for not having acted sooner, not having provided the loving parental support the poor girl so desperately needed. Then they became the subject of intimidation. My *Goddd* – those people!'

'Yes, Rosa, the intimidation. What form did that take?'

'The bastards applied, how you say, physiological?'

'Psychological?'

'Yes. On her dad especially, whose job was in the civil service. Then came the threats. Then a visit in the dead of the night. SNPS. Henry was beaten and dragged away; Geraldine roughed up. Would you believe that two of them even pushed her back on the bed, tore off her nightie, unbelted and unzipped, asked her if she wanted some of what her daughter had got? Can you believe that? *Animals.* They just laughed at her terror. Can you *imagine* the horror?'

'And Henry? Where is he now?'

'*Dead*! The bastards, they *keeell* him…strung him up like a dog… *scarecrowed* him. Hung from the lamppost at the end of the street. Their very own street! I can't—'

'And nor can any sane, reasonable human being, Rosa,' said Ronald, quickly.

Rosa flung herself back, throwing her arms in the air, before falling silent. Ronald allowed the silence to convey the enormity of what Ellie's family had endured, before asking if Rosa had a personal message for her husband.

Dominic sat up in disbelief. A message for him? He looked first to Jo and then to Rebecca.

'I saw your podcast about Chequers, Dom. And the PAD demonstration. What you did. You are hero. *My* hero. God knows you're a sweet, gentle man, not a born warrior. But I'm proud beyond words. Albert and Juan will also be proud. Dominic, what can I say? I want to come home. I *hate* what GB has become but home is where *you* are... I'm coming home.'

She looked into the camera intently and nodded her head slowly, now completely in control of her emotions. 'I'm coming home.'

Dominic stared open-mouthed. He felt a swell of emotion rise within, a tidal wave; it was what he most wanted to hear. *Needed* to hear. His face coloured, his heart raced, and butterflies fluttered in his stomach as they had on that very first date with her. He suddenly felt alive. Very alive. Now he had an imperative to stay alive.

'And do you remember our special anniversary, Dominic? As others celebrate birthdays, anniversaries, first dates...ours is a bit different. *Special.* It's today. Have you remembered? Trust me, honest to *Goddds*, I'll remind you what that's all about when I get back. I love you. I *realllly* love you. Keep safe...'

Jo smiled at Dominic and wiped his eyes, Rebecca leant into him, and her lips brushed his wet cheek before folding him into her arms.

Rebecca re-joined them in the lounge, having taken calls on her mobile, a special mobile, untraceable she had assured them. News of Juan.

'I promised you both the other day I'd level with you. The good news is that Juan's safe and well—'

'Where, how do you know, can I see him?'

'He's not here... I know, I know...please be patient... He's part of FF, one of their leaders. He's a crack shot, he's brave and he's determined to free his brother. He's holed up in the north and will attempt to free Albert with our backup... There's a huge effort going into the co-ordination of FF activities with American support...financial, logistical, firepower. Jinks is behind this with the American president staunchly supportive. They've established a chain of command in the FF with links to the leaders of PAD, all resistance directed strategically. I need hardly tell you that all this is top secret. There are many harrowing stories and many people who have been moved into the rehab or correction centres...'

'But why? Why free Albert? And why help Juan?'

'It's not just Juan...it's many like him freeing hundreds of Alberts,' said Rebecca.

'There's more to it than that. This would happen anyway,' said Jo. Her jaw was set, and her eyes blazed. It was as if she sensed this was the time to elicit the full picture. 'Why help Dominic and his lads at all? Why spend all this time on us when there's so much else going on?' She still seemed to be smouldering from the earlier exchange, thought Dominic, who frowned his annoyance at her interruption.

'Jo—' began Dominic before Rebecca spoke over him.

'No. It's okay.' Rebecca turned away from Jo and fixed her gaze on Dominic. 'Look, your family's experience isn't unique. We all know that. But none has captured the public's imagination or had remotely the publicity you and Albert have. We see you as part of the focused effort to relieve our country of its despotic rulers in the name of democracy, decency, dignity. Your whole story: you and Albert and Chequers and Ellie…your podcasts… your involvement at PAD demos…millions of hits. This is all totemic.'

Dominic stared at her.

Rebecca turned her focus back to Jo and said, 'The messaging's enhanced with Dominic on board. It fits the narrative Jinks is using to help counter the government's hype: NFN is part of the information assault to neutralise the propaganda. You must see that?… And anyway…' Rebecca paused and looked sharply at Dominic, their eyes locking.

'Yes?' said Dominic.

'I owe you my life… I vowed I'd never forget that moment, Dom. Swore I'd always be there for you and, well, you deserve a break and if I can help persuade a few people of the merits of having you on board…'

However seductive it was to lose himself in that period of his past, what was important now was his lads and Rosa. He saw that with crystal clarity, felt it with all his being.

'You keep saying *we*. Who's "*we*"? And Juan's role in all this? Can I see him?' asked Dominic.

'Multiple attacks are planned in different locations simultaneously. The aim is to disrupt and divert the government's attention and stretch their resources whilst also bolstering the public's confidence that this regime's days are numbered. As part of this, the FF are mounting attacks on the various centres daisy-chained across the Northern Pennines and Welsh mountains. You should be proud of him, Dominic… I know, I know… I don't have the precise timings or the details, but I'm heading up there to be part of the extraction process following the attacks. I leave tomorrow morning.'

'I'm coming with you,' said Dominic.

'Me too,' chorused Jo.

'I thought you'd say that. This is dangerous. Stephanie seems to know something's afoot, so we have to assume the SNPS are on alert. But their inherent arrogance may play in our favour. Good planning, a bold strategy will pay dividends. At least that's the theory. Mind you, it's perilous. Your lives may be at risk…many lives are at risk.'

'A bit like being shot at, you mean, or beaten up or chased across London?' said Jo.

'I'm in… End of,' said Dominic.

'As to the political and international dimensions, let's tune in to this…' Rebecca showed them a WhatsApp alert: *The President of the USA and Norris Jinks to broadcast across all social media channels and satellite television across GB, the EU and USA.*

'They'll jam it, won't they, as they did previously?' said Jo.

'They may be able to pull the plug on terrestrial television, but I don't see how they can block Sky News, CNN and all the others. And we know they've tried to disrupt GB access to the internet but that hasn't worked particularly well. They even released a virus to disable smart phones, but the technology companies were ready for that. It knocked a few platforms out for a few weeks, disabled older phones and interrupted some social media channels for a few days,' said Rebecca.

'Did they? Crikey, we have been out of touch, haven't we? Interesting that you know all this stuff.'

Rebecca smiled at Dominic, staying tight-lipped.

I reach out to all American citizens, to our European friends and in particular I speak to the citizens of GB with whom we have a treasured special relationship. You are in our thoughts; it is your government we have a quarrel with. We will stand by the British people. I'm joined today by two special guests.

The camera lens widened to take in the distinctive figure of Norris Jinks, his trademark mop of unruly hair ruffled by his own hands as he spoke into the camera. Then back onto the President.

And now to my extra special guests…

This time the location was an altogether more regal setting as the camera revealed HRH Prince William and Catherine, the Duke and Duchess of Cambridge, with Prince Harry and Meghan, the Duke and Duchess of Sussex. The grouping seemed to underline the American and British special relationship, cemented by royal linkage. William took centre stage and spoke calmly into the camera, a polished performer these days, he, and Catherine – Kate – being popular figures. Harry and Meghan were more controversial but had clearly put old disagreements aside in an impressive, emotional show of unity and allegiance to the monarch.

We have a message from Her Majesty the Queen and the entire royal family...

The messages were delivered in their differing styles, Ashley Jackson's was an emotional rendition beloved of Americans, a bit sweet and sickly to British ears; William spoke quietly in the understated way characteristic of the royal family and Jinks was upbeat, optimistic, his words suffused with lashings of charisma and charm: the deprivations and monstrosities of the Marxist government of Tobin and Connell would soon be consigned to history, normal democratic government would be restored, the monarchy would return and traditional parliamentary democracy would resume. All that was great about Great Britain would be restored and the Union would be resurrected. Once more the British people would stand proud and hold their heads up in the world after this harmful blip in a proud history. Ashley Jackson, the proud forty-sixth American president and the first woman to secure that office, concluded the broadcast:

To Tobin and Connell I have a simple message: it's not too late. Stand aside. To the British people we say this: America will not forget you, we will be there for you in your hour of need. Your deprivations will be relieved, freedoms restored. Those of you who've been terrorised into supporting this foul, odious regime must now find the courage to denounce the Marxists, the SNPS, the red-shirted activists of Mobilisation. You have little time before the day of reckoning. Make sure you end up on the right side. America stands shoulder to shoulder with the royal family, with Norris Jinks, with the British people. Democracy and freedom will win out. You will be liberated – and that is an American promise! Goodnight and God bless.

CHAPTER 35: NORTH

They rendezvoused at a farm on the outskirts of Plumpton where their transport was awaiting them: a lorry containing a cargo of mountain bikes, destination Carlisle. Rebecca climbed up and led them along a corridor of crates, at the end of which was a false compartment spanning the width of the lorry, with a concealed doorway. They ventured in and found the floor covered with mattresses, supplies of blankets, bottles of water, fizzy drinks, snacks, and sandwiches. They each carried a backpack with a change of clothes and bare essentials.

'We leave in an hour. We plan to hole up at a motorway services area in Cheshire. Should arrive at our destination around lunchtime tomorrow.'

'Stopping's dangerous isn't it? Won't we be trapped if rumbled?' asked Dominic.

'More dangerous to proceed beyond the permitted hours of driving. Or to break curfew. We play it cool. The paperwork's all legit, this is all perfectly usual for HGV drivers. The driver's been vetted, entirely trustworthy with an HGV licence and documentation for delivery to a warehouse in Carlisle. There are spot checks in motorway service areas these days and we may encounter them elsewhere, but the cargo is as described on the paperwork. Should be a doddle.'

'And if rumbled?' asked Jo.

'We've got firepower.' Rebecca nodded to a stash in the corner: binoculars, pistols, silencers, ammunition, and commando knives. 'I'll give you instructions on stripping down, cleaning, arming as we head north.'

'A bit like this, you mean?' said Jo, taking a pistol and demonstrating her prowess in a blur of movement.

'Impressive. Full of surprises, aren't you, Jo? Could even get to like you!'

'Steady now…'

'And if it comes to the worst, we've got these little beauties.' Rebecca brandished three grenades. 'You okay, Dom?'

'This is just not my style, girls. Not sure I can wield one of those things. You'd both be in mortal danger. Friendly fire and all that.'

'I'm afraid you may have no choice. Sorry. Decision time. Can't take a passenger. It's not only your life that'll be imperilled if you refuse to defend yourself – we all have to mind each other's back. What's it to be?' Rebecca's steeliness to the fore, combat mode engaged. But Dominic didn't think he had such an option in his personal armoury.

'Man up, Dom,' said Jo. She spoke quietly but firmly. Tough love.

'And we also have an escape route,' said Rebecca. 'Only to be used in extremis. It's tight. We could burn ourselves as it's close to the exhaust system…' There was a trap door towards one side, and she showed them how it worked. It looked more than tight but they were all slim.

Their driver appeared at the door. 'All set?'

'Are we, Dom?'

Pause. A nod of the head.

'Let's go.'

The journey passed through two check points; tense moments as officials probed destination and cargo, the validity of the paperwork. It all passed muster and they relaxed as the lorry resumed its journey, trundling north on the M42 on to the M6. Later they drew into the motorway services area in Knutsford and the lorry came to a halt, having first refuelled. It was early evening, so too much time to burn but they resolved to stay within the safe confines of their secret compartment. Time for a sandwich and a drink. All quiet. Rebecca briefed them as to the itinerary for tomorrow.

'We set off around seven and head up the M6 towards Carlisle. We'll veer off the M6 briefly for our drop-off, lightening the cargo of a few mountain bikes. I hope you know how to ride. We have an onward journey to a remote location.'

'And the lorry?' asked Jo.

'It'll head off to Carlisle, offload and then call in at another depot to load more freight for a return journey.'

'Where *specifically* are we headed? Will anyone be there? What happens *next*?' asked Dominic.

Rebecca stared blankly at him.

'She's drip feeding us, Dom, on a strictly need-to-know basis.'

'Let's get some rest,' said Rebecca, plugging her earphones into a device and tuning in. Sighing, Jo did similarly. Dominic decided he was content with being spoon fed. Best not to get ahead of ourselves. Instead, he sat and sipped at a drink and replayed the Rosa video in his head. It had been a much-desired revelation, but suddenly he felt more vulnerable with more reason to live. And the dread of being forced into a gun battle was balanced only by the thought of being reunited with Juan. Dare he hope that the rescue of Albert could be pulled off? And how soon before he and Rosa could rediscover each other?

As the lorry slowed, Rebecca said, 'We need to be on our guard here. As we disembark, we'll be exposed. Hopefully, it'll be okay. It's an isolated area. But it only takes one SNPS patrol, an over-zealous police officer or a passing informer prepared to trade our safety for brownie points... Weapons to be readied. Okay, Dom?'

'Okay... I think.'

The signal came, a gentle tap on the side followed by the sound of the rear doors opening.

Stay tight.

Brace.

Be ready for the unexpected.

He heard the manhandling of the cargo, footsteps, and then a rap on the panel: the coded rap. It should be fine, should be safe. Warily, Dominic went first. The women would provide the backup. They obviously hadn't fancied him firing from the rear. He respected the wisdom of that call, trying to relax the chill fingers of fear closing around his heart. He certainly did not want to pull a trigger. He was not sure he could.

All clear.

He breathed out, and his heartbeat returned to some sort of stressed normality. They swiftly extricated themselves and stretched. Having been cooped up for over twenty-four hours they were stiff, muscles aching. After the stuffy air of the lorry's compartment from three people living in close proximity the fresh air was bracing and welcome. Rebecca used the binoculars to survey their surroundings. Nothing much to see, just moorland and sheep, she reported. Jo did similarly. Dominic trusted them and took the time to recover his composure. Five bikes were unloaded, and they made the necessary adjustments.

'Why five?' asked Dominic.

'We need to stash two of them. The others will join us later.'

Dominic and the driver climbed over the wall with the bikes, ran up the hill and stowed the two spare bikes in a far field, roughly scattering vegetation over them. They then re-fastened the crate from which the bikes had been extricated and shuffled it to the rear while Rebecca and Jo continued to scan the horizon. When they emerged fifteen minutes later, the two men's breathing was laboured, sweat streaming down their faces, wet patches spreading on their shirts. The doors were slammed shut and relocked. It was time to head off.

'Good luck,' said the driver, as he climbed back into his cab.

The three of them pedalled and wobbled, Rebecca pointing the way, her bike zigzagging disconcertingly. Jo had several false starts and looked decidedly uneasy. But Dominic was a good cyclist, although more used to a road bike. At last he had found something at which he bested the women. He kept the satisfaction to himself, offering guidance to Jo, who had not ridden a bike since her childhood. With some encouragement and tutoring, she soon mastered the bare essentials, and they began to make steady progress, eventually arriving at a remote farmhouse with numerous outbuildings, random machinery, and clucking hens.

A wiry farmer and his wife and teenage son met them, having been alerted by the barking collies who were soon brought to heel. The farmer's wife had a protective arm around her son, whispering reassuringly to him. Responding with a grunt to her encouragement, he took their bikes to one of the barns. As he laboured on his task, moving awkwardly, the three of them were ushered inside. There was no sign of Juan. Or anyone else. A pot of tea and homemade scones was a welcome sight, consumed in front of a roaring fire, which warmed their chilled bones. Having taken the opportunity to wash and use the bathroom facilities, they were shown to the barn that would house them for the night, possibly longer. Yet another temporary home. Settling in the hayloft they reflected on the journey north: a few tense moments but it had all gone surprisingly well. Rebecca briefed them about the immediate plans. Their bikes were to be loaded onto a low trailer of hay bales and feedstuffs, ostensibly food supplements for livestock in distant fields. Their target was one of the Cumbrian curricks on Hartley Moor.

'We offload the bikes, cover with a tarpaulin and head back here. We need to be careful, really careful. There are reports of heightened SNPS activity in this area. And they won't take prisoners... nor will we,' she added gravely. 'On one hand the remoteness is in our favour, but it's quite close to our target rehab centre.'

'How close?' asked Dominic.

'About three miles.'

'Is that where my Albert is?'

'We think so.'

'And where's Juan? I thought he'd be here...'

'He'll be holed up somewhere at the moment and join us after the mission. At least that's the plan. Two teams are targeting Albert's centre. Our focus is the one that will use the bikes to get to the rear kitchen area where Albert's usually assigned. Juan's leading this small group and if we're lucky Albert will be there.'

'How can we be sure?' asked Jo.

'Intelligence...we have someone on the inside,' said Rebecca.

'Wow. So we know exactly where Albert will be and how to extricate him?' asked Dominic, searching her earnestly, seeking reassurance.

'Well...a slight hitch. Our guy's gone quiet, off radar. Might be that he's lying low, might be...'

'Oh, God,' exclaimed Dominic.

'And then there's the mountain bikes? I mean. *Really*? How will the other team be equipped? And how big a force will it be? And what about timings?' said Jo, not masking her incredulity.

'I don't know all the details. I'm just telling you what *our* plan is, what our specific roles are. If you want me to speculate...'

'Yeah. Do that. You know a helluva lot more than we do. And we've got all night. We're putting our lives on the line here too,' said Jo.

'As are my sons,' said Dominic, warming to Jo's theme.

'Okay. What I've told you is what I know for sure. My understanding is there's to be a co-ordinated attack on three centres simultaneously to liberate hundreds of prisoners. How they'll remove them I can only guess but it will be a huge logistical challenge. The first wave is likely to be a full-frontal assault with the focus being on the destruction and capture of SNPS forces. We've arranged for Albert to be extricated as I've said...it'll be a great story if we pull it off and will resonate with the public: a clarion call. It'll be a morale booster for FF cells and celebrated by PAD.'

'They must be using more than just trucks. Surely a fleet of vehicles would be needed and spotted miles away? Are they using airborne forces? Helicopters? And what about the RAF – under whose command is it? And isn't the risk of casualties high?' asked Jo.

'Probably. Good questions, and the answer is I don't know.' Rebecca shrugged. 'Like everyone else I only know what I need to know. And the assaults could backfire on the prisoners, with the remaining firepower turned on them.'

'They can't let that happen. There has to be...'

'That's why I'm assuming a big military backup – much of the armed forces is supportive. But again I'm not sure. Let's get back to *our* plan... We get to the currick, deliver our load, then withdraw to the farmhouse...please, Dominic, let me continue... Juan's team will focus on the kitchen and stores area at the rear of the rehab centre, collecting the bikes from here,' Rebecca said, pinpointing the location on the map spread before them on the barn floor, 'and use them to get to the centre. It might be tomorrow, might be in two or three days. There's a copse of trees to provide some cover, meagre though that is. They'll assemble back here at the farmhouse with us later...'

'On bikes? You've got to be joking. No chance. That's *suicidal*. They'll be picked off...this whole area will be swarming with SNPS. *Madness...*'

'I doubt they'll arrive here on mountain bikes. More likely to be met by backup,' suggested Jo.

'Who knows? Let's get some rest. We have an early start.'

'Look out for the grouse in these parts – red and black. Plovers too...' said the farmer as they loaded up. He looked surprised at Rebecca's and Jo's quizzical expressions. Clearly a nature lover and why not? But their focus was on other matters and their view was to be of each other and hay...lots of hay.

The tractor and trailer set off, the farmer and his monosyllabic son in the cab, the five of them hidden amongst the bales on the trailer. Rebecca's two team members, who had arrived at the farmhouse late the previous night, were positioned towards the rear, while Dominic, Jo and Rebecca sat closer to the tractor end. It was a cold, damp, foggy morning with a constant mizzle, deathly still and eerily quiet. Peeking through cracks between the bales, Dominic could see the mist hanging in ribbons over the moors as the tractor and its payload trundled over pot-holed trails that threaded across the barren, desolate countryside. They were headed towards the heather-covered plateau in the distance, the vegetation at this lower starting point a mix of bilberry bushes, heath rush and sedge. The farmer's attention to fauna and flora had been rather different to Rebecca's. Superfluous information, Rebecca's body language suggested. Dominic thought differently. He needed to be distracted from the risks they were undertaking, which had been spelt out in stark clarity. And anyway, the farmer's and his own professional interests were closely aligned. How he longed for the day when he could return to the more prosaic considerations of building a menu around locally foraged product. It had previously become trendy in high-end cuisine but now was a matter of supplementing diets in the daily battle of survival. The distraction of the natural world was welcome but did not last long as his stomach lurched with the fear and anticipation that raged through him. He glugged from a bottle of water to lubricate a dry throat but had no remedy for his churning stomach.

Rebecca spoke quietly about the task in hand. They needed to ready themselves for any eventuality, be prepared to fight fire with fire. Literally. They checked their guns: safety catches on, ammunition loaded, ready for action – then settled back down to a jolting journey that was expected to take around two hours, during which time they had two lanes to cross.

After more than an hour the journey became mercifully smoother, signalling their emergence onto the first lane. They tensed, needlessly checking their weapons for the umpteenth time. All senses were on maximum alert as they were more exposed to passing traffic here. *It shouldn't be a problem, only used by farmers*, their driver had said. The tractor stopped. A creak of a gate opening. A lurch indicated they were once more heading over twin-rutted tracks of moorland. The next lane was similarly navigated without incident, until at last they drew to a halt.

Rebecca put a finger to her lips.

Quiet.

Wait for the signal.

Two thumps, a pause and a third thump indicated the all-clear and they were soon offloading their cargo, stashing it under a tarpaulin, weighting it down and then covering it with earth, rocks, heather. Dominic raised the binoculars in scanning the horizon, his head throbbing with tension, his heart beating a tattoo in his chest. As the mist swirled and cleared in places, he said he could see nothing but heather and a few sheep from their cairn vantage point on the plateau. He was corrected by the farmer, who pointed out the hare's-tail cotton grass, deer grass, crowberry round-leaved sundew and bog mosses.

'Enough of the nature lesson. Let's go,' said Rebecca. From a distance their cache should pass unnoticed.

Time to head back via two fields to offload, the young farmer dumping a few bags of ewe's feed: nuts and pellets. They set off again, stopping lower down to drop off bales of hay for grazing cattle. Piling back in, they repositioned the few remaining bales as cover but the whole moor seemed deserted, and Dominic began to relax a little. He wondered just when he might see Juan. But the whole escapade seemed hare-brained, dangerous beyond belief. Could it really work? The bone-jarring at last gave way to a more comfortable ride: the first lane. And this time they were to travel on it a couple of miles. *Stay alert, no room for sloppiness*, urged Rebecca, in whispered tones, just as the tractor drew to a halt. They must have reached the next track, and the lad would no doubt be lumbering out of the cab to open the gate. Muffled noises of conversation could suddenly be heard. Strange. They had never heard the son mumble more than the odd word let alone engage in conversation. Dominic suspected he had learning difficulties, had retreated within himself and was happier around sheep and dogs than people. Rebecca took a grip of her gun, their minders doing similarly. Jo also. Dominic steadfastly left his alone. He had only just managed to hit the proverbial barn door in practice.

Thump, thump.

One of her team slipped out the back as Rebecca held her hand up, alarm etched on her features. That is not the signal. But all was quiet. Stay low.

'*SNPS—*' the farmer's lad shouted.

A single shot and a thud.

Then a scuffle.

Rebecca and Jo slipped off the trailer, one each side. Dominic cowered, dithered, but knew he had to do his bit. His heart pounded, the sound of his quickening pulse throbbing in his ears as panic rose in his chest.

Pop, pop, pop.

Muffled shots told him it was their own fire.

Dominic ventured out, gun aloft, just in time to witness Jo taking out an SNPS officer who held the farmer at gunpoint, a high-risk head shot expertly executed. Almost in unison the remaining officer was felled by Rebecca – a body shot, his grey tunic blooming crimson. Then another to the head. Shocked to his core, Dominic's hand shook, everything shook, as he took in the farmer's lad, blood pulsing from his stricken body, the farmer on his knees cradling his boy's head. Two SNPS officers lay on the side, one groaning, the other silenced by death. Jo knelt to administer what aid she could to the farmer's lad, but comforting his dad was all that was possible. Rebecca strode over to check on her guys; one was beyond help. The other had taken a body shot. Thankfully, the bullet-proof vest had limited the damage, but his right arm hung uselessly.

Dominic clocked another SNPS officer in his peripheral vision, saw him struggle to his knees, grab his gun, take aim. At Rebecca. Without thinking, Dominic raised his own weapon with both hands as instructed by the girls and fired once…twice… Rebecca swivelled and finished him off.

Dominic stared, horrified as he took it all in.

A man down.

A human being's life ended by his own hand…

He shook violently, his gun waving around until stilled by Rebecca. A few sharp words to bring his focus back. No time for introspection.

Then he vomited.

Rebecca and Jo inspected the living and the wounded and the dead, taking stock. They surveyed their surroundings. All seemed quiet but they would need to move swiftly. Rebecca barked out her instructions.

The young farmer and Rebecca's dead colleague were loaded onto the back of the trailer, quickly and with as much respect as time afforded. Her other colleague was patched up and joined the bodies in the back. Meanwhile Rebecca directed Dominic and the farmer to dig a grave into which the dead SNPS officers were loaded. Their motorbikes were hidden behind a stone wall. It was all they could do for now. Dominic toiled, sweat pouring off him, unused to this sort of manual labour. Unused to all of this. Then he heard another *pop*, knew at once what that signified: another grey tunic for the shallow grave.

'Will they have called it in?' asked Jo.

'No,' said Rebecca.

'How can you know? You just can't be sure. It's impossible, the whole plan was sheer madness, crazy. They'll be onto us. This place will be swarming…' Dominic was shouting but was unaware of that until he was shushed. Panic mixing with shock, a toxic cocktail.

'I know because I checked, Dom. No radios. They had mobiles, but no calls had been made in the last half hour. Now come on. We need to get away from here…' Rebecca spoke calmly, quietly, with reassuring authority. Dominic looked at her and nodded.

'It'll be okay,' said Jo.

'That's supposed to be my line…'

CHAPTER 36: HARTLEY

Albert was working alongside Chef Whittaker as distant, multiple explosions sounded. It was far away from the kitchens on the furthest side of Hartley. Then the unmistakable sounds of muffled heavy gauge artillery, automatic rifle fire, shouting and screaming, which seemed to be getting closer. Albert silently acknowledged the chef's message, delivered with his eyes, to take advantage of the distraction; they sidled to the dairy fridge, opening the door just as SNPS officers burst into the kitchen areas shouting and hollering. Albert closed the fridge door behind them, and they cowered in the corner as the chef whispered words of encouragement to a dazed Albert. This must be it. Stay calm. Sounds of pandemonium in the kitchens filtered through to them: shouted instructions and screams and running feet. And then the noise came closer, the movement and bellowing emanating from the stores area before dying back down. They stayed stock-still, listening hard. Tightly huddled together, their hearts beat as one. The mayhem had given way to silence. But the door was suddenly flung open and an SNPS officer called out and waved his drawn weapon around as he ventured inside. They pressed themselves hard against the distant wall in a crouched position, making themselves as small as they could behind crates of milk, blocks of cheese, pallets of yogurts. He edged forwards and was soon within arm's length of the two of them.

'Where are you, where are you?' he said quietly, almost to himself.

And then his gun came within reach and Whittaker took his opportunity. He snatched it out of his grasp and launched himself on the officer. Albert shrank back and watched open-mouthed; his face was sheet white. Chef Whittaker shouted for Albert to help him as he struck the officer over the head with a pan. Albert took hold of another pan, upending its contents and stared at it until prodded into action by the chef's pleas as the guard roused. Albert suddenly swung; the SNPS officer's knees buckled, and he collapsed in a heap. The chef tied him up as best he could by pulling his jacket down to his midriff and pulling his arms tight behind him, securing them with the chef's shoelaces and belt. Albert was encouraged to help him, and they relieved the fallen guard of his boots, trousers and belt and stuffed his mouth with an oven cloth that the chef habitually wore tucked into his belt. Just as the officer was showing signs of stirring Chef Whittaker hit him again, harder. He was now spark out as they loaded stores on top of him.

Chef Whittaker opened the door gingerly.

They eased themselves into the large dry stores area that lay close to the dairy and general-purpose fridges, the freezers and the meat and fish fridges, dodging behind a forklift truck as they took in the aftermath of fighting around the loading bay. That was their target. Beyond were the rear gates and the road from which all deliveries came. Reaching the edge of the loading bay, Albert gazed upwards, mouth agape, and would see the leaden skies, real clouds. This would have been the first time since…well he would only be able to guess how long he had been in Hartley. He shivered, a marked contrast in temperature to the controlled internal climate. And then the explosions and heavy gauge artillery could be heard clearly. Presumably, this was all taking place at the main entrance. But the guarded rear entrance was relatively quiet. And then they caught sight of several SNPS officers lying prone, their bodies riddled by bullets and two officers gagged and bound who stared wide-eyed around them.

Albert stared, transfixed for a moment as two figures ran towards him.

'This way…run, no time to lose.'

They jumped down the three or four feet and the hooded figures led them beyond the articulated vehicle out through the gate. Albert cried out and came to a halt at sight of a cadet lying spread-eagled in their path. Blondie. His legs were at unnatural angles and blood oozed from wounds to his abdomen, legs, and head. His face was frozen in a rictus of pain. His gunshot-riddled body made survival impossible, and he would have realised death was only moments away. A grimace at the prospect of oblivion. Whittaker shouted at him, but Albert just stood and stared. The chef ran back and yanked Albert hard and they stepped around Paul 3349 and over another stricken figure to run towards a copse of trees beyond the road. Another cadet, who had been working in the stores and had hunkered down by the bins in the middle of the turmoil, saw his opportunity of escape and tagged along. Reaching the trees, Albert and Whittaker were met by three figures all dressed in camouflaged fatigues and wearing black rib-knit, three-holed balaclavas. One of the figures pulled his off, grinning broadly. Albert's ashen face looked on with wide eyes, not reacting. Juan pulled his brother into an embrace. Albert did not reciprocate. Pulling back he stared at his sibling. But this was no time for family reunions. They needed to get away from here, and fast. The distant shooting was continuing but becoming more sporadic. Albert was pushed towards the end of the treeline and a mountain bike was thrust at him.

'Hope you've not forgotten how to use one of these, Albert,' said Juan, whose smile was brief. They needed to put some miles between the scenes of carnage and themselves. Albert looked at the bike, then at Juan with a quizzical expression.

'Ideal to navigate the worst of the moors. Even Land Rovers struggle there. We only have three or four miles to cover then the next leg will be a bit speedier. Come on, let's get out of here.'

As they wobbled away, Albert slowly getting the hang of it, a shot rang out, a screamed shout from behind piercing the airwaves.

The opportunistic cadet.

But there was no time to stop. Albert offered no objection. He did not pause or slow his exit speed. There was enough for all of them to focus on for now with the rutted track, the springy heather giving way to bogs. Progress was slow and they were exposed as they came upon the plateau on a day of unusually good visibility. They could only hope that any pursuit would be delayed by the confusion.

After half an hour they slewed to a halt. *All good? All good.* They took a breather, checked their maps and co-ordinates before setting off again. On reaching one of the Cumbrian curricks they dumped their bikes and pulled away a heather-covered tarpaulin. Albert looked down and seemed to register surprise, glancing at Juan. Motorbikes. Scramblers. Modern incarnations with 500cc to power them on their way. They were about to embark upon their very own motocross. Juan, who was the cell leader, asked Jason to explain the workings of the machines.

Tutorial over, time to proceed.

The terrain was still challenging, but the trails more obvious; progress was quicker as the bikes screamed across the moorland – ground-nesting birds taking flight, black grouse squawking their protests. There was no sign of pursuit or sight of other human activity. Just moorland, birds, sheep, and a few grazing cattle. They came to a narrow lane. Stopping briefly, they checked the maps again. The plan was to race ahead, risking a chance patrol in favour of speed. A calculated gamble. Then they would veer off onto a lower-level path to their final destination. Jason, Jack, Albert, and Whittaker would lead the way. Juan decided that he and Abdullah would bring up the rear, hanging back a hundred yards or so to watch their backs.

Time to go.

Full throttle was deployed as they enjoyed the welcome relief of tarmacadam surface. Progress was rapid and the sound of the machines reverberated off the stone walls. The risk was paying off. Albert and Whittaker followed the other two. But then, speeding round a hairpin bend, they careened straight into a problem.

An SNPS patrol.

Two motorbikes.

Officers armed, twitchy and dangerous.

The front two applied their brakes urgently, losing control as the bikes slid and skidded horizontally to halt in a hail of sparks from the friction of the engines scraping along the tarmac. They were trapped. Guns were raised; instructions shouted. There was no escape for Jason and Jack. They slowly, carefully extricated themselves from beneath their bikes, laying down their guns as commanded. Hands were raised. Albert and Whittaker had slightly longer to react and had come to a halt twenty yards back. They rolled into the ditch as bullets thudded into the earth, pinged off their bikes and the stone wall.

Whittaker took aim and let off his own flurry of shots.

One of the officers went down as if he had been poleaxed, surprise etched on his features. The other shot clanged off the motorbike. The SNPS officer fired back a volley of automatic fire in the general direction of Albert and Whittaker, who ducked down into the ditch. In that time Jason had rolled over, grabbed his gun, and fired twice into his target.

Both SNPS officers down and out; one of them just a young, clean-shaven lad.

He shouted his orders to Whittaker and Albert and Jack. They obeyed instantly, manhandling the bodies over the wall. Their motorbikes followed them, two shots to disable the engines. Time was not on their side. An inspection revealed their radios. They would have made contact. Their positions would have been given, reporting their interception.

Jason ran back.

Juan had also come under fire from an SNPS officer who had stopped to relieve himself. He was stricken and lay prone but had obviously killed his assailant in the exchange. Abdullah had a cloth pressed hard against an artery that had been severed, attempting to stem the pulsing of blood. Juan's chest was palpitating, one rapid breath after another, eyes already dulling, his body convulsing from head to toe. He bled heavily. Jason offered reassuring words, working calmly but urgently. A tourniquet was swiftly applied to the leg wound. It would hold it for a while. But Juan had also taken shots to the abdomen and there was no way of knowing which organs had been penetrated. Expert medical intervention was urgently needed. Jason bound him with strips of his own shirt as best he could. Albert arrived and knelt down to his brother. He did not touch him; he offered no help. He stared blankly at him but said nothing. He shed no tears. Jack joined them and put his hand on Albert's shoulder.

'Right, guys,' said Jason. 'You stay with Juan please, Jack. We need to get him and the bikes off the road first. We'll go and get help. We're not too far from our destination now. Okay, Jack?'

'Yup.'

'Albert? Whittaker?'

A cursory nod of Whittaker's head. Albert just looked dazed.

'Let's get cracking then. See you soon, Jack.'

'Make it sooner,' he replied, with a grimace.

Albert bent back down to Juan but said nothing. Juan's eyes were closed, and he flitted in and out of consciousness. Albert reached his hand out to him, but it stopped and hovered in mid-air. He stood, looked down, nodded, turned round, and ran back to his bike.

Rebecca informed them that an attack on the camps was in progress. Rebecca had received a call on her radio to this effect. They were on standby. Expect to be joined over the coming hours. Get armed and prepared, have first aid kits at the ready. That was a few hours ago.

They had initially busied themselves as directed. Dominic could only assume that Juan would be heading towards them. With Albert? When? How? How many of them? There were no definitive answers, just hope. Grab something to eat and drink and get prepared. That was all done quickly, efficiently. Rebecca was directive. Jo was brisk, professional, matter of fact. Dominic worked in a daze, fumbling and sighing. Tim, the stoical farmer, was also drawn in, grieving put on hold. He was joined by a farm worker, Dick, also in the resistance. The two of them clambered into a Land Rover and were despatched to the highest point in the immediately surrounding fields with binoculars and shotguns. They had a bag of essentials and a radio. They would call in any sighting and promised not to be trigger happy.

Time dragged. Tension mounted. Conversation was stilted. Dominic immersed himself in his own thoughts. Jo seemed pensive. He imagined her preoccupied with the death of her partner. Surely she regretted ever having agreed to undertake Dominic's assignment, although she had never given any indication of that. And he could not change the past. There was no point in regrets – though he had more than a few. His mind flitted from thoughts of Rosa and his lads to the outrageous events of Chequers, to the scams of Brandon's business enterprises...

The farmer's wife, Annie, was a welcome interruption as she brought them mugs of coffee, bacon sarnies, biscuits, cakes. She had dredged up something close to a smile and had a kindly word of encouragement for them all. And this despite having lost her own son just yesterday. Amazing. What strength of character. It occurred to him that Annie and Tim were characteristic of that great British spirit oft claimed by politicians, leaders, the media. Perhaps that was a bit sentimental, but Dominic was convinced this was what it was all about. The silent, decent majority rejecting everything that Tobin and Connell and Marxism and Mobilisation and the SNPS stood for, all the evil and horrors perpetrated in the name of so-called egalitarianism. The British people would resist and eventually prevail in true Churchillian style. He was convinced of it. It *will* come good. He was right to be positive, optimistic. Someone had to be. This was what they were fighting for. *Fighting!* Dominic Green fighting? Even now it sent a shudder through him. Happy to support the cause, administer first aid, help where he could – but fight? But he had. He'd shot a man only yesterday. Mind you, had his shots hit the target? He hoped not. Perhaps they had simply put the SNPS officer off. The thought of killing someone was simply beyond his comprehension despite recent events, despite the deaths he had witnessed. His meandering thoughts were suddenly interrupted by the crackle of the radio. Rebecca answered as she strode away from the group to take the call in private.

She re-entered the cool of the barn and they all gathered, anxious for news. Rebecca was grim-faced.

'We need to get ready to receive the assault team. Their mission has had some success; they're heading in quickly. No pursuers as far as they can tell. But there was engagement with an SNPS patrol and there have been casualties. I'm not sure how serious. And we need to rescue two of the team. Juan's been hit... No, Dom, we don't know. One step at a time. We just don't know how seriously but bad enough for him to need urgent help. He and another of the FF cell are holed up back on the road...'

'Will he get through? What about Albert? Is he with them?'

'I don't know and yes. Sorry, Dominic, we need to get to it. I've called Tim and he's driving back. Jo and I will go with him in the Land Rover and on to Juan's and Jack's location. I've got the co-ordinates...'

'I'll grab blankets and bandages,' said Annie.

A hiss on the radio.

Rebecca answered and they all heard Dick's rough country voice. 'Four riders coming in...at speed...our boys I think.'

'Let's go,' said Rebecca, as they heard the Land Rover screech to a halt in the yard. They grabbed their guns and packs and joined the farmer. Dominic and Archie, the wounded member of Rebecca's small team, watched them depart. Archie had been patched up, swallowed paracetamol, wore his arm in a sling. But at least he could shoot of a fashion with his left hand. If he had to. He might have to.

It was only a few minutes before four bikes squealed into the yard. They dumped them to one side and were shown into the large barn. They looked exhausted, filthy from the peat bogs, mud encrusted, shellshocked.

'*Albert*! Albert. Son...'

Dominic rushed over, pulling him into a bear hug. Albert did not speak, did not return the embrace. His eyes were glazed. He did not seem to register his father. Dominic stepped back to better take in his son. He was thin, his face pale, scarred and gaunt.

'What *have* they done to you, Albert? Are you alright? Say something, son...'

Silence.

'We'll soon be back with your mum and Juan. We'll be together. So much has happened our end, but I can't imagine what you've been—'

'Come here, my love. Let me get thee something to eat, a drink maybes? Family reunion later, eh?' And Annie ushered him deeper into the barn, mothering and clucking over him. Over her shoulder she whispered, 'Give the lad time, eh?'

Whittaker accompanied Albert, as Jason and Abdullah scouted their surroundings, checked their weapons. First one, then the other, ducked his face into the water trough. They grabbed a coffee and munched on a biscuit, patting Albert's shoulder as he passed, a warrior's reassurance. Dominic approached Jason, pulled him to one side. 'Please tell me. Is it Juan who's wounded?'

''fraid so.'

'How bad?'

'Bad. Touch and go I would think…sorry,' he said, as Dominic crumpled, head in hands.

CHAPTER 37: AFTERMATH

Their stopover at the farmhouse on Hartley Moor had been longer than planned; the fallout from the attacks had created a hot spot down the M6 corridor. SNPS and military units swamped the region as skirmishes with FF resistance and rebellious crack units of the army broke into sporadic heavy fighting. Rebecca had spoken with her commanders, stayed closely in touch with the developing situation. She gradually pieced together the broader picture for them. Two of the three camps had been decimated, with large numbers of SNPS casualties. A second wave of assaults had rescued around a hundred inmates in each camp, although many had already taken flight; groups were fanning out across the moors. Local farmers would offer them refuge, insisted Tim and Annie, but they themselves would become vulnerable.

Dominic spent most of his time at his son's bedside. He mopped his fevered brow as Juan intermittently writhed and lashed out, before lapsing into a deep sleep. He held his hand and whispered loving sentiments as he recalled happier times: family holidays at the beach, birthday parties, Christmas festivities. He could only hope that some of this would reach his son, would permeate his consciousness. Annie and Jo frequently popped in to administer kindly comments and support, and a flow of refreshments that went untouched.

As the evening wore on Juan's breathing shallowed, his strength dissipating like smoke in the wind. The fever seemed to have worsened as infection invaded his body. His leg had swollen and was an angry shade of red. And they could only hope that shots to the abdomen had missed most vital organs. He desperately needed the medical assistance that was beyond their reach. They could hardly turn up at a hospital A&E in the light of recent events.

'Isn't there a local doctor you could call?' pleaded Dominic.

'I suppose I could ring old Dr Douglass. He's been retired for years now but 'e's a good 'un.'

'Can we trust him?' asked Jo.

'Yeah, he's alright. But he's no surgeon and whether he can still get drugs...'

'Call him,' said Dominic.

'Not so fast,' said Rebecca, who had overheard their conversation. 'We need to check his credentials. I'll make a few calls to—'

'No way. Make the call, Annie. To hell with London,' said Dominic.

'It won't take long to check, Dom, and there are lots of lives at stake here,' said Jo.

'I've got some unused antibiotics. We can use them in the meantime, love,' Annie said, as Rebecca retreated to another room to make her call. They may do no good but surely they could not do him any more harm. It was worth a try. But as daylight hours ebbed, his hold on life seemed fragile.

Rebecca soon returned with the news that they were reaching out to Dr Douglass, his loyalties to their cause having been confirmed. But it would take a few hours to arrange his safe delivery once the curfew hours were over.

'Bugger the curfew,' said Dominic. 'Get him *now*.'

'He's based in Skipton, which is swarming with SNPS. If he breaks curfew he'll be spotted and anyway he's knocking on a bit, and we have to make sure he gets here via the lanes without arousing suspicion. It's risky, Dom. But we've got farmers with FF support to get him here by late morning,' said Rebecca.

Dominic sighed his acceptance and settled down to his night watch.

With lookouts in place, the rest of the group settled down to hear the BBC news on the radio, intrigued as to how the government would be presenting the escalation of hostilities. Dominic had been persuaded to take a break from his vigil. Red eyed, he sat next to Albert, reaching out to him. Albert showed no spirit or emotion. Dominic looked at first to Jo and then Rebecca with mournful, damp eyes. It was almost impossible for him to take. Both sons stricken. Rebecca took her place next to Dominic, taking hold of his hand; he eagerly grasped at hers. And the news was further dispiriting. It was all so hard to swallow. First-hand accounts of the various rallies were vivid: of the all-too-familiar red flags, abbreviated goose-stepping, martial music, grey tunics, the ubiquitous red Ms and sounds of gunfire salutes stitched together to the accompaniment of cheering crowds. A government spokesman spoke of the heroic SNPS marching with victorious sections of the military and national police in defeating rebellious enemies of *The People*. Opponents were labelled as traitorous, despicable turncoats in the military turning on their own government; a patchwork quilt of jarring accounts, celebratory language, and confabulations of national pride all in the name of *The People*. An assault on one of the camps was presented as isolated terrorist action. A rogues' gallery of wanted terrorists was summarised, their shameful sins paraded: Norris Jinks for perfidious Albion with pride of place alongside a general in the army and the putative head of the FF. And there amongst the others named and shamed was Dominic. He shuddered as he heard reference to his treacherous terrorist activities, his murder of gallant public servants: a traitor to be hunted down so that justice could be imparted, intoned a government spokesperson.

'Just pure propaganda by a government that long ago lost its moral compass. If it ever had one,' said Jo, appalled at Dominic's portrayal.

'Let's turn it off…' he agreed.

'Hang on, I need to hear this,' said Jo, shushing him. The news reporting had turned to foreign affairs, revealing that a task force of the British Navy had been sent to intercept what was described as a ragtag collection of adventurers from the Commonwealth. In Portsmouth, patriotic crowds were described enthusiastically waving off the *Tobin Red Star* aircraft carrier, the hastily rebadged HMS Queen Elizabeth warship. Bands played, crowds cheered, wet eyes were dabbed. The spirit of the Falklands task force of 1982 was invoked, although today not a single Union Jack was in sight; instead, red flags abounded. Their mission was to deter the approaching armada of Commonwealth nations intent on the invasion of GB. The *Tobin Red Star* was deemed to be the most modern, most powerful aircraft carrier in the world with a fleet of frigates in support with unparalleled air support from helicopter and fixed-wing aircraft. *Certain to repel the pathetic attempts of foreign powers to subvert The People's Revolution. Return to base or be destroyed – the choice is theirs,* declared Jane Connell.

Political correspondents and foreign affairs reporters proceeded to ridicule the verbal assaults of the American president and of the European Union, the contributions of Norris Jinks and the royal family ignored. In an interview Jane Connell dismissed the words of international critics as hot air posturing, while praising Vladimir Putin, the Russian president, and President Xi Jinping of China as loyal friends providing support in the form of food and medical supplies. Arms too, presumably. Reports of foreign soldiers with boots on the ground in GB were flatly denied. *It's not happening. It's not going to happen. The glorious People's Revolution would repulse any such attempts.*

They looked at each other. It was dismaying, and their morale ebbed as Juan's condition worsened over the following hours. And Albert seemed to exist in his own bubble, completely withdrawn, showing no signs of shaking off his malaise. Some sort of PTSD, suggested Jo carefully. A nip of Farmer Tim's brandy helped their mood briefly, but there was no doubting that the overall situation was cause for grave concern. Gradually they turned to their own immediate plans. Given the turmoil, should they lie low or flee? A debate flared as to the balance of risks, views were exchanged, heated discussions soon developing. But Rebecca settled it. 'We stay put for now, no choice.' Rebecca told them she was still awaiting new orders that were expected any time now, alternative routing.

'But Juan won't be able to travel,' Jo had ventured, looking anxiously at Dominic.

He cast her a quizzical look, got to his feet, and returned to his son's bedside, where Annie was keeping a loving watch.

Dr Douglass eventually arrived around midday but by then Juan's breathing was laboured and his pulse weak. He checked his vital signs and gently examined the wounds. He was grim-faced as he relayed his professional opinion and sat with Dominic at Juan's bedside to offer solace and companionship. Juan succumbed a few hours later, his father, Albert, Jo, Annie, and Dr Douglass at his bedside as Juan exhaled his last breath.

Dominic was heartbroken.

Albert simply sat and stared.

Jo later framed the question that had likely been on everyone's mind, speaking softly, carefully, her eyes never leaving Dominic's. 'We will need to hold his funeral here, won't we?'

Dominic was horrified. 'We *absolutely* take him with us, of course,' he insisted. 'Take him home. To Rosa.'

There was an awkward silence in the room, in the end broken by Rebecca. 'I'm so sorry, Dom, but we can't, we have no choice.' She looked at him sympathetically. She could see what it was doing to him. But it might be five or six days before it was safe to head out. Practical considerations made it quite impossible... Jo grabbed his hand and spoke softly, persuading him that Rebecca was right. He nodded his understanding as tears flowed, punctuated by deep, heaving sobs. They had come this far, and they were so close, he lamented. His son had been so brave, had nearly overcome all the odds. So very nearly.

'We'll look after him, love. He'll rest in peace here. With our own son,' said Annie quietly.

Tim was a man of few words, but he nodded vigorously as Annie drew Dominic to her, embracing him tightly. She wept with him. Two parents grieving the loss of two sons. And still Albert just looked on. How much was he taking in? Perhaps he had become inured to death as well as life.

Farmer Tim was determined to dig his own son's grave; he could not be persuaded otherwise. And Dominic watched as Jason and Jack joined in the grim task. Two graves for two boys. The dead boys were to join two others of Tim and Annie's family: young Sal and Kenneth, three months, and eight years respectively when they had perished. Of what? No one asked, no explanation was offered. But Juan was to join the farmer's offspring in the private graveyard. As had Hristo, the fallen member of Rebecca's team the day previously. Albert shed his shirt and joined the gravediggers, perhaps welcoming the chance for manual labour, perhaps needing to simply *do* something. Perhaps he was used to mind-numbing tasks, the graft an outlet for pent-up frustration, a brief escape from his experiences. They could still only speculate as to Albert's personal experiences, although Whittaker had given them a feeling for the sinister, other-worldly sounding cosmos of Hartley. Was he grieving? It was not at all clear to Dominic as he looked on, trying to get his head around what had happened. He struggled himself but could just about do that. As to the why – he had no idea. How could anyone be so ideologically driven to embark on a cruel madness that had catapulted the country into an evil cesspit of horror? What a pointless waste of so many vibrant young lives.

While Abdullah, Archie and Dick took the next shift in maintaining a lookout, the others assembled at the graveside as the warm sun weakened and dipped, dusk beckoning. A simple dual ceremony in the half-light as first the farmer's lad, Derek, and then Juan were lowered into the ground. Temporary wooden crosses had been fashioned, names inscribed, and the mourners gathered in peaceful contemplation. Dominic looked across at Jo as she read a passage from the bible: 1 Corinthians, 13...

> *If I speak in the tongues of me and of angels, but have not love, I am a noisy gong or a clanging cymbal...*

Love is patient and kind; love is not jealous or boastful; it is not arrogant or rude. Love does not insist on its own way; it is not irritable or resentful; it does not rejoice at wrong but rejoices in the right. Love bears all things, believes all things, hopes all things, endures all things.

So faith, hope, love abide, these three; but the greatest of these is love.

Dominic dragged his head up from his son's premature resting place; across from his grave Jo spoke clearly, quietly, respectfully. His heart went out to her as he recalled that she herself had lost a loved one only recently. Not killed in battle for a cause célèbre. But lynched and *scarecrowed* by cowardly sadists espousing vitriol. At least he could say goodbye to his son, had been with him in his last hours. At the end. *Almost* at the end. As he stood at Juan's graveside he felt as if the world was on pause and the fog of grief and emotion swirling in his mind briefly lifted. He felt detached, almost celestial as he looked down on proceedings and found he could cohere his thoughts. Perhaps he was not so weak after all? Or maybe this was the natural process, the very reason for conducting such ceremonies: to allow momentary lucidity and the drawing of a line under the loss of a loved one – the point at which the long healing process would slowly begin. He turned to Albert, but still his eldest son did not speak, did not cry. Dominic took a half-step forwards as if on autopilot, scooped a handful of Northumberland dirt, held his hand over the dark void. He thought of Rosa, of all their plans and dreams. All turned to dust now as he said goodbye to his youngest with their eldest standing alongside him. One of his sons in the grave, the other a broken shell of a young man just about still standing. Perhaps broken beyond repair. A silent tear welled, escaped, slid down his cheek, dropping silently into the grave. And he let his fingers part, watching the soil drop onto his son's final resting place: the dust of plans and dreams.

'Rest in peace, son.'

CHAPTER 38: DESTINATION DAY -2

2027

Dominic's third night spent in the cramped, insanitary conditions in this holding pen in Wormwood Scrubs was no better than his others. Sleep was hard to come by, assailed as they all seemed to be by their nightmares, fears, and trepidations. If he was not being assaulted by his own, he was sharing others'. And then there were the regular toilet visits throughout the night, a necessity of the older males in the room. Dominic seemed to be afflicted these days. He took care not to knock the brimming contents, become the person responsible for any overflow, a not irregular occurrence and one guaranteed to earn the opprobrium of those closest.

And today the guards made an early call, not with provisions but to shout out three more. Each would have known of their ultimate fate and had been in the cell long enough to know the routine, but none of them had been the recipients of so-called special meals the night previously. The callout was a surprise and terror etched their features as they were grabbed and dragged out, one physically beaten as he put up token resistance. This was probably some sort of escalation, a clear-out. Perhaps the urban warfare being raged in the outside world – so close and yet so far away – was approaching some sort of end game. Rupert had brought news of fighting on the streets of London to the south, west and north of the capital. The cockney lady had told them of the continued incursions of the FF and crack army units in and around the heart of London, of their attacks on strategic targets: the SNPS barracks and arsenals in particular, and increasingly on the seat of government.

Celia nudged Dominic, nodding towards Rupert, the cockney lady and the other two. They had drawn tightly together in a conspiratorial conclave, their whispering taking on a more urgent air. And Celia's uncle was one of the named last night now awaiting his imminent time. He had looked on in horror, eyes wide. He had tried to put a brave face on things, but his shaking body betrayed his fear. Celia had comforted him as best she could but in the final analysis the best one could do was simply be there. She held his hand as she whispered to Dominic, 'That lot are plotting something. You spoke earlier with Rupert. Any idea?'

'No. Madness. No chance.'

'Happy's the weak link…the only one displaying any hint of humanity. He might be wavering…'

'Yeah. Not sure he's got the gumption to do anything about it though. It'd be suicide. I guess they'll be back soon. Your uncle okay?'

Celia turned to face him directly, her expression conveying what the voice chose not to articulate: *you kidding? Get real.* Dominic nodded and hung his head. It was all so desperate.

'Thanks for all you did, by the way. Sorry to have—' he said in a low voice.

'All in the past. Tragic how it turned out. But we did give it a whirl, bloodied a few noses, gave them a run for their money. It will all have made a difference in the grand scheme of things, all a small part of the overall victory. We won a few battles. Shame we lost this one, but the war will be ours. Liberation will happen. I'm certain of that. Always have been. Pity we won't be—'

'No.'

Their conversation lapsed, leaving those thoughts hanging in the stale air.

Leaning forwards they grabbed a chunk of bread and half a glass of water. Breakfast. Many wolfed the rations down quickly, hungrily. But Dominic chose to nibble slowly, to savour, imagine it was a piece of French toast. He could smell the spice of the cinnamon, taste the rich butter, luxuriate in the sweetness of maple syrup, detect a scintilla of vanilla, the zest of orange. And his drink was a wonderful brew, Italian roast coffee: dark and strong. He could feel the caffeine fix. To imagine was a form of escapism, although it was becoming more and more challenging as his hunger grew and the aromas of so many unwashed bodies in a confined space was overwhelming; the stink of excrement and urine imbued everything. He had read somewhere that when in the midst of such conditions, you became inured to them, no longer assailed by the filth and stench. He wished that were true for him. He was only too aware of his own odours, let alone everyone else's. It was a ridiculously trivial concern given the context, and he smiled briefly.

*

The door clanged open. Pock, Shorty and Happy all made their entrance. They read the list of names cheerfully. They matched those of last night: Harry Archibold, Jai Kalluri, Kim Harris. Celia's Uncle Harry leaned into his niece; his shivers grew into a spasm. He managed to squeeze her hand, kiss her on the cheek. He struggled to his feet. Dominic stood, faced Harry, whose rheumy eyes reluctantly left Celia for a moment as they shook hands, Dominic placing his left hand on Harry's right bicep, pressing firmly, comradely, before then sitting back down to comfort Celia. Pock hurried him along and out of the door to another waiting guard. Only at the last moment did Harry take his eyes off Celia. She held her composure until he was the other side of the door. Then, for once, it was Dominic administering the sympathy, solace, sensitivity. The other two were also pulled out; Jai Kalluri was wide-eyed but held himself together, Kim Harris less so.

'And as a bonus…a fourth selection…as a reward for his unstinting insolence…' Pock spat his words out with venom, the tip of his tongue snaking around his lips in anticipation of a sweet kill.

'Yeah, troublemaker in chief…Rupert Win-Hughes. Mr La De Da. You get the prize,' added Shorty, grinning idiotically, a contortion of hatred.

'Get him,' he said to Happy, who hesitantly stepped forwards.

And then it kicked off.

Rupert scrambled to his feet and landed a judiciously aimed foot into the crotch of Shorty, who squealed and crumpled; the cockney lady pulled Happy to one side and two of them quickly disarmed him. But Pock was spurred into the sort of action he obviously relished. A baton to the head floored Rupert and his pistol was drawn and fired twice in double quick time into the cockney lady, who was brandishing Happy's weapon. The sound of gunshots and the attendant screams amplified in the confines of the concrete cell.

One of the more recent prisoners started to get to his feet, but thought better of it, settling for shouted oaths and profanities.

Two of the ladies screamed and huddled into each other.

Dominic turned to Celia, held her tightly, fearing she might step into the fray, and then his eyes were drawn back to the cockney lady as blood oozed through the fingers that clutched at her stomach. Her expression was one of profound shock. She sighed and keeled over.

Rupert's two colleagues were swiftly overcome by two other guards who blustered in.

Rupert and the cockney lady were dragged out, the other two walked, hands on head.

The remaining prisoners looked on in stunned silence, a few weeping silently.

CHAPTER 39: PLUMPTON

The FF and Rebecca's teams merged for the journey south. Anxiety levels were high, tension hanging in the air like tendrils of morning mist over the Yorkshire Dales they were navigating through. Tim's trusty, ancient Land Rover stood up to the challenge as it trundled along minor roads. Albert, Jo, and Dominic sat cramped in the back, Rebecca, and Jason up front with the farmer. Whittaker, Archie, and Jack rode a mile ahead in another farm vehicle, Abdullah on a motorbike a mile behind – all in radio contact. They made it to their agreed rendezvous just south of Leyburn. An articulated vehicle was awaiting them. The modus operandi was similar to that of their trip north, which now seemed a lifetime ago. This time the cargo was foodstuffs destined for a depot in South London – the driver's credentials, consignment and paperwork were all legitimate, would stand scrutiny. But this time there was no secret compartment, so a wall of crates was erected behind which the team took refuge, having bade goodbye to Tim. Not a man for sentiment, he briskly shook Dominic's hand, tipped his cap to the women, and climbed back into his vehicle: destination home. Home to Annie, who they had left in tears at dawn that morning. They sat huddled, lost in their own thoughts as they journeyed without incident despite three checkpoints.

On their return journey, Rebecca had continued in her now familiar, professional vein, aided by Jo. They at least seemed to know what they were doing as Dominic tuned out, lost in his own moroseness. Albert just seemed lost to this world.

Having arrived back at Plumpton, Rebecca told them of the plan, the next steps on this perilous journey. 'Hunker down, Dominic. Just remember you're a marked man with a price on your head. It won't take them long to work out your son has been freed. They are bound to label it a terrorist act perpetrated by an enemy of *The People*. You know the sort of trash they peddle. I'm needed elsewhere, my team also. Don't worry, I'll send a couple of guys to watch over you. They'll bring fresh supplies. We have no reason to believe our location has been compromised, but we need to be vigilant. Just lie low. Promise?'

Dominic looked at her with hangdog eyes and then to Jo.

'It makes sense, Dom. I'll be here with you both. You're not getting rid of me just yet.'

He raised the shadow of a weak smile, and his eyes flashed his relief.

'Okay. But for how long? And what about Albert? He needs help. And what about Rosa? Is she headed back as she claimed? How?'

'I'll be in touch, Dom. Sweet Dom,' she said, letting her stance soften. She reached out to him, flashing her sparkling blue eyes.

'I must go. Take care. You too, Jo. Look after him...'

Rebecca and Jo embraced.

Shared dangers, despair, death had bridged the mistrustful gap between the young women. She then kissed Dominic lightly on the lips, brushing away the impromptu return of salty tears before pulling him into a tight hug. He held on to her like a man adrift, desperately clinging to a raft, reluctant to let go.

He watched Rebecca disappear, forlorn at her parting. His mind was in turmoil, emotions tumbling into each other: grief for his son, despair at Albert's psychological condition, panic at being cast rudderless as Rebecca moved on. At least Jo was still here. Trusty Jo.

'Come on, Dom, let's catch up with the news,' she encouraged, taking his hand. They set it up on the specially adapted PC provided. *Untraceable*. As was the mobile they could use, but only sparingly. She had assured them it was secure. The only apps were encrypted, messages impossible to decipher, digital traffic almost impossible to trace. *Almost*.

Dominic refused to tune into the terrestrial television given the bias, the voice of a government determined to inculcate its disinformation. And the NFN video clips told a quite different story of attacks on camps in the Welsh Mountains and in England's Northern Pennines, of the release of hundreds of prisoners. Some regiments of the British Army had been part of the assaults, following the raids of FF resistance cells in a co-ordinated attack. The Royal Air Force had kept their aircraft grounded despite reported instructions to intervene, denied by government sources. Scenes of the decimation of SNPS barracks, offices, encampments across the country were shown. Some pockets were becoming virtually SNPS free in most of Wales and Scotland and in some English cities such as Manchester, Newcastle, and Leicester. Rural areas were solidly monarchist, resolutely opposed to the Marxist regime, passive opponents now becoming proactive. Perhaps in response to the American president's overtures? Possibly. Certainly in tune with their respect and love of the monarch and the royal family, holding HRH William and Catherine in particular regard. But the SNPS remained threatening, were supported by most police forces and parts of the armed forces. How solid this support was likely to prove was almost certainly going to be tested in the days and weeks to come, intoned Ronald Dicks, the hard-working NFN presenter.

Dominic watched agog as a clip was streamed live from the *Tobin Red Star* aircraft carrier; of the red flag being replaced by the Union Jack, of the captain and his crew declaring their loyalty to the Crown and to the British people. Its navigational course was maintained, its purpose the polar opposite to their instructions to engage a supposed enemy. Instead they were to join forces with the Commonwealth of Nations ships with crews from Australia, New Zealand, India, and Canada: destination GB, objective the restoration of peace, freedom, democracy.

'How long before the Americans join this modern-day liberation armada?' intoned Ronald. 'Reports of advance units of the US Army Delta Force teaming up with British SAS crack teams are reaching us, but they're impossible to confirm. And I have just had some breaking news. Norris Jinks has been photographed with British and American forces on British soil, the leader of the Conservative Party receiving a hero's welcome from local crowds in Brighton. More on this later. We can only hope this all heralds the start of the end of this sorry period, but we must all expect difficult days ahead... This is Ronald Dicks from NFN.'

Dominic and Jo reflected on the contrasting news stories, greatly relieved at the turn of events – if NFN were to be believed. And CNN and Sky News reports resembled those they had just been transfixed by. Albert had sat with them but remained impassive. Not even shots of rehabilitation centres similar to the one he had inhabited for so long had stirred him. After a while he wandered off and they could spot him sauntering round the rear garden, hands in pockets, purposeless but peaceful. Dominic later found him sitting stock-still on the bench. He placed a hand on his son's shoulder only to feel him recoil.

*

Later that evening, they checked the mobile device in order to check their WhatsApp group. Turning it on, the familiar tone sounded to indicate a new message. Rebecca.

Hi guys. Your supplies will land this evening and be prepared for a surprise visitor. They'll know how to contact me should you need to. Only use if you have to. Stay safe. Won't be in touch for a while.

'I wonder what that means? It couldn't be Rosa, could it?' said Dominic in a panic, as his heart sank. How could he tell her? What would he say? Oh, *God*, she'll be beside herself. He felt sick to his stomach at the daunting prospect. And then there was Albert...

'Perhaps imminent help is at hand. I absolutely believe the NFN reports, more good news in the pipeline. Then we might all escape this...' said Jo. And then she took in the look of horror on Dominic's face. 'Oh, sorry, Dom. I shouldn't be so insensitive. It will be beyond tough for Rosa, even tougher for you in telling her. I'm not sure there's anything anyone can say to help you. But I will be here for you both. At least for as long as you want me.'

Their frugal tea was a quiet affair. Albert set about his meal with initial gusto but seemed to lose interest and sat back having consumed less than half. It was impossible to reach him despite their attempts to encourage conversation. Nothing could induce him to engage. An uncomfortable silence descended as the evening wore on. They could not face more news reports or concentrate to read. Playing music seemed too frivolous and any conversations soon ran out of steam.

Then the coded knock signalled the arrival of visitors. Jo checked they did not wear grey tunics. Dominic slid the bolts back, opened the door on the chain and looked out.

Rosa.

He rapidly shut the door, unhooked the chain and opened it wide. Rosa embraced him, but it was a stilted, awkward embrace devoid of her usual Latin exuberance, energy or cheer.

'Hi, Dominic. It's been a long time, hasn't it? So much has happened. So much,' she said quietly.

Dominic looked at her sombrely and tears pricked the corners of his eyes.

'What is it? And who the hell's *this*?' she stopped abruptly as Jo advanced to say hello.

'Did Rebecca not say?' said Jo.

'Who?'

'Rebecca. I assume she got you here?'

'I've never met a Rebecca, just these gorgeous hunks here,' she said, tapping depleted reserves of residual energy, gesticulating to her two minders, who carried bags of provisions, grinning from ear to ear.

'And my *Goddd*...I don't *beleeeve* it...*Albert*, my Albert...'

She pushed Dominic out of the way, rushed past Jo and pulled Albert into a bear hug. She used to call it a mummy hug, recalled Dominic, looking on. Mother and son remained entwined for what seemed like ages, punctuated by a commentary from Rosa about him needing feeding back up and expressing all manner of insults and threats at the forces who had inflicted all the pain and suffering he must have endured. And gradually she noticed how withdrawn he was. Gradually it dawned on her that Albert was not well. He had not spoken, and the initial light that seemed to flicker when Rosa first approached him had quickly clouded. Once she could be persuaded to let him go, he ambled out of the room, soon to be heard ascending the stairs.

'And Juan? Where's my little boy?'

Rosa stopped herself mid-flow.

It must have been their expressions and then Dominic could staunch the tears no longer. And he was suddenly stuttering out an explanation his own ears could barely believe. Tears flowed; shoulders heaved. How do you break the news of the death of a son? No one ever expected to be in that position. No head-rehearsal was possible. And in Rosa, waves of emotion followed, the sequential steps of flat denial, disbelief, anger, reluctant acceptance with grief hard on their heels.

Desperate, cloying grief.

CHAPTER 40: ULTIMATUM

Dominic rose at dawn, stiff from a night spent in the bath, thick blankets serving as his mattress, bath towels for warmth. He had insisted that Rosa have his room. She needed her own space after hearing the awful news, although he doubted she would sleep much. If you need me, I'm next door, he had sought to reassure her. It was just so difficult to assimilate what had befallen his family. While he had lived through it, poor Rosa had learnt of everything in a jumble of confused emotions. God knows he understood her shock. It was all so surreal – he kept hoping to awake from the worst nightmare imaginable. Sighing, he pulled on his clothes and headed for Albert's single room, previously Rebecca's. But Dominic found the room empty.

Tiptoeing downstairs, he found that Albert was not in the lounge either. Their minders had already packed away makeshift beds in the front room, having slept in shifts; all was quiet. They must be checking the local vicinity. He presumed that Albert may have ventured outside, and opening the back door to allow the fresh morning air to flood in, he spotted him at the far end of the overgrown garden. He waved but got no response and decided to let him be. It was a glorious morning with a chilly edge; another warm day was forecast. All was quiet, other than the remnants of the dawn chorus and a noisy cockerel, a rural pollution to join the farmyard smells and muck spreading that assaulted his senses, taking him back to his childhood.

He sat in quiet contemplation sipping a mug of instant coffee, letting the cold air wash over him, savouring the tranquillity. He wondered how family life could possibly adjust to their new situation, but he resolved to do whatever it took to reach out to Rosa, to help their son and to start the slow, painful healing process. Rosa was engulfed in grief and incredulity when she eventually joined him, not yet ready to engage. She had not begun to consider how they might secure the professional help their son needed. Albert shuffled in, grunted his recognition – that was something at least – and grabbed a coffee and a piece of toast, which he took back to the solitariness of the garden bench. Jo gave the family some space, took her tea and cereal back to bed.

It seemed that something was on Jo's mind, her forehead furrowed, eyes narrowing as she gently asked Rosa how she had got here. *The hunks.*

'But how did you get from France? Who helped you?' Jo asked.

'I knew people in the resistance cells that supported the FF. They run camps, train people, offer support…all that sort of thing,' she said. Jo frowned. But the absence of locations, the precise nature of the activities, the precise shape the support took, did not seem to be what most preoccupied her.

'And your journey here? You would have needed help. There are no flights or ferries, the ports are closed…'

'A small vessel, manned by supporters.'

'Supporters of whom?'

'FF of course. Who else?' said Rosa.

'Who organised it? Did you meet anyone in command?'

'Not really. They spoke of some woman who had influence who could ensure safe passage.'

'*Who?*' asked Jo. 'Please…this may be important.'

But Rosa just shrugged.

Dominic and Jo exchanged knowing glances. *Surely it was Rebecca? Her MI5 links and networking with the FF.*

Their day passed slowly, Albert opting for his bedroom in the main, the others moving aimlessly between the garden, lounge, and kitchen. Time dragged but at least the weather was kind to them as warm sunshine bathed their garden. This early summer period was punctuated with the sound of songbirds, bees pollinating, baby squirrels playing in the far points of the garden, noisy lambs destined for dinner tables being fattened on the lush grass, tractors working the fields. Their minders came and went, seemingly satisfied they were safe. Books were picked up and discarded, attempted conversations were sporadic, stilted. A game of Scrabble fell into disrepair, participants drifting off. As dusk fell, they set about a tea of cold meats and salad, and Jo lightened the fridge of a bottle of Sancerre. Dominic sipped and played with his cutlery disconsolately; Rosa slurped more enthusiastically, topping up generously; Jo was pensive. Albert picked at his food, ignored the wine. It was as if a dark cloud hovered low, draping them all – darkly claustrophobic.

Jo turned the PC on, intent upon catching the news.

'Bound to be depressing,' said Dominic, as he joined her. But at least it was something to do. Rosa disappeared upstairs with another glass of wine; she seemed to be self-medicating. They listened to Ronald Dicks deliver startling news. The HMS *Queen Elizabeth* – name restored and blazoned across the vessel's stern – was joined by its sister ship, HMS *Prince of Wales*, and two frigates, all of which were accompanied by Commonwealth vessels plus two American frigates. Each of the Queen Elizabeth class of aircraft carrier carried thirty-six F-35B strike fighters and four Merlin helicopters. The British Navy was proving itself to be solidly supportive of the Monarchists; opposed to the pariah government, loyal to HM Queen Elizabeth II and the British people. As they sailed towards the coast of GB, the seas were absent of ships that might pose any threat. Instead, a reincarnation of the Dunkirk spirit was taking root, shoaling in the form of a flotilla of fishing trawlers and boats, both small and large, joined by leisure crafts. All heading out to meet the British fleet, most proudly displaying Union Jacks. NFN also reported the USS *Gerald R Ford* aircraft carrier and auxiliary fleet exercising in the Atlantic, itself conveying a clear message to the British government. A formidable force.

The news then turned to London. A clip showed two frigates with high-speed commando vessels zipping up the Thames. As they approached the SNPS centres on both sides of the Thames they came under fire. But the firepower returned by the frigates as they deployed their missiles on the complexes revealed the stark inequality of these opposing forces. SNPS troops were forced to beat a swift retreat, leaving behind a battle-scarred trail of debris, destruction, devastation. *A modern-day assault by British forces on British targets in the name of the restoration of the monarchy, of democracy and freedom: the early quest for a modern-day restoration not seen on these shores since the seventeenth century* intoned a foreign affairs expert interviewed by Ronald Dicks.

'The government can't possibly cope with the military capability of the Monarchists with the majority of the military now declaring in support of the Queen. And it seems impossible they will be able to withstand the onslaught of criticism from around the world – the notable exceptions being Russia, North Korea, and China. The calls on the government to surrender are mounting from the European Union to the Americans to the Commonwealth nations of Australia, Canada, India, New Zealand,' said the expert.

'Will Tobin capitulate?' asked Ronald.

'Very likely but the question is when. It's not imminent but the tension notches up daily with the danger of escalation.'

'Are you suggesting the superpowers on the world stage could all be dragged in? USA, Russia, China even. A third world war? Surely not?'

'Tobin and Connell have been bailed out by Russian roubles – no doubt whatsoever. They are in receipt of Russian and Chinese aid, armed with Russian artillery and their so-called advisers are to be found in London. Their focus is the destabilisation of GB, their active support of Tobin. None of that is surprising. But will they take on American firepower? Risk a world war? I think not. The odds are heavily stacked against them. They'll melt into the background, resume their covert undermining of democratic nations, wait for a future military opportunity to attack the West. And conversely, America will do whatever it takes to ensure a Marxist regime in their sphere of influence is removed.'

'So we've entered an end game?'

'I think so, but nothing can be taken for granted. There can be no *certainty*. A moment of madness is always possible, an error of judgement, a cataclysmic mistake to spark a crisis to match that of the Bay of Pigs in the 1960s or worse. But that apart, there's evidence to support my analysis.'

'You mean the Russian fleet turning around?'

'*Part* of the Russian Northern Fleet led by the *Kuznetsova* aircraft carrier with its eighteen fixed-wing aircraft and helicopters had been steaming towards British waters but seems to have altered course. I don't believe the Russians will risk a confrontation with the American forces in the Atlantic. And British airspace has been cleared of encroaching Russian aircraft too. Until the last few days they flew with impunity, landing on British bases at will. A few aircraft and crew still remain. I would expect them to be allowed to leave quietly. To do otherwise would likely spark a reaction. I would also say that the crucial, critical game-changer – along with American interventions – has been the armed forces chain of command abandoning Tobin and Connell.'

'And the European Union – how will they act?'

'Oh, I would expect them to splutter fine words, issue communiques, hold summits, produce wordy declarations…'

'In other words do *nothing* other than wring their hands.'

'I couldn't possibly comment,' the expert said with a smirk.

Another clip showed foreign and British Army boots on the ground, advancing on the city of London. Fierce fighting was reported but there was little doubt the SNPS, and police were ill equipped to counter without the support of the military. Even those regiments that had remained loyal to the government were noticeable by their absence. The strength of the message, the power of the forces seemed impossible to resist and yet, according to NFN and CNN, the reprisals inflicted on members of the population, senior civic leaders, captured military figures were growing. Scarecrowing was now commonplace, official public executions on the greenery of Parliament Square a daily occurrence, kangaroo courts presided over by pliant members of the judiciary ever more cursory and inevitable in their conclusions and sentencing.

'Oh, my *Godddd*. The *bastarrrrds*,' said Rosa, who had re-joined them. The exclamation had energy and the rolling of her r's exaggerated. Good signs or the influence of alcohol? Whatever the reason it was good to see a glimmer of the real Rosa.

'*Shush*. What was that?' said Jo, suddenly alert.

'What? Didn't hear…'

Knock, knock.

The front door.

'Stay calm, it may be a nosy villager or farmer. Check it out, Dom…the window. Careful,' whispered Jo. She naturally assumed the absent Rebecca's command position.

'You're not going to believe it…oh, *hell*…'

'Dom? What is it?'

The three of them assembled in the hall as the letter box opened.

A sweet, female voice hailed them. 'Don't be tiresome, Dominic. You're not going to leave a girl out in the cold, are you?'

'Is that—' began Jo.

'Yeah,' confirmed Dominic.

'*Who*? What's the matter with you both…open the bloody door,' said Rosa. She strode forwards, pushing Dominic out of the way, and slid the bolts back, unhooked the chain, swung the door open.

'I *knew* I'd like you. How nice to meet at last,' said Stephanie, as she slipped past Rosa. 'But I wouldn't do that if I were you,' she said, her eyes narrowing as they focused on Jo's hand reaching into her pocket. Her voice had dropped a level, and she shuffled to one side to allow two heavies to intervene. They roughly frisked Jo and extricated her gun, handing it to Stephanie.

'Nasty things these,' she said, holding it by an extended little finger curled around the trigger guard. 'Jo, isn't it? But of course. We've met before, haven't we? Yes. Perhaps a more social opportunity to get to know each other this time. More civilised. What do you say? Yes,' said Stephanie, answering her own questions as usual. She brushed past Jo, standing on her tiptoes to plant a gentle kiss on Dominic's cheek.

'*So* good to see you, Dom. All those memories. Too long. Are you going to offer me a drink?'

Rosa glared, hands on hips.

'What have you done with our guys?' demanded Jo.

'I've no idea what you're talking about.'

'So explain your Neanderthals.'

'They're just friends of mine. I'm afraid it reflects a sad state of affairs, but all sorts of dangerous folks are out and about these days doing all manner of horrible things. You wouldn't believe it. It seems a girl needs her pet rottweilers.'

'And what have they done to Rebecca's men?' asked Dominic, following Stephanie as she breezed through into the lounge.

'I've no idea, but I'm afraid if you keep mongrels, they really are no match for…well, you get the idea…mind if I do?' Stephanie asked, reaching out simultaneously for the bottle of whisky.

'What do you *want*?' asked Rosa.

'It would be *marvellous* to get to know you, Rosa. Dom has told me *soooo* much about you. I just know we'll get along famously. How are your mama and papa? And I do hope poor Albert is recovering. Such a shame about Juan. Poor lad…' Stephanie looked from one to the other, slowly shaking her head as she raised an immaculately shaped eyebrow before saying, 'Do I detect a frisson of hostility? I'm here on a mercy mission. Mother Theresa and all that. Your saviour. Anything to help my Dominic…'

'*Yours*, is he? That so?' said Rosa, with the volume turned up.

Stephanie smiled and turned back to Dominic.

'On to business then, I suppose. The thing is you've got yourself a bit of a reputation. I'm sure it's all a terrible mistake. A man of your sweet nature. A terrorist? It's all a terrible gaffe – and so easy to correct. And I do have some *influence* in certain quarters…'

'At last the duplicity is cast aside. The pretence of supporting Jinks and democracy and freedom and…and…'

'Look, it's all frightfully simple. You've had bad press. Interviewers who twisted your intentions, misrepresented your beliefs. Fake news and all that.

There's so much of it around these days. You simply need to declare in favour of the government…your country…and all will be well.'

'Just look what they've done to my family. Juan's gone, Albert damn near destroyed, they've taken our house, raided our bank account, wrecked my business…I've been vilified, abused. How can you…how can you even begin to… *No*! I have *always* supported my country, always will. And monarchy and freedom win over your repugnant Marxists. *Always*. No, Stephanie, I simply won't do that…get the hell out of here…' said Dominic.

Rosa stared, open-mouthed. She stepped forwards to stand close to Dominic and placed her hand on his arm. Turning to Stephanie she said in a hushed tone, 'Please leave now.'

Stephanie looked on impassively, seemingly unmoved, unsurprised. She finished off her whisky, uncrossed her shapely slim legs and stood. Her hazel eyes locked onto Dominic's as she said in an unhurried voice, 'Twenty-four hours, Dom. That's all the time I can secure for you. It's the best I can do. BBC or NFN – it's all the same to us. Please get the message straight this time. Safe passage until then…just as you had across the English Channel,' she said, turning back to Rosa. 'He'll do the right thing by his family. I just *know* he will. After all, we wouldn't want Albert going the way of Juan, would we now? Oh, and I really do hope we can get to know each other, Rosa. I just *know* we'll be friends. And you should know he really loves you. After all, when you've known a man *carnally* you just *know*, don't you?'

Rosa stepped in front of her, visibly shaking. Her eyes tightened, eyebrows knitted together, and her face flushed. 'You know *nothing. Nothing.* Did you think my husband hadn't confided in me the error of his ways? You just prey on blokes for your own ends.'

Stephanie cut an ethereal figure and wore an enigmatic smile. She exuded calmness and a condescending, contemptuous air of superiority.

Rosa paused and then launched herself.

She slapped Stephanie with all her force, an explosion of pent-up emotions finding release to send her target staggering backwards, blood appearing at the corner of Stephanie's mouth. Composure erased in a single swipe.

The two women faced each other; Rosa glared.

Stephanie dragged her attention away from her assailant and looked intently at Dominic.

'Twenty-four hours if you don't want your eldest son to end up like Juan.'

Stephanie turned and walked away.

Rosa slammed the door behind her.

'Where's Albert?' asked Jo.

Rosa flew upstairs, Dominic frantically searched the house, while Jo checked outside, soon re-emerging with the news that Albert had been in the garden, occupying the wooden bench. Perhaps old survival techniques had kicked in. When trouble kicks off: head down, stay low. He seemed happier outside, so Jo chose to sit with him in silent reflection having first grabbed the emergency telephone. Dominic looked pensive, and presumed she was going to call Rebecca.

'She can't help. Rebecca's obviously on ops of some sort. But I know someone who can. We have to move, and fast, Dominic.'

He nodded but had even more pressing matters to attend to.

Rosa.

Needed to straighten this out.

No idea how.

Had to try.

'Rosa...' began Dominic.

She swung again, her second victim floored, as she erupted, her colourful Spanish and English expletives tumbling into each other as the tears flowed.

CHAPTER 41: BROADCAST

'We bring you breaking news of further atrocities. Fierce fighting is also breaking out in the Midlands and the Northern Home Counties with the Monarchists having the upper hand – SNPS barracks are being abandoned; the SNPS are on the retreat to their heartlands of London and the Southeast. Troops advancing on London have liberated the Southwest and the M4 corridor. More on these events as they unfold. In the meantime I welcome a familiar face – a government-declared terrorist, but a hero to Monarchists, FF, PAD, and his loyal fans. He's gained widespread acclaim from large sections of the British public. His interventions have become emblematic of the fight for freedom from the tyranny of the Marxist government – *peaceful resistance* being his mantra. Of course I refer to our celebrity chef Dominic Green aka Dominic Diamond. *Welcome*, Dominic. I understand you have a message to your supporters. *And* to the government?'

'I do.' Dominic paused, licked his lips. He reached for his glass of water, gulped deeply, placed the glass down clumsily.

'The thing is…an *ultimatum…*' he said, as he reached again for his glass. He looked over to Jo, who smiled her encouragement. Rosa sat and scowled. It had taken a lot of pleading to dissuade her from marching out of their marriage. It was probably Jo who saved the day, pointing out just how much Albert needed her at this moment. Needed both of them. *One mistake, Rosa. Are you going to destroy everything in punishing him for that?* It seemed to have given her pause for thought. But still Rosa was a brooding, dark force prickling with hostility one moment, grieving the next. She glared at him now. Albert was impassive. Was he listening? It was hard to tell. They had set up the interview to be held virtually, the four of them being trapped in their rural retreat – a retreat devoid of protection other than Stephanie staying the hand of the SNPS by exerting political influence. For now. As dusk approached, so did the expiry of their ultimatum. Dominic twiddled his wedding ring, fiddling with his truncated finger, while watching Albert.

'Take your time, Dominic. We understand you've been through a lot.'

'Okay…here goes. The thing is, I've been given an *ultimatum*. Our lives are at stake: Albert's, Rosa's, my own. My friend Jo's too. I'm required to confess my guilt…' Another gulp of water. 'I see a government that has changed this country beyond recognition. That's what it promised. But it never said how that would be achieved, it never secured a mandate for their version of socialism – communism, *Marxism*. In the name of egalitarianism of all things. *Egalitarianism*! I realise that our experience is but a small example of the terrors our people have been subjected to. Along with thousands of others, my business has been attacked and ruined. My best friend has been killed. *Scarecrowed*. My new absolute best friend's partner…' He looked up at Jo and cast a sympathetic half-smile. 'Her partner was dragged out of their bed, beaten and…*scarecrowed*. My youngest son's girlfriend was *gang-raped* at Chequers. It seems almost trivial to complain that my house was stolen from me, my bank account raided by the government. I know these acts have been replicated throughout the country to tens of thousands of people. These are heinous crimes, inhuman acts against ordinary people going about their daily lives. Then they threw my Albert into prison – a so-called rehabilitation centre. For the purpose of *re-education*. *Ha*! He was subjected to brainwashing, denied all freedoms, subjected to the most horrific mental pressures and drug therapies, which have left him almost comatose…he's lost his mind. A mere shell of a man. I don't know how to help him. I don't know what to do… Our youngest son, Juan, was killed in the act of freeing his brother. Rosa and I…we are trying to keep it together for Albert's sake…life's hardly worth the candle. And now I'm expected to declare in support of the government…despite all this. Our lives are threatened. They've explicitly said they will…they will…kill my son. *Our* son…the love of…' Dominic broke off. He took a drink and fought to control his emotions, rubbed a wavering hand across his forehead, pushing his hair back.

'We understand, Dominic…do you believe the threats to be real?'

'No question.'

'So what do you have to say to your supporters, to PAD, FF and to the government?' Ronald asked the question gently. His empathy was obvious, but he was still a broadcaster, he still wanted to complete his story. Uncover the punchline.

'I say this…am I guilty of opposing Marxism? *Yes.* Am I guilty of fighting for my family? To my shame I was slow to act, but in the final analysis – *guilty.* Am I guilty of trying to secure the release of my son from his illegal incarceration? *Guilty.* Am I guilty in supporting PAD, FF, national agencies that are seeking to release us from a despotic, cruel, inhumane regime? *Guilty as charged.*'

'And do you regret all of that?'

Silence stretched out…

'Dominic? Viewers will understand the unfair, appalling pressures you are being placed under. They will understand a survival instinct…'

He glanced at his son, who was wearing a quizzical expression. Dominic's heart missed a beat. It seemed another baby step in the right direction. Rosa looked at him and smiled, her eyes just about managing to get there too. He and Jo locked eyes. Hers glinted. What were they communicating? Defiance? Contrition? Submission? Then she nodded.

'Not a bit of it… I will *not* repent my supposed sins. I will *fight* to my last breath for my family, my country, for my Queen. I *love* my Rosa and Albert and my dead son, Juan… And dear Jo… But I do have a message to anyone out there who may be listening… The time has arrived. *Now* is the time for British values and compassion to prevail. *Now* is the time for the decent, silent majority of the British public to show their colours, to surface in resistance. Let humanity conquer evil and the time is…*now*! At my son's funeral… I can't believe I'm saying those words…as I gazed down on my son's last resting place… Corinthians… *Love bears all things, believes all things, hopes all things, endures all things.* Well, *now* is the time for love to conquer. If we believe in freedom, human rights, democracy and Queen and country *now* is the time to show it. *Fight* for your beliefs. *Fight* for our families. *Fight, fight, fight.* And to Stephanie Meadows…'

'Can you tell our viewers who she is, Dominic?'

'Stephanie Meadows is related to Tobin…she posed as a supporter of all that is decent and humane, inveigled herself into the orbit of Norris Jinks. She duped him. Deceived me. Many others too. She has betrayed many of the people she claimed to support. Better men than me fell under her bewitching spell… I have a direct message for you, Stephanie: *I've never met such a duplicitous, scheming, manipulative psychopath* as you. I can't hate you though…I feel sorry for you. Sorry for what you have become, sorry for your lack of compassion, your absence of human empathy, your inability to love – I mean to *really* love. I appeal to you to step away from your course of action, to think again. Somewhere deep inside I know there's a good person. Please don't subject my family or any other family to yet more horrors… But if you must, you must. The choice is yours. I won't abide by your demands or your distorted perspective of reality… I've made my choice.'

Dominic closed his PC lid slowly, thoughtfully. Jo was the first to embrace him, before standing aside as Albert took a half-step forwards, stopped and looked intently at his father.

Staccato movements.

'Son? What is it? We love you *so* much, son – what can we do to help?'

Albert suddenly stretched his hand out to Dominic.

It was grasped with alacrity. First a quizzical expression. Now a handshake.

And then father and son were embracing each other. They held on tightly, each to the other, as if to a lifeline. Rosa's hand went to her mouth, but she somehow maintained her silence as tears flowed freely. Albert pulled back from Dominic, looked round at his mum, then his gaze fell back on his father.

'Spot on, Dad. Well said.'

And that was the cue for the release of all their emotions, Rosa's to the fore. Very soon the three formed one in a bear hug. A single entity. A seamless family unit. Jo was soon pulled in. They had been through so much together.

As dark fell, they completed their preparations under Jo's tutelage. They wore backpacks containing bare essentials: spare clothes, water, sugary snacks. Jo distributed arms. Rosa declined. Dominic accepted reluctantly. Albert stepped forwards and took a rifle and a handgun. He spoke little but at least there was some communication now. Jo described the plan: exit route was via a public footpath accessed from the rear of their cottage, beyond the next field under the cover of darkness. But they knew they would be pursued.

'Destination?' asked Dominic.

'We head south towards Brighton where we can find safety with the Monarchists, where troops are clustered readying themselves for the final phase. But we need to get a move on. Three or four hours of walking, minimum. The SNPS are gathering somewhere between London and the south coast with a government-compliant military regiment to take a major last stand. We need to skirt around them. It's dangerous, so we'll avoid the towns and villages. We're heading towards a golf course the other side of the A27. That's probably the most perilous pinch point. Okay? Ready?'

They nodded.

All lights off, they ventured out, Jo and Albert taking the lead.

'Wait for my signal,' Jo said.

A tear in the clouds allowed a gibbous moon to penetrate the blackness of the night, casting a silvery hue as the damp grass reflected the moonlight. The light was unnerving, and he felt exposed. And Dominic was undoubtedly Stephanie's quarry now. He havered and was grateful for the reappearance of thick cloud, blackness once more enveloping them. His senses were on full alert, nerves jangling at the night sounds he could not identify, the susurration of the trees amplified.

'What was that?' whispered Rosa.

He stopped sharply. It could have been the rustling of a badger or a fox. His eyes had not completely adjusted but he thought he could just about make out two dark figures disappearing over the garden boundary, slipping from view. It must be Jo and Albert. Yes, Jo. She stood beyond the fence, and he could just make out her waving them on. They edged forwards stealthily, Dominic scouting the path beyond the terrace, wincing at every sound of his errant footsteps. A twig cracking, a small stone inadvertently kicked, the rustle of leaves all seemed magnified. Rosa followed closely. Dominic's head throbbed; his hands moistened.

Suddenly, the night was suffused by a wall of light.

He was blinded.

Drop your guns or die, a gruff voice called out.

And then figures stepped in front of them. Rosa reached out to Dominic. They froze.

'Drop your arms…*now*,' spoke a voice behind them.

Trapped.

Nothing for it.

All his fears fizzed to the surface. His heart thumped, filling his throat as it pushed into his mouth. He could hear his blood pulsing and felt Rosa's grip tighten.

'Put it down…*now!*'

No options, no escape, no rescue possible.

Get away from here, Jo, Albert, he willed them.

And then the finality of the situation hit home. No more running, no more shooting, no more fighting. All uncertainty removed. His tension slowly ebbed, and his heartbeat settled, and then a wave of fatigue overcame him. His destiny was no longer in his own hands. The end was in sight, a conclusion to all this.

'*Now!*'

He gently eased his gun to the ground. It was a relief to get rid of it. He drew Rosa tight to him.

'I love you, Rosa, whatever happens.'

'How sweet,' said a cultured voice, as she appeared from the blinding light, a spectral figure. He would recognise that voice anywhere. Stephanie stepped directly in front of them and cast them an enigmatic look that morphed into an ugly, tight-lipped hardness he had not seen in her before.

'I owe you, Rosa...'

She signalled to one of the guards who stepped forwards; he swiped Rosa across the face, first one way, then the other. Rosa yelped, stumbled, but managed to remain standing.

'*Bastarrrrds,*' she screamed.

Dominic pulled her into him, dabbing away the speckles of blood, shushing her.

They were pushed back inside the house. Dominic was torn away from Rosa, who was roughly pushed aside, prodded with an AK-47. Dominic's hands were secured: plastic cable ties, pulled tight. His and Rosa's eyes never left each other, silent thoughts communicating so much. His love transmitting, rising above all his regrets, all his sins, all his failings.

'Oh, Dominic – why did you not save yourself? I gave you *every* chance. Pulled *every* trick in the book – and then some. Such a shame. But such is life, no point in remorse or regrets. You got all your lines wrong yet again. But there's no point in looking back, harping on the past. Mind you, that spring morning...' said Stephanie, allowing the sentiment to hang in the air. And there was Mona Lisa making another appearance. Except that now she seemed demonic, distorted, demented. Dominic shuddered, suddenly seeing the reality behind her beauty starkly revealed, feeling a sudden wave of remorse and disgust. How could he have been so blind?

'You've no idea how to love, Stephanie. You play with people. Me... Rebecca...'

'Mm, Rebecca. Now there *was* a girl. Loved her dearly. A great shame she opted for the wrong side; you do know it was a close-run thing?'

Dominic looked aghast.

'Yes, we were sisters in arms for a long time. Until she made a fatal error of judgement. Traitorous. She's gone now, Dominic. She was captured, tried, sentenced. She's awaiting...well, I'm sure you can imagine... Oh, you didn't know that either! It seems I'm the harbinger of yet more bad news. She led us a merry dance and was quite good for a spook. But her luck ran out. Tragic...' A pall of sadness passed across her features momentarily, and then the half-smile returned, and the eyes lit up. 'Just shows, you can't win them all.'

'You really are deranged,' said Dominic.

Stephanie suddenly turned back to Rosa, slapped her hard, caught her by surprise, and this time she lost her footing and was sent sprawling. From her supine position she spluttered, '*Bitchhhh.*'

'You have spirit. I knew I'd like you. *Go*, Rosa, before I change my mind... Well, that's almost my final present to you, Dom. Just for you. Your wife's freedom...for now at least. Such a shame.' And as the guards held him tight, Stephanie rose onto the tips of her toes and planted a gentle kiss on his lips.

'Goodbye, Dominic. We won't see each other again...'

'*No*! Dominic, *Dominic*, please, please don't...please let him go. *Please...*' pleaded Rosa, on her knees, looking up imploringly at Stephanie. Dominic's last sight was of the return of Stephanie's supercilious, imperious disdain as the guards roughly bundled him out to a waiting van.

The last sound was of Rosa screaming his name.

CHAPTER 42: JUDGEMENT

Dominic was quickly dealt with at the police station without offer of legal representation. The charge was of terrorist activities in relation to Hartley Camp, citing his own words on NFN as evidence; treason for working with a foreign enemy to overthrow the government. The only surprise was that the charge was not for high treason, but Dominic thought he recalled that only applied to disloyalty to the Crown. The recollection opened a window on the irony of his supposed crimes. The charges seemed lazy, but he supposed they hardly needed to corral too much evidence to satisfy the emergency laws. What had he to say to the charges? He acknowledged the former, denied the latter. On being pressed, he admitted sympathy with the cause of restoration of the monarchy. His answers were offered wearily, transcribed by a bored officer with no attempts made to pursue any of the details. He had expected his fingerprints to be obtained but they weren't. The emphasis seemed to be upon photographing him while holding a card with his name and a caption in bold letters, "Enemy of the State." The presumption of innocence until proven otherwise was clearly a nicety jettisoned in favour of expediency, efficiency, effectiveness. He assumed his face would soon be emblazoned across national media as a government prize, evidence that the terrorists and usurpers of the Marxist rule were losing the battle. But the fighting he had heard on the journey back to the capital suggested a different story.

At Wormwood Scrubs he was soon wearing a prison uniform, having been processed speedily. His own clothes were stuffed in a plastic bag. He signed for them, mildly surprised that such procedures had survived. Dominic was bundled into a cell with others also awaiting trial. Conversation was minimal, the mood sombre. They would all know of their likely fate.

*

Caged within a prison van, the journey to the Old Bailey took around twenty minutes. Muffled sounds of engagement reached him in his confined space. Perhaps liberation was close? Was it cause for hope? But he could not allow himself that, quickly banishing the thought. Mr Micawber's days were finally behind him. Hope only brought false expectations, all too quickly shattered. His avowed wish was that liberation would soon happen – but he was realistic in accepting it would be beyond any timescale that might help him.

Hands and feet securely manacled, he debouched blinking into bright sunlight, a strong SNPS presence, and a noisy scrum of reporters and photographers. Rather than be squirrelled into court via the back entrance he was afforded a frontal entry: like a prize bull paraded round the ring at a county show. And a show trial was too good an opportunity for the propaganda machinery to miss. He grimly looked on at the circus. Images of Dominic Diamond in cuffs, flanked by SNPS officers, of jeering crowds drowning out his few supporters, of red flags waved jubilantly as he stood on the steps of the Old Bailey. The scene would no doubt grace the front pages of newspapers and feature as a lead story on television. NFN would also inevitably highlight it, but with fairer reporting. It was something to muse on as he was made to pause, present himself, an enforced pose.

He was brought to his feet as the court welcomed the newly appointed Lord Chief Justice, who was to preside in a panel of three, flanked by Justice Ellery to his left and the Recorder of London to his right. The seniority of the judges would lend a veneer of legitimacy to proceedings. There was no right of appeal. The verdict of the court would be final. And the requirement for a jury had been dispensed with. His appointed legal counsel – little more than a callow young barrister visibly unnerved by the prospect of leading such a high-profile case for the defence – explained that under emergency legislation the convening of a jury was no longer a requirement. Of course not. The introduction of a panel of people might bring an element of doubt to the outcome; it would be less efficient, consume too much time. And his barrister was to face an eminent prosecutor with Queen's Counsel status, the only surprise thus far being in the retention of such a position, that a change to the tag had not been conferred on QCs. A briefly diverting thought. After all, if they could think to change the *Queen Elizabeth* aircraft carrier into the *Tobin Red Star*... Dominic had been allowed two hours with his own barrister. He was told to expect a guilty verdict and was asked to consider submitting a plea of guilty while citing extenuating circumstances. He had been hazy as to what these might be considered as being. *Throw yourself on the mercy of the court.* Dominic's hollow laugh had caused consternation from his despondent young barrister.

The proceedings featured all the judicial trappings, pomp and circumstance of the English legal system as developed over the centuries with the wigs and flowing scarlet robes of the judges: the Lord Chief Justice had the distinction of a scarlet train; the QC wore his black, silk court coat with turned down cuffs adorned with the distinctive three buttons and also wore a wig. The finest legal minds in the land had gathered to prosecute, defend, and judge Dominic's crimes. That he had pleaded "not guilty" seemed to be a matter of mild irritation, even to his own barrister and supporting team, an inconvenient transgression from perceived wisdom in the face of overwhelming evidence.

The QC was soon in full flow, delivering the prosecution's arguments before proceeding to dismantle the flimsy case for the defence. Dominic viewed proceedings with an almost out-of-body experience: detached philosophical interest. He found the process surreal. The prosecution's case was succinct, the case for the defence briefer still, but the dismantlement of the defence almost leisurely: vultures picking his bones clean, savouring every morsel.

As the Lord Chief Justice briefly consulted with his colleagues, they prepared to deliver their verdict; it had obviously been deemed unnecessary to withdraw to consider their judgement or to balance any arcane legal arguments. It was hardly surprising as the case against him was straightforward, the defence compliant in bending to the QC's will. Dominic had not chosen to take the stand and had declined to make any statement. He would reserve what he did wish to say until the final moment.

There was nothing left to do but deliver the verdict and proceed to sentencing.

The Lord Chief Justice, with a tendency to slouch one moment, lean forwards the next, now drew himself up with a ramrod-straight back. His hands thrust forwards on the bench like a priest gripping the edges of the pulpit about to deliver his sermon. His glasses balanced on the end of his long, aquiline nose.

'*Silence in court,*' an official demanded.

The hubbub died down, and soon the court awaited the verdict in hushed silence. The priest cast eagle eyes around the court before delivering his tub-thumping address: pompous words emphasised his own loyalty to the rule of law. The unspoken sentiment was one of absolute loyalty to the government of the day, whatever its dubious credentials. He whipped himself into a frenzy of legal argument, masking any professional misgivings at the undue haste of the legal process in meting out what he declared as justice. As an educated man with a long career, surely he would be aware of the fig leaf of judicial process he was presiding over? It was pointless dwelling on such niceties as the absence of a jury or any chance of a credible defence or of any right to appeal. All such matters had been swept away along with the solicitors, barristers, judges who had sought to express their concerns.

Dominic was found guilty on the charges levelled.

In sombre tones, he was invited to address the court before sentencing.

The judges seemed surprised that he chose to do so.

'My lords and lady…you deem me guilty. But it is I who remain loyal to Queen and country. I'm not propelled by ideology or high principles. My actions have been driven by the cruelties inflicted on my family and friends by SNPS and police thugs. The government had no mandate to morph into Marxism, no electoral legitimacy. My family and friends have been abused, terrorised, tortured and killed by this despotic, odious regime. Along with tens of thousands of other law-abiding British citizens. Was I to stand back and do nothing? But I do have regrets…that I could not have saved Juan, could not have prevented harm to Albert, that I've been separated from the love of my life, my Rosa. My lords and lady…I'm no terrorist; I've never had a treasonous thought in my life. You have found otherwise in the loyal service of your political masters, and you must all live with your own consciences… Mine is clear.'

That he was allowed to speak freely without interruption was a surprise. A relief. He hoped his sentiments would be captured for posterity and might one day be regarded fondly by those he knew and loved; he hoped the sentiments might resonate.

He was asked to stand again to receive his sentence.

He remained calm, although a few butterflies stirred.

After a long gap the Lord Chief Justice reached down to his side and was soon placing a black cap on his head, the restoration of the practice obviated by the abolition of capital punishment in 1969, now restored for the crimes he had been found guilty of in a trial lasting just a few hours.

CHAPTER 43: DESTINATION DAY -1

The atmosphere was oppressive as a shroud of gloom and despondency descended following yesterday's cell battle. Rupert had provided a lift as their D-days loomed ever larger. His team's irreverence and preternatural optimism had lifted morale a notch or two; their departures had left a void, the bloody stain that was the legacy of the cockney lady a constant reminder of her demise. Their numbers were also dwindling. Dominic counted just twelve remaining. There had been no additions following Rupert's recruitment to cell block H, so dubbed by one of their number.

His roast pork meal ominously portended tomorrow's destiny. He gazed down on it in silence, taking in the gelatinous grey mass, soggy crackling and a grey puddle that was a poor imitation of apple sauce. Or was it sage and onion stuffing? And the soggy vegetables did not tempt his taste buds either, salivation kept firmly at bay. He shuddered at having almost arrived at his pre-determined destination, struggling to retain his equanimity.

'Star attraction, top billing to our celebrity chef *hero...*' The word was laced with contempt. Dominic thought that unseemly, unnecessary. But then how much of what the country had experienced recently had been anything less than unseemly? There was no point looking back. It was so painful. Except, come to think of it, there were positives, it suddenly dawned on him: a remarkably close friendship with Jo, the stoicism and bravery of Farmer Tim and Annie, the acquaintances in PAD and FF...and then there was Celia. *Rebecca.* He must ask her about the Celia moniker. His snagged thoughts were dragged back to the here and now as Shorty continued. 'And our MI5 snake in the grass...our traitor. Good crowd guaranteed. Midday – peak time viewing.' And then he rattled off four more names, which would halve their number by the time tomorrow was over. Unless they planned any more surprises. But it would not be of any interest to him by then, he thought grimly. He quivered, provoking Celia to place a comforting hand over his. They sat so close together her fear reverberated through him; two ex-comrades in arms hermetically sealed into a single unit. At least for now.

Morsels of his meal were picked over, most of it left untouched. The guards had long since retreated and silence descended as some slumbered; others retreated within themselves. Dominic could not sleep. Celia seemed to be similarly afflicted.

'Why Celia?'

'My real name – always hated it. Only my close family call me that. Or at least used to... I didn't want Uncle Harry to know how we'd met, what we'd been doing. He chastised me for putting myself in harm's way as it was. I just couldn't put him through more than he'd suffered already.'

'What was his story? But only if you want to...if it's too painful—'

'A silent hero was Harry. A quiet, unassuming man just going about his business. And then they came for his son in the middle of the night. It's a now familiar story. You know the form. He was later found *scarecrowed* at the end of his street. It completely destroyed Aunty Margaret. She was ill anyway, but she just gave up the ghost; withered and died within months. He vowed revenge and was soon helping in various FF raids. But of course he eventually got caught. The rest you know, or can imagine,' said Rebecca.

'And *you*? What happened after you left us?' asked Dominic.

'In a word – *Stephanie*! I thought we had her and her cronies, but they had the drop on us. We'd tailed the team. Despite taking extra precautions she simply outsmarted me. *That's* the bit that hurts most. It hurts like hell... And you, Dom?' she asked.

'The same really. Stephanie found us; her guys topped yours. She gave Rosa a slap, me an ultimatum: repent my sins and avow allegiance to Tobin – publicly... BBC or NFN...or...well...*this*!'

'You refused...'

'Yeah...I had my interview on NFN, declared my allegiance to Queen and country...love of my family. A fat lot of good any of that did. Except my conscience is clear. I made my choice a long time ago. I just couldn't let Rosa down again...nor you...nor Jo. Stephanie stopped our escape. Mine and Rosa's. Jo and Albert had slipped away as the advance guard, thank God. She slapped Rosa again. Then said she liked her spirit and let her go...you do realise she's quite mad, don't you? I'm sure she must be a psychopath.'

'Certifiable.'

Rebecca seemed to slip into some sort of trance for a while and Dominic's thoughts drifted off. He wondered where Rosa and Albert might be and how they would cope. His only solace was in the final exchanges with Albert and his last conversation with Rosa. How he wished they could be reunited. But it was too late. At least there had been a coming together at the end. That was something. His private reverie was suddenly interrupted by a gentle prod in his ribs. He turned to Rebecca and the two looked into each other's eyes.

'You weren't a natural freedom fighter, Dom...' Rebecca said, in a sombre tone.

'No,' he said as his friend Tim's plight and Rosa's accusations sprang to mind.

'But that makes your bravery all the more impressive. Don't get me wrong, as a fighting machine you – well, you were pretty hopeless. Definitely not cut out for guns. But to stand up to the bullies, to call out Stephanie and declare yourself publicly in favour of Queen and country in the face of...well, you know. And Rosa seems a great character... I'm sorry that I caused her so much pain...'

Rebecca's words dried up, but Dominic was moved, emotion bubbling to lodge in his aching throat. The last time he could recall that sensation was... well, come to think of it – very recently. *Juan*. The emotion akin to grief spiced with a burning, loving intensity that physically hurt. He and Rebecca had gone through so much over recent years: from brief illicit lovers to strangers to companions in arms, to warm, sibling-like friends. Quite a journey. He shifted uncomfortably and fought to hold back the tears that were only too ready to make their appearance.

He needed to prick the moment.

'Oh, she's a character alright!' he said, shrugging his acknowledgement of the weak humour. *The best I can do at the moment*, his expression conveyed.

He slowly broke into a full smile and Rebecca joined him.

They shared a momentary spike of happiness – emotional warmth.

The pleasure of full-on friendship.

CHAPTER 44: DESTINATION DAY

The clanking and scraping of the door announced the start of their last day. But the demeanour of Shorty and Pock seemed subdued, their usual delight in the imminent demise of their charges absent. Even Pock's delivery of his boot on a careless rear seemed half-hearted. Rations were dumped in the middle of the cell, and they sloped off, more surly than triumphant, banging the steel door behind them.

'I wonder where Happy is,' said Rebecca.

'Don't suppose he's that popular with them now... You okay?'

'Spirits have been higher...'

'Yeah.'

They lapsed into doleful silence, disconsolately chewing at lumps of bread and cheese, sipping water. Dominic tried to imagine a luxurious serving of eggs Benedict, but this time his imagination failed him; he could not conjure up the aroma, struggled to imagine home or a holiday hotel, so gave up trying.

'Can I ask you about Stephanie?' he finally said.

'Now or never.'

'Mm. It's something she said about you having changed sides. She implied you originally supported Tobin and Connell, Mobilisation, the whole agenda...'

'That's Steph. A grain of truth, but it falls a long way short of the whole truth. Remember that I was employed by a government agency – Spooks Ville. Just a foot soldier really. Tobin was democratically elected; I had no reason to think my allegiance would be tested. Who could have imagined how things would develop? As to being on the same side as Steph...she never spoke of politics, never declared any allegiances. At first, I'd no idea she was connected to Tobin.'

'How did you meet, then? I've come to assume you infiltrated her company as some sort of MI5 ploy.'

'I stumbled on her at a social event. She was fun…beguiling. I'd never had a friendship like it. And we discovered a shared love of the arts—'

'Stephanie? Really?'

'You now know she's manipulative. And how she behaves for you guys is so clichéd. You know, those big eyes flutter, she shows a shapely leg, flutters her eyelashes, oozes sexuality. And you all bloody well fall for it! But that's not the whole Stephanie. It's an act of course. She's actually a highly intelligent, well-educated woman. We quickly found a shared interest which spanned much of the arts: Shakespeare, Renaissance painters, classical music, theatre. And we both had a passion for watercolours. She had studied art at university and we both admired the likes of Turner and Constable. She was actually incredibly talented, and I dabbled a bit. In fact, you might remember back in Devon…'

'I do. Your seascapes and the tors of Dartmoor…and in your Mayfair pad the walls were festooned with artwork.'

'A few were mine, but most were Steph's. We had a room done out as our studio and whiled away many an hour in there – as unlikely as that now seems. Our friendship became a social whirl that took us to the Louvre, Musée d'Orsay, Pompidou in Paris as well as the V&A and all the various iconic venues in London. I loved it.'

'I never saw any of that in her…not beyond what I took as a genuine interest in haute cuisine. How sincere was that do you think?'

'Undoubtedly so. We did lots of top restaurants in Paris, Barcelona, London. And she genuinely liked you, set her stall out for you. Not that Stephanie has much of a grasp on normal human feelings.'

'You obviously worked her out…so why the relationship?'

'That just grew out of friendship and mutual shared interests, and she was good fun to be with. I sort of fell under her hypnotic spell. I could hardly believe I was falling for someone of my own gender. I'd never imagined…never suspected such leanings, but we just clicked. It just sort of happened naturally. At first, anyway. If someone had suggested I might… I'd have laughed. But it happened. And at first it was wonderful. Now I look back on it I realise she saw me as being potentially useful, given where I worked. I slowly came to suspect her motives and she was so vague about what she did and spun lies about her family background.'

'Is that when you started to follow her? Discovered Tobin?'

'Sort of.'

'Why didn't you just get up and walk away?'

'I nearly did a couple of times, but there was something addictive about her character...intoxicating, if you like. You should know all about it...and Jinks... Gender didn't seem to matter. If someone interested her...and she would pull me into her playful games – remember the restaurant and the times we were together in the flat?'

'So, when did it go sour? When did you suspect something sinister?... I mean...why did she drag herself into politics...how did it become cat and mouse between you two?'

'Oh, crikey, Dom. Who knows what her game was? I'm not sure she ever did either. She just alights on one scheme after another. Then she mentioned your name and I was a bit shocked, and she dragged our story out of me. From then onwards you became a cause célèbre. She claimed it was harmless, flirtatious fun, and I just watched from the side-lines a bit bemused.'

'And you didn't think to object? To warn her off? Or me?'

'I tried to at first, but you know what she's like. Told she can't have something, and she doubles down. I'm sorry, Dom. Terribly sorry. I should have warned you. We were long since done, but I always remembered our time in Devon with misty-eyed fondness. And I liked you. I never wanted you to become some sort of pawn in her game. But even now I'm not sure what I could have done to stop it. She certainly wouldn't have taken any notice and I doubt you would have either.'

'No.'

'Then it became something more. I saw what she was doing to you – and you never had a chance, by the way. A blood sport to her. You were a naïve innocent... It gradually occurred to me that what she was doing was cruel, that it could ruin your life. Little did I know to what extent. But by the time she had pulled you into her web, politics had turned nasty. I deployed some of my craft to dig a bit deeper into who she was, having begun to suspect something. Despite living with her I knew little about the real Stephanie and yet she seemed to know all about me. Anyway, that was when I uncovered her family connections. And someone had taken to tailing me. It all spiralled down from there. I wanted out, but a colleague persuaded me to try and benefit from her family link.'

'You're saying MI5 were taking sides with Jinks...against the government?'

'Not officially. Most of the top brass sat on the fence. Waiting to see how things might transpire. Weighing up the competing forces. It's a fallacy that they always work for the government. If they're supposed to, no one ever told them! But a few were more proactive, and I was appalled at what was happening, so I wanted to help. And I could see how Steph was manipulating you…and simply saw me as being at her beck and call. I began to resent that too.'

'But remember she was trying to persuade me to join the resistance at that time…'

'Just as she had recruited celebs and others. You yourself said they all seemed to disappear having declared their colours. And, you know, I'm not even certain she knew which side she was on at that time. Perhaps playing with both, keeping her options open.'

'But in the end family ties were decisive?'

'Perhaps. Who knows? The irony is that you doubted *me*. How many times did you challenge me? Even after the PAD demo which nearly ended in disaster, you weren't able to trust me completely…'

'I feel bad about that, but Stephanie had messed with my head, and to be fair you were ambiguous time after time…my head never did make the decision.'

'Jo?' she asked.

'Nah. My heart if you must know. You were the only person who showed sympathy, who cared for me when I was at my lowest. It just felt genuine. You became the little sister I never had. And you showed everything I lacked – bravery, leadership and what you'd call tradecraft. I just instinctively trusted you.'

'Shame it all failed in the end…but we gave them a run for their money, Dom. We made a difference. Tobin and Connell and Stephanie *will* all founder. Their demise is certain and that wouldn't have happened without people like us. And you captured the imagination of swathes of Middle Englanders.'

They lapsed into silence once more, Dominic dwelling on his loved ones: his family, Jo, and Rebecca uppermost, but Bill also featured in his grim recollections. At least Albert and Rosa had escaped. They would be able to piece together a life. He wondered if she might take him to Spain with her. Rosa would do whatever was best for him, of that he was in no doubt. And that was a comfort.

The sound of boots signalled the arrival of their time. They offered no resistance, went quietly to their guards, joined their guarded escort in the corridor. Their hands were secured with cable ties. First Rebecca and then Dominic were loaded into adjacent cages in the prison van. Dominic was a dazed zombie, slowly walking through his own nightmare. As the van bumped its way through the streets of London his brain seemed incapable of coherent thoughts, his head full of cotton wool. No words were exchanged between the two prisoners.

Dominic could not have said how much time had passed, but after a while the vehicle pulled to a halt. The doors were flung open, and they were led down the steps into an open-air courtyard with SNPS guards all around. While his eyes adjusted to the light and he took in the wave of coruscating heat from yet another scorching hot day, his captors seemed to be taking last-minute orders. But there was none of the usual strutting officialdom, hectoring or intimidation. They were strangely muted in their exchanges. The guards shuffled constantly and fidgeted with their weapons. A few looked around, seemed anxious. Then his ears were assailed by cheering, and in the background the sounds of battle. His senses struggled to take everything in: first the brightness, then the heat, then the body language, the cheering and fighting. Layer upon layer gradually unfolding to reveal their stage. He glanced at Rebecca, who seemed to have been distracted by a flurry of activity in the far corner of the courtyard. She had probably taken it all in instantly. Perhaps even now she was assessing her surroundings, concocting some sort of plan, impossible though that seemed. He preferred to cast aside thoughts of somehow being spared the sanction of the courts.

They were offered counsel with a priest. Rebecca shook her head; Dominic nodded and was led to a corner for a private session. He bowed in supplication as his priest muttered prayers for his soul. He barely heard a word. But the private moment seemed fitting, and he said his own silent prayers for his family's future; a final chance to allow the idea of a God to hear his wishes, even forgive him his sins and inadequacies. A final goodbye to Juan. Unspoken words to dear Jo and to Rebecca. Two amazing women. He considered himself privileged to have met them, to count them as his friends.

Then it was time.

They were led through a corridor of scaffolding into Parliament Square. As he emerged onto the green and they came to a halt, his knees gave way. Guards either side took tight grip of him, prevented his slumping to the ground. There, in the middle of the area, were three wooden structures standing side by side: gallows, one with a figure already swinging from the gibbet.

Rebecca gasped.

'See what you lot did...' said Shorty, pointing to where the hapless guard swung: Happy. The loss of his firearm in the melee in their cell the other day – the loss of his life today. Dominic stared open-mouthed. His forehead beaded with pinpricks of sweat; his armpits were wet. And then he took in the backdrop – Westminster Palace. The traditional home of democracy was to witness his fate.

And then the noise hit him.

Looking around, he was stunned in his recognition of the purpose of the metal scaffolding he had stepped through into this arena. Surrounded on three sides of the square: temporary stands erected to house the public. The sort of structures he had sat in himself: at a country summer fair at Chatsworth House, at the open golf tournament at Turnberry. And they were baying for the spectacle of their daily ration of morbid curiosity. Then Rebecca nudged him, drawing his attention to one small section where his own smiling picture was displayed on posters held aloft. Supporters cheered him, chanted his name and then in unison rose to their feet and lambasted the nearest guards, letting loose bags full of red M badges. But their calls were soon drowned out by the majority assembled for their blood sport. SNPS guards rushed into the stand, hauled out the perpetrators, rid them of the pictures of a treasonous terrorist. They were thrown out, beaten as they were being evicted. And their place was taken by more members of the public wearing the ubiquitous red shirts and Ms, bearing the look of Wimbledon tennis fans handed prized late tickets for Centre Court.

Dominic watched this unfold, his mind momentarily distracted from his imminent demise. As the red shirts had flooded in, he became aware of guards to one side gesticulating to the stand opposite Westminster Palace, as the sounds of an encroaching gun battle grew louder. Officers were energised, soon shouting their commands. Firing was drawing closer, punctuated with deep-throated explosions. The volume had definitely been turned up. People in the upper tiers of the stands cast their eyes at events unfolding behind them and a steady stream of spectators heading towards the exits soon turned into a flood, just as Parliament Square was breached.

FF resistance fighters now poured into the area as confusion reigned; members of the public screamed, many choosing to hunker down below their seats, many running directly into the firing line. SNPS officers barked their instructions, many guards ran haphazardly towards exits to be met by more resistance fighters, civilians with their blood-curdling screams, blazing gunfire. Many guards fired indiscriminately as panic took hold and they were gunned down from all sides as the breaches in the stadium admitted columns of fighters and soldiers to the killing ground. Mayhem ensued and soon the stadium was strewn with bodies, mainly SNPS but some FF fighters also succumbed.

Dominic fell to the ground as a gunshot fibrillated the air around him, only to have a figure falling across him. He struggled to free himself – warm, cloying blood flowing over his face and arms. A civilian figure rushed to him, offered a quick toothless grin, and in a swift movement wielded his knife to slit Dominic's cable ties. A series of shots sounded out and his rescuer landed in an untidy mess, his body riddled. Dominic heard a shout and looked up: Pock. He stared at the gun pointed at his head just a foot away, its owner delighting in his shock, his face breaking into a fiendish, cruel grin.

A loud retort sounded out.

Dominic flinched reflexively, and then gaped in astonishment as a hole punctured Pock's forehead, a mirepoix of tissue, bone fragments and bloody grey matter exploding from the back of his head. His stricken body was propelled backwards, collapsing in a brief spasm as his lifeblood pooled around him.

Suddenly Rebecca was at Dominic's side, armed with Shorty's AK-47, having despatched their owner to what they later imagined would be eternal purgatory. She knelt down to his stricken form. He had not felt anything as the adrenalin surged through him, assumed the blood was that of those who had fallen on top of him. That of Pock too. His eyes dulled and he drifted off…

When he came round, medics were kneeling at his side, Rebecca too. He was told to stay still. He could not do otherwise. A stretcher appeared and after the administration of calm but urgent first aid – tourniquets, bandaging, splints, intravenous fluids – he was eventually loaded onto the stretcher and transferred to an ambulance.

Dominic woke up the next day in a hospital ward attached to drips, machines monitoring his essential organs, his oxygen levels, and heartbeat. He had been hit several times, the most serious being a shot to the abdomen, which had required surgery. Fortunately, it had missed the liver, bladder, and kidneys, but there was damage to his stomach and intestines. He had lost a lot of blood and was the recipient of a transfusion. A broken arm and a flesh wound to his leg had also been treated. He later learnt that he had been operated on within an hour of being admitted and had been heavily sedated to help him recover. It was several days before he was able to focus and converse, then only stutteringly.

His first words were to enquire about Rebecca. Had she survived? Good news. She had fared much better than him and was waiting to see him. And Rosa? Albert? Jo? The nurses smiled, reassured him all was well and were soon ushering Rosa to his bedside. She was unusually calm, soon telling him the doctors had said she could come in for a brief period but that he needed peace and quiet. She made a conscious effort to remain in control of her emotions, but the tears were soon flowing as the dam burst with the relief and sheer joy at their unexpected reunion.

'Where's Albert? How's he doing?' Dominic asked.

His voice was thin, concern engraved on his features as he squeezed her hand.

'He's coming on. One of your PAD contacts got in touch with me. Said he heard your broadcast, knew Albert would need help. He put me in touch with an expert who specialises in stress disorders, and he's now holding regular sessions with Albert. He seems to be responding, but it will be a long period of recuperation and he'll be mentally scarred for the rest of his life. He wouldn't take a fee. He said they all owed you, it was the least they could do,' said Rosa, stroking his hand.

Dominic smiled, but his eyes were heavy, and a nurse called time on the visit.

Rosa bent over and kissed him, wiping away tears forming at the corners of his eyes. She turned, scooped up her coat and made for the door, stopping briefly to deliver a parting shot, 'Muy bien, Dom…such big cojones! *Mucho grande!*' with which she blew him a kiss, and he smiled at her retreating back.

CHAPTER 45: RENEWAL

AUTUMN 2028

The family had gravitated back to London, finding a two-bedroom flat to rent as a temporary arrangement, while both Dominic and Albert convalesced. Slowly, he and Rosa picked up their relationship, learning how to cope with their grief at Juan's passing and being encouraged by the progress of Albert's rehabilitation. He had even begun to take an interest in culinary matters, which drew father and son closer as master and apprentice reconnected. Dominic was delighted at Albert's latent flair, as he began to take special interest in the pastry section. He even started his craft qualifications part-time at college. This process of recuperation and renewal at the family level reflected what was happening in wider society and politics.

The government had capitulated, and Tobin's attempt to flee had been thwarted; he was intercepted heading towards the ports on the south coast. Connell had remained in Westminster awaiting her inevitable arrest. The royal family had returned from Canada to popular acclaim. Their return seemed to lift the national mood, a sign of hope, a symbol of the imminent return to normality. Norris Jinks was asked to form an interim national government of unity to pave the way for the resurrection of the civil service, the restoration of democracy and a general election. The interim government was hastily assembled, and modified emergency legislation quickly approved, soon receiving royal assent, and so passing into law. The more extreme measures of Tobin's regime were repealed along with the abolition of capital punishment. The SNPS were abolished as a force but had long since dissipated, their members fading into the background of society; a minority formed dissident, armed groups, and made occasional noisy, violent forays but their outrages were spasmodic and lacked traction.

Jinks' government was quick to establish its libertarian credentials, embracing basic human rights, freedom of expression, the restoration of government agencies. It reached out to the international community, where it was warmly received, by major Western and world alliances: the United Nations, NATO, the World Health Organisation, and the European Union. Members of the government included senior politicians from the Conservatives, Liberal Democrats, Greens, SNP, and old grandees from the pre-Marxist Labour Party. It also had leading figures from business, the professions, religious groups, and environmentalists; a quasi-political, technocratic government with a shared mission to reach consensus across Great Britain. But the top priority was to restore peace and to prepare for the return to a full parliamentary democracy. A conciliatory approach was taken to the healing of the wounds of conflict with an amnesty for the surrender of firearms, the extension of an olive branch to those that had been sucked into the extreme version of socialism. It would take generations to heal the wounds completely, but the process was begun in earnest. As for senior figures like Tobin and Connell, they were to be tried; the precise details as to process and timescales were to be determined by a special commission to be led by judicial review. The previous Lord Chief Justice took the chair, his successor having been allowed to quietly retire along with other pliant figures who had bent to the will of Tobin and Connell.

Dominic was surprised and delighted to receive an invitation to a garden party at Buckingham Palace being held to recognise the nation's resistance heroes. King William V and Catherine, the Queen Consort, were to be in attendance following his coronation. His ascent to the throne the result of the royal family choosing to leapfrog a generation; a popular, youthful monarch in tune with the need for renewal and regeneration.

Rosa was wildly excited at the prospect of meeting the monarch, hoped desperately to meet Catherine, and spent weeks anticipating the event. They stretched their meagre budget to splash out on an outfit that would best set off Rosa's vibrant Spanish heritage: her black shiny hair and dark eyes. It was always likely to be in her favourite colour, red. Dominic also insisted on her having her hair done at a top salon and a luxurious facial treatment, which she turned into a day out complete with a champagne lunch. And on the day prior to the garden party she had her nails manicured. Dominic insisted she looked a million dollars, and she fizzed with nervous excitement as they set off for their special day. What a contrast to their recent travails.

'Need to get going, Rosa. You ready? Wow, you look stunning. Do we have time to...'

She hit him and a mock scowl was accompanied by a threatening wag of the finger.

'Okay, but first stop Westminster.'

'Why Westminster? What you up to now...'

'Just a routine meeting I have to attend to, love.'

'Oh no you don't, not on today, of all days. Since when have you had business meetings? Dominic Green, if you dare spoil today, I'll have your cojones on toast, I swear.'

'You really have a thing about my cojones, don't you? It won't take long... 10 Downing Street please,' he said to the taxi driver.'

'My *Goddd* – what's going on?' Rosa said.

'All will be revealed.'

Rosa was in a state of shock as Dominic led her up to the most famous number ten in the world. As he approached, the door opened and they were immediately met by the imposing, mildly dishevelled Norris Jinks. His welcome was warm and informal: *call me Norris*, he said, pulling his hand through his unruly mop of ginger corkscrews. He complimented Rosa on her outfit, expressing mild concern that she would relegate the Queen Consort to a mere supporting role on the haute couture stakes. Rosa positively glowed, and for once struggled to find words. Dominic's attention was drawn by the photographs of the various prime ministers through the ages that adorned the walls of the sweeping staircase. Noticing, Norris Jinks insisted on being their guide through the history of British prime ministers as they picked their way up the famous staircase. He selected a few characters who were particular favourites of Dominic's: Churchill, Lloyd George, Asquith, Clement Attlee. Jinks had a word or two about what made each special and then picked a few nineteenth century figures he considered worthy of special mention: Disraeli, Gladstone, Salisbury. Back at the bottom of the staircase, Jinks insisted on taking them into the cabinet room. They were encouraged to sit at the famous table, taking chairs opposite the provisional prime minister. He then turned his attention to Dominic, clasping his hands together as he leant forwards across the cabinet table.

'We have a garden party to attend...mustn't make you late for that. You would never forgive me, Rosa. So I'll get to the nub of it...' He proceeded to invite Dominic to become an ambassador – the advocacy of freedoms of expression and human rights being the focus for a role that was to reach out to communities throughout GB with a strong media presence. 'A Tsar of Freedoms if you like. How does that sound?' Dominic stared back at him, momentarily flummoxed.

'I'm hugely flattered...hugely...but I'm not sure it's me, Prime Minister...'

'*Norris.*'

'Err, Norris. I'm not a public figure—'

'Nonsense! Quite the contrary. You were an icon for decency, freedom, and democracy in the struggles. Never off the screens. A good-looking man like you with a great fan base. Perfect for the role. No one more passionate on the subject. I want to mark your contribution somehow and it's an *important* job.'

'That's kind, although I fear you're overstating my role in the struggles. It's a great honour... But I have my reward. I have my Rosa back and Albert is recovering, slowly but surely. He needs us full-time. We want a simple family life. We've a lot of catching up to do, a lot of healing...'

'Well, I must say I can't blame you for that. Very well. So be it. But what can we do to thank you? Needless to say a gong will be forthcoming – your name's towards the top of the list.'

'Well...'

'Yes? Speak up, man. Ask away...'

'It would be a huge honour to cook for you; run the kitchen for a banquet or a dinner at your country residence, Chequers. It holds so many terrible memories. Perhaps a rebalancing of the scales, putting the previous experience behind us...although the nightmares will never leave me. It would be the pinnacle of my professional career to...'

The prime minister had pulled his bulk out of the chair and paced up and down as Dominic spoke. He wore a frown and then came to an abrupt halt opposite them. Ruffling his hair again, he shifted his weight from one foot to the other.

'Sorry, too much to ask for. It's just a privilege to meet you and we are so looking forward to the garden party,' said Dominic, colouring.

'Not at all. Just turning the options over in my mind. Yes, I know what we'll do. *Right.* You'll be hearing from me,' he said. 'Now I really ought to let you good people get to the party. And I need to smarten myself up, though I fear I'm a bit of a lost cause on those stakes. Need to report back to Pamela the haute couture standards you have set, Rosa. My dear wife's a fine woman, very handsome, but I fear it's an impossible challenge. Don't tell her I said so – get me in frightful trouble.'

The garden party proved to be a big hit despite finding the socialising daunting at first. A couple of glasses of Pimm's soon took the edge off, allowing him to relax into the occasion. And he did not have to work hard as Rosa came to the fore, finding an outlet for her exuberance, delighting in the attention she received. She also indulged in celebrity spotting and took the opportunity to meet a famous actor. Undoubtedly, the highlight of the day was in meeting Catherine, the Queen Consort, who was charming, relaxed, and informal.

As Albert's mental health improved, they soon hatched a plan for their future. Rosa's parents had sadly passed away during the latter part of the troubles, leaving her a small inheritance. They had also been in receipt of compensation for the loss of their property; not a large figure but a welcome surprise. The newly elected government, with Jinks at the helm with a decent working majority, chose a path of compensation for wronged previous homeowners as being reasonable and expedient. As the government owned the houses that had originally been confiscated from the likes of Dominic and Rosa, they set upon a challenging task to rehouse the current occupants, a process fraught with social challenges and opposition. It had seemed only fair to act swiftly to compensate the previous owners in the meantime.

Brandon tried to convince Dominic of a fool-proof business opportunity – several options, in fact. It was impossible to be anything other than impressed with his enthusiasm, but Dominic remained steadfast. *We have other plans, not prepared for any more of your madcap schemes.* Brandon expressed surprise at the rebuttal, and turned on the charm turbo chargers, but to no avail. Rosa similarly shunned the overtures from her partners at the legal practice, announcing that she was drawing a line under her professional career to focus on her family's future.

The three of them set about their new life in North Yorkshire, a local hostelry transformed into a gastro pub. Albert was transferred to a new doctor in the locale who would continue to guide his recovery, and he passed his craft examinations with flying colours. They threw themselves into their new life, meeting locals who readily welcomed them into the community, no doubt helped by Dominic's reputation and Rosa's outgoing character. Dominic and

Albert focused on menu and recipe development, establishing local suppliers of the finest indigenous produce, while Rosa took on interior design and front of house. Their ethos reflected their own renewal as a family: *simplicity and authenticity*. Gone were the days of elaborate Michelin-starred food, complex dishes, starched linen, and formal service.

At last *'D&A at Green's'* was ready to throw open their doors for the locals to sample their fare; initially meals were offered free of charge as the family sought to establish a routine, iron out teething problems, grapple with a new computerised system of billing and stock control, train local staff and ensure the new chef could reach their standards, adapt to their style. In the second week, they began trading for real and were visited by local food critics who were largely complimentary in their reviews.

But they had always intended to mark their official opening in a manner that would bridge the years of terror and their new world order. Dominic and Rosa put everything into the planning of it from the special menu to the guest list. Albert was content to focus on the pastry section, leaving organisational matters to his parents. The day of the event duly arrived and brought with it fine autumnal weather. The passing of the equinox had brought shorter days, weaker sunshine and fading light as the trees that surrounded and draped the stone pub slowly shunned their green cloak, seasonally transforming to spectacular hues of reds, yellows, and russets. Illuminated by the golden sunlight, they provided a magical autumnal spectacle, a magnificent backdrop to welcome their special guests as the long-anticipated day arrived. Accommodation had been arranged locally for those who were staying over, the vista spectacular with views towards the North Yorkshire Moors in the distance and of the gastro pub, which was looking spick and span. The kitchen brigade had all their mise en place completed, the tables had been set, the bar stocked, wines at the ready. They were ready to go.

The stone-flagged floors, wooden beams and a roaring log fire added to the atmosphere, and the arrangements for the reception in the bar were in keeping with the ethos of their new venture, featuring local fare. English sparkling white and blush wines were served alongside glasses of locally brewed bitter from an artisan brewery; Yorkshire gin infused with foraged woodland produce from the Dales, and freshly squeezed local apple juice and Yorkshire mineral water, also featured. As the staff picked their way through their special guests with a selection of pre-dinner nibbles, Norris Jinks was particularly appreciative of the black pudding, baby beets and blue Wensleydale rustic canapes and mini pork pies made by Albert; Pamela opted for the champagne-soaked strawberries with a milk chocolate dip; Farmer Tim was completely at home with the beer, black pudding, and pork pie options, as was Annie.

In the midst of the bubble of conversation, Dominic and Rosa were pulled to one side by Rebecca. Her sparkling eyes clouding momentarily.

'I have news for you, Dom. *Stephanie.*' She paused as Rosa bristled, an eruption of bile stayed by Dominic's gently placed hand on her arm. He nodded, not thinking he could find the right words to express residual feelings.

'She escaped to the continent and is now living the life of Riley in the Caribbean, but she reached out to me recently. Said she had always worked for the overthrow of Tobin and Connell—'

'*What?*' Dominic exclaimed.

'I know. She said she was sorry for having hurt you. That she had worked with the Americans to ensure our rescue. She recognised it had gone down to the wire and was sorry for that. And she promised to see you one day soon. Rosa too.'

'*Unbelievable.* One sick lady. You can't believe any of this?'

'No…no…not really…' But she wore an expression that said *who knows?*

'Well, I don't *belieeeve* her. *Bitchhhhh* of the first order. Enough. I won't hear her name uttered in my presence or my home again.' With that pronouncement, Rosa bustled off.

'You don't, do you, Becks?' said Dominic.

'It's Stephanie, *anything's* possible…but no.'

She shrugged, leant over to Dominic, and cupped his face, delivering a light kiss on his lips. Her blue eyes sparkled as she pulled him to one side to introduce him to her new partner, Tessa.

Dominic went in search of Rosa, concerned at the impact of the mere mention of Stephanie's name. Surely that woman was not destined to haunt their future as well? His thoughts were shunted to one side as he saw Rosa in conversation with Ellie and her mum, Margaret. Rosa had been so pleased they had decided to come to the event, fearing it might pull to the fore the awful memories of Chequers and of course the demise of Juan. Dominic smiled, as he overheard Rosa at her kindest, empathy oozing as the three chatted quietly, slightly adjacent to the main hubbub.

Twenty of their friends had gathered and enjoyed a splendid meal: a refined version of Whitby fish and chips as a starter; Farmer Tim's lamb served three ways – roasted saddle, individual shepherd's pie, and herb-stuffed lamb belly;

bramble and apple crumble with a raspberry ice cream; and finally a Yorkshire cheeseboard. Simple food cooked to perfection with fabulous ingredients: *simplicity and authenticity*. Beer, wines, and juices flowed, and the conversation effervesced as alcohol intakes rose. As Dominic, Rosa and Albert re-joined their guests, spontaneous applause rang out and Norris rose to his feet.

'Friends, new friends if you permit, I will say a few words – a brave step, mark you, as I was under strict instructions from Pamela to fade into the background. Well, I *tried*! Friends, let me make a short toast...' said Norris Jinks.

But Dominic stood and waved a hand in his direction.

Norris acknowledged the interjection. 'I give way to my honourable friend.' He pulled his hand through his curls, made an inviting gesture, and sat down heavily.

'Norris, if I may be so bold...'

'Quite right, quite right my...'

'Order, *order* – let the honourable member for D&A at Greens have his say,' shouted Pamela, producing the loudest laugh of the night.

'I'm no orator, unlike my right honourable friend, the prime minister... but I would like to thank you all for coming tonight. All of our thoughts will be with those loved ones who *can't* be with us... To witness such a gathering of joy and laughter – well, we all know how unthinkable that was not so long ago. A few special thanks if I may. Tim and Annie – you placed yourselves in peril and in so doing lost your young son; you will always have a special place in our hearts... And you harbour and tend the grave of our youngest, Juan. Words can't do justice to our feelings, to our gratitude... Prime Minister, when politicians speak of the decent, normal, silent majority I can think of no better examples than Tim and Annie... To our long-standing friend, Mary, wife of my closest colleague and dear, irreverent, brave friend, Bill, we share your pain and extend our love to you... I marvel at your fortitude, the compassion you extended to Rosa and me in the loss of our own son coming as it did so hard on the heels of the loss of Bill... To Norris and Pamela – Rosa and I are so grateful for your kindness, for you providing the stage for the pinnacle of my career in cooking for you and the King at Chequers. My words can't convey the pride I felt in being extended such a privilege. And for sparing the time to spend an evening away from Westminster at such...' Dominic paused as Norris started to rise to his feet but was unceremoniously hauled down by Pamela, cueing more mirth.

'Thank you, Speaker,' he said, nodding to Pamela, 'I shan't give way this time…now to two ultra-special people with whom I have shared darker moments than I care to recall. Their forbearance, bravery, inventiveness, tradecraft, and resilience are impossible to exaggerate. But Rebecca and Jo, it is your compassion, sympathy, and kindness in the darkest moments…your sheer humanity…which will always live with me… I feel honoured to have met you both and count you as our friends. It's so good to see you moving on from your own losses, finding your own new lives and partners. Tessa and Thomas, I truly hope you realise just how special these two ladies are…' Dominic had flushed and wiped his eyes; Rosa was less discreet as tears flowed and she rushed to embrace Dominic. And the room reached an emotional crescendo as Albert appeared from the shadows to embrace his parents.

Eventually they recovered and Dominic rose to his feet to propose a toast.

'To family and friends; to recovery and renewal.'